"THIRTY SECONDS TO SRB STAGING."

Something suddenly speared through the sky in the distance, darting across the windshield like a laser-bolt effect from a movie. Schwarz tensed, but the angle was all wrong for something coming after the *Arcadia*.

"What the hell is going on?" Cole growled.

"Darkest night…" Broome gasped. "Mission control, are you tracking that on radar?"

"We're trying. It came within twenty-five miles of your course," Thet said on the other end. "Its trajectory is toward the Caribbean."

"What is it?" Cole demanded.

Lyons closed his eyes, his jaw set firmly. "It's the opening shot. This war has reached the hot stage."

DON PENDLETON'S

STONY

AMERICA'S ULTRA-COVERT INTELLIGENCE AGENCY

MAN®

SPLINTERED SKY

A GOLD EAGLE BOOK FROM

W🦅RLDWIDE®

TORONTO • NEW YORK • LONDON
AMSTERDAM • PARIS • SYDNEY • HAMBURG
STOCKHOLM • ATHENS • TOKYO • MILAN
MADRID • WARSAW • BUDAPEST • AUCKLAND

First edition October 2008

ISBN-13: 978-0-373-61981-8
ISBN-10:   0-373-61981-2

SPLINTERED SKY

Special thanks and acknowledgment to
Douglas P. Wojtowicz for his contribution to this work.

SPLINTERED SKY

PROLOGUE

Near Yuma, Arizona

Sabrina Bertonni winced as she clutched her hand to the bloody gap in her side. The raider's bullet had merely grazed her, but her clothes were soaked through from what had only been a little nick. Other than keeping her hand clamped over the injury, she didn't move. The limp bulk of Harold Maguire slumped against her body, casting her in shadow. Maguire's body shook violently as the raiders emptied more bullets into the group of rocket scientists who had tried to escape out the back of the laboratory.

The men were masked, clad in black from head to toe, wielding automatic weapons that made almost no sound. They moved with a similar eerie silence. Bertonni's lucidity was hampered by blood loss and the concussion she'd received when her head smacked a rock on the desert floor with the added momentum of Maguire's corpse, but from the way the assault force moved, it was as if they were living excerpts from her worst nightmares. Their speed and coordination, and just how quietly they had laid waste to the Burgundy

Lake Testing Facility gave her the impression of shadows come to life.

Though none of the black-clad raiders had spoken, their goal was clear to Bertonni, especially since she was one of the scientists working on brand-new, high-mobility steering thrusters for precision orbital maneuvering. Compact and fuel-efficient, they would be very important in the next generation of spacecraft replacing the aging, worn-out space shuttle. The maneuvering thrusters would make the expansion of the International Space Station easier, and provide the ability to perform round trips to the moon. Bertonni had no doubt that the thrusters could provide extra maneuverability for combat-oriented suborbital fighters and bombers, or armed satellites. The military potential couldn't be underestimated. The kind of firepower and professionalism displayed by the armed marauders lent credence to what the enemies of the United States thought of the design.

The security force was provided by the U.S. Air Force, heavily armed and trained soldiers who were responsible for protecting nuclear bomber groups. These men had trained hard against Navy SEAL Opfor units to hone their combat skills and antiinfiltration awareness.

Fat lot of good that did, Bertonni thought. In the distance she heard the blast of C-4 detonating. The ground shook under her, and Maguire's corpse slid off her prone form. She stirred, looking around. The shadowy raiders were nowhere to be seen, but with their bombs going off, she knew that they weren't going to stick around. She fished in her pocket for her cell phone and hit Send to 9-1-1. The lighted LED screen showed she had no bars. The remote Burgundy Lake facility had been chosen for its distance from civilization and privacy, but the administrators had set up a cell tower to make things easier for the staff. Bertonni knew that the calls were monitored through that tower, the better to prevent sensitive data from being transmitted outside the testing laboratories, but right now she needed help.

The phone didn't ring. The raiders had been too efficient, probably taking out the cell tower first.

Bertonni pocketed the phone and crawled, scurrying deeper into the desert, away from the dormitory building. She'd gotten twenty yards when the apartment shook. She looked back to see a cloud of dust and debris swell, escaping through shattered windows and burst doors. The vomitous wave of ejecta hit her hard and knocked her off her feet. Her head swam and she stumbled on the uneven ground. She wrapped her arm around her nose and mouth, filtering out the choking dust with the cloth of her sleeve.

With a kick, she pushed herself forward and struggled to get farther from the building, hugging the ground, trying not be seen by any straggling marauders.

The air popped and crackled with weapons fire, and her instincts threw her flat to the dirt again. The cloud hadn't dispersed, but someone opened fire into the airborne dust. It was the raiders, and they had to have seen her in the shadows just before the exploding dormitory obscured the scene.

Bertonni crawled, scurrying back toward the destroyed housing, knowing that once the dust settled, she'd be out in the open, an easy target for the brutal gunmen who had visited destruction on the testing facility. When the swirling wisps of the cloud finally dissipated, she was snugged, caked in dust, under the low remnant of a wall. Her breathing slowed, her shoulders tensed as she did her best to impersonate rubble.

A voice cut through the night. "I told you, I saw someone!"

"Fuck it, we've got to go. Time's wasting," another answered.

"But…"

"Now!" the other ordered. "We won't be ID'd." In the distance, she heard large trucks grinding into gear. "You want to walk to Mexico?"

There was a sigh of exasperation and then the sound of running feet.

Cargo trucks grunted and grumbled, rolling away before she could even dare to relax. She sucked in a breath of clean air, exhausted, and light-headed from blood loss.

No one was visible.

Bertonni was safe, for now, but she rolled onto her back, looking at the sky. Stars twinkled above her. She gulped air and looked at the cell phone in her hand.

She had one bar of signal. She thumbed 9-1-1 and hit send.

"Nine-one-one dispatch. What is the nature of your emergency…"

"I've been shot. Everyone else is dead. Burgundy Lake Testing Facility," the woman gasped. "Help me."

Her strength gave out and her fingers loosened on the phone. She could hear the dispatcher's voice, tinny through the tiny speaker, and she held on, saying, "I'm awake" every few seconds until she saw the flashing glare of red lights.

CHAPTER ONE

Ten miles north of the U.S.-Mexico border

Hermann Schwarz watched the stars sprayed across the black night as Jack Grimaldi piloted the Hughes 500 NOTAR across the Texan sky. The inky-black background with the glittering field of pinpoints reminded the Able Team electronics genius of one of his lifelong dreams—to soar among the stars. And he had been one of the lucky few who had done just that.

Schwarz's other lifelong dream was more pedestrian. He wanted to help people. Though he was one-third of one of the world's most highly experienced and blooded combat teams, the ultimate goal of Able Team wasn't to engage in bloodshed. It was to protect the citizens of the U.S. Schwarz had been called an assassin by various enemies, but the term "assassin" implied a callous disregard for human life. Certainly, he had a measure of ruthlessness, but it was only displayed against opponents who were demonstrably hostile and violent. While he had no qualms about shooting heavily armed men in the back to end their potential to harm himself, his partners or noncombatants, Schwarz was not murderous.

Killing was just an aspect of his job, just as much as tinkering on new electronic surveillance devices and security countermeasures. Schwarz turned from the starry night sky back to his Combat Personal Data Assistant, a compact little computer that provided the gadgeteer with a suite of powerful tools to make his work easier. He kept the illumination low on the monitor as he scanned the screen. Its powerful satellite modem, akin to the satellite phones, allowed him Internet access even without a WiFi source for miles around, even though a backup transceiver would allow him to piggyback on someone else's modem if necessary. The CPDA was connected to Stony Man Farm, thousands of miles away in the Blue Ridge Mountains of Virginia, allowing him to be plugged into the network run by Aaron Kurtzman and the cyberwizards of his team.

"Hey, Nerd Man." Carl Lyons spoke up, interrupting Schwarz's reveries. "You getting this?"

"I am," Rosario Blancanales announced, answering for his friend. He had a pair of light amplification binoculars scanning out the window. "To the north."

"Minimal profile on the terrain radar," Lyons answered. Sitting shotgun in the Little Bird helicopter, his hard blue eyes scanned the screens devoted to the Forward Looking Infrared—FLIR—and Terrain Looking Radar, both keen electronic sensors installed in a bulbous nose projecting from the front of the helicopter's teardrop shape, lending it the appearance of a porpoise whose snout had been punched off center. "But we've got headlights on the FLIR."

"Low-light headlights," Blancanales said. "Probably Ultraviolet or IR illumination to make it easier for them to run dark. I didn't see the vehicles directly, but I saw the ground lit up."

Schwarz looked to where Blancanales was sweeping the

horizon. He ran his stylus over the CPDA, popping open a window that displayed a satellite view of their immediate surroundings.

Lyons turned in his seat and Blancanales leaned over. They all saw, through the IR imaging of a National Reconnaissance Office satellite, a cone of illuminated terrain with tiny stars of light one after another.

"IR beacons so they can follow each other," Lyons suggested.

"This way only one vehicle has to have its illuminators on, but the others can follow," Schwarz said. "We got lucky. If you hadn't seen the ground lit up by IR lights and given Bear a heading, we'd have completely missed them."

Schwarz's mind continued to race, analyzing the situation. This night, Able Team was in the air, racing to intercept a smuggling operation that the Farm had heard whispers about. Someone had been monitoring Border Patrol schedules, tailing Jeeps as if looking for holes. This was something more than just a coyote operation snooping for a gap in the defenses. The human smugglers bringing illegals across the border didn't need to track the USBP's agents and vehicles, and wouldn't even dream of tickling their computer system with hacker fingers in cyberspace.

Whatever this operation was about, it wasn't smuggling illegal immigrants. Able Team had come into conflict at the border several times before, and it could have been anything from a large shipment of drugs to nuclear weapons.

Schwarz's headset warbled with a beep from his communicator. He keyed the com unit, hearing Aaron "The Bear" Kurtzman's voice in his earphone. He immediately switched it so everyone in the helicopter could hear their support back at the Farm.

"We've got a call. Someone hit Burgundy Lake Testing Facility," the Stony Man cyberwizard said. "Nine-one-one call center got the news five minutes ago. A lone survivor says that the raiders just bugged out."

"We believe we have their convoy in our sights," Lyons announced. "And you already know Gadgets has them highlighted on satellite imagery."

"Affirmative," Kurtzman returned. "Still creepy how that little box of his keeps him plugged into our network."

Schwarz smirked. "You know me, I'm five bucks and a nuclear weapon short of controlling the world."

"Which is why I'll never pay you back anything you lend me," Blancanales quipped. "Burgundy Lake, that's not far from the border, relatively speaking. This has got to be a part of what drew our attention down here."

"What are they testing there?" Lyons inquired.

Schwarz tapped the CPDA screen a couple of times with his stylus. "They're on a NASA grant. High-efficiency rocket thrusters."

"Give the man a cigar," Kurtzman stated. "You'll put us out of business with that thing, Gadgets."

"Nah. I'm just piggybacking on Carmen's workstation. She pulled up the information a moment before she got it to you," Schwarz stated.

Kurtzman chuckled. "So you let us do all the work, and you look brilliant."

Lyons snorted. "It'll take a lot of work to make Gadgets look anything close to brilliant."

Schwarz lifted his middle finger to inform Lyons that the Able Team leader was still number one in his book. Lyons grinned and turned to Grimaldi. "Jack, see that wash down there? It's the only path through these foothills that'll give the convoy a quick route south. Land us right there. We'll set up an ambush."

"Good spot," Grimaldi mentioned. He grimaced with regret. "Wish this thing had some guns on it."

"Take off and pull back to an overwatch. We might need a quick pickup, but the convoy could have the firepower to deal with aircraft."

Grimaldi swung the Little Bird around, depositing Able Team at Lyons's suggested position. It was several miles ahead of the convoy, but still in their path. The helicopter had been set up for quiet running with engine baffles and sideways projecting speakers that canceled out the racket of the rotor by interrupting the noise with the same sound, aimed back at the rotors at a perpendicular angle. When the two sound sources crossed, they nullified each other, rendering the aircraft no louder than an idling automobile.

There was no doubt that the convoy was up to no good. A line of trucks running on "invisible" headlights and tail beacons at night were the tactics of thieves and smugglers, not of innocents. Burgundy Lake was less than twenty miles north of the border, but directly to the south there was a range of uneven hills without anything more than a goat trail wending through them to cross into Mexico. Schwarz pulled his CPDA from its pocket on his load-bearing vest, checking on the satellite view from above. Something was wrong.

Lyons looked over his shoulder at the small but crystal-clear screen. His big fists clenched and relaxed, tendons popping like firecrackers as his adrenaline kicked into his bloodstream. "They're operating on strict discipline. The beacons have cut out. It was a refresher flash so that the convoy could maintain its formation. Only the headlights are still running hot."

"The right place at the right time with the right kind of eyes," Schwarz mused. "One thing wrong, and they would have gotten away. And we were only here because they were so professional and thorough in their planning and recon, they left enough fingerprints to make us wonder what was going on."

"Okay," Lyons said. "We've got six vehicles. One truck and several SUVs. They're running dark and they've got radar-absorbent materials rendering them almost invisible. We can also assume they've got armor on their rides, and considering the destruction they've wreaked, they're heavily armed and ruthless."

"Bear, do we have any images of the actual assault?" Blancanales asked over his communicator.

"No," Kurtzman replied. "We have some NRO satellites looking at the area, but we were looking at the border, not any facilities. I have Hunt and Akira scanning recordings to see if we can see the raiders in action, but nothing yet."

"This has got to be what drew us down here," Lyons interjected over his headset. "A hit on Burgundy Lake? Wonder why they didn't take out the communications."

"We received a report of a sudden blackout in the facility's cell tower coverage. It's still out, but somehow the survivor got a signal," Kurtzman told him.

"Steel-framed buildings," Schwarz said. "Usually the steel understructure isn't preferred because it acts as too good of an antenna, pulling down all manner of interference. However, out in the middle of nowhere, the prefabricated structures are exactly what are needed to set things up on the cheap. If the raiders set explosives and blew up the place, then they undoubtedly left wreckage behind. Our survivor must have huddled among the wreckage, and a remaining girder of the freestanding superstructure formed an impromptu antenna."

"Wouldn't be too efficient," Kurtzman mentioned. "The specific frequency range—"

"All you'd need was at least one bar of signal. The survivor'd be better off with a walkie-talkie," Schwarz advised, cutting him off. "Shit…Bear, check the satellite imagery from when I first high lit the convoy. I think one's missing."

"Checking it," Kurtzman said. "One beacon has cut out."

"They're altering course," Schwarz told his partners. "Something's up."

Lyons ground his teeth in frustration. The trucks were veering back toward the north when he looked over to Schwarz and the dim glow from his CPDA screen. He then turned his gaze skyward, switching his com link to the Stony Man Farm cybernetics crew.

"Bear, check to see if you're the only ones on the NRO's party line. The bad guys are changing course, and they might be keyed into the same eyes in the sky."

"Good instincts, Ironman. How'd you guess?" Kurtzman asked.

"Because we're the only ones watching them," Lyons returned.

"One vehicle just dropped off the grid. I can't even find it by its illuminators," Schwarz replied. Using a stylus, he dragged the focus of the camera, and stopped. "We're visible to our own satellite. Damn it…"

Lyons and Blancanales returned to scoping out the darkened landscape, alert that they were literally in the spotlight, the National Reconnaissance Office satellite's unblinking electronic eye pointing them out to the very force they had used it to spy upon.

"They'll come in hard and fast, and we're sitting ducks," Blancanales replied. "At least in comparison to them."

"We could call Jack back, but we might only expose him to fire," Schwarz returned.

"And we'd lose track of the convoy," Lyons snarled. "No, we get ourselves some wheels and continue the chase."

Blancanales and Schwarz smiled. When it came to the burly blond ex-cop, the simplest solution was always his choice. There was one vehicle in the area that they could use to chase down and intercept the escaping convoy. The fact that it was filled with heavily armed gunmen was no hindrance in the Ironman's mind. Lyons had no problem sitting on the gore-soaked bucket seats of an SUV while chasing after high-tech raiders.

Fortunately, the men of Able Team were prepared for a war. The trio had opted for DSA-58 carbines, compact versions of the FN FAL. Normally, the team utilized some form of the M-16 rifle, but with the long ranges and flat terrain of the desert they were in, they went for the 7.62 mm NATO round for the excellent reach it possessed over the 5.56 mm NATO. The smaller, lighter bullets would be blown off course by a stiff desert wind at farther than 500 meters, and at that range, a reliable kill was an iffy proposition. For the FAL, it was child's play to cause a lethal injury at twice that distance.

The American-made FALs were supplemented by Smith & Wesson Military and Police pistols. The M&Ps were sixteen-shot, .40-caliber autoloaders in a package no larger than a 1911. Attached to Picatinny rails under the pistols' barrels were white light and laser aiming modules, as much for recoil control as for illumination purposes. Able Team had chosen a proved border-fighting load, the 165-grain jacketed hollowpoint round, as accurate and powerful as a .357 Magnum round out to one hundred yards. The trio opted to leave the suppressors off the thread-barreled handguns, not needing stealth at the cost of increased range. Blancanales had added an M-203 grenade launcher to the forearm of his DSA-58 carbine, while Lyons wore a Mossberg 500 Cruiser pistol-grip pump shotgun in a sheath on his back. The Cruiser had no shoulder stock, but the big ex-cop had a Knox Comp-Stock installed, as well as a stabilizing single-point sling. Schwarz's extra load had been taken up by his various electronics gear.

Lyons changed out the dutch-load of shot and slugs to go completely to Brenneke slugs, which turned the compact scattergun into a large-bore rifle spitting out devastating .72-inch slugs. Anyone coming at them would catch a face full of big bullets that hit hard.

Even though Able Team knew that a single vehicle had broken off to break their ambush, it still came as a surprise when they heard the warbling whistle of a 40 mm grenade arcing through the sky.

"Cover!" Lyons bellowed, throwing himself into a rut on the uneven ground.

Schwarz dropped behind a berm that rippled up at the base of a foothill instants before the world broke apart around him. Six and a half ounces of high explosive detonated only a few yards away, the lethal concussion wave and shrapnel deflecting off the small slope. No jagged bits of segmented wire tore through his flesh, but the powerful ripples of force coming off the detonation expanded, rolling into him.

The stars above swirled chaotically as he struggled to retain consciousness.

CHAPTER TWO

Carl Lyons saw Schwarz flop on the ground in reaction to the grenade detonation and cursed under his breath.

"Pol! Gadgets is hit," he hissed into his throat mike. "Cover him."

"One sec," Blancanales responded. His own 40 mm launcher popped off a shell. Instead of returning fire, it threw an M-583 parachute flare into the sky. Burning at 90,000 candlepower, it lit up the general area where the enemy grenade had come from, illuminating a spot two hundred yards in diameter with night vision–frying light. Even bare, night-attuned eyes would have trouble adapting immediately to the sudden blaze of white light slashing a hole in the dark.

Lyons spotted two gunners flinch from the sudden brightness, and brought up his FAL carbine, triggering a burst of high-powered rifle slugs at them across the distance. One of the enemy shooters jerked violently, crushed by the devastating 7.62 mm NATO bullets shredding through body armor and churning up vital organs. The other ducked quickly toward the cover of the uneven ground at roadside. Beyond the 650-foot circle of light descending from the parachute flare, with his

DSA-58's muzzle-blast dampened by an efficient flash hider, the Able Team leader had the opportunity to chase the enemy gunman with another burst as wild rounds snapped randomly through the darkness.

The enemy gunmen hadn't been ready for their night game to be cast in a high-definition 90,000-candlepower spotlight, and only seven seconds had passed in the 40-second burn of the parachute flare. Through the holographic reflex sight, Lyons picked up a third rifleman who exposed only a small portion of his head and shoulders around the side of a big rock. The sight was a quick reaction design, and didn't provide an increase of magnification, just a tiny, projected red dot in the middle of a glass screen that gave the big ex-cop a faster focus point. The projected red dot obscured the enemy shooter's head and shoulders, and Lyons milked the trigger. At 650 rounds per minute, the carbine chewed out a blistering salvo of bullets that spat dirt and stone splinters up in a cloud.

Another 40 mm grenade sizzled through the sky, and Lyons glanced back to Blancanales and Schwarz.

The electronics genius had recovered his senses, but Blancanales had instinctively hooked his arm under Schwarz's and yanked him along. Lyons bellowed, equalizing the pressure in his ears as he stuffed himself into the bottom of a gully beside the goat path.

The darkened desert shook with a thunderbolt strike, and Lyons could feel his load-bearing vest ripple as the concussion burst swept across him. Blancanales's grenade launcher burped again while Schwarz's own DSA-58 carbine snarled a vengeful response. This time, the Puerto Rican Able Team veteran popped off an M379-A1 Airburst grenade. Instead of providing a miniature sun dangling from a parachute, the Airburst shell looped into an arc, landed on the ground and a black powder charge propelled the main grenade five feet into the air before its fuse wound down to detonation. At a height of five feet off the ground, the Airburst exploded, spraying out a sheet of lethal shrapnel that would kill anything within a sixteen-foot radius of the blast, but still could wound as far out as four hundred feet.

A wailing scream of pain as shrapnel tore through body armor and fragile flash and bone beneath provided the testimony to its effectiveness. Lyons spotted the gunman who had dodged his initial burst, clutching his shredded face and neck. He'd lost his weapon when Blancanales's shrapnel had scythed across him, and Lyons was about to put a few mercy rounds into the gunman when Schwarz nailed him.

"Can you run?" Lyons asked over the headset.

"Yeah," Schwarz replied. "The concussion wave only knocked the wind out of me."

"We've lost the element of surprise." Blancanales spoke up, pointing to the flare as it sputtered through the last of its forty-second lifespan, burning down to a lifeless ember that flopped under its parachute on the ground. "That baby was seen for miles."

"I saw their truck," Lyons told him. "It did its job. Gadgets…"

"I'll get Jack on station," Schwarz returned.

The trio raced across the desert, wary that they might not have finished off all of their opponents.

Charging up the goat path to the SUV took only another half minute. Lyons paused at roadside for a heartbeat to pop off a single round into a sprawled corpse to ensure it would never rise again. He noted with grim humor that Schwarz had been the one to nail the enemy gunman wielding the grenade launcher.

The enemy's SUV had a guard with a compact machine pistol. The man rushed to get back behind the wheel of his vehicle, firing across the hood, but Lyons and Blancanales stitched him with twin bursts of autofire. Blown nearly out of his boots, the guard's corpse flopped in a boneless mass, door wide open.

Blancanales checked the dead man and peeled the night-vision goggles off his face.

"Keys are in the ignition," Lyons announced, crawling into the SUV's shotgun seat.

"Good," the Able Team commando replied. He slipped behind the wheel, fired up the engine and spun out.

Schwarz was in the back, picking up the FLIR camera feed from Grimaldi's helicopter, correlating the image with his GPS data. "They're looping around, going for a second run at the border. They're either certain their boys did the job, or they're going to come in hot and heavy."

"I'm not going to wait to see what their response is," Lyons said. He wedged his Mossberg shotgun into the seat well and rolled down the window, providing himself with room to shoot his carbine with its stock folded. "Nut up and do it."

"It's worked this long," Schwarz agreed.

Blancanales nodded. He could see the beacons on the enemy convoy blink out, their headlights flaring to life in an effort to blind him, but they were so far away, and the wily Able Team expert was so familiar with low-light operations, he avoided any discomfort. Turning his head to observe the cast-off infrared illumination instead of staring into the "invisible" light sources directly with his NVGs, he was able to keep his course to intercept the enemy trucks.

Lyons had traded his carbine with Blancanales and stuffed an M-433 HEDP shell into its grenade launcher. The SUV jostled him, rocking hard in an effort to throw his aim off, but Lyons had earned the name Ironman due to his phenomenal strength. He'd braced himself in the passenger seat, pointed at a raider's SUV and touched off the grenade. The high-explosive, dual-purpose shell spiraled toward the enemy vehicle at 350 feet per second, smashing into the grille of the on-rushing Jeep. The M-433 exploded, a spit-back assembly built into the shell focusing a blistering-hot jet of molten copper, propelled by several ounces of A5 explosive through the engine block and into the cab of the SUV. The raiders' driver and shotgun man were killed as the dashboard, speared by liquid metal and high explosives, turned to a mass of jagged, burning fragments that tore through their chests, legs and faces. Driverless, the enemy Jeep swerved into a rut and somersaulted in the air before it could bleed off speed. The men in the back seat, merely wounded by the cone of deadly shrapnel that used to be their ride, screamed for a moment before the airborne SUV slammed, roof-first into the Texas desert. The SUV had been designed to handle roll-overs, but no maker could have predicted their vehicle would be lifted up and hurled at the ground like a toy. The survivors' screams cut off instantly as their bodies were compressed to ground beef under three-quarters of a ton of off-roading metal.

The remaining three escorts for the big trucks swung out, gunners ripping off streams of autofire. Schwarz had targeted one of the Suburbans as they swung parallel to Able Team for a moment, his hammering carbine carving a bloody swathe through the open windows that the enemy gunners fired from. The vehicle that Schwarz raked swung wildly off course, a lifeless body flopping half in and out of the window he'd used as a turret. Schwarz, a veteran of countless gun battles inside of a vehicle, had known to tuck himself low, using the window-reinforced door as his shield, rather than expose his head and shoulders in an effort to utilize the opening as a turret.

Blancanales swung the front of Able Team's captured Suburban on an intercept course for a second of the raiders' vehicles, giving the wheel a jerk at the last moment to stab the corner of the front fender into the rear wheel of the passing enemy. The fender deformed on Able Team's ride, but the rear axle of the hostile Suburban snapped like a twig under the force of the SUV hammering into it. The mysterious marauders wailed in dismay as their truck spiraled through the desert, back wheels flying off.

"Last one's keeping its distance," Lyons noted. "I'm only getting glancing shots on it. Their driver's good."

"Forget him for now," Blancanales snapped. "We've got the main trucks to deal with."

Lyons glanced back at the pair of trucks. They were two-and-a-half-ton M35 trucks, and they were lumbering toward the goat path as fast as they could roll, taking advantage of the distraction provided by their escorts. The Able Team leader sneered and pushed home another M-433, then remembered the possibility that the marauders had taken captives.

Rather than risk noncombatants, he pulled his Mossberg Cruiser 500. The Brenneke slug load would be devastating in close quarters, and not as risky as buckshot to bystanders. "Swing up close on the lead truck. If we can stop it while we've taken up the roadside…"

"Good plan," Blancanales agreed, and he gunned the engine, zooming past the second transport truck. Schwarz scanned the back, but could only see black-clad troopers in the shadows of the canvas tarp.

Blancanales swerved between the two big M35s, putting the passenger side in close contact with the tailgate of the lead vehicle. Lyons threw open the door and launched himself from the shotgun seat, his Mossberg gripped tightly in his right fist. His beefy left hand wrapped around the top of the tailgate, and he hauled himself up as his partners veered away. Swinging over into the tarp-covered bed, he spotted a quartet of gun-toting men surrounding a pair of crates. In the corner, a coverall-wearing man, his head bleeding from blunt trauma, curled up.

Lyons evaluated the scene in half the time it took for the gunmen to react to his bulk surging over the top of the tailgate. The Knox pistol-grip Comp Stock gave the Able Team leader all the leverage he needed to swing up the Mossberg Cruiser 500 like a handgun and fire a single 12-gauge slug through the chest of the closest gunman. A .72-inch missile ripped through the raider's breastbone, reducing it to free-floating splinters as the solid hunk of lead tore his heart from its arteries like a miniature bulldozer.

Lyons immediately shifted his aim and stabbed the next of the armor-clad raiders in the breastbone with the point of his Cruiser 500. Since Lyons had John "Cowboy" Kissinger modify the muzzle of the weapon with a Tromix Shark Brake Door Breacher, and, given his awesome strength, the shotgun became a spike-toothed spear that made ribs crunch even through body armor. The hapless enemy grabbed the shotgun instinctively, bracing the slide. Lyons thanked his opponent for playing into his hands by quickly wrenching the Cruiser 500 back and forth, his foe's grasp enabling him to pump the shotgun one-handed. A second solid 12-gauge slug exploded from the muzzle, tearing into the bruised sternum of the marauder and exploding out of his spine. The shooter behind him was bobbing and weaving, trying to get an angle on the burly killing machine attached to the tailgate when the Brenneke slug sliced across his biceps and glanced across his ribs.

This time, the gunman's body armor protected him, if only because the deadly slug had been slowed down by the armor and torso of another person. The impact still threw the guy off balance and he let go of his grip on his rifle, one hand tearing through the canvas cover in an attempt to get an anchor to remain standing. Unfortunately for the raider, the force needed to tear through the tarpaulin had shattered several of his fingers, and with only one digit to maintain a hold, the next jolt of the truck sent him reeling across the crates in the middle of the bed.

Lyons's legs and support arm surged with power and he hurled himself over the tailgate. He somersaulted to cushion his landing on the bed where the injured raider had fallen. As the enemy shooter struggled to bring up his rifle single-handed, Lyons foiled his efforts at self-defense by spiking both of his heels down into the murderous marauder's chest. Aching ribs snapped under the ferocious power of the Able Team leader's devastating kicks, and the gunman's mouth became a crimson volcano of burbling blood and bile.

Lyons took the opportunity to rack the action of his Mossberg with his now free left hand, just in time to see the head of the last of the hostiles in the truck poke up.

"Don't do it!" the raider shouted. "I'll kill—"

Lyons pulled the trigger on the shooter before he could even complete, let alone make good on his threat to shoot the cowering figure in coveralls sharing the carnal pit. One and three-eighths ounces of rifled lead struck the loudmouth between his eyes and popped his skull like a balloon filled with gray gelatin. It was a vicious, ruthless action, but the Able Team leader knew that the black-clad gunman wouldn't have worried about shooting either Lyons or the helpless hostage. He got to his feet and moved over to the bloody-faced man in the corner, clicking on a pocket flashlight to get some intel on who the victim was.

"Who are you?" the balding hostage asked. Just beneath his high hairline was an oval-shaped section of livid skin. Lyons recognized the injury as caused by the steel tubular butt stock of an M-4 assault rifle, just like the black-clad gunmen were wearing. He gripped the man by the chin and checked his eyes.

The pupils dilated as the flashlight's glare stabbed into them, so the head trauma was only superficial, torn skin seeping blood from a glancing impact. Lyons was glad for that, because he wasn't in the best position to deal with a victim suffering from a major concussion or slipping into shock.

"I'm a friend," Lyons answered. "Stay here and curl up. We're going to make certain you are safe."

"Where are you going?" the man, Leon Paczesny according to his Burgundy Lake Testing Facility identification badge, asked.

"Truck's still moving. I'm going to schedule a stop to let you off," Lyons told him. He returned the Mossberg to its sheath on his back and pulled the Smith & Wesson MP-40 from its holster. "Sit tight, literally."

Paczesny nodded, tucking his knees up to his chest and resting his bloodied forehead between them. Lyons unsheathed his combat knife and sliced an exit hole through the canvas. He climbed through the tarp and grabbed onto the back of the cab.

Able Team's captured Chevy Suburban was at Lyons's side, Schwarz firing his DSA carbine through the back window of the armored raider vehicle at the two remaining enemy SUVs which were struggling to keep up with the racing convoy. Lyons grimaced as he heard the rip-snap of the FAL's high-velocity rifle bullets spearing through the darkness. By now, all pretense of stealth had disappeared, and the Burgundy Lake raiders had switched on conventional headlights. Lyons stiff-armed his MP-40 and fired a volley as fast as he could work the trigger, six 165-grain jacketed hollowpoint rounds striking the windshield behind a pair of enemy headlights. The Able Team commander focused his fire on the Suburbans, not certain if the other truck had a hostage, as well.

Safety glass deformed and whitened under Lyons's barrage, shocking the driver into slamming on the brakes. The second Chevy flashed forward to take up the slack, but its hood smoked, pouring out thick clouds from where its shattered radiator and shot-up V-8 burned. The fact that the Suburban continued to rattle onward to keep up with the rolling battle despite a magazine of .30-caliber bullets in it was testament the truck's engineering. Unfortunately, no amount of SUV design excellence could have provided the raiders with protection from a 40 mm buckshot grenade.

Firing the equivalent of three 12-gauge shotgun shells' worth of number 4 buck, the M-576 turned Blancanales's M-203 into a supershotgun. At maximum dispersal, the M-203 could put out a cone of death almost one hundred feet wide. At the range between Schwarz in the back of Able Team's Suburban to the enemy vehicle, the spread only ensured that a seven-foot diameter hose of death collapsed the windshield and perforated the surviving gunmen in the Jeep.

The smoldering vehicle rolled on, glancing off the fender of the second M-35 cargo truck before rebounding into a ditch. As tortured steel collapsed under its own inertia, gasoline squeezed out of severed fuel lines and turned into a blossom of fire licking into the night sky.

Lyons returned his attention to the cab, only to see the shotgun rider of the lead two-and-a-half-ton truck climbing out the passenger door, a Glock in hand. Lyons swept the MP-40 back toward him and triggered a pair of slugs. The bouncing truck was too much for Lyons to maintain his aim, so the bullets went high and to the right. Only one wide-mouthed round clipped the enemy gunman's shoulder, gouging a deep laceration through the muscle. The impact was still enough to throw the raider's aim off, his Glock punching holes through the roof of the cab. A sudden spray of blood darkened the driver window, and the M-36 cargo truck lurched violently. Lyons tightened his grasp on the iron rib holding up the tarp, and though his feet left the thin ledge he was using as a running board, he wasn't thrown from the vehicle.

"Hang on!" Lyons bellowed to Paczesny. "We're going to crash!"

The truck swerved off the road and Lyons twisted, hurling his Smith & Wesson into the bed and using both hands to haul him through the tear in the canvas. He tucked his legs up and behind him just as the two-and-a-half-ton truck lurched and skidded onto its side. The steel ribs held as Lyons flopped against the bottom of the seats. The packing crates shattered, spilling prototype motors onto the canvas where shredding tarpaulin snagged them and ground them to useless metal splinters under the cover's ribbing.

Lyons looked around for Paczesny and saw the balding, bloody-headed man holding his Smith & Wesson.

"Had to go and fuck up everything didn't you, Blondie?" Paczesny snarled, jabbing the pistol toward Lyons. The faux hostage took in a breath, but Lyons straightened his legs, using the bench he laid on as a launch pad, slamming into the gun-toting fake and knocking them both out the back of the sliding truck. The pair hit the ground, tumbling, MP-40 flying clear of stunned fingers as the second two-and-a-half-ton truck whirled past, missing them by inches.

Paczesny's fists rained on the Able Team leader's neck and shoulders in a futile attempt to dislodge Lyons. Without leverage, the blows were merely annoying, and Lyons whipped his forehead forward, striking the balding man's nose at the bridge, hard enough to make him see stars under the impact without doing any fatal damage. Lyons needed this man for information. Grabbing Paczesny's wrist, Lyons twisted. The pop of joints was accompanied by a wail of pain.

"Are there any hostages in the other truck?" Lyons bellowed.

"Piss off!" Paczesny answered.

Lyons twisted even harder, and he could see the knob of his prisoner's ulna stretching the skin of his elbow. "Wrong answer. I'll rip this fucking thing off and feed it to you if you don't answer."

"No. No. I was the only one with them," Paczesny said.

"How'd you get the stock burn?" Lyons asked.

"Air Force guard gave me a whack in the head when I pulled a gun on him. My partners burned him down," Paczesny said.

Confronted by the balding man's betrayal, Lyons gave a hard final twist, then punched him in the temple. The blow rendered Paczesny unconscious, and Lyons secured his wrists and ankles with cable ties. "You two get that? No friendlies are on truck two. Free fire!"

"We've got it," Schwarz answered. "Let me just take care of this."

Hundreds of yards away, Schwarz fed another magazine into his DSA-58 tactical carbine and hammered off another burst through a pursuing Suburban. Finally, despite the unstable platform of his own ride and the uneven road, he was able to score a direct hit with the autorifle. Schwarz's burst struck the enemy driver in the head and exploded his brains. The shotgun rider lunged, grabbing the wheel, but the vehicle fell back without any pressure on the gas.

Schwarz had an easier time aiming at the stilled SUV full of gunmen, burning off the rest of his 30-round magazine into the cab. One of the enemy raiders was leaning out the window, returning fire with his M-4 carbine, but his efforts were cut off by the Able Team genius's slashing storm of high-velocity bullets. The vehicle was out of the play.

"Okay, the last of the escorts are done," Schwarz called. "Wish you were here for this."

"Just do it," Lyons growled over the com link.

Schwarz fed another HEDP round into the M-203's breech and aimed at the second M36. He pulled the trigger and the 40 mm armor-piercing round hit the grille and detonated. A small gust of flaming gases appeared around the nose of the cargo truck, a display of the impact point as the real light show went on inside of the engine compartment. The shaped charge liquefied the interior cone of copper and turned it into a flaming bullet that shredded the engine block. The twelve-cylinder motor disintegrated into a wave of shrapnel that obliterated the bellies and legs of the driver and the passenger, killing them instantly.

The vehicle skidded to a halt, kicking up dirt as it slid sideways. Blancanales hit the brakes, and the two Able Team commandos got out of the captured SUV using it as a shield.

"I've got movement," Blancanales announced. He opened fire at a fleeing shadow, but the enemy figure was just too fast. He disappeared into the rough, broken face of a cliff. "Ironman, try to cut him off."

"You're too far down, and I don't have a shot," Lyons replied. "More movement at the back of your truck…"

Blancanales and Schwarz saw three black-clad marauders exit the rear of the truck, their weapons up and spitting fire, but the two Able Team operatives were ready for them. Their rifles vomited hot lead, dumping the hard men into the dirt.

Blananales returned to looking for the mystery shadow, launching another parachute flare, but the uneven ground had too many shadows, nooks and crannies for a determined fleeing opponent. The fact that he hadn't returned fire was indicative that their foe was not interested in a fight.

"We'll find him," Schwarz promised. "Whoever set this up has something planned."

Blancanales nodded as the parachute flare sputtered and burned out. In moments, it was as cold as the trail looked.

CHAPTER THREE

Yuma, Arizona

The aftermath of the border battle wasn't the end of Able Team's business. First, they had to stash Paczesny away in their safehouse. Since Grimaldi had the use of a small airfield that saw only moderate use, Lyons decided to keep him in a broom closet in the hangar that Stony Man Farm had reserved for them. Paczesny glared daggers, his mouth stuffed with a rag that was duct-taped in place. Anchoring the rag partially inside and outside of his mouth would keep him from aspirating the cloth and choking to death on it.

"We'll talk to you when we're rested," Lyons said. He slapped pieces of duct tape across the prisoner's eyes and set a pair of headphones on the man's ears. The other end of the phones was plugged into an MP3 player that ran a twenty-minute loop of a digitally produced, low-pitched squeal. Completely blinded and deafened, the prisoner would be softened up by the time Able Team was ready to interrogate him.

The trio reported in to the Farm, giving what they knew and

learning of a full-court Homeland Security press on investigating the brutal raid.

"We'll put you on the roster to join in with the task force," Barbara Price, Stony Man's mission controller, told them. "You'll be Justice Department agents."

"Good," Lyons said. "I'd like to get a quick look at the crime scene."

"You'll get as much as you want once daylight hits," Price responded. "We'll see what we've got on file about Leon Paczesny and do some forensic financial documentation on him. Whoever paid him to be the inside man at Burgundy Lake will have left a trail."

"While Aaron and the gang play CSI Grand Cayman, don't forget to have them let us in on parallel rocketry developments in the works," Lyons added.

"You think this was a ploy to interrupt our ability to develop maneuvering thrusters that could compete with an enemy power?" Price asked.

"Wouldn't be the first time we were in on something like this," Lyons replied. "Does HS have an investigation team going to the border?"

"To pore over what's left of the raider team that hit, yeah," Price answered. "Fortunately, we do have the fingerprints and facials you sent us via digital camera."

"Keep working on that. I don't mind interagency cooperation, but HS tends to trip over its own dick when it comes to actually putting clues together," Lyons grumbled. "We can toss them a few hints when we're on the way home from wrecking the perps."

"Trust me," Price said. "You'll be the first ones to know anything about this."

"Good," Lyons replied. "I'm going to get cleaned up and

get some food in me. By the time I'm done, Paczesny will feel like he's been in sensory deprivation for a whole day."

"Don't forget to break out your Fed suits," Price reminded him.

Lyons wrinkled his nose. "Yeah."

Watching him over the Web cam link, he saw Price's face brighten with gentle but mocking humor. "Just when you thought you'd gotten away from the suit and tie look…"

"Yeah," Lyons said, rolling his eyes. "It's the price I have to pay to get a look at Burgundy Lake."

"We'll be able to reconstruct the raiders' hit when we're on-site," Blancanales added. "The tactics they used might give us a clue as to who trained this group."

Lyons nodded. "I hope they're local. I'd hate to lose a shot at them because they're overseas."

"Phoenix Force is prepped and ready to move out," Price told him. "Your job this time around is to work inside our borders."

Lyons sighed. "Used to have the whole world as our beat map."

"You've been getting more chances to step out and play, Ironman. Don't worry. This doesn't seem close to finished," Price promised.

Lyons glanced toward the broom closet where Paczesny was being softened by Schwarz's home-brewed sonic assault. "Not with Paczesny. Right now, I'm melting his brain. In a few minutes, he's going to wish he didn't have one."

The Able Team leader broke contact and freshened up.

CHRONOLOGICALLY, LEON PACZESNY was left in the sensory deprivation for only forty minutes total. However, due to the white noise and utter lack of sensation except for the tearing agony in his ruined elbow, it felt as if he were penned up in the broom closet for forty hours.

The first hint he had of the real world was when the duct tape was ripped off his mouth and eyes. Gag free, he let out a yell that was cut off when Lyons punched him just under the sternum. The blow interrupted the shout and cut off his breathing for a few seconds.

Just long enough for the Able Team commander to slide the headphones off Paczesny's ears. Then the turncoat felt the back of his head crack against the broom closet wall, iron-hard fingers squeezing his jaw until it felt as if the mandible would snap.

"Welcome back to the land of the walking dead," Lyons snarled. "I'm the Ironman, and I'll be your host on the scenic tour of hell."

"You can't do this. I'm an American citiz—"

"You, Mr. Paczesny, are nothing anymore," Lyons growled. "You are listed among the corpses stacked like cord wood back at Burgundy Lake. As such, you are a non-entity, only useful for as long as you are giving up information. Do I make myself perfectly clear?"

"I have no rights?" Paczesny asked, already knowing the answer.

"You're acting as if I'm some kind of cop. I'm the Grim Reaper, pal. It's just been a busy night, thanks to you, and I want to play a little before packing you off to hell."

"Damn it, you can't do this. You have to have some kind of authority, some rulebook…" Paczesny said. "This isn't Camp X-Ray."

Lyons slammed his forearm down on Paczesny's. "Camp X-Ray? That's amateur hour, dip shit. It's kindergarten, while this is the graduate class. Get it?"

"Yes. Yes, sir," Paczesny whimpered. "I got it!"

Lyons started the digital recorder, and began asking questions. Paczesny spilled his guts.

Stony Man Farm, Virginia

HUNTINGTON WETHERS LISTENED to the download of the MP3 file that Able Team uploaded to him. Paczesny's confession made the process of forensic accounting easier, enabling Wethers to locate the trail of funds.

Naturally, the identities of the mysterious donors remained vague. Paczesny didn't have faces or voices, only e-mail contacts and a few shadowy meetings with men who hid their features and utilized vocal distortion technology. The trail of cash in Paczesny's Cayman Island account also followed a tangled snarl of jumps from front company to front company, all of which were new and lacked any ties to previously known espionage or organized crime groups.

Wethers squeezed his brow as he went over the financial autopsy on the screen before him, scanning line by line for the name of a front company owner who would register on any of a thousand law-enforcement watch lists. Though the plodding, meticulous cyberdetective was utilizing his search engines to look for a familiar name, his own vast reserves of memorized information churned in his mind, working as fast as the powerful processors of the Cray supercomputers in the Annex.

For all of the technological power in the Stony Man cybercenter, the computers were still only pale duplicates of the human brain, lacking intuition or the ability to correlate something that didn't quite match what came before.

Wethers blinked his eyes, realizing he hadn't done so in several minutes. Tears washed over his parched orbs, flooding down the side of his cheek.

"Doing okay, Hunt?" Akira Tokaido asked from his workstation.

Wethers picked up his pipe and chewed on the stem, sitting back to allow his subconscious to digest the images burned into his retinas. "Just slow, steady work. I need to rest my eyes a little."

Tokaido nodded.

"Nothing's shown up yet?" Carmen Delahunt asked, stepping over to Wethers' station.

"The money that ended up in Paczesny's account has been immaculately sanitized," Wethers responded. "I've gone over every single penny, and can't make head nor tails of where it came from, despite all the front companies."

"Maybe you're looking at too large an object," Tokaido responded. Wethers glanced over at his younger partner, gnawing on his pipe stem.

"You mean that this might have come from another source?" Wethers asked. "Someone might have found a way to pick up the fractions of pennies in interest and convert the digital leftovers into real money?"

"It's happened before," Tokaido replied. "But you'd have to be very good to break into that kind of a slush fund."

"Wait…fractional cents of interest?" Delahunt asked. "Sure. Bank computers round down the interest they're offering, keeping the leftover bit for themselves. But surely, it would take a large bank to accumulate that kind of money."

"You'd be surprised, especially since we're talking how many banking franchises in the U.S.?" Tokaido asked.

Wethers nodded his understanding. "So someone has a tap on banks, and they're using that to create a clean form of money. And of course, the banks won't say anything, because they don't want the public to know that they're being short-changed. Instead of getting thirty-two point eight-five-two cents, they only get the thirty-two, and the bank keeps the slop over. In the course of a year, that can add up to ten cents an account, times however many hundred customers per branch, over the course of several years…"

"Big money tucked away for the guys up top," Delahunt said. "And it's completely independent of the FDIC insurance on any account."

"So Paczesny ended up with forty grand in his account," Wethers mused out loud. "And it's made up of withheld interest surplus from a banking franchise, which can't mention the disappearance of that kind of money, unless they want to pay taxes on it."

"We're dealing with a good hacker," Delahunt noted. "The dummy companies that filtered those funds also have nothing much to give in terms of who set them up. Akira, think you can do something about that?"

"I'll hit it hard," Tokaido said, accepting the challenge. "There's no way to make a dummy without leaving one fingerprint on it."

"It could be that they left a fingerprint, but we just haven't recognized it as such," Wethers added. "Some signature that would be so obscure that while we've been looking at it, it just simply blends in."

"Your fine-tooth comb has eliminated a lot of options," Tokaido mentioned, looking at the relevant data that Wethers collected. "It's going to take some hairy-ass cyber monkey action to break this open."

Wethers snorted. "Thank you, Akira, for introducing an image of your hirsuteness that I shall need to gouge from my mind's eye with a spork."

Tokaido and Delahunt chuckled at the scholarly computer expert's subdued shudder.

"Hunt, work with me on trying to back-trace the origin of the trucks," Delahunt said. "It'll be something new for your brain to work on to clear the cobwebs."

"Unfortunately, Able Team didn't leave much in terms of trace evidence on the vehicles," Wethers lamented, looking at

Delahunt's notes. "And what Carl and the lads didn't wreak, the marauders themselves contributed. VIN plates removed, and no accumulation of personal items that could betray origin. Even the odometers were taken out."

"Thorough," Delahunt agreed. She took a deep breath, returning to her workstation. "With the odometers, and a rough estimate of the distances traveled, we could have at least narrowed down the trucks to wherever they were stolen or purchased."

"How about the electronics?" Wethers inquired. "Surely the IR illuminators should have betrayed a point of origin."

"Chinese military equipment, top of the line for special forces," Delahunt said. "It doesn't show up on any catalogs, but we've had enough dealings with the Security Affairs Division to know what their gear looks like."

Wethers observed the screen, looking at the night-vision equipment that had been photographed by Schwarz. Images of the complete unit, then dissected, were displayed. Chinese knockoff transistors were in the design. "It's pretty damning. Red China is the only concurrent power to the United States to have a burgeoning aerospace industry devoted to orbital craft."

"We've also got an international mix of operatives among those bodies not burned or mutilated beyond the point of recognition," Delahunt mused. "China does have the kind of budget to…"

Wethers glanced over to her as her train of thought trailed off. Her green eyes flickered and Wethers knew she'd hit a hunch.

"Akira, put the bank search on hold," Delahunt noted. "Take a look at brokers who make large dollar to yuan conversions."

Tokaido nodded slowly. "Why didn't I think of that in the first place?"

"That's why we're a team, Akira," Wethers admonished. "Still, what would the PRC benefit by this? This kind of activity could result in trouble for them once an astute investigator figured this out."

"You think that this is circumstantial evidence left to implicate Beijing?" Delahunt asked.

"It's a possibility. Or, it could be a double-blind. The U.S. wouldn't believe China to be so arrogant as to leave these traces, and thus waste energy confirming such a setup," Wethers explained.

"One step at a time," Delahunt said. "We find the evidence, and then see where it points. As setup or as genuine."

"Fair enough," Wethers stated. He went to work, going over transistor lots and equipment manufacture manifests. Though it looked as if he were in a trance, mentally slowed to a stop, his brain raced at the speed of light.

In the back of his brilliant mind, the eldest member of the Stony Man cybernetics crew wondered if the speed of light was still too slow to prevent Armageddon.

Midway Island, U.S. Naval Cleanup and Reclamation Center

PHOENIX FORCE HAD BEEN returning from an operation in India when they received the alert to go on stand-by due to another crisis. David McCarter waited in the hangar at what was a covertly operating Naval Air Station, stubbing out a Player's cigarette. The U.S. Navy had been publicly ordered to clean up the contamination of the Midway Station National Wildlife Refuse, but there were still low-profile facilities available for the United States Special Operations Command to use as forward staging areas. Phoenix Force was taking advantage of the top-secret station to recuperate from the first half of a long flight when they'd received a stand-by alert.

"Thank you, David," Rafael Encizo said, waving the fumes away from his face.

McCarter winked and pulled another from its pack, lighting up. "Anytime, mate."

Encizo rolled his eyes. "This is Hawaii. Fresh air, crystal-blue water, verdant green…"

"Yeah. But I'm workin' as fast as I can to fix that," McCarter joked.

"Give me strength," Encizo groaned. He walked out onto the tarmac. The breeze blowing spared him from suffering McCarter's secondhand smoke. "Think we'll have time to head home, or will we have to resupply here?"

"Your guess is as good as mine," McCarter answered. "But I'm betting that it'll be a little while until we're back at the Farm. Hope you didn't have any hot dates waiting."

Encizo shrugged. "You know me, David. A girl in every port."

McCarter didn't know whether that was an exaggeration or not, but he didn't particularly care. The Cuban had his relationships that had survived the social-life-strangling strains of covert operations, as McCarter had his own.

"We've got an update," T. J. Hawkins announced. The youngest member of Phoenix Force had been manning their satellite uplink-equipped laptop, waiting for news.

McCarter crushed the half-smoked cigarette and joined Encizo beside Hawkins, Calvin James and Gary Manning to observe the electronic briefing from where they'd been occupying themselves.

"Currently, all we have is circumstantial evidence," Barbara Price announced on screen. "But put together, it's pretty damning. We've got several million dollars missing from People's Republic of China banks. The money disappeared from facilities that were converting dollars to yuan and vice versa."

"Added to the SAD-style night vision, it does look damning," James, a former San Francisco police officer, agreed.

"But circumstantial evidence doesn't hold up. We need something stronger."

"Try this image we've got from an NRO satellite," Price added. An image appeared on the screen, a photograph of a launch facility. The image enlarged and focused on a corner of the launch campus. "It was observing a facility referred to in the records as the Phoenix Graveyard."

"Glad I'm not superstitious," McCarter muttered.

"Looks familiar," Gary Manning said, cutting off his friend's gloomy proclamation. "The same kind of terrorist combat training facilities that litter Asia from Syria to Pakistan."

"Too disorganized to be conventional army barracks, and this tank," Encizo mentioned. "I recognize that kind of water tank. There's one at Cape Canaveral."

"A zero-gravity, space-suit training tank," James agreed. "The water duplicates the relative lack of gravity, as well as operating in a self-contained atmosphere, preparing people for extra-vehicular activity."

"And it's not for astronauts, because this is a second tank in addition to one for the Chinese astronauts," Manning said. "The Chinese don't normally send people into orbit, and when they do, it's on the QT. Mostly, their facilities are rented out to launch satellites, but they do have their own space program, complete with a knockoff of the shuttle that's a little better than the Russians'."

"So they're training terrorists for zero-gravity combat in a space suit?" McCarter asked. "That narrows down the targets considerably."

"The International Space Station," Hawkins concluded. "Isn't there supposed to be a shuttle launch and rendezvous?"

"It'll be going up in three days," Price answered. "Take a look at this setup here…"

The photograph increased in detail, and it was a maze of

tires. Utilizing computer wizardry, the picture blended with the layout of the ISS. The commandos of Phoenix Force were immediately aware of the PVC pipes that simulated the crawl-spaces between the station's various modules.

"Still circumstantial evidence," James stated. "It's too thin to make a rush into the People's Republic."

"One more bit of evidence. We did a sweep for radiation on the scene," Price concluded. "We picked up high-energy gamma radiation signatures."

James winced and McCarter knew that the Phoenix Force medic had heard something terrible. McCarter checked his memory for problems that would have a high gamma radiation signature.

"Iridium 192," McCarter stated.

"You got it, David," James answered. "It's a very credible threat for a dirty bomb. External exposure to Ir-192 pellets can cause radiation burns, acute radiation sickness or even death."

"They wouldn't need explosives," Manning interjected.

"What do you mean?" McCarter asked.

"Iridium is a highly dense metal. We're talking a higher friction resistance than the toughest steels around. Plop it into the atmosphere on a proper trajectory, when it hits the ground, even the pencil-size sticks of Ir-192 used for industrial weld-ing gauges will survive and merely fragment," Manning said. "Put it in a barrel, and reentry will heat the drum up enough that when it strikes a solid surface, like a building, it'll pop like a balloon, spitting shards over the center of a city."

"A radioactive shotgun round," McCarter mentioned. "Anyone not killed by a splinter of the stuff would receive a dose of radioactive shrapnel. With the amount of casualties possible from an air burst over a city, you'll have hundreds, perhaps thousands, suffering from both fragments and the ra-diation they put out."

"They wouldn't need a barrel, and they'd have their delivery systems on the ISS," Hawkins noted. "Right now, our shuttle is going up to augment the ISS satellite maintenance duties. At any time, there's a half dozen satellites docked to the station, and there are remote operating thrusters to return the satellites to their proper orbits. It'd only take a minor bit of programming to turn a satellite into a weapon, especially with a load of Ir-192 in its guts."

McCarter took a deep breath. "When do we take off, Barb?"

"There's not too much activity now, but the timing of the hit on Burgundy Lake with the launch of the current shuttle mission is just too suspicious," Price told them. "If it's Beijing looking to make an official move, or renegades at work, we need to get you in the air now."

"What's our ride?" McCarter asked.

"The Gulfstream's been refueled by naval aviation, but the closest approach to the Chinese launch facility is in Thailand. The Gulfstream's not set up for HALO, nor a stealth border crossing, so you'll transfer to a dedicated craft in Thailand, and then infiltrate the Phoenix Graveyard, approximately 250 miles west of Canton," Price responded. "I'll arrange for gear to be ready when you get there. Good luck."

"We'll need it," Hawkins muttered.

"All right, team, load up," McCarter ordered.

CHAPTER FOUR

Yuma, Arizona

Leon Paczesny was turned over to federal Marshals, glad to
be away from the big, menacing blond cop who liked to pound
on his arm. It had only taken a gentle reminder, dozens of
color photographs of the corpses Able Team had created the
night before, to ensure that Paczesny was going to keep their
part in the apocalyptic border-crossing quiet. Hal Brognola
had a Justice Department detachment, independent of the
Burgundy Lake investigation, take care of the turncoat. The
deal was a simple one. Paczesny would eventually be turned
over by Brognola's baby-sitters, and the traitor would confess
to his part in the operation.

In return for not contesting his espionage charges, he'd get
to live. It would be an existence in an eight-foot-by-five-foot
cell until he was old and decrepit, but it would be life. Any
deviation from the deal would result in pieces of Paczesny
being mailed to all of his living relatives, each part harvested
from his screaming body.

Lyons told the traitor that they had excellent life support

machines. He amended the threat with a story of the last fool who blew his free pass to continued existence. With grudging respect, Lyons noted that the turncoat had survived until he was trimmed down to an eyeless, earless, noseless head attached to a torso that had been carved down to just above the navel.

"It was the most incredible six months of my life, slicing a traitorous bastard up like lunch meat," Lyons confessed.

It was all a lie, but Paczesny didn't know that.

"Intimidation has a name," Schwarz quipped after Paczesny left in the back of a Justice Department SUV. "Lyons. Carl Lyons."

The Able Team leader snorted. "This isn't a game, Gadgets."

"No, you sure talk a good nightmare," Schwarz answered.

"I don't like it, but when it comes down to saving noncombatants and breaking apart some thug who's in on a bunch of deaths I can prevent…"

"The needs of the many, bro," Schwarz replied. He bopped the ex-cop on the shoulder.

Lyons looked at his watch. It was just after dawn. "Please. It's too early for that *Star Trek* crap."

"Speaking of which," Blancanales interjected, "what's the plan? Stick around poking at any support structure for the mercenaries who hit Burgundy Lake, or do we go to Florida?"

Lyons frowned. "We'll spend a few hours here snooping around. We might hit something, but I doubt that the raiders' backup would stick around longer than sunset."

"That's including the guy who ran off," Blancanales reminded him.

Lyons nodded. "Our mystery opponent took off, and we still haven't assembled much in terms of ranking on this group. Chances are, the escapee was either the highest ranking, or the most experienced in the marauder party. Either way, that will make him valuable enough to be useful in Florida."

"A hit on Cape Canaveral would be insane," Schwarz stated. "The security forces on hand are well-trained."

"So were the Air Force guards at Burgundy Lake. Besides, we've penetrated NASA security before, too," Lyons countered.

"Okay. We hit the bricks and try to catch our boy on the way out of town," Blancanales said. "I'd make it a safe bet he'd try a charter flight."

"Check on it," Lyons told him. "I'll be at the battle site. Gadgets, check out the warehouse where the combined task force has the wreckage. A closer look at the stolen technology might tell us if this was an effort to steal and reverse-engineer the thrusters, or just getting it out of the way."

"Knowing the state of international rocketry research, it's a good bet that they already have their own version of the operating thrusters Burgundy Lake was working on," Schwarz agreed. "And where will you be?"

"You don't run into anything larger than a few homes or a roadhouse until you reach the coast," Lyons replied. "The north is the eastern suburbs of Yuma, so there'll be airports, but the only major airfield in Mexico is pretty deep behind the border, about halfway to the coast."

"Your Spanish sucks, Ironman," Blancanales mentioned.

"I know enough to get by. I'm just going there to see what they've got set up. Bear took a look on satellite and saw only single seaters, but these engines are supposed to be small maneuvering thrusters, so they can't take up a lot of space on something like a ninety-nine-ton shuttle. Transporting a few examples via a puddle hopper won't be difficult," Lyons surmised.

"What about the mercenaries?" Schwarz asked.

"Cessna Stationaires hold six passengers. They dump their assault load out, and they can pack on two thruster prototypes a piece with the 180-pound luggage capacity. I saw only four in the one truck, so given the two we found in the other, we can count three Stationaires, eighteen mercenaries and six thrusters in the air toward the coast," Lyons pointed out. "That accounts for half the force we eliminated. Don't forget that in Mexico, whatever flight-plan paperwork exists is literally on paper, not something we could get with a hacker."

"That's quite a distance," Blancanales noted, looking at the aerial photo map Lyons pointed to. "One man, doing it on foot, that'd be a hump, even to the nearest road, which would be Route 8, cutting from Sonoyta to Puerto Penasco."

"You or I could do it," Lyons replied. "A disciplined soldier could make Route 8 by sunrise, and there is traffic on the road."

Schwarz spoke up. "And if he and his buddies thought ahead, they could have had a spot to dump off the heavy vehicles and transfer to less conspicuous rides before they got to the airport."

He summoned up a satellite map on his PDA and began calculating distances from the previous night's battle and the road to the coast.

"Foothills?" Lyons asked.

"Yup. Found it. Seriously broken ground where you could stash a used car lot and keep it invisible from the air," Schwarz answered. "I'm going to check on the thrusters, but I think I'll talk to Dr. Bertonni. Something tells me that she's not out of danger yet."

Blancanales thought for a moment. "Give me a few minutes on the phone, then I'll hop out with you and Jack to the airfield to check it out."

"Good plan," Lyons replied. "The less dicking around we do here, the less chance we have of losing our wayward punk."

"Good hunting," Schwarz told his partners.

"Thanks," Lyons answered. "This guy looks like he's dangerous game."

SABRINA BERTONNI DIDN'T feel any more comfortable after having her side stitched shut, but she was alive, and no longer bleeding.

She was tired, having been up for a long time, but the investigative team looking into the Burgundy Lake raid had brought her to the warehouse where recovered hardware and wreckage from the battle scene were assembled on long tables to be examined in depth for forensic traces. After a grueling inventory, the exhausted rocket scientist took a seat on a bench in a corner. A deceptively baby-faced, mustached man with a mop of unkempt brown hair and sparkling brown eyes held a bottle of cold cola out to her.

Bertonni took the bottle with a smile and he sat next to her, opening his own drink. "Thanks."

He wore a badge naming him as Henry Miller. Sabrina raised an eyebrow as he took a seat beside her without drilling her with questions.

"You look like you could use the caffeine," Gadgets Schwarz told her.

"Thanks, Deputy Miller," Sabrina replied.

"Call me Gadgets," Schwarz replied. "Deputy makes me sound like I belong in a Western."

"Gadgets," Bertonni repeated. "So you're a tech-head?"

"Ever since I was a kid," Schwarz replied, taking a sip. "I'm mostly electronics, programming and robotics, but I've dabbled in rocket science."

Bertonni nodded, drawing a sip from her soda. "So what department are you with?"

"The Justice Department," Schwarz answered. "But I'm more a tech-head than a field agent, despite the gun on my hip."

"So I don't have to dumb down answers to any questions you have?" the woman asked.

Schwarz shook his head. "Nope. Though I already know about the basics of your compact hydrogen cell."

"How much do you understand?" Bertonni prodded.

"Enough to be impressed at your fuel to energy conversion formulas," Schwarz responded. "I'm more solid-state technology, but I've got a solid grounding in chemistry and physics. The important thing we need to know is, how recoverable are the engine parts?"

"The thrusters were made to withstand considerable shake, rattle and roll. These were going to be tested out on the next ISS mission. We had everything set up to transport today," Bertonni said. The words caught in her throat. "It's so hard to believe that only a few hours ago…"

Schwarz rested his hand on her shoulder. Bertonni gulped, trying to dislodge the constriction in her windpipe, but her voice still crackled with tension.

"A plane was supposed to be coming in to pick up the test modules at Burgundy Lake this morning," she explained. "Burgundy Lake… Stupid name for the test facility. There wasn't anything for forty miles that was inhabitable, let alone moisture. Flat desert with just that compound, and the outskirts of Yuma safely shielded behind a mountain and…"

Schwarz gave her a gentle squeeze as she began to ramble. Bertonni wiped a tear and smiled gently at him. "Sorry."

"It's okay," Schwarz said. "It's going to be all right."

He frowned, then pulled his CPDA. An aerial view of the compound betrayed a landing strip not a mile away. "You didn't happen to see what went down at the airstrip?"

"No, but explosive charges were placed around the dormitories for the staff, as well as the testing and administrative buildings. All we knew was that the trucks rolled up, and then my partners started…started…"

Schwarz gave her shoulder a reassuring pat. She rested her

hand on his, smiling at the gesture. "You need to get some sleep. I've got a pair of well-armed federal Marshals who will keep you safe."

"Could have used them six hours ago," Bertonni said with a sob. "You're going to make sure whoever did this won't get away with my friends' murders, won't you?"

"Someone already took care of most of them," Schwarz informed her. "The killers are smeared across a five-mile stretch of desert along the border. They've been shoveling bodies into bags for identification."

Bertonni nodded. "I thought I'd have felt better, knowing that the men who did this are dead…"

"It doesn't take the pain away. It rarely ever does. But later on, you'll know that the monsters behind this won't hurt anyone else again," Schwarz replied.

"And the guys who put them up to it?"

"They're going down. I'll see to it."

Sonora, Mexico

SPEEDING OVER THE SONORA desert in a Bell JetRanger, Carl Lyons heard his cell phone warble.

"What's up, Gadgets?" the Able Team leader asked.

"Lot of shit's not adding up, Ironman," Schwarz responded. "There's an airfield right by the test facility, call it a mile away, but with an access road. And a NASA transport was scheduled to pick up the test modules that the marauders stole. They could have hit the airstrip this morning and taken the transport if they'd only waited a few hours."

Lyons frowned. "They have the pilots, especially if they intended to use any airstrips in Sonora. And the NASA crew wouldn't notice bullet holes in the test facility. The raiders could have hit the plane, then taken it through one of the regular dope smuggling flight routes, and refuel it for a dash to a port or to an island refueling station."

"Carl, Gadgets," Blancanales interjected. "I just got off station with the Farm. The Justice Department forensics team going over our leftovers have reported in. It's an international crew. It's a mix between Europeans, Orientals and Semetic operatives."

"Hired mercenaries, or perhaps a sanitized strike group assembled by a major power," Lyons muttered. Outside his window, the sands of Mexico rocketed past at well over 100 miles an hour. "How soon till we reach the first of the airfields I looked at, Jack?"

"About ten minutes," Grimaldi answered.

The terrain rippled, and Lyons was heartened by the fact that it would be difficult to even use a dune buggy or a motorcycle to cross it. The wrinkled furrows would make any rapid progress a stomach-churning, neck-snapping journey. The unmarked tops of windswept dunes showed no tire tracks, and both Lyons and Blancanales used their binoculars to scan for tracks or dust clouds of any sort. Frustration gnawed at Lyons's gut as he hunted for clues. Then he spotted a glimmer against the pale blue sky in the distance.

Jack Grimaldi had seen it, as well. "An Ultralight."

"Pushing the limits of its range," Blancanales noted. While he didn't have a PDA to calculate distance, the wily veteran was as good with a map and compass as any highly trained soldier. "He probably resorted to gliding to conserve fuel, which is how we caught up with him this far."

"If it's him," Lyons countered. "Jack, get us closer. We can resume the search pattern if it's a false alarm."

"Got it," Grimaldi replied.

"We're closing in on the first airstrip," Blancanales stated. On his map was a marker of a position that had been provided by Lyons's contacts within the U.S. Border Patrol. "And he's circling for a descent."

"Doesn't mean anything," Lyons replied. Still, he reached for the DSA-58 carbine he had stashed under his seat. He kept its stock folded, for better maneuverability inside the confines of the helicopter. He idly wished for the nose sensors on the Hughes 500 NOTAR they'd utilized only a few hours before, but the JetRanger had the kind of speed and range Grimaldi required to ferry them on their search of the desert. The airstrip was quiet and still, but camouflage netting could have concealed a small battalion from unaided eyes. FLIR and Terrain Radar would have given them a better heads-up. He clicked on his open line to the Farm.

"Bear, got anything on satellite?"

"The sun's been baking the area enough to make any thermal imaging a mess. Radar shows you following something, but its signature is faint and indecipherable," Kurtzman answered. "It's an ultralight?"

"Yeah," Lyons confirmed. "It could be made of any one of a dozen materials that wouldn't show up well on a radar scan. Even its engine would be masked by the superstructure. Are there any vehicles in the area?"

"Anything outside is probably covered," Kurtzman told him. "The signal isn't coming back clean, so it's possible that someone's got camouflage netting with radar-absorbent material in it. Expect trouble, but I don't have any magic figures for you."

"I've got the outline of a hangar," Blancanales called out. "It looks large enough for half a dozen Cessnas. It's covered in camouflage netting, and low profile to blend into the hills."

Lyons squinted. There was motion near the airstrip as the Ultralight suddenly banked hard, powering into a climb to push above the altitude of the JetRanger. Grimaldi was watching their aerial quarry, but the movement on the ground was fluid motion of fabric tossed aside.

"Ironman, we've got signatures!" Kurtzman shouted. "Looks like…"

"Machine guns," Lyons bellowed, jolting Grimaldi into a hard juke to one side. Spearing tracers burned through the air only inches from Lyons's window, twin streams of glowing streaks confirming the dual-mounted .50-caliber machine guns raking the sky. Another position fluttered to life farther down the strip, and Blancanales shoved his folded FAL's barrel through the window port, holding down the trigger for half of the 30-round extended magazine.

With Grimaldi engaging in evasive action, the Puerto Rican's fire only swept the machine-gun nest with a few glancing shots, but it was enough to force the antiaircraft position to miss the JetRanger. Still, Blancanales was satisfied with the results of his suppression fire.

Lyons had his DSA-58 burping out rounds to harass the other antiaircraft nest, but he knew that there wasn't much of a chance of scoring an easy hit, not with Grimaldi weaving through the sky. "Jack, we need to get out of here. At least set us down out of range of the twin mounts."

"Make me a hole, guys," Grimaldi said.

Blancanales thumbed a round into the breech of his grenade launcher and fired. The shell hit, spewing a noxious-looking green cloud that obscured one of the machine-gun nests. In the meantime, Lyons unslung his Mossberg Cruiser 500, ejecting its load of Brenneke shells and quickly thumbing in a load of ferret rounds. The 12-gauge shell spit a tear-gas bomb toward the other twin-mounted Fifty. Being a solid round, the shotgun tear-gas shell had the range to pepper the enemy gunnery position. By tromboning the slide as fast as he pulled the trigger, Lyons saturated the nest with a blinding, stinging caldron of capsicum gas. The machine gunner, his sinuses and respiratory passages swollen in reaction to the horrendously hot-pepper extract, held down the spade trigger on the heavy machine gun, firing uncontrollably. His tear ducts felt as if they were filled with scalding hot acid, and he swept the half of the sky that was empty.

Blancanales's smoker was followed by a second, thickening the turgid green cloud, giving the helicopter room to maneuver.

"Put us down," Lyons told Grimaldi. "If we back off, they won't stick around."

"Roger," Grimaldi answered. "Luckily, Pol laid down a good landing marker."

Lyons looked to see that the ace Stony Man pilot had swooped the helicopter over Blancanales's thick green fog. The rotor wash pushed away the cloud, and Grimaldi let the aircraft drop right on top of the second machine-gun nest. The starboard landing skid hit the frame of the twin mount and tore it from its moorings, digging it into the sand.

Lyons and Blancanales snapped out of their harnesses and were out the chopper's doors in an instant. The Able Team leader paused only long enough to ram the pistol grip of his Mossberg into the jaw of one of the antiaircraft crew they'd landed among. Bone shattered under the impact, the gunner's head flopping loosely on a rubbery neck. Blancanales's FAL carbine burped out a short burst, churning 7.62 mm slugs through the intestines of a second gun crewman.

Lyons didn't have to tell Grimaldi to take off, as the helicopter popped into the sky like a cork. Already the tear gas was wearing off on the first machine gun nest. "Pol!"

Blancanales whirled, feeding his M-203 again. Snapping the shoulder stock straight on his rifle, he triggered the grenade launcher. A 40-mm round spiraled through the air between the two antiaircraft positions, the shell's travels seeming to take forever as Grimaldi struggled to gain altitude. When it felt like the first crew of enemy gunners could have recovered and taken a nap to sleep off the effects of the tear gas, the grenade landed at their feet. Six-point-five ounces of high explosive converted from solid potential chemical energy into a thunderclap of pressure and heat. The twin-mounted machine gun was shorn into its component parts by a wave of force that turned its crew's legs and lower torsos into a rocketing halo of jellied meat. Their top halves were simply lobbed out of the sandbag ring, bouncing on the tarmac.

Lyons traded his Mossberg for the DSA carbine to deal with a group of newcomers to the battle, teams of men exploding through two doors of the hangar, brandishing automatic weapons. Lyons's full-auto fire lanced into the squad, stitching torsos with high-velocity bullets that exploded through bone and vaporized tunnels through muscle and organ tissue.

"Damn it! Get them!" a voice shouted. Lyons narrowed his eyes and spotted a short, balding man with lean, cruel features, tripping a memory in the Able Team commander's mental mug book. He dismissed his familiarity with the enemy leader, swinging his DSA's chattering stream of automatic fire toward his slender opponent. The enemy leader charged ahead of the scything arc of supersonic lead, saving his own life, but causing Lyons to mow down three of his forces.

Blancanales added his autofire to the conflagration, but the fleeing leader was inside the protective walls of the hangar. Rather than being deterred, the Able Team grenadier stuck an M-433 HEDP round into his launcher and fired. When the dual-purpose round touched the wall of the hangar, its copper armor-penetrating shrapnel charge spit out the prefab wall material and molten metal in a cone of lethal devastation that slashed through whatever defenders stood on the other side of the door. Screams of agony split the air.

Lyons emptied his DSA through the hole, then transitioned to his six-inch Colt Python. The airplane access doors groaned ominously and buckled as a thunderous force exerted itself. Moments after the doors deformed, they toppled over, concussive force shearing them from their moorings. Inside, a Cessna Stationaire idled, its propeller sucking smoke from the detonations into spirals of inky grayness. The dark-clad, blond figure stood in a half-open door and brought up a pair of flashing Uzi submachine guns.

Lyons and Blancanales dived for cover as a salvo of 9 mm slugs stabbed at them. The Able Team leader grunted as his body armor stopped a pair of slugs, and he triggered the Colt Python, knowing it wouldn't be enough to stop the prop plane. He missed the twin-machine-pistol-wielding enemy leader as the Cessna shot forward. Another plane closed its access door and followed the lead plane, but having started later, it was slower, enabling Blancanales to cut loose with his FAL rifle.

The engine belched smoke as 7.62 mm slugs tore into it. The high-velocity bullets shattered the pistons, freezing up the propeller. Lyons let the Python drop to the tarmac and he unslung his Mossberg 500. Tromboning the slide, he hammered a blast of slugs into the fuselage and passenger cabin. Twelve-gauge missiles punched through fiberglass and flesh, tearing into the gunmen jammed into the back of the plane.

Blancanales's grenade launcher chugged loudly, a third Cessna disappearing in a cloud of flame and splinters.

All the while, Lyons watched the lead plane, and the enemy commander, the same slender figure who'd raced into the darkness before. The Cessna climbed until it was a tiny speck in thousands of miles of empty sky. It was out of eyesight in a minute, but it was not out of sight of the satellites that the Farm had watching the airstrip.

"That's twice you've gotten away," Lyons snarled. "But we'll see where you're going. There won't be a third time."

CHAPTER FIVE

The Pacific, en route to Thailand

As they were making their preparations for the penetration into China, there were a few things on Phoenix Force's side.

The first was the requirement that orbital launch stations be as close to the equator as possible, which limited the facility to being on the southern coast of the nation, far closer to the equator than even NASA's launch center in Cape Canaveral. While Florida was below the 25th Parallel, the south China coast was well below the 20th Parallel, the Tropic of Cancer. The nearness to the equator added to the facility of getting to orbital velocity by using the Earth's rotation for help. Since space vehicles orbited simply by missing the Earth's surface and atmosphere in their million-mile "fall," it required less energy to attain the altitude necessary to enable that skillful task of throwing themselves at the ground and missing.

Considering the nature of Stony Man Farm's previous conflicts with the Chinese government in their sponsorship of terrorism and espionage against the United States, Phoenix Force and the Farm had developed dozens of infiltration protocols to get into the nation, contingencies that had been set up for other enemy nations that sponsored the atrocities McCarter and his men spent their lives fighting against. Actually using one of those contingency plans wasn't something that McCarter relished, but there was the chance that this operation might be coming to the Chinese government's rescue.

McCarter mused on that for a moment as he reassembled his CZ P.01 pistol. A modern update of his favored Browning Hi-Power, with its safety replaced by an easy-to-reach decocking lever, it had the same ergonomics and high capacity as his preferred Browning, but its Czech origin meant it wouldn't be traced back to the U.S. if it was lost in the heat of battle. He'd field-stripped the gun to ensure the mechanism was sound, with no burrs on any springs or bearing surfaces that could have compromised reliability. He loaded a 13-round magazine into the butt of the gun, racked the slide, thumbed down the decocker and holstered it. The P.01s were Czech police issue, but used 9 mm ammunition available around the world, including China. The same went for Phoenix Force's Type 95 assault rifles. The compact bullpups were ugly, and oddly balanced, but they were tough, reliable and used Chinese military ammunition, the 5.8 mm cartridge easily garnered from enemy forces. His and Calvin James's rifles were fitted with 35 mm under-barrel grenade launchers, while Gary Manning eschewed the compact bullpup for the NORINCO Type 79 self-loading sniper rifle. The Phoenix Force marksman preferred having a long-range weapon, and the 7.62 mm round had an effective range of 1300 meters.

There would be no disguising their appearance, so the team was decked out with a variant of the Land Warrior combat suit. Stony Man Farm had helped them out with the camouflage pattern that would match the area they were inserting into. The Land Warrior suits were complex weaves of Kevlar and Nomex that T. J. Hawkins and Gary Manning were currently stenciling camou patterns onto. The rifles were being color detailed with camouflage paint by Rafael Encizo while Calvin James went over his medical kit to ensure that they were ready for whatever infections and injuries they could incur. Radiation poison inoculations were also being set up, given the chance of external exposure to lethal Iridium-132. The dense, radioactive metal could cause gamma radiation burns and poisoning.

A layer of charcoal filtering underneath the Land Warrior suits would provide some protection, but gamma radiation was of a powerful, high-frequency energy wave that required high-density materials, such as lead aprons, to stop it. Unfortunately, that kind of protective covering would prove too bulky to wear into a stealth operation, and would hinder movement to such a degree that a firefight would leave them as practically stationary targets.

McCarter's satellite phone warbled and he picked it up. "News?"

"We've been digging into SAD internal communiqués. We ended up with a few discarded, zero-filed memos in their trash," Barbara Price announced. "Someone's keeping information in SAD from getting out about anomalies in their military launch programs. The higher-ups are not getting discrepancies in field reports on their threat matrix because someone's deleting them."

"I knew it didn't make sense for the Chinese to try something big against the International Space Station," McCarter said. "It's too risky a move that could start a nuclear exchange."

"Renegade factions inside Chinese intel?" Price mused. "Or someone who tapped into them?"

"We'll have a chinwag with the blokes running the joint when we drop in, Barb," McCarter returned.

"We'll keep tracing SAD communications to see if there's

evidence of a larger conspiracy within the government," Price said. "So far, the way they're smoke stacking the information, it looks like it might just be a small cadre involved, probably reinforced by international support."

A beep sounded, distracting Price. She put McCarter on hold for a few moments.

"We've got confirmation of activity in Mexico," Price broke in. "Able encountered a group of enemy soldiers in Sonora, utilizing an airstrip. They reinforced it with antiaircraft machine guns and a full squadron of aircraft on hand."

"Any escapes?" McCarter asked.

"Carl has confirmed that the same one who got away from them at the border was at the strip. He took off under a wave of suppression fire, but he was the only one who did," Price said. "We've got satellites tracking their plane."

McCarter rubbed his chin. "Then he won't get away."

"You sound doubtful," Price noted.

McCarter looked at the satellite photographs of the Phoenix Graveyard launch facility. "They obviously have to know that their activities are being watched by us. We've got enough eyes in the sky—"

"Image failure," Price interrupted. "Bear's reporting that we've lost satellite imaging on your insertion point."

"Looks like the Chinese have found their own copy of the antisatellite laser that Striker took out a while ago," McCarter commented. "It's no surprise that the Chinese 'borrow' technology from the Russians, whether Moscow wants them to or not."

"Damn it!" Price exclaimed. "Bear, we need to get on the horn to NRO now. Shift orbits for their birds over Sonora now."

"It'll take time to shift aim to take out anything in the sky over Mexico," McCarter stated. "We're talking vastly different orbital arcs."

"Not necessarily," Price returned. "So far, our flyer is heading due south and skimming the dune tops, hoping to lose himself in ground clutter through Mexican airspace. Obviously, our boy will have a refueling point somewhere in his operational range, and the time it takes to reach that distance, the laser might be recalibrated and ready to take down those satellites."

"Do you have anything else?" McCarter asked.

"We're monitoring VOR and local airfield radar, but again, he's flying nap of the earth," Price stated.

"He'll keep his radar footprint faint until the satellites are knocked out," McCarter grumbled.

"Have you prepped for insertion?" Price asked. "Maybe you could figure out where the laser came from."

"The camouflage paint will cure on the rifles and gear during the flight," McCarter replied. "There's nothing on the ground in China indicating a laser with the kind of reach to knock out a satellite. The Skysniper was a huge piece of machinery, the size of a railroad car, and it needed a lot of power. I don't see anything indicative of such a system."

"Maybe not on the ground in China," Price said. "Though I wouldn't put it past the Chinese to have a laser system."

"What about the plasma engine missiles? Striker destroyed their production facility, but perhaps enough technicians survived who remembered the basic layout. Those things had enough energy to reach escape velocity."

"We're scanning for possible launch sites in Southeast Asia," Price returned. "So far, nothing matches any signatures that we're familiar with. The missiles were fast, but that kind of velocity produces sonic shock waves. Listening posts are directed across mainland China to see if there have been such devices still in service, but we're talking a large land mass, with plenty of valleys to hide those tests."

"So it's up to us to go up to our elbows, sifting through the entrails," McCarter stated. "All while the Chinese government might be setting up a trap for us by making it look like they don't know about this."

"Watch your back, David," Price admonished.

"I will, Barb," McCarter returned.

The transport plane had given the signal. They were going to take off on a route toward Thailand. Along the way, Phoenix Force would disembark, provided they weren't blown out of the sky by Chinese interceptors or antiaircraft installations. Then there was the Phoenix Graveyard itself, full of armed guards and potential terrorists.

All of this taking place on a deadline that, by every indication, would run out when the next shuttle from NASA was sent up to the International Space Station.

In one way or another, the stars were going to be bloodied. Whether that blood would drip like venom across the Earth was up to the warriors of Stony Man Farm.

Kennedy Space Center, Cape Canaveral, Florida

CAPTAIN JORDAN BROOME went over the preflight checklist, looking for the slightest discrepancies that could ground the shuttle flight. The loss of *Colombia* due to broken heat shielding was proof of the fact that every detail had to be gone over with a fine-tooth comb. Even before the other shuttle disasters, the NASA crews performed "belt and suspender" checks to back up maintenance technicians.

His desk phone rang, and Broome picked up.

"Jordie? We've got a problem with the upcoming flight," Dr. Alexander Thet, the ground control coordinator for the upcoming mission, spoke hurriedly into the line. "Could you pop over to my office?"

"You can't tell me over the phone, Xander?" Broome asked.

"Your office doesn't have a secure link. Mine does," Thet answered.

"Secure link?"

"That bad. And the man on the other end doesn't want to run up a phone bill," Thet told him. "Move it."

Broome hung up and rushed down the hall to Thet's office. Thet was a small, pale man with a receding hairline and washed-out blond hair, so light it could almost be white. In comparison, there was a large, burly guy in a rumpled suit.

"Jord, Hal Brognola. Hal, Captain Jordan Broome," Thet said by way of introduction. He gestured to the video monitor with a small camera on the top. "I suppose I don't have to introduce the President, do I?"

Broome shook his head. "What's wrong?"

"Around midnight, there was an incident at a scientific testing facility in southern Arizona," the President said.

"The new hydrogen cell maneuvering thrusters?" Broome asked.

"Exactly. We lost the shipment," the President told him. "Mr. Brognola is going to be my liaison to you on this. We believe this might be more than just a sabotage attempt against technology."

"Why not handle this through Dr. Griffey?" Broome inquired.

"I appointed Stewart to manage the scientific end of things. Hal, here, is one of my most trusted associates in regard to matters of national and international security," the President said. "He is my right hand, and he can make any decision as if it were under my authority."

Broome nodded and offered a hand to Brognola. "It'll be good working with you."

"I hope so," Brognola answered. "But I rarely show up at pleasant circumstances."

"I'll leave the important details to Hal," the President told Broome and Thet. "I just wanted to make certain that there is no ambiguity as to how important Mr. Brognola's input is going to be."

The pair nodded, and the screen went dark.

"We have a feeling that there might be a problem on the International Space Station," Brognola announced, getting right to the point. Broome frowned at the implications as he looked at aerial photography of a Chinese launch facility. Broome could tell what it was because of the effort to duplicate the NASA facilities, as well as the equipment. If there was one thing that the Red Chinese could do, it was to replicate "borrowed" technology, and it was in full evidence here.

Brognola pointed to a training camp off to the side, and a scale-model layout of what could only be the ISS. "It's not concrete evidence, but we've been running this particular mock-up against every other facility, and nothing but the ISS matches it. And because it's a tire house, we can only assume that combat training exercises are being conducted inside."

"Can't be firearms based," Thet stated. "This isn't like an airliner where one bullet only adds another vector for depressurization. We'd be talking a major atmosphere leak, as well as a weakening of the station integrity."

"What's this that you have circled?" Broome asked.

"Those are deposits of Iridium-192," Brognola replied. "Whoever is responsible for the training camp setup—"

"It's not the Chinese?" Broome interrupted.

"We're digging. And while there might be elements of Red Chinese security involved, we don't believe that they are acting alone," Brognola stated. "Which is why I want to make a substitution on your shuttle crew."

Broome raised an eyebrow. "At the last minute?"

"He's a highly trained asset," Brognola told him. He handed over a file, heavily edited. Broome picked it up, looking over the dossier for "Henry Miller."

"I'm going to have to take some time on this," Broome replied. He glanced at Brognola. "He had been previously cleared for a shuttle mission?"

"Two in fact. Only one incident was meant as a ruse. The shuttle never launched," Brognola explained.

"So he's experienced. I do want to meet him. There's only so much that a piece of paper can tell me, and in case you haven't noticed, Mr. Brognola, we're going into space. Even if he's somehow managed to get on a shuttle before, this 'Miller' cat had better be on top of his game," Broome said. "I know you're only an administrator…"

"Hands on," Brognola countered. "And I am well aware of unit integrity. Ideally, we'd have loved to have Miller gain more experience with your crew, so that you could operate together more fluidly, but we just don't have the luxury to do so. As it is, he will be arriving here inside the hour."

Broome nodded. "We'll have to have Komalko sit this one out then, Xander."

The administrator nodded. "At least this guy has the creds to sit in for him."

"On paper," Broome retorted.

"That's another thing," Brognola said. "The crew going up to the ISS check out well on paper. But have you been getting any bad vibes from them?"

"Bad vibes? The crew is full of U.S. military personnel who have passed extensive background checks, Mr. Brognola," Broome protested.

Brognola sighed. "I know it seems like I'm insulting people, but in my line of work, I've run across a lot of sinners posing as saints."

"And in my line of work, you have to have good instincts about your people and your equipment," Broome countered.

"So no one on your crew has made you suspicious," Brognola surmised. "Good. That's all I wanted to know. Just keep your eyes and ears open for anything that might be suspicious."

Broome relaxed. He realized that it wasn't the Fed's intention to offend, that he was looking at every possible angle on how the opposition might want to damage the International Space Station. "I've got a shuttle to go over from nose to engine cones," he replied, the anger drained from his voice. "It's hard enough being suspicious of circuits and frame welds when you have to add in possible terrorists posing as astronauts."

"I know. That's why I'm bringing in Miller. He's not only qualified to ride with you, he's got a good sense for whoever might want to sabotage this mission or help hijack the ISS. Besides, you'll need someone with training on the station in case this group does launch a takeover attempt from China," Brognola explained.

"Takeover?" Broome asked. "You mean they'd send up a shuttle full of soldiers to take over the ISS? Why not just blow it out of the sky?"

"Because otherwise, they'd have no way to drop large amounts of highly radioactive isotope with a high resistance to reentry on the cities of the world," Brognola answered.

"Iridium 192… It's an externally hazardous material, but doctors use it all the time to treat certain forms of cancer," Thet advised. "Because it's so dense, however, it passes through without leaving trace amounts."

"But as shrapnel, it'd be hazardous because it would be embedded in the environment, giving off gamma radiation to irradiate survivors," Broome concluded. "Externally it produces radiation burns and induces radiation poisoning."

Brognola spoke up. "That's a dichotomy I'm having a little trouble wrapping my brain around. You'd think it'd be more hazardous inside a human body."

"We're talking different amounts," Thet replied. "The seeds that are ingested are tiny seeds. Internal radiation burns could occur in the digestive system if a quantity of industrial pellets were ingested. It's not completely harmless inside the body, otherwise it wouldn't be used to burn out cancer. As a shrapnel injury, exposure would be far worse."

Brognola nodded, understanding. His teams had had several close calls with various forms of radioactive material, and so far, they had all gotten through without major incapacitation. The foes of Able Team and Phoenix Force usually weren't so lucky, and the head Fed had seen the results of massive radiation exposure.

Thet's phone rang and he picked it up. "Miller's about to land," he said after hanging up.

Brognola looked to Broome. "Want to come meet him? Or do you still have checks to run?"

Broome shook his head. "It can wait a few minutes. I do want to meet your man and see if he'll fit in with the team."

"Can we get a driver, Xander?" Broome asked.

"I had one on standby when Mr. Brognola told me he was coming. I called before you came in," Thet explained.

"Thanks," Broome said. "I don't want to waste too much time."

"I certainly hope it is going to be a waste of time," Brognola stated. "Because if it isn't, the next few days are going to be hell."

Broome nodded in agreement, believing that the big Fed was correct.

"I KNOW YOU'RE NOT in love with the idea that we're splitting up," Schwarz told Lyons over his satellite phone as they approached to Cape Canaveral, "but Hal needs someone inside the shuttle."

"Yeah," Lyons mumbled. "I remember the last time we were an official part of the shuttle crew. That was a plain fucked mission. I just wish we still had you on the streets with us."

"There's always a chance the launch will be scuttled," Schwarz offered.

"I don't think so," Lyons replied. "They'll need someone up there. Right now, you're the best option. Shoving all three of us on the shuttle will make things too crowded, and will tip off any infiltrators at NASA that we're on to them."

Schwarz sighed, knowing that his friend was right. "Just be careful out there."

"Careful gets you killed, Gadgets," Lyons returned. "I'll just have to put a little more ball to the wall to make up for you not being at my back."

Schwarz chuckled through a nervous shudder. "You been holding back all this time, Ironman?"

"Just watch your ass. We'll be fine," Lyons admonished.

Schwarz hung up and looked out the window as the plane taxied to a halt. A silver Hummer with blue trim rolled up to the tarmac, and he saw Hal Brognola looking out one of the back windows.

Sabrina Bertonni stirred in her seat, looking up at him. "We're there?"

Schwarz nodded, grabbing his gear. "Yup. Are you sure that you're up to this?"

Bertonni shrugged. "Someone has to implement the upgrades on the samples we sent on ahead. Besides, I'm not the one riding tons of thrust into space."

Schwarz rolled his eyes. "When you put it that way, it sounds scary."

The scientist's lips tightened. She'd been brought into this knowing there was the possibility of sabotage or infiltration on the flight to the International Space Station. There was a good chance that this flight would end up in flames, just like the *Challenger* and *Columbia*. Instead of voicing her doubts, she picked up her bag and disembarked with Schwarz. They clambered down the roll-up steps as Jordan Broome and Brognola got out of the NASA Hummer.

"Captain Broome, this is Henry Miller," Brognola introduced. "Miller, Captain Jordan Broome, the commander of the USS *Arcadia*. Have you met Dr. Sabrina Bertonni, Broome?"

The astronaut nodded. "On a few instances, usually while going over testing protocols for the thrusters."

Schwarz offered his hand. "Permission to come on board, Captain?"

Broome took the offered hand and shook it, a moment of challenge rising as he applied a strong grip. Fortunately, the Able Team electronics genius was used to such testosterone-soaked rituals. His own hand was tight, and Broome's efforts to make the handshake uncomfortable were foiled by his own strong grasp. "Permission granted, Lieutenant Miller."

Schwarz grinned. "Call me Gadgets."

Broome nodded. "Kind of figured that Miller wasn't a real moniker."

"Oh, it is. But people keep wanting me to recite from *Tropic of Cancer*."

Broome chuckled. "So, how is June?"

Schwarz winked. "I'm sure you've seen the movie, Captain Broome."

The astronaut laughed. "Call me Jordie." His tone returned to seriousness after a moment. "You're going to have some trouble. The rest of the crew isn't going to like Pie Komalko being kicked to have you put in."

"Is there an official explanation as to why?" Schwarz asked Brognola.

"You're one of the few Burgundy Lake survivors in any condition to work with the experimental prototypes that survived the assault," Brognola replied. The big Fed glanced at Sabrina Bertonni, whose expression had darkened at the mention of the incident that had claimed the lives of so many colleagues.

"Right. A few had been sent on ahead," Schwarz replied with a nod, giving Bertonni's hand a reassuring squeeze. Her green eyes flicked to him, and her mouth turned up in the closest thing to a smile she could manage. Schwarz sympathized with her. "We'll work on upgrading the test samples to meet the current generation that was lost."

"We?" Broome asked. "So the nickname fits. You can work on the thrusters?"

"I've been discussing the work with him on the flight over," Bertonni noted. "He's a quick study, and assisting me, we'll get everything running better than the modules you were going to take up."

"Of course, that's between my preflight responsibilities," Schwarz noted.

"Komalko will help you out with that. With the two of you working on it, you'll be able to halve the time needed for the checks, freeing up room for the module upgrades," Broome stated. "But first, you're going to have to meet the rest of the crew."

Schwarz nodded. His introduction as an outsider would leave him vulnerable to anyone in NASA who could have been a turncoat. If the enemy had been able to slip an insider into Burgundy Lake, a top-secret facility with only a small staff, the sprawling Cape Canaveral could potentially be a minefield of danger.

That was Schwarz's job, though. To flush the enemy by setting himself up as bait. Glancing at Bertonni, he realized that she would be under the gun, as well, so he had more than his own life at stake.

Staring into the bright blue Florida afternoon, he knew both of their lives were on the line to keep the sky from falling.

CHAPTER SIX

Union Park, Florida

Andre Costa took the glass topper off his carafe of brandy to pour his third drink in as many minutes. His phone had rung five minutes ago, informing him of a new arrival at Cape Canaveral, taking the place of one of the crew of the space shuttle *Arcadia.*

It was supposed to be because of a need to upgrade the experimental prototype thruster modules that had been lost at Burgundy Lake. His hand shook, liquor sloshing around inside his crystal tumbler, and he wished that the alcohol would take effect faster. He took a hard pull on the brandy, then choked as he drank too quickly. The brandy burned in his sinuses and he wiped tears from his eyes. A sneezing fit left him dizzy, compounded by the alcohol burning through his bloodstream.

He'd performed a quick relay of phone calls to the next contact down the line after he'd gotten the call. It had taken only a minute of dialing, but he was shaken, wondering how the hell he'd gotten hooked up in all of this. Costa stood up, trembling from his burning nostrils and tear ducts, wishing that the allure of easy money as a drug lawyer hadn't brought him to Orlando. Though it wasn't the kind of hot spot that Miami was, it still received a lot of cases. The lion's share of cases he took were on behalf of the students at the University of Central Florida, charged with possession, not intent to sell. Of course, this attracted the attention of El Toronado, one of the biggest suppliers in Union Park, who took an interest in some of the students who were selling for him to get a little extra cash on the side for their extracurricular activities.

El Toronado was the only name Costa knew him by, but it was enough. One of the most feared businessmen in Orlando, he had his fingers in cases that stretched from Winter Garden on the shores of Lake Apopka all the way to Titusville.

More than once, Costa had been asked to help out at Cape Canaveral Air Station with civilian employees who had attracted attention. Costa was glad that the Judge Advocate General and the code of Military Justice kept him out of protecting whichever Naval airmen were involved in El Toronado's operations, but he still had staff members running research to assist the JAG defenders in those cases.

Costa was glad he never was involved in defending any of El Toronado's shooters, but that pleasure ended when he was approached by a man with photographs of his meeting with the Union Park drug lord.

"You'll be our conduit," the man stated.

"For what?" Costa asked.

"Just take the calls and pass them on. You'll be protected from prosecution under attorney-client privilege," the stranger told him. "Fail at any point…"

The stranger handed him a shotgun shell.

Costa looked at the brass and red-plastic cartridge, turning it over in his fingers, hearing the buckshot rattle inside.

"You've already got enough to disbar me and make me use-less to El Toronado."

The man reached out and took the shell. Costa noticed his latex glove.

"This will end up at a crime scene," the man told him. "You just need to know that when forensics takes your fingerprints off this shell, El Toronado will not be happy with your con-tinued existence."

The man set down a stack of photographs. As he saw through smears of crimson puddles, Costa's eyes widened at the horrors that could be inflicted on a human body.

"That man was still alive when those photographs were taken. I am told he lived two days afterward," the stranger stated. "As you can tell, his quality of life was…negligible."

Costa looked at the photographs. Toronado's agent turned and left after depositing a small, nondescript black-leather notebook on the table in front of Costa. It contained the num-bers he had to call. The ones he'd spent the past few minutes dialing.

His gut burned with brandy, and he wished that he was somewhere else.

A THOUSAND MILES TO the north, Aaron Kurtzman was lead-ing the effort to pick up any phone calls from the Titusville area. There were hundreds of calls going out, but only one call came from a pay phone all the way to a lawyer's office in Or-lando. While the pay phone was geographically easy to track down, its user wasn't. The call was only fifteen seconds, hardly a business call. The brevity of the communication, plus the call to a lawyer who was on the DEA's radar, raised a flag. It was one of twenty calls that could have been suspi-cious in the hour since Schwarz landed at Canaveral.

It was a warrantless search, and it would have been

frowned upon in the press, a mass net thrown out looking for something suspicious. Kurtzman kept rolling on the searches, poring through dozens of phone numbers, correlating the checks between the digits and their owners. In the second hour after Schwarz's arrival, five more suspicious phone calls were made out of the phone junctures at Titusville, and the Stony Man staff was hard at work tracking everything from point of origin to length of call. Even with Wethers, Tokaido and Delahunt working on it, the twenty-five phone calls that rang their alarms took another hour to go through, checking phone patterns of the callers of landlocked lines.

The only oddball in the stack was the pay phone call to André Costa, but even by then, Lyons, Blancanales and Grimaldi had their helicopter waiting at Space Coast National Airport in south Titusville, ready to move on anything that the cybernetics team had worked up. It was after sunset by the time Kurtzman had narrowed down the phone calls.

Tokaido and Wethers turned their attention to Costa's phone logs. They picked up a phone call to a cloned cell phone that had a Miami-Dade area code. While it might have given Able Team a lead going into Miami, the ability to hack cellular signals meant that the cell phone could have been anywhere in the country, and being on a cloned line, could have been any one of half a dozen units. If there was a GPS designation associated with the cell phone, it wouldn't carry over into the hacked duplicates.

LYONS'S ONLY LEAD BEGAN and ended with André Costa. The Agusta helicopter was one of the fastest craft in the air, much quicker than the Bell JetRanger they'd used in Mexico. The Able Team commander wondered if it would get him onto Costa fast enough to give him something to work with.

Lyons and Blancanales wore loose-fitting, summer-weight

jackets, not out of place in the relatively balmy winter months of Florida, but the oversize garments helped them to conceal their urban fighting kits. The Able Team commandos had their Smith & Wesson .40-caliber pistols tucked into waistband holsters, as well as shoulder harnesses from which hung micro-Uzi machine pistols on extendable slings. The sling would provide a brace for the stubby chatterboxes when pulled to full extension, but remain tucked out of sight, a hidden ace in the hole in case they encountered a firefight. Flush 20-round magazines nestled in the butts of the minichoppers, but were backed up by a quartet of 32-shot sticks.

"My gut's telling me this might be a sucker play," Lyons said as the Agusta passed over the University of Central Florida campus on its way toward Union Park, where Costa had his home and office. "This is just too noticeable."

"Or just noticeable enough to attract our attention," Blancanales agreed. "Just like the airfield in Sonora."

Lyons nodded, his jaw firmly set. "We went into that thinking we had the upper hand."

"We weren't packing light, Carl," Blancanales countered.

"No, but we thought that we had the advantage of surprise. And when we saw the ultralight still in the air, we sprung at it like a fish on a worm," Lyons explained. "We barely broke that ambush because we thought we got there in time, not after they set up a trap for us."

"Their response still wasn't quite enough," Grimaldi said from the pilot's seat.

"Only because we had you as a pilot," Lyons returned. "Anyone less, we'd have been knocked out of the sky, no matter how quickly I noticed the antiaircraft nests."

Grimaldi nodded. "I also had you and Pol as my gunners."

"So this setup, narrowing down our possible leads to a drug lawyer, could just be another trap," Lyons told them.

"We left our heavier hardware back in Titusville," Blancanales said. "Not that we'd want to cut loose with thirties and grenade launchers in a residential neighborhood."

"No," Lyons agreed. "The Uzis and our handguns will have to be enough on that count. Jack, I'm going to find us a place to park this bird, and we'll take the rest of the route by foot."

Grimaldi smirked. "Gadgets got you using his PDA?"

"He made one for each of us," Lyons returned. "I might not be able to do his fancy programming, but I've been able to handle technology more complex than flint spearheads and bearskins."

Lyons ran his stylus over the screen while Blancanales used his Combat PDA to contact Kurtzman.

"Bear's setting up a satellite to work on real-time imaging of Costa's home," Blancanales advised. "The bird's going to be recalibrated inside of a minute. He'll have thermal giving us the layout and the makeup of the reception committee on hand."

Lyons nodded. "I went high magnification on the map of Costa's neighborhood. His house actually has got a good flat roof for us to touch down, if you feel up to dropping us off into a hot LZ, Jack."

"I'm up for a little barnstorming," Grimaldi replied.

Lyons pocketed his CPDA. Pol, anything on satellite imagery?"

"Nothing," Blancanales answered. "Bear told me that they lost contact with the NRO satellites in operation over the southeast coast."

"All of them?" Lyons asked. "There's no way the enemy could have hit spy satellites over Florida and hit the bird watching China."

"Not with a laser, but we might be talking about some other means," Blancanales retorted.

"Not the satellite killers with the kinetic launchers again," Lyons mused.

"Something more down to earth," Blancanales answered. "Simple hacker interference."

"That kind of hacking isn't simple," Lyons retorted. "If it was, we'd be seeing a lot more actresses down-blouse photos from horny computer geeks. We're talking someone with a good crew and some killer applications."

Blancanales nodded. "So the cameras are still working."

"And they're going to see us coming, real-time, a mile away, tracking us, and with good infrared they'll know how hot we're rolling," Lyons continued.

"You were right, it's a trap," Blancanales answered. "We could have Orlando P.D. pick up Costa."

Lyons shook his head. "I'm not risking any cops when I can take the hit instead. And I'm not going to take the hit because I'm going to pour boxes of bullets down the hitter's throat."

"Same plan?" Grimaldi asked.

"Same plan," Lyons answered. "It's not an ambush when you know you're going to get your ass shot at."

The Agusta thundered through the sky, skimming the treetops on its date with the enemy hit team.

JASON MELLERA HAD BEEN ordered to stake out André Costa's home, and he was told to bring a dozen of the meanest bastards he knew, all loaded up with the best hardware they could find.

Mellera, Toronado's best local enforcer, was not one to want for manpower or firepower when it came time to kill. He'd been responsible for the disappearances of twenty streetcorner dealers who were encroaching on Toronado's turf. In one instance, Mellera had even been able to hook up with a box of fragmentation grenades, three of which he'd thrown at one dumb ass who thought that he could sling flake on someone else's corner. The first grenade made a mess. The other two reduced the dealer and his compatriots' shredded bodies to unrecognizable pulps, unidentifiable even by dental records.

Mellera still had those grenades, and he handed them out to the muscle he'd brought in. The miniature bombs and their assortment of assault rifles, submachine guns and shotguns would have made them a match for any fighting force in Florida. Anyone who didn't have his own heavy artillery was given a piece of firepower from the enforcer's own collection.

"How many are we expecting?" Mellera asked.

"Two or three," came the response on the phone. "We're not certain of the exact numbers."

"Twelve men to take down two?" Mellera pressed.

"Don't knock the odds. We want overwhelming force against these two. Start shooting and don't stop firing until they're bloody smears, got it?"

"And they're worth a million a head?"

"A million a head, and another million on completion."

Mellera's instincts rang out. That kind of money and that kind of overkill were not called for lightly. This wasn't a case of simple nerves.

"Anything?" Mellera asked into his walkie-talkie, nestled in the shadows of some bushes on Costa's estate.

"I hear a helicopter coming in low and fast."

"That's gotta be it," Mellera said. "Everyone, ready. Don't fire until we see them disembark. We need to hit them as one."

"Gotcha," came the responses over the radio.

The Agusta thundered overhead and Mallera tensed.

"Hold it!" he reminded his troops.

Smoke grenades popped on Costa's lawn, vomiting out thick clouds in the helicopter's wake. Mellera grimaced as the rotor wash twisted swirling tentacles of chemical fog in the aircraft's wake.

"Fire now!" Mellera shouted, lifting one of his Krinkov submachine guns and bracing it to his shoulder. He pulled the trigger, aiming at where he suspected the Agusta's course would take it, but it was already popping up above the obfuscating smoke it had dropped. For a moment he thought that he'd driven off the mystery men, but realized that the helicopter was peeling away and soaring into the night.

If the veteran commandos were here to lean on Costa, they wouldn't go far.

"Focus on the roof!" Mellera ordered, leaning on the subgun to control its writhing recoil. It felt like he was wrestling a miniature fire-breathing dragon, but he kept the muzzle blazing hot and heavy, sweeping Costa's roof with a murderous slash of 7.62 mm rounds. Brass somersaulted out of the breech, tumbling to the grass at his feet, the tiny assault rifle's mouth opening wide and unleashing a fiery strobe of rage that lit the night.

Around Costa's estate, other weapons barked and flashed, creating a cacophony of light, lead and thunder. If anyone had been dropped on the roof, they were either pinned down or already shredded by a storm of unrelenting bullets.

Something sailed from the darkness, striking Mellera between his shoulder blades, and his Krinkov popped out of his hands. The Cuban enforcer sputtered, gasping from the impact and he struck the grass face-first. A brawny hand grabbed his neck and yanked him up, tearing the other slung Krinkov from its shoulder sling.

SATISFIED THAT HE'D GOTTEN a better weapon, Carl Lyons shoved the man hard into the low property wall he'd been hiding behind. The guy's nose and cheekbones cracked violently, flesh torn from his brow and cheeks, leaving a stringy smear of shredded skin behind on the rough cinder block. The blow had knocked the man senseless enough for Lyons to restrain his wrists and ankles with cable ties. A quick pat-down produced a KG-99 machine pistol and a big, 9 mm stainless-steel Taurus, which he handed over to Blancanales as he dropped from the property wall.

"Good diversion," Blancanales noted. His micro-Uzi was a better weapon than the KG-99, so he tucked it into his gear bag for backup. The Taurus found its way into his waistband, since it was a familiar variant on his favored Beretta. "They paid attention to Jack, not realizing we'd been dropped off half a block back."

"The trees helped to mask the sound of our drop-off," Lyons said. "See? I learn things from you military types now and again."

"You know, you might have some hope as a squad leader," Blancanales quipped, knowing that the ex-L.A.P.D. cop had been a good part of the reason why Able Team had survived countless missions in hell zones around the world. The wily veteran picked up the man's fallen radio, hearing its tinny sound. "They're wondering where the hell their boss went."

Lyons looked down at the bloody mess lying unconscious at his feet. "Good score on this one. How good is your Cuban accent?"

Blancanales smirked, remembering how he and Phoenix Force's Rafael Encizo worked on being able to mimic each other's Spanish dialects. He pushed the speaker to his mouth and broke into fevered, Cuban-flavored speech. Lyons understood enough to realize that Blancanales was warning the rest of the ambush team about how two men had tried to sneak up on him, using silenced weapons.

Lyons took back the KG-99 and raked the stone wall to emphasize Blancanales's ruse.

"Fall back!" Blancanales ordered, knowing the macho, loyal gang toughs would rush to their master's side.

Lyons flipped the KG-99 back to Blancanales who raced out from behind the wall. Obscured by the swirling smoke from their grenades, and firing the machine pistol into the shadows, Blancanales looked enough like their boss to assuage their suspicions as five of the Cuban toughs ran up to his side.

The quintet of gunmen concentrated on the section of perimeter foliage Blancanales was firing into. The eldest member of Able Team let the KG-99 drop to the grass and pulled his micro-Uzi, turning it toward the toughs who had come to their boss's aid. Triggering the machine pistol, its cyclic rate snapping the bolt back and forth 1100 times per minute, he unleashed the compact 25-round magazine into the knot of gangsters, burning down four of them mercilessly before they even realized that they had been duped. The last gunman swung his weapon to shoot Blancanales, but the Able Team commando brought up his foot, jarring the assault rifle out of the Cuban criminal's hands. A quick stab of the unyielding barrel into the hollow of his throat, and Blancanales put him down, the micro-Uzi's hard steel muzzle mangling his windpipe. The gunman collapsed, clutching at his throat, blood burbling over sputtering lips.

The ambush had sacrificed Blancanales's momentary cover and two men swung their rifles toward him. Before they had a chance to trigger their weapons, Lyons ripped off a figure eight of autofire from his appropriated Krinkov, the stubby submachine gun ripping the duo to ribbons, giving his partner enough time to rush to cover and reload his Uzi.

Lyons scanned for more of the Cuban gunmen and spotted another three, but Blancanales opened up on them first, rak-

ing them from their right flank with his machine pistol. The
ex-Black Beret tapped off short bursts from the Uzi, conserv-
ing its ammunition despite its breakneck cyclic rate of 1100
rounds per minute. Taken down by precision fire, the hired
guns collapsed in perforated heaps of lifeless muscle and bone.

Automatic weapons barked from the tree line, muzzle-
flashes betraying the enemy's positions and count. Four more
gangsters remained, and they were laying down suppressive
fire on Lyons, who'd taken cover behind a large marble
planter. The Able Team commander made a hand signal to
Blancanales to watch his flank, because the indiscriminate fire
was meant to harass and distract.

Blancanales nodded and disappeared into the shadows,
brown eyes sweeping the darkness until he detected movement.

The remaining five had picked this particular gunman to
try to outflank Able Team because of his stealth. Had Blancanales's seasoned senses been less sharp, or his mind less
aware of avenues of approach to take Lyons by surprise, the
lone Cuban might have stood a chance. Blancanales lurched
from his position, micro-Uzi rattling out its death song. A
flaming hose of 9 mm lead lanced into the gunner's back,
stitching him from the base of his spine to the back of his
head, ripping him open and hurling him to the ground. Blancanales extended the length of his burst to distract the gunmen at the tree line, who'd paused on seeing their partner fall.

The diversion gave Lyons the opportunity to swing around
the planter and pour a stream of full-auto tracers from the extended Krinkov drum. He raked two of the enemy positions
before the remaining Cubans opened up, one aiming at Lyons
crouched behind the planter, the other squeezing off a few des-
peration shots toward Blancanales. The pair was too far behind the curve, both Able Team aces hammering the last two
from their covered positions.

As quickly as the gunfight had burst to life, it had ended.

"Jack, get back here," Lyons ordered. "We're taking Costa on a little trip before the cops show up to this little party."

"Coming in, Ironman," Grimaldi answered gusta.

Lyons kicked the French doors to Costa's den, shattering them off their hinges. Inside, the drug lawyer was frozen in a prenatal ball of quivering flesh.

"Wake up, baby," Lyons growled. "You've got a flight to catch."

CHAPTER SEVEN

Kennedy Space Center

For someone who had been bumped from his chance to fly into orbit, Marshall Komalko, nicknamed Pie by his friends, was friendly, cordial and professional with Hermann Schwarz. The two of them were working hard on preflight checks of the systems as Schwarz was taking his place as a flight engineer.

"You don't seem disappointed in not going up," Schwarz observed as they were going over the circuit on one of the maneuvering rockets on the shuttle.

Komalko shrugged. "Hey, this would have been my hat trick. I've had my chance, and you guys need to make sure the experimental modules are operating according to plan. You have more familiarity with the updates than I do."

"Pretty practical," Schwarz stated.

Komalko grinned. "Hell, who'd have thunk that an Inuit kid like me could have gone into space once, let alone twice? I've lead a charmed life. Besides, you're just being pushed around by the bureaucrats. It's not your fault that I'm grounded."

Schwarz nodded, returning his attention to the volt meter testing the circuit. "The readings are showing a little variation here. Not outside normal parameters, but it didn't show any wobble on the previous test according to your notes."

Komalko's face darkened with concern. "C'mon, let's get it out and take a look."

Between the two electronics geniuses, they had the control panel for the thruster out and the leads checked. It turned out that there had been a scratch dug into the foil grid pattern, compromising the circuit.

"Deliberate?" Schwarz asked.

Komalko raised an eyebrow, then shook his head. "Probably someone slipped with a screwdriver."

"That's a thin tip for a screwdriver. Looks more like a pocketknife; besides, this board is secured by Allen-head screws. When have you ever seen a pointed Allen wrench?" Schwarz asked.

Komalko frowned as he sent one of the maintenance crew down for a replacement board. "Stranger things have happened."

"Sorry, just paranoid," Schwarz returned. He hated to tell a lie, but he continued on, explaining himself. "It's not every day I survive an attack by raiders."

"I figured as much," Komalko answered. "Probably another reason why I'm grounded and you're going. You're more security-minded than I am."

"You noticed?" Schwarz asked.

"You stand bladed to people you're talking to, providing a smaller target, and your feet are usually planted in a T, to provide a strongly secure footing. Those are peculiar to martial artists and cops who've dealt with a lot of violence," Komalko answered. "My uncle was an Inuit Nation Police Officer, and he held himself like you do."

Schwarz fought off a self-recriminating grimace. He dramatically pulled off his eyeglasses and raised an eyebrow. "So you know my secret identity."

Komalko winked. "Don't worry. I'm good with secret identities."

"Thanks," Schwarz said. "Anyone's ego I have to watch out for on the crew?"

"Not everyone is as cool as I am," Komalko answered. "Captain William Cole really thinks he's a cut above everyone."

"Bill Cole?" Schwarz asked.

"Oh, don't ever call him Bill. Or even just Cole. It's William, or Captain Cole," Komalko said. "He says he's earned his rank, and doesn't take kindly to us inferior personnel engaging in familiarity."

"Well, there's nothing against the law about being an egotistical bastard," Schwarz replied. "If that were the case, Billy would be joining millions in jail."

Komalko picked up on Schwarz's use of the most diminutive version of Cole's name and smiled. "Yeah. Unfortunately, every crew has its assholes. But he's so clean cut and by the book, he's practically a saint. Director Griffey thinks that Billy could walk on water."

"Friends in high places?" Schwarz asked.

"No, just an embarrassment of possibilities for Cole to show how worthy he'd be of being the team commander. It's eating him that Jordie's in charge," Komalko answered. "Jordie's just a normal kid who busted his ass through the Air Force Academy. He didn't graduate at the top of his class, but he still made it through. Cole sailed through as if the Red Sea opened for him."

"Broome works for a living. Cole had his handed to him," Schwarz noted.

Komalko nodded. "The best tutors and teachers. He was spoon fed."

"Nobody else pops up on your radar as someone to watch?" Schwarz continued.

"Well, there is this nosy engineer with a round face, but he's been grounded already," Komalko said with a wink.

"Personal issues with Cole already?" Schwarz asked.

"Cole wanted his pal, Armin Mustafa, to be placed as flight engineer in my place. Said this mission was no place for some hotshot and his kid sidekick," Komalko explained.

Schwarz nodded.

"I know Mustafa, and except for him being hooked up with a complete jerk, Armin's a decent guy. Another hard worker, quiet, gets along with everyone," Komalko said. "And they run us all through deep background checks. I don't think he's al Qaeda."

Schwarz shrugged. "I don't judge on names, Pie. I've been through enough to know that worrying about someone's name sounding vaguely like a paperback terrorist without solid foundation is just plain stupid. Never mind that I've worked with plenty of folks, and encountered the best and worst of everything, Arab, Asian, white, black. People are people. Some are dicks, some are just plain bad, but most are just folks doing their job."

At that moment, a young, handsome black man came up the scaffolding.

"Oh, Armi, we were just talking about you," Komalko said.

"Hi," Schwarz greeted. "What's wrong?"

"You guys had a problem with the old circuit board," Mustafa answered. "I brought up a new one. You must be Miller, the new guy."

"I am," Schwarz told him. "I guess you heard us talking."

Mustafa shrugged. "I'm used to it by now. I've got a name that brings up some bad images to ignorant folks. Luckily, you're not ignorant."

"Still, you were next in line to go on this bird," Schwarz said. "Sorry for bumping both of you."

"I'm still young and still part of the program," Mustafa replied. "Double check the board."

Schwarz looked at the open box, the clear Mylar bag intact and protecting it from its packing material. He took it out and hooked it up to the test meter. It worked fine, without variance. He did a quick eyeball on the circuit board itself, checking for inconsistencies, then handed it off to Komalko who screwed it into place. Another circuit test, and it was done.

"Nice teamwork," Schwarz complimented.

"That's the whole point," Mustafa said. "We've got a large team here, working to put ninety-nine tons into orbit, then bring it back down to Earth, and we can't make any mistakes. I'm part of something really big and important. This is us, the whole human race growing up and learning to leave our nest. All parents want their kids to go out into the world. God wants humankind to go out into that big infinite, which is why He made that for us. You know?"

"I've known it since I was a kid," Schwarz answered. He could feel the excitement in Mustafa for just being a ground engineer for the space program. The day-to-day work was hard, and Schwarz only had a small taste of it with Komalko's help, but this time, like the last time he worked undercover in NASA, there was an electric tingle that ran through him. It was like being plugged into a live wire. This *was* the stepping-stone to the next great frontier, the next great age of exploration. He took a deep breath, feeling a tinge of disgust at the idea that someone might be undermining the future this program represented. The International Space Station was a conglomeration of multiple nations, working together to run tests that would take science to the next step. Traditional enemies from the cold war had become lab partners, and even ally nations who had recently become bitter, mocking adversaries in the political arena, were still coworkers in forging a future.

"That's the last we've got for today," Komalko said. "Want to join us for some drinks?"

Schwarz shook his head. "I've got last-minute updates to run on the modules with Dr. Bertonni."

Mustafa chuckled. "Why hang out with fellow nerds when you can hang out with a hottie?"

"It's work, honest," Schwarz replied, but he did agree with the young astronauts' assessment of the Burgundy Lake survivor. He wished that he had more time to spend with the pretty rocket scientist, but there was work to be done.

Orlando, Florida.

JASON MELLERA TRIED TO breathe when he recovered consciousness, but his arms and legs were bound tightly to him by tough cables. He was folded into a tight ball and wrapped in a burlap sack. Thick, musty humidity assaulted his nostrils, an oddly familiar smell.

"See, we're not making it exactly easy to feed you to the alligators," Carl Lyons's voice intruded on his assessment of his surroundings.

"What?" Mellera asked. His mouth felt full of cotton, and he realized that his knees, bound and folded up to his chest, were covered in bile. Mellera also noticed that he was nearly naked. His head pounded uncomfortably and he realized from his gentle bobbing motion that he was in a boat.

"I said, we're not making it easy to feed you to the alligators. They need arms and legs loose to grab on to, so that they could twist your limbs out of their joints and swallow them," Lyons explained. "Now, if we'd had time to take your ass out to the coast, I wouldn't be regretting binding you up like a turkey."

"What are…"

A hard kick rocked him in the burlap sack.

"We don't need you," Lyons growled. "And you shot at my pilot. Nobody fucking does that to my people."

"Wait!"

"Ironman," Blancanales interrupted. "I see some. And as the man used to say, 'cor blimey, they're beauts!'"

A low, intestine-shaking rumble that Mellera recognized as the excited, hungry moan of an alligator shook through his bones. He swallowed.

"Wait a second!" Mellera cried.

Lyons kicked the sack again. "Just keep making noise. They're not quite excited enough to see us."

"I said wait!" Mellera howled.

"See, if you'd waited to go to the coast, we could have dropped him, already dead, into the water to let the bull sharks snack on him," Blancanales complained. "Sure, he's bound up in a tight ball, but shark jaws go through anything, even bone."

"Eh, fuck off, Lopez," Lyons said. "Give me a hand dumping this bastard overboard."

"Screw you. I'm not going to throw my back out feeding a bunch of shoes," Blancanales grumbled.

"You let on that we're at an alligator farm," Lyons gritted.

"So? He's going to be gator shit in a few hours," Blancanales countered.

"Goddamn it! I can tell you who sent us to cover Costa's place!" Mellera screeched.

"What can you tell us that a bit of forensic examination of your clothes and personal belongings couldn't tell us?" Lyons asked. He gave the burlap sack a nudge with his big hand.

"Listen, El Toronado has some friends who are pretty high up on the food chain," Mellera said.

"No kidding?" Lyons asked. "High enough that he'd have

contacts inside Cape Canaveral? That he'd be spying on any new arrivals?"

"That's just relay info from that little shit lawyer Costa," Mellera responded. "He's clueless about the whole organization. I'm El Toronado's right hand."

Lyons opened the neck of the burlap sack, glaring at him. "Nah, you're bigger than a hand. Otherwise we'd just dump you down a garbage disposal."

"Listen, El Toronado has been expanding his interests of late. People higher up on the food chain have been asking him to do some snooping. He's got people watching research at UCF, at the Cape, at a lot of the aerospace production centers," Mellera said, pleading for his life.

He looked at the edge of the boat and saw an alligator lift up its head, blunt jaws snapping shut, splashing stagnant, algae-thickened water all over the boat. His bowels and bladder loosened at the sight. "Oh fuck…"

Mellera spilled his guts about El Toronado's new activities. Going by the phone logs and Costa's confession in a Justice Department safehouse, it was a slam dunk that Able Team had its next rung on the ladder in sight. Tracking down the conspiracy threatening NASA had yielded another result.

It also told Lyons and Blancanales that the enemy was aware of their presence. The Stony Man commandos didn't think that their names and true identities were known to their foes, but given the opposition they'd faced already, whoever was behind the conspiracy had been brushed by the three-man death squad before, and they remembered the conflict.

Taking down the hijackers wasn't going to be easy, but then, Able Team was never called in if it was going to be a cakewalk.

Stony Man Farm, Virginia

KURTZMAN SIGHED AND POURED himself another cup of his high-test concoction that only nominally resembled coffee. He took a sip and felt the rush of caffeine blast through his bloodstream. Frustration gnawed at him, the plane that had escaped from Sonora having disappeared after flying south.

Lyons and McCarter had a good point when they suggested that since the enemy had revealed its own ability to tap into satellite communications during the border intercept, it was likely that instead of utilizing antisatellite weaponry, they simply killed access to the computer network relaying imagery. Kurtzman had already considered the possibility when they broached it, and was looking into it. Sure enough, there was a shield of black ice around the satellite surveillance network they'd been accessing. It was a subtle, impressive program, so nearly invisible that it made it seem that the satellites had ceased to exist. Only streams of phantom data appearing at other nodes betrayed the fact that the eyes in the sky still existed, untouched by any high-powered antisatellite laser cannon. The enemy program was well-designed and updated in real-time response to the Farm cyberteam's attempted hacking into their defenses.

Stony Man Farm's electronic warfare specialists were among the best in the world, but this was a case of them meeting their equals. The brainpower behind the satellite hacks had to be considerable, rivaling Kurtzman, Tokaido, Wethers and Delahunt on an intelligence and experience basis. Such black hats would have to be known somewhere, so Kurtzman set Delahunt on tracking them down while Tokaido continued his frenetic assaults on the black ice, hoping to find some dent.

"Bear, we've got some new data to put into the mix." Lyons's voice came over the com link. "What do we have on a drug dealer by the name of El Toronado? He works near Orlando, and is mainly based in the Union Park area."

Kurtzman rolled over to his computer, taking the call. "We've been running checks on him since he popped up as one of Mellera's known accomplices. He's got his fingers in a lot of pies, but mostly he seems like he's just a midlevel drug dealer who only popped up about five years ago."

"Only popped up five years ago?" Lyons repeated, musing. "These guys don't just appear."

"That drew my attention, as well," Kurtzman said. "I'll transmit everything to your PDA."

"Nothing in regard to where he might be working out of?" Lyons asked.

"No…wait. We've got a flag going up on the file," Kurtzman noted. "We almost set off someone's trigger. Hunt, follow that trip line!"

"I'm on it," the former Berkeley professor replied. His fingers moved over the keyboard as he began his meticulous dissection of the watch alert program.

"Is it an internal trigger?" Lyons asked. "Or a hack?"

Wethers fielded the question as he went over the traceback. "It's a Justice Department approved watch. We've got a special agent in Baltimore looking for El Toronado."

"Baltimore," Lyons mused. "Who's the agent?"

"Gilbert Shane," Wethers responded. "He's tasked to Homeland Security."

"Can you tell me if there's any other flags that have crossed his desk?" Lyons asked.

"It'll take a while. Why?" Wethers asked.

"El Toronado might be a resource of his. Look for patterns connecting him to any of Shane's older assets," Lyons suggested.

"You've got an idea about El Toronado?" Kurtzman asked.

"I remember a case in Baltimore, five years back," Lyons said. "We didn't have any involvement in the investigation, but he popped up on a threat matrix I'd set up. He looked like he'd be a potential problem that we'd get involved in since he had acquired a bunch of ex-KGB operatives as his leg muscle. He was moving large amounts of contraband through the ports, including sex slaves, plastic explosives and the chemicals needed to process heroin."

"I vaguely remember that. He was called Apis, right?" Kurtzman asked.

"That's the one," Lyons returned. "He disappeared before a combined task force in Baltimore could take him down. He disappeared, as well as much of his muscle. There were a few guys caught, and the smuggling operation was dismantled, but not without a witness being murdered because Apis found out about him."

"That was a union steward at the docks?" Kurtzman asked.

"Absolutely."

"What's got your interest in this particular guy?" Kurtzman asked.

"Toronado is a nonsense term, but its base term is Toro, Spanish for bull," Lyons said. "Even I know that much. Apis, however, drew his name from the Egyptian god of fertility, who was a bull."

"That's thin," Kurtzman mused.

"This guy has sublimated his outward appearance to the point where he's only known by reputation as the biggest bull in the pen. He's the one who delivers a shot in the arm to any criminal enterprise, a living fertility god of smuggling, so to speak," Lyons explained. "It could just be a coincidence, but

I'm thinking this guy's ego got the better of him when he selected his new title."

"I don't know which is more disturbing, the reasoning behind this guy naming himself, or the fact that you just gave me a lecture on magical bull inseminations," Kurtzman returned.

Lyons chuckled. "Just check this out. Any news on our escapee?"

"Zilch," Kurtzman replied. "The satellites watching his plane went dark. We've found them, they weren't knocked out by a laser, just garden-variety hacking."

"Hardly common hacking," Lyons returned.

"Just trying not to disturb you," Kurtmann admitted. "These guys are good, so breaking into the ice they set up around the satellite network will be a bitch and a half."

"No Easter eggs left in by the code writers?" Lyons asked.

"You've been hanging around Carmen too much, Carl," Kurtzman responded. "But no, this is clean and tight code. No ego signatures anywhere in sight, but we haven't even penetrated half of it."

"Keep us posted," Lyons said. "We're going to lean on El Toronado's operation to see what we can uncover."

"Good luck," Kurtzman returned.

"Save the luck for David and Phoenix," Lyons told him. "We're just knocking heads in Orlando, not busting into China. What's their ETA?"

Kurtzman checked his counter. "They're an hour outside of Chinese airspace."

Lyons took an audible deep breath on the other end. "Don't let David know I'm worried about his operation. He might actually accuse me of being a nice guy."

"Hey, you guys are mellowing after all these years, Ironman," Kurtzman responded.

Lyons grumbled. "We're going to have a central Florida crime scene who won't agree with you in a few hours. Able, out."

The connection was severed

"Good luck to you guys anyway," Kurtzman offered.

CHAPTER EIGHT

Kennedy Space Center

Schwarz was glad that Sabrina Bertonni was given other members of the NASA ground crew to work with while he familiarized himself with the shuttle and his responsibilities as Komalko's replacement. Still, her face lit up when he joined her.

"Hi," she greeted with a lighthearted lilt. "Welcome to thruster central."

Schwarz looked over the setup modules and frowned. "What a mess."

"I slave over a hot engine module all day, and this is all you can say?" Bertonni asked.

"Sorry," Schwarz replied with a grin. "What needs to be done?"

"I'm having a hard time trying to return the remote throttle to baseline so that we can recalibrate the fuel mix. Got any ideas?"

Schwarz looked at the laptop hooked up to one of the thruster modules and examined the code for the command sequences. While he wasn't exactly a rocket scientist like

Dr. Bertonni, he did have a good handle on programming. He checked her notes on what she wanted to do with the thrusters. "Give me about fifteen minutes. I might have something that'll work."

The woman nodded. She looked pale, and her eyes were sunken and dark.

"Get something to eat or take a nap," Schwarz said. "You look ready to fall over."

Bertonni took a step. The Able Team electronics genius knew the smell of fresh blood and looked at her slacks. Though they were dark in color, they seemed wet, and glancing down at her ankle, he saw it was red and slick.

"Sabrina…" Schwarz called, reaching out to grab her just as she passed out. "Call an ambulance!"

Technicians scrambled around, some going to get a first-aid kit, another getting the wall phone and dialing for help. Schwarz accepted the kit and opened Bertonni's blouse. Her bandage had bunched up and was drenched. Her stitches were torn from too much effort, and he pressed a gauze pad to the open wound.

"Oh, God," someone said. "What happened?"

"She overworked herself and opened her stitches," Schwarz explained. "She's been losing blood but didn't notice."

Bertonni's eyes blinked, fluttering as they struggled to focus. She looked at Schwarz as he applied a new dressing to her side. "Oh wow… So this is what it takes for you to go to second base."

Schwarz suppressed a grin. "Usually takes a firefight to get me in the mood to go all the way home."

"I'll buy a Beretta," she muttered drunkenly.

"Quiet, Sabrina," Schwarz cautioned. "We've got an ambulance on the way. A transfusion, a little sleep, and you'll be as good as new."

Bertonni coughed, then smiled. Her skin felt burning hot to the touch, and her eyes were wide and unfocused.

"Has she been acting strangely?" Schwarz asked.

"Just a little giggly, but we attributed that to everything that's happened to her," a technician said. "We had plenty of soft drinks, and she was sucking them down like a fish."

Schwarz looked around and saw a liter bottle of diet soda at the side of the scientist's workstation. There was a little still sloshing in the bottom, but he saw gritty residue clinging to the wall of the plastic container. He picked it up as a NASA ambulance rolled up.

"What's wrong?" one of the paramedics asked.

Schwarz looked around. "Someone spiked her soda with ecstasy."

"What?" a technician asked.

"She pushed herself too hard, didn't feel it when she opened her stitches, and her current state of dehydration and fever all point to it," Schwarz surmised.

"We'll get an IV into her," the paramedic said. "Saline will help with the blood loss and dehydration."

A figure at the back of the group shifted his weight from one foot to another, looking wide-eyed at the bottle in Schwarz's hand. When the man noticed he'd attracted the Able Team commando's attention, he whirled and bolted for the ambulance.

"Stop him!" Schwarz shouted, dropping the bottle. The NASA staff was too bewildered at Bertonni's collapse and the arrival of the paramedics to make sense of what was going on as the guilty worker rushed to make his escape. Schwarz couldn't blame them, they had no idea that there was a strong possibility of an infiltrator in their midst.

Mustafa and Komalko were outside the laboratory when they saw Schwarz racing in hot pursuit of another man. Mustafa broke into a run, his legs pumping, rushing to keep up with Schwarz.

"What's wrong?" the engineer asked.

"He spiked Dr. Bertonni's soda," Schwarz answered as he charged after the runner.

"Got it," Mustafa said, and he lowered his head, pouring on an extra surge of speed that cut the distance between him and the infiltrator. Once he was inside two yards of the fleeing technician, Mustafa kicked out and hit the man with a shoulder block, slamming them both down hard on the sidewalk. Wind escaped from the tech's lungs as Mustafa's tackle bowled him over.

Schwarz dropped into a skid, feet-first, as if he were sliding into second base, except instead of a bag, his feet speared into the technician's side, flipping him over even as he tried to get up. The Able Team specialist scrambled to his feet, then lunged forward, spearing an elbow between the tech's shoulder blades and pinning him to the ground.

"Don't move," Schwarz warned, wrapping his arm around the man's neck. "I can break your neck and still leave you alive and talking."

The technician swallowed hard, seeing the anger in Schwarz' eyes. "Yes, sir…"

Schwarz grimaced at Bertonni's near brush with death, but relaxed when he looked back, seeing the paramedics walking her to their ambulance. If she could walk, she'd be all right. Still, he'd check on her after he was done talking to the tech.

Orlando, Florida

YANOS PROHASKA PUT A pile of twenties into a neat stack, smoothing out the tower of bills so that each edge was flush with the other. That the money in the stack added up to five thousand dollars didn't matter so much as how neat it would be. Apis had chided him that there were counting machines that would do that job, but Prohaska didn't care.

A machine, counting money, was just a soulless item. Prohaska had been cooking books and ledgering illicit cash for years. Apis was certain that the accountant had obsessive-compulsive disorder, part of what made him such a wizard with money, and made him absolutely trustworthy with large amounts of cash. Taking a paper wrapper, Prohaska wrapped the block of bills with a precision that would put a robot to shame, then placed it in a gym bag with gentle care, setting it in place like a piece of marble into a tapestry. It was part of an ever-growing brick of money.

More money was strewed about the table, bills waiting to be sorted. Prohaska itched to wrap them all in neat, perfectly counted stacks, assembling each 250-bill packet until they were part of his perfect square of cash.

All hope of organizing anything else disappeared in a clap of thunder as a hole tore through the door. The concussion wave produced a cloud of splinters, the doorknob flying through the mountain of money on his table and scattering it in the wind.

Carl Lyons kicked open the damaged door, racking the pump on his Mossberg Cruiser.

The security men Apis had watching over Prohaska lurched to their feet, grabbing for their handguns. Lyons emptied a 12-gauge burst into one's center of mass. The gangster's white shirt shredded and became jammed into the bloody, pulped wound of his torso.

Rosario Blancanales swung around the door frame and engaged the other bodyguard, popping off two rounds from his .40-caliber Smith & Wesson. Both bullets struck home, dumping the hardman back on the sofa. The hollowpoint gouged through flesh and bone until they reached his heart, bursting the tough-skinned pump with their brutal passage.

"The money!" Prohaska shouted.

Lyons lowered the Cruiser and turned to Prohaska, who was

scrambling after flying bills. Lyons grabbed a handful of the man's shirt and heaved him back in his wooden chair. "Sit down."

"No! It's a mess!" Prohaska wailed. "I have to clean it up!"

"You do anything other than breathe without my say-so, I'll take your legs off," Lyons growled.

Prohaska looked at the scattered bills, his lips trembling. "Messy, messy, messy…"

"Let me take a crack at him," Blancanales offered. "I don't think the hard approach will work on him."

Lyons nodded, recognizing the emotional trauma besieging the accountant. "All yours, Pol."

Blancanales righted the table and began picking up the money, setting it in front of him. Prohaska started sorting the bills, settling them into neat stacks.

"Have to keep everything in order, you know," Prohaska muttered. "A place for everything and everything in its place."

"Absolutely," Blancanales answered. "Disorder is the worst sin of all."

Prohaska looked up, his bleary blue eyes lighting up from within. "Exactly!"

Blancanales smiled and continued to set the bills in front of their prisoner. Prohaska showed no sign of wanting to make an escape, only to put things in order. The neurotic accountant looked over to the bodyguards, slumped in their chairs, and sighed.

"Sloppy, sloppy…bad posture is not good for you," Prohaska explained.

"Ironman," Blancanales said.

The Able Team leader nodded and went to the dead gunmen, settling them on the sofa, seated straight up, hands folded in laps, feet straightened. "How's that?"

"Best they've ever been," Prohaska said with a disconnected smile. "Always so sloppy, and the bad posture. I must finish with the money, though. It's supposed to be delivered on time."

"Punctual," Blancanales agreed.

Prohaska nodded with spastic, bobble-head intensity. "Absolutely."

"Keep working," Lyons ordered, even though the accountant ignored him. He stepped closer to Blancanales. "Do you think he's autistic?"

"Probably equal parts OCD and autism. He doesn't care about the bloody messes over in the corner, but calmed down when we helped him put everything in order," Blancanales agreed. "Probably why El Toronado trusts him with the money. Those bills aren't currency, they're building blocks that need to be put together."

"He'd be less likely to stuff some cash in his pocket for his own personal use," Lyons noted. He pointed to the gym bag. "Those corners are square enough to cut leather."

Prohaska looked at his watch. "Almost time to take the money in."

"We'll take you," Lyons offered.

Prohaska looked to the bodies. "Apis won't like strangers."

Lyons smirked, nodding to Blancanales. "I was right."

"We're sorry," Blancanales offered. "We didn't mean to be improper."

Prohaska's lips tightened and he put another stack in the bag. "Things must be done. Not good to change the order of things, but worse not to try at all."

Blancanales gave the accountant all the help he needed, and Lyons watched grimly as they finished counting another forty thousand dollars in cash.

"An exact half million," Prohaska announced, zipping the bag shut. He looked at the pair. "You're going to kill me for this, aren't you?"

The obsessive-compulsive money manager had returned to lucidity, his lips drawn tight in concern.

"Why?" Lyons asked. "You've never murdered anyone, and you didn't react violently to us."

Prohaska chewed his upper lip, glancing to Blancanales.

"We just want your boss," the Puerto Rican told him. "Where is the money exchange going to be?"

"And if I don't cooperate?" Prohaska asked, eyes flitting between the pair.

"I don't think that you will be in a good position if you're in general population," Lyons stated. "That's going to be such a mess. Your neurosis won't be able to handle it."

The shudder that rocked Prohaska's shoulders told Lyons that his ploy was dead on the money. "And if I do help you?"

"There are some very nice facilities that will help you cope with your disorder," Lyons offered. "You might get over many of your fears with proper medical assistance and can rejoin society as a productive citizen."

Prohaska nodded. "But I am a criminal."

"You're a glorified adding machine," Blancanales responded. "You can't be held accountable for someone abusing your skills. Like my partner said, you're not a violent criminal."

Prohaska took a deep breath. "There are car keys in Carmine's right front pocket. We'll take their Cutlass. It's what Apis would be expecting."

Lyons smiled, thumbing two shot shells into the partially spent Mossberg's magazine. "Thanks for seeing things reasonably."

Prohaska looked at the floor and lead the way out into the hall.

China

THE HALO JUMP INTO CHINA had gone off without a hitch, but T. J. Hawkins was glad to touch the ground again. He scooped up his parachute, folding it into a compact ball. David Mc-Carter had begun digging the burial hole for the chutes, while Manning, the second one down, set about stowing their oxygen bottles and rebreathing units. The shallow graves for their skydiving equipment would keep them from being discovered by the Chinese military. It was likely that the Red Chinese wouldn't want an American-backed special operations team in their backyard, even if they were working at the same purposes—clearing foreign terrorists out of one of their most highly guarded facilities.

He joined James and Encizo, guarding the perimeter while McCarter and Manning concealed the evidence of their arrival. Their Type 95 bullpups were equipped with foot-long suppressors, but the three of them were supposed to avoid hard contact with PRC forces. McCarter didn't want to be involved in a potential act of war against China without positive proof that it was the Red Chinese who were in on the intrigue to sabotage the International Space Station. If soldiers did come into the area, the plan was to engage in harassing fire and retreat under that cover.

Manning and McCarter joined the others after completing their digging.

"We're in the clear. No one's going to find our pits," McCarter assured them.

Hawkins looked back and saw that the Phoenix Force pair had tamped down the squares of grass they'd cut and removed. The sod pads helped to settle the surface they'd dug up, and as the elements worked on the digs, the grass, roots and clinging dirt would melt and meld back together with the surrounding soil. He couldn't see where the grass had separated, Manning having raked the grass so that it blended in perfectly.

"Move out," the Briton said.

The Phoenix Force commandos, their Land Warrior body

suits digitally camouflaged to match the Chinese countryside, disappeared into the wilderness. Moving stealthily, with both Hawkins and Manning utilizing their forest experience to ensure that they left no tracks, they moved at a pace that would take an hour to go the five miles from where they'd landed to the Phoenix Graveyard.

After a mile, Manning halted the group. "Motion sensors."

McCarter checked his map. "We're still four miles out, which means this is an early warning system. Can you figure an override for it?"

Manning dug gently around the ground unit. "It's a seismic monitor, and it's connected by land line to a central source."

"So walk softly?" James asked.

"It's an imperfect way of beating it," Manning replied. He looked back. "This is only the first ring we've encountered, so they knew we landed."

"And nothing has been dispatched to look for us," Hawkins said. "Yet."

"Could be that central security isn't watching," Manning noted. "Though, we passed a trail about a quarter mile back. Wildlife is common in this area, so we could just be registering as livestock."

"But if we advance closer, they might figure we're more than just wandering sheep," McCarter mused. "If the launch facility is paying attention to its security perimeter."

"That's a lot of ifs," Manning returned. "Hang on."

The Canadian stomped the mud next to the sensor, popping the land line loose from its moorings. "Take cover along the tree line. Standard operating procedure should have a patrol here inside of ten minutes."

The Stony Man warriors faded into the shrubbery, disappearing from sight. After fifteen minutes, there was no sign of a maintenance crew. Just to be safe, Phoenix Force pulled away from the damaged sensor, circling wide of it and keeping to the trees as they advanced toward the Phoenix Graveyard.

"Circumstantial evidence." McCarter spoke up. "But it's a good chance that it isn't the Chinese government behind this mess. If they were still in charge of the launch facility, they'd have been on a security breach like Gary said."

"Still no sign of a patrol, and the seismic sensors aren't precise enough to home in on us so they're not setting us up for an intercept," Hawkins added. "We might be in the clear."

"Makes no sense to leave themselves wide open," Encizo noted.

"It does," James said. "Sending out maintenance crews would expose them. They're looking toward their closer security, rather than make the locals curious why a repair crew isn't made of Chinese soldiers."

Encizo nodded. "Good point. So they could know we've messed with their seismic sensor, but are keeping a low profile, just hardening up in case we—"

The air began to rumble. In the distance, the Stony Man warriors saw thick white clouds rising from the ground, a long tusk spearing through the top of the frothy white wall.

"—drop in," Encizo concluded.

"They're launching?" McCarter asked. "The shuttle shouldn't be launching for another thirty-six hours."

"Second exhaust trail," Manning pointed out. "Two rockets."

"Two loads of potential terrorists," McCarter stated. "Hold up. I'm phoning this in."

The team looked to him, concern on their faces. They were breaking communication silence, but the threat posed by the two rockets heading to the International Space Station outweighed their own personal safety.

"We'll secure a perimeter," Manning said. "Call it in."

McCarter nodded and took out the team satellite phone. With each mile the rockets rose into the sky, hope drained away.

Kennedy Space Center

HERMANN SCHWARZ PACED IN the offices of the Kennedy Space Center police force. He was wound up and ready to interview the technician, Andy Knopf, and his involvement in trying to kill Sabrina Bertonni with an overdose of ecstasy.

"Relax, KSC P.D. has everything under control," Hal Brognola informed him. "He's not going to get away."

Schwarz shook his head. "She nearly died on my watch. I was supposed to be looking out for her."

"You were doing your job. Your other job," Brognola told him. "You, Komalko and Mustafa fixed a faulty thruster on the shuttle."

Brognola's cell warbled and he plucked it from his pocket. "What's up?"

Schwarz watched as Brognola's features fell. He could only guess as to the news.

"I'll see what we can do about moving up the launch," Brognola stated.

"What happened?" Schwarz asked.

Brognola leaned in close, his voice low. "Phoenix saw the Chinese facility launch two vehicles into orbit. This has gotten bad, Gadgets."

"So we'll try to move up the launch?" Schwarz asked.

"Yeah. And we'll see if we can fit Carl and Pol onboard," Brognola added. "Two orbital vehicles means you'll be facing some pretty hard odds all on your own."

"There's no way we're going to be able to hide those two being commandos in case we have an infiltrator on board," Schwarz told him.

"We've gone from sneaking around to needing to get things done now," Brognola explained. "I've got Cowboy on task at getting weaponry ready for taking back the station if it's already been compromised."

"There's a good chance it will take a full day for those vehicles to catch up with the station," Schwarz replied. "It's a long flight, and they have to match the ISS's speed to dock with it."

"The team is crunching numbers to check the trajectory information," Brognola said. "We'll figure out the window we've got, but even as we're talking, it's closing."

"How are Carl and Pol doing?" Schwarz asked.

"Still trying to track down El Toronado," Brognola stated. "But we've learned from his accountant that he was a smuggler from Baltimore who went by the street name Apis."

"Ironman gave us a workup on him," Schwarz told him. "But someone in Homeland Security dropped the ball and Apis disappeared like smoke."

"I was happier when Able Team was only in a pissing contest with the CIA," Brognola grumbled. "Homeland Security is supposed to be—"

"What it is and what it's supposed to be are two different things," Schwarz returned. "You've got this pregnant, drunken yak of a bureaucracy flopping across the board, muddling real investigations and blowing them to shit. We might step on some toes, but we close cases and get results."

Brognola sighed. "I know. But right now, Homeland Security is supposed to be our best bet to protect this country."

"Yeah, so explain why a drug smuggler from Baltimore has his fangs deep inside Kennedy Space Center?" Schwarz asked. "Get me in there. I want to talk to Knopf now."

"You're going to go all Ironman on me?" Brognola asked. "Because I don't know how much I can cover for you."

"Fine. When we have American citizens pulling splinters

of Iridium 192 out of their asses and dying of radiation poisoning, you'll be glad you avoided the paperwork, Hal," Schwarz snapped.

"Yeah, you're going all Ironman on me," Brognola huffed. "Including being pretty damn convincing. I'll swing you ten minutes alone with Knopf."

"I won't need that long," Schwarz replied. "I'm going to get my gear bag."

"Gear bag?" Brognola asked. "For what?"

"My Dremel tool and my CPDA," Schwarz said.

"You have the bits to turn that into a drill?" Brognola questioned.

Schwarz nodded. He plucked a thumbtack from a detective's desk. "It's not as bad as you think, but it'll look and feel really bad when I work on him."

Investigator James Roston came out of the interrogation room. The collar of his shirt was unbuttoned, his tie flopping around his neck. His forehead was glistening with sweat, and his eyes were heavily lidded with exhaustion. "He's not giving us anything."

"I'll get something," Schwarz told him. "Just turn off the camera. I've got my own digital recorder. I'll get him to talk, and his rights won't be violated. And it's all going to be smoke and mirrors."

"You sure it'll work?" Roston asked.

Schwarz nodded. "Trust me. I've done this all before."

Roston sighed. "I'm not gonna ask how."

The Stony Man electronics wizard went out to his car to get his bag.

CHAPTER NINE

China

From their vantage point, the men of Phoenix Force had a good view of the Phoenix Graveyard launch facility, especially Gary Manning, who made good use of his Dragunov knockoff's scope. The telescopic power allowed Manning to get an up-close look at the men who were patrolling the base. He lowered the scope and drew out a digital camera, affixing a telephoto lens designed for the unit. He snapped several shots of various guards, then brought up the images on the display screen to show to the others.

"One Caucasian, and we have what looks like an Indian or Pakistani," McCarter noted, looking at the screen. "I'll send the images through the uplink. We'll see if these match any known terrorists or mercenaries on record."

"It's only a few out of the patrol shift," Manning stated. "The rest appear to be Asian and at least half of them are wearing official uniforms."

"Half means that they did have someone on the inside," McCarter said. "But it also means that this isn't the government's idea."

"Beijing won't like us hosing down even renegade soldiers," James noted.

"Considering we entered the country illegally and are intending to infiltrate one of their military installations, that would only be the icing on the cake at the show trial," Encizo quipped.

Hawkins shrugged. "If they even give us a trial."

Manning took more shots of the base with the telescopic-lensed digicam. "Why would they want to pass up on the chance to embarrass a foreign government?"

"Like the man says, if you're gonna cheat, don't get caught. We've got work to do. Give me the camera for a data transmit," McCarter said.

Manning plugged a fire wire into the camera, which McCarter attached to the sat phone. "At least the Farm will have something close to real-time intel on this place after their observation was knocked out."

McCarter looked at the sat phone. "Not getting a signal. Something's jamming it."

"I thought our version was supposed to be unjammable," Hawkins said.

McCarter nodded. "But then, we did lose connection with the satellite keeping watch over this place. And this is a satellite communicator. The bad guys must have knocked out the bird relaying our signal. We tipped our hand when I called in about the launch."

"So, we have no official support," James said. "Oh well. What else is new?"

"Movement at the hangar," Manning answered. "Looks like they're preparing another launch vehicle or two."

The men of Phoenix Force watched two trailers with rockets rolling slowly out of a massive underground hangar.

"They resemble Atlas rockets," Encizo said. "I've seen

enough of them when I lived in Florida. When I was working underwater salvage, I was contracted to bring one up. The guy with me told me it takes a dedicated work crew two hours to raise one."

"And the trucks can't be topping five miles an hour. We've got time to stop a second flight," Hawkins added.

"Why stop the launch?" McCarter asked. "They're giving us a ride. We go up."

"Our guns aren't going to do any good on the space station," Hawkins noted.

"Knives," Encizo offered. "Every one of us is a skilled unarmed or knife-armed combatant. Gary doesn't need a blade, since he can apply enough force to twist a man's head from his shoulders without breaking a sweat. And from the ISS, we can also get a communications link to the Farm."

"But first thing's first. We take care of the launch facility," James noted. "Don't count your astronauts before they hatch, Rafe."

Kennedy Space Center

HERMANN SCHWARZ ENTERED THE room silently as Andy Knopf sat clutching the armrests of his chair. He was handcuffed, one wrist to each rest, and his ankles were similarly bound to the legs of the heavy metal chair.

"Who're you?" Knopf asked.

Schwarz didn't answer, unrolling his tool bag and pulling out a battery-powered Dremel tool. He opened the neck slot with an Allen wrench and dropped in a slender drill bit, twisting the chuck until it was tight. He triggered it, letting it whirl.

Knopf tensed, then looked at the electronic unit with the probe. He recognized the basis for the device, a common voltmeter. The narrow electric probe was attached to an insulated wire that transmitted electrical current readings to the main device.

"We don't have time for niceties," Schwarz said. "I'm just going to implement some emergency cybernetics and get what you know right now."

"Emergency cybernetics? What…"

"Sit still. I don't want to damage your brain stem," Schwarz warned, pushing Knopf's head forward so that his chin was jammed down against his chest.

"Brain… Wait!"

"Simple process. I open up your head with a pinprick hole and insert the probe. My PDA will analyze your neural impulses, and I'll know if you're telling the truth or not," Schwarz explained.

"You're crazy!" Knopf exclaimed. "You can't just drill a hole in someone's skull and stick a wire in to read their mind!"

Schwarz grabbed a thick handful of Knopf's curly black locks and dragged his head back. "Oh, so all those prosthetic limbs hooked up to nerve endings to mimic real body parts are just science fiction? Granted, this is a field improvisation, but if I took you back to headquarters to hook you up properly, it'd waste too much time."

Schwarz let go and Knopf twisted, kicking hard enough to move the heavy chair he was in.

"Wait! I've got my rights!" Knopf pleaded. "I was just waiting for my lawyer."

Schwarz pushed on the back of Knopf's head and triggered the Dremel tool. However, instead of sticking the drill bit into the back of the prisoner's head, he poked the thumbtack against the skin, piercing all the way to the bone. It hurt like hell, and with the body of the Dremel pressed to the flat top of the tack, the vibration made Knopf believe that the drill had just been pushed through his skull.

"No!" Knopf shouted, his shoulders tensed, not daring to move.

"Now, there's a chance of infection, and there's also a good chance that the exposed lead will cause nerve damage, but considering you tried to murder a government operative under orders from an enemy combatant…" Schwarz began.

"No, he was just someone I bought X from," Knopf said. "That's all."

Schwarz looked at his CPDA and pressed his stylus to the screen. He showed the monitor to Knopf, blinking "truth."

"What do you know, the computer believes you."

"I was just ordered to make her a little sick. You know that ecstasy isn't normally dangerous," Knopf sputtered. "I didn't realize she'd rip her stitches and start bleeding to death."

Schwarz gently pushed on the tack, upping the pain in Knopf's neck. He gave a squeal. "Check the computer! I'm telling the truth!"

"Fuck the computer," Schwarz snapped. "She still nearly died because of you."

"Please. That thing's hurting me," Knopf whined. "I don't want to become a vegetable!"

Schwarz continued to apply pressure to the thumbtack, keeping up the pain. He shrugged. "Then maybe you shouldn't have betrayed your country to an enemy power."

"He's just a drug dealer!" Knopf said. "I just know him as El Toronado. He phoned me personally."

"El Toronado?" Schwarz asked. "What kind of a stupid fucking name is that for a drug dealer?"

"I don't know," Knopf sobbed. "He just sent a man to my house. Not a big guy, but he was nasty as fuck."

"What was his name?" Schwarz asked.

"Argus. That's the only name I know him by," Knopf replied. "He said he'd always be watching me. If I screwed up, he'd know, and my family would be dead."

Schwarz pulled the tack out and threw it on the table. "Well, now we're talking."

Knopf swallowed. "You didn't drill my skull?"

The Able Team electronics genius set his tools on the table. "No. Can you point out Argus if I showed you a photo sheet?"

"How would you know I'm not lying?" Knopf asked.

"You stuck with your story when you were sure I'd drilled a hole in your brain and stuck an electrical probe inside. That kind of distress and maintenance of detail is real hard to fake," Schwarz told him. "Plus, we need to be able to track down Argus before he goes after your family."

Knopf nodded, staring at the thumbtack he was certain had been a hot wire plunged into his brain. "Just please, save my wife and kid."

"Where are they?" Schwarz asked.

"My home," Knopf said.

"You got an ecstasy contact, and you've got a wife and kid? She not good enough for you?" Schwarz asked.

"No, I don't use the X to pick up girls," Knopf replied. "I use amphetamines. To keep my edge…"

"Uppers. And you were given X to take care of Dr. Bertonni?" Schwarz asked.

"I thought it was a lot, but they said it wouldn't kill her," Knopf answered.

"They had to assure you that you weren't killing anyone, and they have your wife and kid hostage." Schwarz asked, "Would it have mattered?"

Knopf shook his head. "They said they'd kill my wife and kid, but they don't have people on the scene. Not yet, I don't think. They just said…over the phone. They left the X in my locker."

Schwarz looked to Detective Roston through the observation mirror. "So they only talked to you over the phone?"

Knopf shook his head. "Snail mail. I kept the notes in my desk at home."

"All right. I'll make sure your family is okay," Schwarz told him. "We'll check your locker for prints, too. See who dropped the X off for you. You save the container for it?"

"The K.C.P.D. took it from my pocket," Knopf replied. He shook. "I'm fucked, aren't I?"

"We find someone's out to threaten your family, I'll make sure you get off on exigent circumstances," Schwarz explained. "And knowing El Toronado, he'll have something ready for them."

Knopf looked up at Schwarz as he started to leave the interrogation room. "Where are you going?"

"To save your wife and kid," Schwarz said. "So quit wasting my time."

Orlando, Florida

LYONS CHECKED HIS PDA as they closed in on the meeting with Apis. A fresh image popped up on his screen, identifying Jan Pantopoulos, also known as Argus. Now Lyons knew where he had seen the man from Sonora before, but couldn't place him. His mental mug file was centered on criminals, while Pantopoulos was a Greek special forces expert.

"Keep an eye out for this guy," Schwarz said. "He's Apis's main enforcer, and he's got Greek counterterrorism training."

Lyons heard background static. "You sound like you're in a helicopter."

"Andy Knopf's home," Schwarz explained. "His family's got a deathwatch, and we're not wasting time."

"Watch your ass," Lyons told him.

"You're the ones going after a crime boss who has a Stony

Man qualified combat specialist as his right hand," Schwarz returned.

"Closing on the meet," Lyons said. "Over and out."

Schwarz got off a quick, "Good luck," before the call ended.

Lyons's cold blue eyes scanned the lot as Blancanales pulled them off the street. The Able Team leader had the Mossberg tucked into the seat well next to his leg. His Colt Python rode in its shoulder holster, and on his hip was the .40-caliber Smith & Wesson. Blancanales was wearing his Uzi pistol in a shoulder rig, and packing his favorite .45-caliber 1911 and the new Smith & Wesson MP-40. Together, the two Able Team experts had eighty-eight rounds on tap before they had to stop and reload. They'd fitted Prohaska, who sat in the back seat, into a protective Kevlar vest, and wore their own body armor.

"There he is," Prohaska said, pointing out the pickup vehicle. His stubby sausage finger aimed right at a slender, white-goateed man in a plain brown linen suit with a dark blue polo shirt. He was braced by wiry, hard-faced young men with close-cropped hair.

"Apis is still hanging with former Soviet army," Blancanales noted as the car coasted closer to the Greek mob boss and his quartet of defenders. "American blue jeans and clean white gym shoes are practically uniforms for *mafiya* operating on American streets."

"Windbreakers," Lyons said. "It doesn't look like they're packing folded rifles, but they might have something else. Bizons perhaps."

"Any sign of backup protection?" Blancanales asked.

"Good chance there is," Lyons noted. "Let's get the ball rolling. Do your countersniper evasive driving."

Blancanales hit the gas and Lyons whipped up the Mossberg, triggering a single Brenneke slug into the chest of one of the Russian army thugs. The high-powered combat missile flipped the man onto his back, piercing through his sternum. The mobster's white linen shirt blossomed a gory flower of blood on the front.

Distant rifles opened up, asphalt exploding behind them as Blancanales accelerated the Cutlass to fifty miles an hour in the parking lot. By weaving in a serpentine path, he prevented the backup riflemen from drawing an easy bead on their car. Blancanales spared a breath to shout, "Tuck your head under the money bag, Prohaska!"

Lyons glanced back to see the criminal accountant hugging the back seat, the duffel bag stuffed with cash hung over his unprotected head like a pillow. "Funny how your worries about making a mess disappear when there's a rifle spitting at you."

Lyons tromboned the slide of the Mossberg, punching out two more 12-gauge blasts. The second round out of the weapon vomited a cone of .36-inch pellets into the upper chest of another Russian hardman as he pulled out a Bizon submachine gun, a compact gun that looked like a shrunken AK-47 with a cylinder in place of its banana clip. The high capacity weapon dropped from lifeless fingers as the Able Team commander's third shot took another gunman through the biceps. Unfortunately, the Russian's other hand held a Bizon, and he clamped down the trigger, a stream of 9 mm rounds tearing from the stubby muzzle, pinging along the side of the Cutlass. Lyons twisted to pump off another shot, but Blancanales swerved to avoid the snipers.

Apis showed a spry swiftness belying his bony frame, racing away from the battle sight as the fourth Russian opened up with his own Bizon to track the Cutlass. Blancanales stuck his Uzi out the window and ripped off a blast that stitched the last bodyguard with the final rounds of a sweeping burst. The two hits were enough to drop the gangster to one knee, clutching a sucking gut wound. Blancanales swerved again, but not before an enemy rifle punched a hole in the sedan's hood. Smoke poured from the engine, but the Able Team wheel man swung the car's front bumper toward the wounded bodyguard. At forty-five miles an hour, the impact jolted Lyons and Blancanales in the front seat and dumped Prohaska into the rear seat well, but the Russian gunman's body flopped bonelessly to the ground, leaving one shooter on the parking lot, the Greek mobster running for his life, and two snipers pumping high-powered rounds at Able Team.

Lyons thumbed Brenneke slugs into the Mossberg's tube magazine, knowing he'd need the range to take on the snipers. He pressed his earpiece tighter to his head. "Jack, got eyes on the riflemen?" he said into his throat mike.

"I have a muzzle-flash at the stop-and-rob to your west, and another coming from an apartment complex balcony," Grimaldi said. The ace Stony Man pilot was five hundred feet up, and watching over his friends with a pair of night-vision goggles. Even the dimmed flares of a silenced rifle were amplified through the NVDs enough to be noticed in the hot Florida night.

"Right," Lyons replied. He quickly relayed the snipers' positions to Blancanales, then handed over his six-inch Colt Python. "I'm bringing down Apis."

Blancanales nodded and swerved toward the fleeing mob boss. Lyons popped the door and then gave it a kick. The door snapped out violently and struck Apis across his back, tossing him harshly to the tarmac. Lyons kicked out of his passenger seat and rolled to a halt five yards from the stunned Greek.

The sniper on the apartment balcony triggered his rifle just a little too soon, a .30 caliber bullet gouging up asphalt a few feet to Lyons's right. He swung up the Mossberg and punched a 12-gauge slug toward the enemy. The Able Team leader's initial round was low at ninety-eight yards. The Brenneke slug passed between two bars of the rail and struck the rifleman just above his knee. At the extreme range, the Brenneke lost the vicious penetration that severed the bodyguard's arm with one hit. Against the heavy femur, the .72-inch monster bullet simply stopped without fracturing the bone, but the sniper flopped, losing his rifle and ramming his jaw against railing.

The stunned gunman rolled onto his side, clawing for a long-barreled revolver cradled in a tanker-style chest holster. Lyons pumped his Mossberg and fired again, his second slug ramming one of the steel bars, bending it. The deformed missile missed the sniper as he jammed the long nose of the heavy Magnum weapon through the grating. A huge muzzle-flash flared and Lyons stepped back in reflex, a .44 Magnum slug chopping into the ground at his feet. It would only be a moment before the balcony sniper could adjust his aim, so Lyons pulled out his Smith & Wesson MP-40.

"Time to see if you're any good at a football field," he muttered, powering through the take-up of the six-and-a-half-pound trigger, letting his index finger snap back forward to reset and fire again. Three 165-grain .40-caliber hollowpoint rounds leaped out at close to 1200 feet per second, one sparking on black-painted steel grating, the other two disappearing into the shadowy lump on the floor of the balcony. The two .40s that didn't strike metal speared the gunman through the heart. The deflected round ricocheted into his groin, and even if the heart shots hadn't been instantly fatal, a fountain of arterial blood jetting out would have been.

Across the parking lot, Rosario Blancanales stood on the brake, spinning the car to a halt. He brought up the Colt Python in both hands, aiming at the roof of the convenience

store where the second sniper was located. Thumbing back
the big Magnum revolver's hammer, he gave himself a hair
trigger, lined up the sights and fired once. The enemy rifle
barked, the bullet punching through the Cutlass door. It
skimmed a few millimeters over Blancanales's thighs, so close
he could feel the heat and shock wave coming off the deformed bullet, splinters of plastic from the car's interior door
spraying his leg.

The Able Team driver's single round leaped across the 125
yards in a heartbeat, cutting through the rifleman's clavicle.
The high-powered handgun round shattered bone and severed
the Russian's aorta. Blancanales swallowed, realizing how
close he'd come to having his own femoral arteries severed
by a single rifle round. An inch in any direction, and he'd be
crippled with a shattered femur or pelvis, or trying to hold in
his boiling intestines. Only blind luck and a car door saved
him from a slow, painful death.

Apis, born Thanos Burzyck to a Greek father and a Bul-
garian mail-order bride nearly sixty-five years ago, recovered his senses from the jolting impact of the car door. The
gunfire had died down while his head was still reeling, but
he couldn't tell who was the winner. He spotted one of his
Russian bodyguards, a hard-eyed, raw-boned young man
who had spent time in the Special Forces. The ex-Spetznaz
fighter limped across the parking lot, trying to reach the
cover of a parked van, while trying unsuccessfully to hold
on to his Bizon with the flopping mess of a shattered left
arm. Finally, the Russian gave up and threw the Bizon
down in disgust, clawing for the Glock he had stuffed in
his waistband.

Burzyck looked around and saw a big blond man closing
in on the bodyguard, a pistol in his hand. The Russian fired,
single-handedly, and Burzyck could see the guy's wind-

breaker flutter under the impact of bullets. Instead of falling over, wounded or dead, the blonde continued to charge, triggering his Smith & Wesson on the fly. The Russian hard man jerked as high-velocity, large-caliber bullets bore through his torso, churning vital organs into ragged, shredded lumps of useless tissue. The one-armed Russian collapsed, Glock clattering from lifeless fingers.

Burzyck struggled to his feet. His back hurt, and his legs felt wobbly beneath him, but he still managed to achieve a stooped-over stance. He knew that it would take a long time for him to recover his energy. While he was old, he still was fit and could run like the wind, but after being rammed by a speeding car's door, it would take his old bones longer to stop complaining and allow him to flee. He took one step, then turned to look back to see if there was a sign of the men who'd tried to ambush him. The big blonde that had gunned down his last bodyguard was coming toward him.

Burzyck grimaced, realizing that he was smart not to carry any weapons on him. Fighting this man would be suicide, and considering that his pursuer hadn't opened up on him, he would be destined for jail, not a coffin. The Greek crime boss straightened and held his hands up, palms facing the Able Team commander.

Glassy blue eyes sized up the commando, lip curled in a sneer for the American who had destroyed his guardians. "You've made a mistake, fool. They'll have me out of jail before you finish eating breakfast."

Lyons lowered his Smith & Wesson, holstering it. He shook his head. "Jail? You're not going to jail, Apis."

Burzyck squinted as he realized that his facade as Florida crime lord "El Toronado" had been torn away. "Then what do you want of me?"

Lyons grinned mirthlessly, his cold blue eyes burrowing into Burzyck's heart.

The Greek grunted in pain as Lyons reached out, whirled him around and handcuffed him. "You and me need to shoot the bull."

CHAPTER TEN

Stony Man Farm, Virginia

Barbara Price was all business as she entered the War Room. Looking up at the main screen, she saw that Phoenix Force was triangulated in southern China, but instead of the green "in contact" arrow, they were under a red wedge.

"Still nothing?" Price asked.

"Satellite comm isn't giving us any love, Barb," Kurtzman replied. "We're trying to get an angled signal beam, but currently we're running into active resistance. Akira's been pushing at the defenses that have denied us communication with the satellites we've lost, and they've picked up on our control signature. Every time we try to bounce a signal from one satellite to another, they intercept us."

"Whoever this guy is, he's good. I'm trying to crack his coding and he's left nothing in his programming that would have his identification," Tokaido announced. "He's reacting to keep pace with me, but so far it still feels like a one-man deal."

"How about blocking us in Florida?" Price asked.

"Akira's hitting them too hard in the Southeast Asian

satellites for them to establish a decent defense," Wethers explained. "We wiggled in and managed to regain control of the eyes in the sky supporting Able Team. We haven't had much of a chance to utilize that, but given the feeble efforts thrown at trying to retake the surveillance birds, we're concentrating on maintaining our uplink."

"With all this activity, I'm surprised that the National Reconnaissance Office isn't alerted to the fight going on in their network," Price said.

"It's essentially the same kind of operation going on in China," Kurtzman countered. "Both Stony Man and our unknown enemy are keeping a low profile and invisible to the main opponent. If we directed more bandwidth to trying to outmuscle them, we'd be spotted by the NRO's cyberdefenses and they'd come down on us like antibodies. The same fear of NRO attention has them keeping their head low."

"I could get us a legitimate presence on their mainframe," Price stated. "Then we'd force their hand."

"If we do that, then we open ourselves up to attack," Kurtzman explained. "The reason why we're doing this covertly is that we don't want the firepower ramped up in this fight. Carmen…"

Delahunt nodded. "While Akira's been giving the enemy hell, I've been tooling around a logic bomb that they've dumped into the NRO mainframe. In layman's terms, this thing is a MOAB."

"Mother of All Bombs," Price muttered. "It'll cripple the whole National Reconnaissance Office if we drag this out too much."

"I'm tickling its triggers, trying to defuse them, but one wrong move, and we blind the nation," Delahunt said. "We've got other eyes in the sky, but nothing that's as good as the NRO's satellites. The images we pull off them enable us to give the teams an idea what they're up against."

"But we're not using NRO for our communications, right?" Price asked.

"Every time we switch satellite frequencies, we're jammed. As it is, the base is under a heavy blackout. According to Chinese intelligence chatter, the launch facility, which isn't even supposed to exist, has disappeared. Radar and their own satellites have been blanked out," Kurtzman responded. "They have apologies for the blackout, from the people who've been covering up other information about the facility, and everything will be back up in the space of an hour."

"An hour…just long enough for them to launch another flight," Price said. "They send up a fighting crew and a supply rocket loaded with their isotopes with each two-shot launch."

"It seems likely," Kurtzman said. "David was trying to get in touch with us a minute after he sent us digital imaging on the first launch."

"What about the local countryside? No one reported the smoke contrails?" Price asked.

"The nearest local habitation is beyond the horizon," Kurtzman answered. "It's far enough inland to be invisible from the coastal villages and ports, but still close to the equator."

"There's four other space program stations in the north," Wethers stated. "And our view of them and their activity has been left alone."

Price grimaced. "Carmen, Hunt, could you find out if there's a similar logic bomb inside SAD's mainframe?"

"It's not going to be much help if we do," Delahunt began.

"Just pop it off. Chinese intel goes completely off-line," Price suggested. "We leave them blind and deaf…"

"And then we can just hit the area with a blanket communication from whatever sources we can get without fear of Phoenix Force being traced," Kurtzman added. "Carm, give me the recognition profile on the bomb."

"It shouldn't take too long for the Chinese to get back on line with their backup systems, but it'll give us a window of opportunity," Price said. "And, without the ears that the conspirators have put up inside SAD's network, they'll be hampered in fighting against our incursions into the system."

"It'll give us an opportunity to lay some sensors within their system, open links that we can tap at any time," Kurtzman added.

"There you go," Delahunt told Kurtzman. "There's the profile."

The Stony Man head computer technician triggered the booby trap inside the Chinese Intelligence Network, and the steady flow of data from behind the Bamboo Curtain spewed out in a twisted snarl of garbled digital gibbering. China went dark.

"We've got contact with Phoenix!" Tokaido shouted.

China

MCCARTER GOT A SIGNAL on the satcom, so he aimed the telephoto lens of the digital camera at the base, showing the Farm the efforts of the enemy to get the second flight on its way into orbit. He also hurriedly transmitted earlier images he'd taken of non-Chinese sentries on the base.

"We're getting your data," Price said over the line.

"You're taking a risk doing this on an open line," McCarter replied. "The Chinese might hear us."

"They can't even hear themselves," Price said. "We set off a logic bomb the enemy had put in their system and left them blind, deaf and dumb."

"And it'll put the Chinese government on alert when they recover their senses," McCarter replied.

"We'll let them have the imaging you just gave us," Price stated. "It'll put them on cleanup duty looking for the ones who were covering for the takeover."

"They're getting close to launching," McCarter warned. "We're going to try and take a seat on the next rocket up after we clean out the forces that have taken over. If we're lucky, they have prisoners hostage who know how to continue the launch process, and if we rescue them and make allies among them, we can take the next ship up."

"That's one way to get out of China," Price replied. "What's your progress?"

McCarter looked at the broken-necked body crumpled at his feet. He took a quick shot with the digicam, feeding it live into the satellite phone. The features of the corpse betrayed a Slavic background. "That's my fourth sentry. The others are taking out perimeter guards, as well."

"No gunfire?" Price asked.

"So far, so good," McCarter answered. "You've got all the data you need from my camera?"

"Yeah. We're trying to take over local Chinese spy satellites and get images off of them. With the system thrown into disarray, slipping through the cracks is making it easier. We'll work on setting up a communication signal so the team can coordinate," Price promised.

McCarter kicked the body into a bush, knocking visible limbs behind branches. He tucked the camera away and continued to leave the phone's hands-free set running. "Here I thought we were going to do this the hard way."

He bent and retrieved his combat knife from the chest of a second guard, this one a local Chinese military man. The blade had been stuck in his breastbone when McCarter had stabbed him through the heart, necessitating the broken neck on the second man.

"You're pulling this off without gunfire so far," Price answered. "If that's not hard, then I don't know what is."

"What's the progress on sorting out the hodgepodge of soldiers here?" McCarter asked. "I've seen Arabic, Slavic and Hispanic features."

"We've been lucky in one regard. Thanks to Able's interception at the border and in Sonora, we've got a known associates list to help narrow things down on the facial recognition software," Price said. "The gentleman you just sent us was a member of the GRU who was drummed out on corruption charges. He's been making his money as a gun for hire. Two of his compatriots were at the border, and another was in Sonora."

McCarter grimaced as he caught sight of another sentry. The man, an Iranian by his appearance, saw the ex-SAS man at the same time and opened his mouth, hands dropping to the Iranian-built Heckler & Koch MP-5 hanging on its sling. McCarter cursed, realizing that he couldn't cross the distance, nor throw his knife in time to stop the Iranian from triggering the assault weapon. The Phoenix Force Commander dug in to make the effort when steel whistled through the air, shining flashes of reflective metal glinting in the sunlight before they lodged in the enemy commando's right eye and cheek, blood gushing. The Iranian forgot about his MP-5 and clutched quickly at his face, screaming as he jarred the five-pointed throwing stars jammed in his eye socket and cheek.

McCarter took the brief respite and lunged, his Ka-Bar knock-off biting deeply into flesh at the base of the gunman's throat. Windpipe speared, the Iranian clawed at McCarter's face, but the Phoenix Force pro whipped his polycarbonate-protected elbow around and struck the two metal stars jammed into the Iranian's skull. The curved elbow-protection shell skidded a bit on one of the stars, but hammered the second five-pointed blade half of its three-inch diameter into brain matter. The intrusion of solid steel into his central nervous system sent the Iranian into a seizure, bile and blood bubbling through paralyzed lips. He collapsed.

McCarter took the handle of his knife and whacked the two throwing stars out of his victim's face. He noticed Rafael Encizo off to one side and gave him a low-key salute of thanks. Encizo's close friend, and the first Phoenix Force commando to die in service, Keio Ohara, had taught the Cuban the art of shuruken-*jutsu,* the way of hurling a variety of throwing blades in combat.

"Thank you too, K.O.," McCarter whispered. "Still watching my arse after all these years."

"David?" Price asked.

"Sorry," McCarter said. He took a quick snapshot of the dead man. "New confirm."

Encizo, now armed with an MP-5 SD, closed with McCarter and handed a Fire wire plug to him. "Process mine, too."

McCarter was glad that the phone unit had multiple ports for the Fire wire connections for the digital cameras as he jacked Encizo's camera into his system. The size of a pie plate, it rode on McCarter's right hip and had the power to upload information back to the Farm, as well as download and process large files. In its bullet-resistant shell, with solid-state electronics to survive the harsh jostling of combat, it was an integral part of a Land Warrior commander system. The flat communicator also kept him in contact with his teammates, able to transmit visual information over heads-up display-equipped goggles. The only limit was the memory-intensive digital camera information his partners picked up. He gave the voice command for the camera dump and he saw the progress meter running on the left lens of his goggles. "You've got more data coming in."

"We're getting it. Aaron's got eyes operating in the sky," Price responded on the other end.

"That's good news," Calvin James's voice cut in. "I've nearly been spotted twice. A little extra intel would make this easier."

"What've we got on the infrared?" McCarter asked.

"We've got a major contingent of guards surrounding a building full of warm bodies," Price answered. "Transmitting digital map."

McCarter received the aerial imaging and gave the vocal command to disseminate to the rest of the team. "Looks like twelve guards, all appearing fresh, and something along the lines of thirty hostages."

"Indispensable technical crew," Manning said, anger tinting his tone. "The disposable staff were murdered and shoved into a mass grave by a bulldozer from the looks of it."

"Visual confirmation?" Price asked.

"I'll upload it when this is finished," Manning told her. "Not particularly happy to have documented that atrocity."

"Take it out on this group," McCarter said. "Any info on the Arabic bloke I got the pic on?"

"We have a false positive," Price answered. "Apparently it's an Iranian security officer who died two years ago."

"Hell, Barb, Gadgets and Pol are officially dead, too," McCarter countered. "And let's not even go into Striker."

"Sanitized," Price translated. "He disappeared a few years back on an op in the U.S. that Striker had broken up, but we never picked up his remains."

"He crawled out of the rubble and ran with his tail between his legs. He's reported dead, but this was his way to get out of the shit house," McCarter said. "He helps get this operation off the ground, and he wouldn't be awaiting a sickle haircut back home."

"Too bad you gave him too close a shave," Encizo noted, looking at the horrific knife wound in his throat. "These MP-5s are Iranian-license built guns. They didn't even bother to work the serial numbers."

"How can you tell they're Iranian built?" Price asked.

"The serial number range of the three that I acquired," the Cuban explained. "Don't forget, I'm Phoenix Force's resident HK expert. That includes historical data, such as which factories produced which guns."

McCarter accepted one of the silenced machine pistols, and Encizo handed off the third to T. J. Hawkins who joined the pair.

"Gary, have you got a suppressed weapon?" McCarter asked.

"I've got the suppressor and subsonic 7.62 mm Russian rounds for my SVD all ready," Manning stated. "I've got a three-hundred-yard lethal range with that combination."

"Enough to provide fire support against the defensive perimeter they put up around the hostages," McCarter said. "Rafe, hook up with Cal and come around side three. T.J., on me for side one. You've got the overwatch, Gary. Start the ball rolling, then bat cleanup."

"Side three doesn't have that strong a concentration of sentries," James responded over the headset as Encizo stalked away from Hawkins and McCarter.

"T.J. and I will be distracting the main guard force," McCarter answered. "Rafe will be your security while you run triage on the hostages. If we're going to get them on our side, we need to save as many as possible, including any wounded or ill."

"It's more likely I'll run into dehydrated or malnourished captives," James said.

"Then break out the bottled water," McCarter told him. "Anything to let them know we're friends."

"Gotcha," James answered. "Rafe's here."

"Okay," McCarter replied. "Time's wasting. We've got killing to do."

CAPTAIN YUAN HAU WINCED as he sat up. The Iranians and their western mercenary puppets had given him a harsh beating when they took the Phoenix Graveyard. The Chinese government had given the covert satellite launch facility an innocuous, dead-end name when they'd constructed it. Everything referring to it in the official records had it listed as a dead-end research center for weather observation, where the dredges of the SAD were thrown when they'd failed in observing the west's aerospace industry.

However, even being labeled as a failure, the SAD was too savvy to let Hau's expertise and gathered rocket science intel go to waste. He'd been able to copy Atlas rocket data and upgrade the performance of the launch vehicles by a full thirty percent, while keeping costs down. Utilizing cast-off materials from cold war intercontinental ballistic technology, modifying them and upgrading what he could, he'd saved the Chinese government millions in development costs. His fellow scientists had also been responsible for similar leaps and bounds of progress.

Then, Colonel Wing opened the front gates and allowed some "investors" into the Phoenix Graveyard. When they pulled out machine pistols and gunned down specifically targeted security and command personnel, Hau realized that the Graveyard would become his soon. He'd tried to resist interrogation attempts, but as his sore, limp arms betrayed, Wing's invaders were skilled in breaking people. Hau was just a scientist, and after one of his rotator cuffs had been destroyed by a bar crucifying him between his folded elbows, he surrendered and gave them assistance.

"Only a few more minutes before the second flight goes up," the Iranian commander said with a grin. He spoke in the only language that they both knew, English. "Then we won't need you anymore."

Hau grimaced. "Big man with a machine gun."

"God gives us the weapons to strike down our enemies,"

the Iranian, Wahri, he'd been called, replied. "Your multi-stage rockets. German-designed machine pistols. International mercenaries."

"And Colonel Wing," Hau grumbled.

"And your Colonel Wing. God is generous, as is our sponsor," Wahri stated.

"And when the last two Dragon Knives go into the sky?" Hau asked. "You're going to kill us?"

"Not much use left for you," Wahri stated. The radio on Wahri's belt beeped and he plucked it to his ear. Hau could see shock blank the cockiness from his features, anger filling in the void left behind. "Everything's down?"

Wahri glared toward the Chinese rocket scientist, his finger curling around the trigger of his black German machine gun. "We'll do what has to be done. Any word from our perimeter guard?"

The buzzing reply over the radio was unintelligible as the Iranian held the speaker to his ear. Hau tensed the muscles in his good arm as he knew that Wahri was being told to start shooting as soon as there were signs of trouble. Though the muzzle of the black gun was aimed at the ceiling, the finger on the trigger was a sign of impending violence.

A clenched left fist, with no real finesse and a fraction less pure muscle, was the only weapon he had to use against Wahri. Even if he somehow managed to cold-cock the Iranian commander, there were two more mercenaries in the barracks, also heavily armed and placed so that the three of them could hose down the hostages in moments. Hau knew that the minute he punched Wahri, his back would burn with a relentless storm of hot lead.

Better than dying as a sheep, he told himself, legs tensing as he prepared to make his move.

The back door slammed open and Wahri and Hau whirled

as one, watching as a pair of strangers burst through, weapons up and tracking. One was a stocky Hispanic man and the other was a tall, lean black man, both clad in camouflaged skintight suits.

The Hispanic man exploded into action first, his HK knockoff ripping off a quick burst that took Wahri in his shoulder and gun arm. The Iranian's weapon clattered to the floor and Hau leaped across the distance separating him from his captor, firing off his cocked left fist like a rocket. The Chinese scientist could feel his knuckle bones crack and split as he drove the blow down hard into the side of Wahri's head, crippling pain shooting up his forearm.

The black commando pumped a suppressed burst of 9 mm slugs into a Filipino mercenary who was tracking the lunging Hau with his own weapon. The bullets cut through the gunman, killing him instantly before he could pull the trigger and murder the Chinese officer. The Hispanic man's machine pistol erupted again, taking down Wahri's other mercenary backup, a stream of Parabellum rounds chopping through the man's skull, literally blowing his brains out.

Wahri struggled to sit up, still dazed from the shoulder hit and Hau's punch, but the black man crossed to the commanding officer and snapped a kick under the Iranian's jaw.

"Are you all right?" Calvin James asked Hau in his passable Cantonese, learned from his friend and martial arts instructor John Trent.

Hau shook his head. "They tore up my shoulder, and my good hand feels like a cow stepped on it."

"Is anyone in immediate need of medical attention?" James called out in Cantonese.

Hau lifted his mangled left hand, gnarled, broken-knuckle fingers aiming at a few figures in the corner. "We've all been beaten badly, but those men are the worst off."

"I'm a medic," James told him. "I can check out their injuries. How are you all on water and food?"

"We haven't eaten in several days, but we've got water, as filthy as it is," Hau answered, pointing to a brackish, green-tinted soup laying in a trough. "If you have antibiotics…"

"Rafe!" James called in English. He tossed him a small resealable bag full of pills. "Start administering this. The water they've been drinking looks like it was emptied from a drainage ditch. Who knows what kind of bugs they've got swimming in that sewage."

"Gotcha," Encizo said. "Ask if anyone else knows English. My Chinese is pretty limited."

"I speak English, as do several of my comrades," Hau stated.

Hau jolted as he heard the sound of a body crash against the wall near him. James held his hand to his earpiece and listened. "Who's a good shot?" the black man asked in Cantonese, not wanting to waste time on translations.

Three bruised, limping Chinese answered the call, and James handed out weapons he'd confiscated from the invading force, Iranian submachine guns and Beretta-style handguns. The trio took them. "Cover the back entrance. My man outside is observing enemy movement, and there are gunmen trying to take the building. They don't know that you've been liberated."

James quickly crossed to the corner of the room, Hau joining him. He found one of the prisoners was pale, his normally golden flesh turned ashen and gray. Clammy sweat smeared his black hair to his forehead, and the Phoenix Force medic knew the man was in shock. Hau cooed to the badly wounded Chinese in Mandarin, reassuring him.

"Thanks, my Mandarin's not so good," James explained.

"You're helping us. It's the least I can do with my injured hand and arm," Hau said.

"I'll take a look at that as soon as we get the chance," James stated.

"You think you have time? The countdown for the next flight of rockets is in at least the final half hour," Hau told him. "That's the way Wahri seemed to be acting."

"We've got an estimated forty minutes," James corrected him, checking the wounded man. His guess as to the wounded man's injuries were correct, the prisoner's ribs were broken, and from a quick stethoscope examination, he was operating on only one lung, the other either filled with fluid or collapsed from being speared by a broken rib. Pulling out a thermal blanket from his pack, James unfolded the small square of foil until it was large enough to engulf the patient. "He needs to be kept warm and hydrated."

James handed over his canteen to another Chinese technician, and Hau translated the instructions. He pulled a morphine syrette out and gave the agonized, shocked prisoner a small dose to take the edge off the pain. "Make certain he has the antibiotics, as well."

The prisoner's face regained some color, the tension melting off of his expression as the morphine relaxed him. Sleep took over in an instant.

"So that's thirty-eight minutes left to stop the second launch," Hau said.

"You know the specifics of who went up?" James asked.

"They only needed us to install life support systems on two of the rockets," Hau explained. "The other two were presumably for cargo. There were biohazard barrels brought in a few days ago."

"How long have they been here?" James asked.

"Six days. Colonel Wing and his loyalists have undoubtedly been keeping up appearances for the top brass, while their allies have been smuggling in both mercenaries and supplies in lieu of our ordinary material."

"Does he have anyone who might be considered a prisoner near the launch pad?" James continued. "Techs who he didn't have under control, but was holding the rest of you to keep them on a short leash?"

"A dozen men," Hau said. "But the orders seemed to be that we would die as soon as the second launch was through. Then, I think they were going to abandon the Phoenix Graveyard and head back to wherever they wanted to go."

James touched his earpiece again. "Our partners have cleared the guard force outside the building. This part of the compound is secure for now. Now, tell me what you know about the invaders."

Hau nodded, starting from the top. "They were mostly Iranian…."

CHAPTER ELEVEN

Central Florida airspace

"I'm an old man, so I'm not afraid of death," Thanos Burzyck told Carl Lyons as the helicopter accelerated back toward Kennedy Space Center. "If you intend to intimidate me, you can't. I've been worked over by the worst the Turkish government had to offer."

Lyons merely stared at the Greek crime boss for a long, silent moment.

"I also suppose you're not afraid of incarceration for the rest of your life because of your pal in Homeland Security, right?" Lyons asked.

Burzyck smirked. "Ah, you finally caught on to the fact that I have friends."

"Not friends, Apis," Lyons countered. "A puppet master. And this one has his hand jammed so far up your ass, he can tickle your tonsils. Fertility god, my ass."

Apis narrowed his eyes. "I'm no man's puppet."

Lyons didn't bother to fight off the laugh. It came out as nearly a roar.

"Men who laugh at me don't live long," Burzyck warned.

Lyons shrugged. "Everyone who tells me that ends up as a missing person or an unidentified corpse rotting in some field. You tell me not to intimidate you when the truth is, you couldn't hope to get any leverage on me. I'm God, and you're just a sack of shit who has some pertinent information that I'm too lazy to cut out of your skin."

"I have people…"

"Like Mellera and Gil Shane?" Lyons asked. "Mellera and fifteen of his closest buddies are either mulch or holed up in a Justice Department safehouse. Actually, Mellera's the only one still alive. His men, the punks you had looking out for Prohaska, and the Russian meatheads who were supposed to be covering your ass are all dog food. And don't count on Shane giving you any support. He's skipped town."

Burzyck tensed. "Skipped town?"

"Since yesterday, no one has seen or heard from him in his office. Either he's in his apartment hanging from a noose, or he's on his way to Argentina hoping to avoid extradition for selling out our space program to terrorists," Lyons pressed. "I just don't see a case where he'll be in the mood to bail out your wrinkled ass when we stake it out for the wolves."

Burzyck grit his teeth. "You're making shit up."

Lyons handed over a digital camera. He pressed a button and the LCD displayed a slide show of Mellera's murdered acquaintances, and the bodies from the subsequent two battles between Able Team and Apis's organization. "I'm speculating as to what happened to our missing Homeland Security fink, but you're looking at the gory mess that's left of your street soldiers."

"That's just a small fraction of my army."

"Sure. Twenty-five gunmen isn't much to a guy who supplies Central Florida with tons of contraband a year. You could call down an army as big as the one the Persians sent into Thermopylae. Well, Molon Labe."

Burzyck narrowed his eyes at the infamous challenge King Leonidas gave to the million-man army that tried to push itself past a force of three hundred Spartans. Molon Labe. The closest translation in modern times was "Bring it, asshole."

"Two men against twenty-five gunmen in the space of a few hours. You see a bullet hole in my partner?" Lyons asked. "Or me? Outnumbered thirteen to one, and we don't have a scratch on us, and you're a tied-up old man who I can toss out of this helicopter and not give a fuck if they find you with my signature and social security number scratched into your face with a Bowie knife. In fact, here…"

Lyons handed Burzyck a cell phone. "Call every single person with a gun that you've ever heard of. Have them meet us on a beach north of Cape Canaveral. Tell them you'll pay a million dollars to anyone who can kill us. You won't even be out a nickel when we're through, though we'll be saving the taxpayers millions in the scumbags we snuff."

Burzyck's mouth formed into a tight, bloodless line.

"Go on. I'm giving you your shot at me. Shane's bugged out on you, probably because he figured out we're on your case," Lyons continued. "We're not too well-known, but Homeland Security knows our pattern pretty well. We show up, and the scumbags start filling body bags like they're trying to dam a flood in hell. And Homeland Security? They get told to fuck off and stay out of our way, even if we have to saw the head off a crooked cop or some CIA agent who sold out the country. The only trace Shane left behind was the piss stain in his office chair when he saw we were interested in you."

Burzyck closed his eyes.

"Or maybe you want to call Shane's cell. Maybe he didn't ditch it yet while he's running scared off to South America,"

Lyons said. He smiled wistfully. "I hope he's in Brazil. I liked it when I was down there, slaughtering the rancid cops who kill homeless children."

"All right," Burzyck huffed. "Gilbert Shane set it up for me to move in down here in Orlando. He's the one who put me in charge of looking out for an operation that Homeland Security was running.'

Lyons tilted his head. "Kind of figured you were working for them."

"I used to be working for the CIA. I was their asset here in the U.S.," Burzyck replied. "Because the Company isn't allowed to operate on U.S. soil, I was one of their necessary evils. Someone they're trailing shows up in the country, and he needs to die, I'm the one who throws his funeral. As long as I leave the cops alone, they keep me solvent, helping me out. I could be warned of a major federal joint task force looking at me cross-eyed here in Orlando, and by the end of next month, I've got a new identity as the Minotaur in Los Angeles or Longhorn in Houston."

"All the while, you just rake in money, importing drugs, stolen electronics, cars, weapons," Lyons offered.

"Good pay, though the Kennedy Space Center thing started eating into my time, so I passed the minutiae off to that shyster Costa," Burzyck explained. "I had to step up my personal involvement because my right hand took off."

"Argus." Lyons supplied the name.

"The same," Burzyck said. "He was a gift from the CIA. Seems they didn't want him to join some rival operation, so they offered him the high life with me. They have a highly trained killer in their pocket on U.S. soil, and their competition in the National Security arena doesn't get to use him."

Lyons laughed.

"It was you?" Burzyck asked.

"Pretty good possibility," Lyons told him. "Though, if he had the moral bankruptcy to work for a soulless bastard like you, then we really didn't want him."

"I wish I knew how to get in touch with him. I'd be willing to trade him for my freedom," Burzyck answered.

"You want freedom?" Lyons asked. "There's only one way out."

Burzyck sighed. "I'm just negotiating for something fast."

"A fast exit, or free room and board for the rest of your miserable life," Lyons offered.

"Shane wanted me in on watching the Kennedy operation. I was his main contact, though there was someone inside NASA that he didn't even tell me about," Burzyck explained.

"What was it all about?" Lyons asked.

"Throwing a wrench into China's space program," Burzyck told him. "He said that when this shuttle mission launched, the U.S. was going to have everything it needed to smash the hell out of China with impunity."

Lyons shook his head. "With the assets tied up in the Global War on Terror, we don't have time to fuck with the Chinese."

"All I know is, I've been getting a lot of my product through the Middle East. Guns, drugs, supplies," Burzyck said. "Argus told me that the guns were Iranian manufacture, though I thought they were supposed to be German."

"Heckler & Koch?" Lyons inquired.

"Those guns the SWAT teams all used. The MP-5?" Burzyck asked. When Lyons nodded, he sighed, continuing to talk. "I just pull the trigger, I don't care about anything except if they work. Ever since they went with these ugly square guns instead of revolvers, I don't care."

"You ever meet the Middle Easterners?" Lyons asked.

"Argus did once or twice," Burzyck explained. "He told me at least one of them was an Iranian. Not quite official, though."

"Not quite?" Lyons prodded.

"Official, but not official," Burzyck answered. "Not exactly working in league with the administration's best interests, if you know what I mean."

"Yeah, I know," Lyons replied. "So we've got elements of the Iranian government working with elements of the U.S. government, and in the end, China is going to end up looking like a world-class villain, ending it all up in a major war."

"I hope not a war," Burzyck said. "I want to be a very old man, and if China doesn't like how it's being fucked over, it will make the world a hard place to live. I'm still healthy and tough, but would you want to risk finding out how you survive a nuclear winter?"

Lyons stayed silent, noncommittal.

Burzyck took a deep breath. "So whatever cell you dump me in, it's better than a grave. I've had a good run."

"Let's hope you survive your little betrayal," Lyons warned. "I guarantee, if one citizen dies because of this shit, no hole will be deep enough for you."

Burzyck started revealing all the specifics he knew.

HERMANN SCHWARZ AND FOUR members of the Kennedy Space Center special tactics team arrived at Knopf's home and were relieved to find his wife and children unharmed. Schwarz ordered the team to get them back to the Space Center where there'd be dozens more cops on hand to protect them. He explained that he wanted to check around for evidence.

As soon as the cops and Knopf's family were away in the helicopter, he established contact with the Farm over his Combat PDA, utilizing the Knopf family's phone hookup. Using the CPDA as an anchor, Aaron Kurtzman and his team were able to sink their cybernetic claws into Andy Knopf's communications, at least land line and Internet-based.

"He's got a cable connection," Kurtzman explained to Schwarz over the phone. "I'm having Carmen dig into his Internet Service Provider to pick up the trail."

"I'll look around for any other forms of contact," Schwarz said. "Knopf's cell was with him back at Kennedy, but that didn't give us much. He might have an alternate cell phone on hand…"

"And you're hoping to get a shot at the intimidation crew El Toronado or Argus would have sent to kill Knopf's family," Kurtzman said.

Schwarz didn't respond to the obvious question. With the Smith & Wesson on his hip, and a Remington 870 entry model slung at low ready on his shoulder, he was ready for violence.

Going through Knopf's home office, Schwarz found everything to be neatly organized. Schwarz went through the desk and found a small stack of unmarked envelopes. He opened them up and laid out the contents; examination revealing messages from El Toronado.

"Find anything?" Kurtzman asked Schwarz's ear set.

"Yeah. El Toronado preferred to do his communication the old-fashioned way. Unsigned orders to Knopf, including the note informing him about tonight's activity," Schwarz explained.

"He did his communication via snail mail?" Kurtzman asked.

"Only with people outside his control. He'd know if his phones were being tapped, but he wouldn't be on top of his pawns so easily," Schwarz said. "Thus, he went with courier messages."

"They wouldn't be able to call him back, or know how to get in touch with him without—" Communication was cut off.

Schwarz tapped his earpiece He knew that the batteries were new and fresh, so he had only one option.

The Remington slid into his hands, his trigger finger pushing off the safety. A round rested in the chamber, so he didn't need to rack the slide. He clicked on his flashlight and set it on the desk, balanced between two pens in a holder. He took a quick sidestep after setting his firefight bait, waiting for the enemy to betray its position.

The chair that Schwarz had been standing near a moment before suddenly jerked and flipped onto its back, riddled by a stream of full-auto bullets. Schwarz watched two shadowy figures, armed with machine pistols, concentrating on the cone of light from his flashlight, wondering why it hadn't been knocked over.

Schwarz triggered the Remington, hitting the closer man at hip level. A storm of buckshot smashed the gunman's joint to splinters, two balls shredding the juncture where the femoral arteries branched from the end of the aorta. Instantly crippled by the close-range shot, the shooter collapsed, screaming, his legs useless lumps, his groin gushing hot streams of arterial blood. The farther gunman whirled in surprise, but was jolted off balance by his collapsing ally, the assassin's initial burst missing Schwarz by inches.

Racking the slide, Schwarz decided to whip around the hard fiberglass stock. Its steel reinforcement kept it from collapsing as it crashed against the jaw of the shooter. The black polymers cracked loudly, but not as loudly as the shattering mandible bone. Collapsing, the gunner was senseless, blood pouring where he'd bit his tongue in two with the assistance of the buttstock strike. From down the hall, more gunfire filled the air, forcing the Able Team electronics genius to throw himself to the floor. Firing from a prone position, he decided to risk a blast to the chest of the silhouetted shooter, hoping that the enemy hadn't brought along body armor. The gunman jerked under the impact, holding down the trigger and sweeping the air over Schwarz's head.

"Body armor," Schwarz noted. He racked the Remington

and aimed higher, triggering another burst of buckshot at face level. The gunman's protective shooting glasses weren't enough to stop the streaking pellets that burst the eyes from their sockets. The Able Team veteran hadn't yet encountered eyewear that would provide proper protection from a point-blank blast of buckshot.

Still, the injury was only a glancing one. The enemy gunner's helmet and skull protected his brain and he howled, thrashing blindly on the floor.

"We have armed resistance!" came a cry at the base of the stairs.

"Pull out! Pull out!" another voice answered.

Heavy metal clunks struck the floor and Schwarz recognized the sound of grenades hitting hardwood. There were at least two that he heard, but he didn't bother counting as he lurched to his feet, racing for Knopf's den window. With a hard kick, the Able Team commando threw himself through the glass, head tucked low as he somersaulted in the air. Behind him, heavy concussive blasts whipped at his armor-covered back. Fortunately, he'd leaped far enough from the blasts' epicenters that he was safe from shrapnel, the shock wave pushing the glass he'd broken farther ahead of him and away from his vulnerable flesh.

With a heavy thud, he hit the grass on Knopf's lawn and spotted a pair of black SUVs on the driveway. One man, dragging the gunman that Schwarz had blinded, was heading to the rearmost SUV while black-clad shooters ran for the other vehicle. Schwarz scrambled to his feet, racing toward the enemy.

The guy who was dragging his wounded buddy along spotted the Stony Man warrior and dropped the blinded assassin, reaching for the submachine gun hanging on its sling.

Schwarz had transitioned from the shotgun to his Smith & Wesson, and tapped out four quick shots toward the juncture between his opponent's head and torso. One of the bullets slammed to a halt, stopped by reinforced layers of Kevlar, while the other three walked up the armed marauder's chin and jaw, pulverizing bone and tongue to splinters and mush. Choking on the gore pouring down his windpipe, the gunman flopped on top of his blinded friend, eliciting more screams of fear.

Schwarz charged toward the second SUV where the driver was stunned, half in and half out of the vehicle, realizing that one of his partners had just been cut down before his eyes. Torn between getting behind the wheel or pulling his handgun from its holster, the driver's indecision extended into eternity when the Able Team commando whipped the MP-40 around and fired two bullets into an exposed leg. The driver screamed, collapsing out of the SUV as the other vehicle tore backward down the driveway, its rear end catching a family sedan's front end where it was parked.

The driver clutched at his ruined shin and knee, giving Schwarz the opportunity to leap over the fallen wheel man and slip behind the wheel. "Thanks for keeping it running."

Schwarz threw the Chevy into reverse, and he felt a bump as the front tire ran over the driver's good leg, snapping bones brutally, but accidentally. He felt an ounce of regret for crippling a fallen, out-of-combat opponent, but his attention was focused more on the second truckload of bad guys who were trying to extricate their rear bumper from the parked sedan.

Stomping on the gas, Schwarz aimed the SUV like a missile, catching the enemy vehicle in the driver's door. The impact stunned the Able Team fighter, slowing him enough that the other vehicle got torn loose from where it had been jammed. The Suburban's engines roared, and the remaining driver tried to race away at top speed. But a crumpled fender slowed the SUV's progress, sheet metal catching messily on the left front tire.

Schwarz threw his captured vehicle into drive, aiming at the enemy taillights, gunning the gas again. He'd traveled a few yards when the windshield suddenly burst into a mass of cracked safety glass. Throwing himself flat behind the dashboard, he was glad that the assassins were armed only with submachine guns. The initial bursts, had they been from rifles, would have shredded him instead of showering him with polymer-coated chunks of glass. Schwarz popped up and unleashed a salvo of rapid-fire bullets from his handgun, raking the back of the enemy SUV and scoring at least one hit on a black-clad gunner. A machine pistol fell into the street beside the marauders' vehicle a moment before a jolt of power from the engine tore the mangled fender loose, along with chunks of tire.

The front left rim sparked as it ground on the asphalt, but the Suburban picked up a surge of speed and raced off into the distance. Schwarz cursed, then used the barrel of his shotgun to pound out and sweep away broken windshield so that he could see to drive. He hit the gas and took off in hot pursuit.

The assassins whipped a right at the nearest corner and gunned it onto the straightaway, taking advantage of a lack of traffic to pour on as much speed as possible. Schwarz rode the brake as he cranked on the wheel, his Suburban skidding in a drift until he was pointed right at his speeding prey. He jammed the accelerator to the floor and rocketed forward. One of the hit squad poked out a side window and opened fire with his machine pistol, but the bouncing SUVs conspired to make any accurate shot impossible. Bullets tore up the hood, but they glanced away from Schwarz.

Using a shredded patch of dashboard as a brace, the Able Team commando racked the slide on his Remington and triggered it. The buckshot pattern struck the rear window of the enemy vehicle, not doing much against the thick safety glass, but it stopped the door gunner from firing, encouraging him to duck back into the black SUV. Schwarz had the advantage on the straightaway, powering his vehicle up through the gears until his front fender mashed into the torn and tattered back end of the escaping truck. The impact jolted the Remington onto the floorboards and out of Schwarz's reach, and the enemy driver twisted his wheel, sparks spraying wildly as the flattened rim vomited metal shavings under hard contact with the asphalt.

Schwarz tromped the gas again, his SUV's front fender kissing the back of the enemy SUV, momentum transferring from one vehicle to another and vaulting the assassins out of control. Instead of spearing into a cross street, the limping Chevy pivoted too far and glanced off a street-lamp. Concrete and steel peeled the grille off the Suburban. The hit squad's driver struggled for control as sparks flew not only from the concrete-grinding flat tire, but off the driver's door as it ground itself hard against the wrought-iron grating of a yard.

Schwarz hit the emergency brake, allowing his vehicle's momentum to whirl his borrowed ride 180 degrees, aiming at the battered assassins as they bounced over the curb and back onto the street. Releasing the brake and hitting the gas, Schwarz launched his SUV like a missile, eating up the distance between them. His front fender struck the right rear tire with tons of force. Unable to withstand the hammer-blow impact, the rear axle of the marauders' Suburban snapped like a twig. Without the power train spinning the rear wheels, the enemy vehicle screeched in a wild half-circle before it rammed against the far curb.

Schwarz hit his brakes and retrieved his fallen shotgun. Thumbing in shells from the sidesaddle as he got out of the vehicle, he kept himself shielded by the wheel well of the sturdy SUV. One of the enemy gunmen poked a machine pistol out the window and fired, but accuracy had abandoned the shooter. Schwarz triggered the Remington at the muzzle-flash. The buckshot ripped the machine pistol from the man's grasp, and he screamed.

The Able Team commando worked the slide and fired again at the wrecked vehicle, this time aiming for a spot just behind the driver's mirror. A storm of pellets smashed through glass and plastic and into the steering column, rendering the vehicle completely useless.

"You can live!" Schwarz shouted. "Throw your weapons out the window!"

A weapon was tossed out, a small metallic cylinder. Schwarz cursed his luck and dived away from his captured Suburban. The grenade rolled beneath the undercarriage before it detonated, earth-shaking force lifting the SUV off its wheels before it collapsed back onto the street. In the dive, Schwarz had lost his shotgun, but he pulled out his Smith & Wesson, firing through the driver's window. Forty-caliber thunderbolts tore into flesh and bone. The driver's head was split in two by three bullets that had chopped a line from his ear to the top of his skull. The front-seat passenger screamed in anger, firing his submachine gun blindly, eyes caked in splattered blood and brains. Schwarz continued to work the six-and-a-half-pound trigger of the MP-40, burning off more of the weapon's fifteen-round magazine until the sub gunner stopped shooting.

A lone figure got out on the other side of the obliterated vehicle, limping toward a property-line fence. Schwarz could see his opponent was down to a handgun, but he knew that would be enough to take a Floridian family hostage. He scurried to his feet, reloading the spent Smith & Wesson on the run.

"Stop!" Schwarz bellowed.

The last gunner paused at the authoritative command.

Schwarz could see the man curse himself, and he brought up his pistol. The Able Team commando fired twice, bullets ripping into the shooter's shoulder, blowing the joint into a pulped mass of shattered bone and tenuous tendons. The assassin's pistol dropped from his grasp as he dropped to his knees. Schwarz caught up with the wounded man, kicking him onto his back.

"Give up," Schwarz ordered.

"Peace…" the man slurred.

Schwarz holstered his weapon and frisked the wounded Russian for additional weapons. Sirens wailed in the distance, the Titusville police department responding to the violent high-speed chase and shootout. He pulled out his Justice Department credentials and let them hang around his neck on a thong.

Time for another visit with the friendly neighborhood police.

Schwarz hoped that Brognola was ready to bail him out of the consequences of this gunfight.

CHAPTER TWELVE

China

Phoenix Force had managed to assemble a good-size force to augment its ability to regain control of the Phoenix Graveyard. Captain Hau was badly injured, making him useless as a combatant, but that didn't keep him from giving the five international commandos a direct course toward the command center for the launch facility.

"We'll need someone on hand to give us some backup in the control room," McCarter said. "If they've already sent up their assault force…"

"The men were sent up first," Hau told him. "There are a couple of pilots for the launch vehicles, and the manned craft will be able to guide in the remote-controlled cargo ships. The pilots of the manned craft were going to sneak in on the blind side of the International Space Station."

McCarter could tell by the look on Hau's face that he was doubtful of how much of a blind spot a space station could have. "As far as we can tell, the Iranians and their allies have access to a team of hackers who have been able to blind satellites, or simply edit out radar data that might point to them."

"Then the two orbiters could slip up on the visual blind side of the station before deceleration and docking," Hau surmised.

"Sounds like a reasonable assumption," McCarter said. "How long would it take to install life support on one of the orbiter rockets?"

"Stop the launch, and we'll have you up inside of an hour," Hau told him. The Chinese rocket scientist took a deep breath. "Besides, we owe you our lives. I figure that one of those rockets might be the best way for you to get out of here before the military shows up."

McCarter nodded. "Thanks. But we haven't done anything yet."

Gary Manning showed Hau the back of his digital camera. "There are a lot of pipes here. Is there something that might cripple one of the rocket crews just enough to delay the launch?"

Hau looked at the sniper rifle that the big Canadian had slung over his shoulder. "These particular pipes are liquid oxygen. If you put a bullet through one of these, you'll have a leak that no one will want to hang around."

Manning nodded. "Liquid oxygen vaporizes quickly on contact with atmosphere, but even in the moments while it's still in its liquid state, and early in its gaseous state, it can destroy tissue as completely as any flame thrower."

"It also can render metal as brittle as fine crystal, too," Hau said. "You'll need a spotter to check if there are any of my people in the area."

"Not a problem," Manning admitted. "You have a suggestion?"

"Kinan," Hau called. A Chinese Red Army corporal jogged over. Hau explained everything in rapid Cantonese.

"A pleasure to work with you," Kinan said, bowing to Manning. Kinan was one of the few infantry-trained members of the Phoenix Graveyard facility. He'd taken a scoped HK from one of the dead Iranians, and wore it with pride.

"Likewise," Manning returned.

"We make good team. Fuck the Arabs!" Kinan said with a wide grin.

"That's the spirit," Manning replied. "I'm going to take my gung-ho partner with me and we're going to raise some hell at the launch pad."

"Good. We'll take on the command center through this access pipe," McCarter returned. "Hau, keep your people in a tight perimeter around this barracks. This big lug will watch over you in case the Iranians decide to lob some mortar shells at the building."

"Good hunting," Manning said to McCarter.

"You, too," McCarter replied.

The Phoenix Force warriors split up, ready to take back the facility.

RAFAEL ENCIZO, WEARING A blood-spattered Iranian's uniform over his Land Warrior camouflaged armor, was on point through the access tunnel. He'd blackened his jaw and upper lip with oily soot, which would enable him to pass as an Iranian commando in the shadows of the half-lit corridor. The disguise was imperfect, but it was enough to give the opposition a moment of pause. Stocky and swarthy, his Hispanic features gave him enough of a resemblance to the Arabic looks of the Iranians to make the ruse feasible.

He held the Iranian-built MP-5 in one hand and affected a limp to match his blood-smeared clothing.

Enrizo heard the clack of a bolt and froze. He spoke quickly in his limited Farsi. "Don't shoot! Don't shoot!"

BUSINESS REPLY MAIL

FIRST-CLASS MAIL   PERMIT NO. 717   BUFFALO, NY

POSTAGE WILL BE PAID BY ADDRESSEE

GOLD EAGLE READER SERVICE
3010 WALDEN AVE
PO BOX 1867
BUFFALO NY 14240-9952

NO POSTAGE
NECESSARY
IF MAILED
IN THE
UNITED STATES

"What happened?" the gunmen at the other end asked. Encizo stumbled and dropped to one knee, his MP-5 clattering on the stone floor of the tunnel.

"Intruders," Encizo rasped as two of the Iranians rushed to his side. "Wahri and the others are dead." Then the Phoenix Force commando flicked both hands, combat blades snapping into them. With a hard double punch, he speared each of the Iranian soldiers.

The sudden movement brought cries of fear and terror from the other end of the access tunnel, and Encizo hauled his two dead opponents on top of him as a shield. MP-5s sputtered, bullets striking Encizo's lifeless barrier, and he snaked out his CZ P.01 pistol, triggering fire at the end of the tunnel. McCarter and the rest of the team opened up from the shadows down the tunnel, high-velocity 5.8 mm projectiles spearing the air over the prone Cuban. McCarter, Hawkins and James had taken advantage of Encizo's startling distraction to fire into the remaining soldiers who had been flushed by their partner.

A Tehran-hired mercenary plucked a grenade off his belt, hands coming together to pull the pin. Encizo grimaced as he raised his CZ, fearing that he might be too late to stop an explosion that would tear his partners to pieces. The Czech pistol barked out two hot bullets, one 9 mm round slashing through the wrist of the grenadier, rendering him incapable of pulling the pin on the grenade. Encizo's second shot tunneled into the bomb-throwing maniac's breastbone. The 9 mm slug deformed, knocking splinters of bone free as it deflected through the man's heart, broken rib shrapnel whirling wildly through lung tissue. The grenadier flopped onto his face.

Hawkins returned Encizo's favor by rescuing him from a rifleman who focused his machine pistol on the downed Cuban. In exposing himself to take out the grenadier, Encizo's head and shoulder were vulnerable, presenting a tempting target. The Type 95 rattled out its silenced bullets, slicing the machine-pistol wielding mercenary from crotch to throat. A bullet from the dying gunner glanced off Encizo's shoulder, knocking the CZ out of his grasp. The trio of Phoenix Force warriors rushed to their friend's side.

James knealt by Encizo. "You okay, Rafe?"

"I'm good," the Cuban answered, digging out from under the corpses. He patted one dead body's back. "These idiots make good insulation."

"What about your shoulder?" James asked, handing Encizo his rifle and handgun.

"The Land Warrior armor's pretty good. The shot hurt, but nothing penetrated."

James helped his buddy to his feet. "Still hate seeing you as bait."

"C'mon, you two lovebirds. We have arse to kick," McCarter announced. He popped up the ladder, the Type 95 leading the way. The Briton slithered to the surface, scanning for trouble. Fortunately, all he saw were imported ground crew attending to the launch scaffolding, preparing to dock the second of two Atlas-style rockets, topped with the experimental orbiters. The guards were busy overseeing the activity as a multinational crew of technicians worked on the massive boosters.

As soon as McCarter broke the surface, Manning went into action. He took aim and fired his SVD, a single round punching into a liquid oxygen conduit. The polymer pipe popped, a jet of liquid oxygen spearing into a trio of technicians next to it. The closest man didn't even have time to scream as superchilled fluid froze his flesh until it was so brittle, he fell apart under his own weight. The man next to him did have time to howl as he caught only the barest edge of the gouting liquid oxygen, parts of his face flaking off as he screamed. The third man leaped, preferring broken bones to the horrendous pain of having his skin and flesh turned to self-destructing crystal. The tech hit the ground, shoulder snapping out of place, not dislocating but actually shattering as the joint was hammered by the ground.

The venting liquid oxygen caused a wave of concerned voices to rise as the launch pad crew scrambled. Armed sentries stood back, giving their unarmed allies some breathing room, realizing that their assault weapons were nothing against a cloud of bone-shattering, supercold liquid.

Unfortunately, the diversion wasn't quite enough. One guard, a Chinese traitor, turned to see the battle-armored Phoenix Force commander rise from the tunnel. He opened his mouth to scream, dragging up the muzzle of his rifle to greet the intruder with a burst of autofire, but McCarter was already tracking him. Suppressed 5.8 mm bullets stitched across the Chinese turncoat's chest, shattering ribs and churning lungs and heart into chunky soup. The soldier flopped backward, dying reflex tightening his finger on the trigger. The dead-man's gunfire raked across a catwalk, sending technicians jumping for cover.

"Bollocks," McCarter rumbled as three more soldiers noticed the brief skirmish. One of the soldiers was bringing his rifle to his shoulder when a bloody red crater was hammered into his forehead by Manning's precision rifle fire. The second and third gunmen were caught in a cross fire from Encizo and Hawkins as they exited the tunnel, spreading out. James was the last one up to the surface, but his attention was settled on the command center bunker.

A pair of guards were at the bunker entrance, but they were distracted by gushing steam that billowed from a pipe Manning had ruptured, giving his partners a smoke screen as they came into hard contact with the enemy. James could see under the column of superheated fluid, spotting the pair of riflemen by their legs and their rifles held at low ready. Adjusting his aim, James raked the pair with two short bursts, smashing them back against the wall. Even as they slid slowly down the entrance, James rushed through the steam, nomex and Kevlar protecting him from all but the slightest of discomfort from the scalding jet. Encizo, his helmet pulled back on, came through the burning cloud right on James's heels, followed by their two partners.

Manning clued them in over their headsets. "Kinan told me that one of his hostaged co-workers is outside the building. The two of us are treating the second launch pad as a free fire zone."

James and Encizo listened to the explanation as they went over the lifeless soldiers, looking for access cards. The Cuban found one first and swiped it through the electronic security lock. The door released with a hiss, and McCarter put his boot to it, slamming it open. Hawkins rolled a stun grenade through even as the door smacked the limit of its hinge, McCarter ducking back out of the doorway. Hawkins whirled out of the inevitable concussion wave path, noting that the lobby was filled with gun-toting Iranian commandos, mercenaries and turncoat Chinese soldiers. The concussion grenade went off, a shearing sheet of hyperpressure slamming bodies through furniture and into walls. Debris gouted through the opened door, papers and dust choking the air.

"Move!" McCarter growled. He was first through the door. Stunned and disoriented enemy soldiers were strewed about as if someone dropped them through the roof by pouring them out of a giant sack. One Iranian, choking in agony, the concussion grenade detonator jammed through his throat, received a mercy bullet to end his suffering. McCarter felt another hand wrap around his ankle, and the Phoenix Force leader stomped down hard, crushing forearm bones to paste. A follow-up kick tore the mandible off the mercenary's face and used it to guillotine the man's windpipe. It was ruthless and bloody, but if the hired gun had recovered enough sense to grip McCarter by the ankle, he'd be able to retrieve a weapon and shoot his teammates in the back.

Suppressed gunshots popped as Hawkins, Encizo and James cleaned up the other gun-toting murderers splayed throughout the lobby. The butcher's work went quickly, corpses replacing stunned bodies within thirty seconds of Encizo unlocking the door.

McCarter hoped, for the sake of the hostages, that Phoenix Force was killing the enemy fast enough.

COLONEL CHOW WING heard the grenade detonation down the hall, and his spine froze. He glanced over at his Iranian counterpart, Commander Ibrahim Asmadi, who had heard the blast.

"We need to get out of here, now!" Wing said.

"Those rockets have to go up. Without the isotopes, we won't be able to accomplish our goals," Asmadi said.

"We'll be dead if we stand our ground," Wing snapped back.

Asmadi sighed, then whipped the point of his knife across Wing's face, slashing him from cheek to chin. "Shut up, you sniveling little ass. You are being paid well to risk your life for the cause."

The Chinese soldiers under Wing's command tensed, Asmadi's Iranian followers and hired guns outnumbering them. The eleven uninjured hostages had their attention on the sheer abundance of assault weapons ready to cut loose.

Chong Ximan knew that unless he did something quickly, his friends would be dead. It would be a fair trade, Ximan thought, one life for eleven. He tensed, eyed a Westerner and started a countdown in his mind. The gunman had his finger on the trigger, a violation of safe handling procedures, but that was understandable in the tension of the moment. Ximan hoped that a reflexive jerk would give him an advantage in saving his friends. A sudden jolt would cause the gunman to trip the trigger on his assault rifle, pouring bullets into Wing's crew.

Ximan lunged from his chair in a blur, fingers wrapping around his target's wrist. Sure enough, reflexive tension set off the MP-5 on full-auto, bullets raking across two of Wing's turncoats. The 9 mm rounds threw them to the ground, never to rise again. Wing and Asmadi, however, were distracted from their standoff, jolted back to reality by the attempted escape of the hostages.

"Kill him!" Asmadi snapped, turning his MP-5 on his own man, pumping Ximan's captive full of copper-jacketed death. Ximan pushed on his dying captive's arm, trying to swing the muzzle at the Iranian commander. The machine pistol took out both Asmadi and one of his gunners before running dry.

It had been worth a shot, Ximan thought when the door to the command center burst open.

David McCarter was first through the entrance, his assault rifle chattering out a burst that swept three of Asmadi's mercenary reinforcements from life. Hawkins tapped off single shots with his Type 95, punching 5.8 mm holes through the chests of two Iranians and a Chinese soldier, taking care not to cause damage to the computer terminals that would guide Phoenix Force into orbit.

Encizo and James braced themselves on either side of the doorway, focusing their marksmanship to create an impenetrable cone of high-velocity lead that would protect Ximan's partners.

Chow Wing knew that discretion was the better part of valor and slammed through a back entrance to the control center, his shoulder powering the door open even as Hawkins and McCarter both tried to tag him. Fear had given Wing extraordinary speed, and he proved too difficult a target to tag.

"Get him!" McCarter called to Encizo and James. "We've got this lot."

Hawkins's rifle barked one last time, coring the last of the gunmen in the control center. He glanced back at McCarter. "David?"

"Check on our hero," McCarter ordered.

Hawkins rushed to Ximan's side and looked him over.

"It's not my blood," the Chinese man said. "It's his…"

Hawkins looked toward the corpse of the mercenary Ximan had jumped. Bloody holes were torn in the gunman's torso, but none of the 9 mm rounds had penetrated through the man's body. Ximan had been saved by his human shield from certain death.

"Good, you speak English," Hawkins replied. "Is anyone else hurt?"

"No."

"Tell the others that we're here to help. Captain Hau is on our side, and we need to get the undamaged rocket set up for a flight crew to take up to the International Space Station."

"We've got the course already laid in," Ximan answered. "You're American?"

"The less you know, the less you'll have to tell your bosses about the guys who rescued you," Hawkins said. "We'd appreciate as much ignorance as possible."

Ximan nodded. "What about outside?"

"That's being taken care of," McCarter explained. "By yours and our own."

The Briton spoke into his helmet communicator. "Cal? Rafe?"

There was no answer.

CHOW WING RACED DOWN the underground tunnel. He turned, looking over his shoulder as he reached an intersection, starving lungs sucking down air as quickly as they could. The sudden influx of oxygen into his bloodstream made the world spin. He was light-headed from the increased oxygen burning through his brain.

With almost laser clarity, he spotted two figures charging after him.

"Shit, we had contact from the last tunnel to Gary," James swore. "We've got bupkis here."

"Electrical conduits," Encizo said. "All the wiring and the shielding on the wires is blocking our communications signal. The other tunnel didn't have any wiring like this one does."

"Still inconvenient as hell," James complained.

A bullet sparked wildly through the tunnel, and the black Phoenix Force commando had to fight the urge to return fire. Encizo crouched while James tucked back behind one of the conduits that had been inconveniencing him.

"Options?" Encizo asked.

James looked at the pipes, then drew his CZ. He leveled the compact pistol and pulled the trigger, firing at a steam pipe next to Wing's leg. A scalding spear lanced into the turncoat colonel, and he leaped out into the open, injured leg collapsing beneath him. He crashed face-first into the concrete floor of the tunnel.

Encizo darted out and kicked aside Wing's fallen pistol. "You've been a bad boy, soldier. And we need to talk to you."

CHAPTER THIRTEEN

Kennedy Space Center

Captain Jordan Broome and Dr. Alexander Thet were present as Hermann Schwarz returned from Titusville. With them were co-Captain William Cole and two visitors, Deputy Marshals Carl Dutse and Paul Rosales.

"Oh, I see you've met Moe and Curly," Schwarz quipped as he got off the helicopter.

"Which is which?" Broome asked.

Schwarz pointed to Lyons. "That's Curly."

Broome nodded. "Ah…yes. I see the preponderance of bone in his head. The other must be Moe?"

"Call me that and I'll murderlize ya," Blancanales replied with a wink.

"You two are here, so, there must be one reason," Schwarz said.

"Yeah. They're gonna launch me 'bone head' into space with you," Lyons grumbled. "Our cousins are trying to arrange their own trip upstairs, but the home office felt they needed to put some dangerous people on the space shuttle."

"I'm plenty dangerous." Schwarz sighed, displaying mock hurt.

Lyons shrugged. "Seriously, Miller. There's at least one orbiter full of terrorists on its way to the ISS. If our buddies can't make it up, we're talking three to ten, not one against ten."

Schwarz nodded. "Glad to be back with my bros."

Cole spoke up. "Two new crew members are going to throw off our calculations."

"Considering that we're now undergoing a rescue mission, any research programs have been grounded," Thet explained. "We'll keep a little of the research material on board as ballast against the projected launch vectors, but these two are taking priority as part of the delivery system."

"And the launch? We're trimming twenty hours off the timetable," Cole added.

"That's why we really should bump more cargo and bring up both Komalko and Mustafa," Broome suggested.

Lyons looked to Schwarz. "The engineer you were taking the place of?"

Schwarz nodded. "Both are good guys. They're a little geeky…"

"Coming from you, that's saying something." Lyons grunted.

Schwarz rolled his eyes. "Oh, now that you're Curly, you're a comedian?"

Lyons tried to mimic an innocent smile, but on his face, it wasn't going to work. "Don't hate the player. Hate the game."

Schwarz squeezed his brow. "I think it's a good idea to bring up Pie and Armi. Between the two of them, and with my help, we'll be able to solve any problems that arise. Plus, there's the possibility that the terrorists might have already caused some damage to the station."

Cole sneered. "I can't believe that you two didn't let me in on this spook and his mission."

"It was 'need to know,' Bill," Broome said, eliciting a glare from the uptight astronaut. "You didn't need to know at the time."

"What's with the dagger glare?" Blancanales asked.

"He hates any diminuation of his name," Schwarz commented. "According to Armi, he's just an uptight jerk, not someone we have to worry about."

Lyons cleared his throat. "Captain Cole, we really don't have time for a bureaucratic pissing contest. If you're that angry and offended that we've been slipped onto the *Arcadia,* you can just sit behind here at the Cape."

"You don't have the authority," Cole decreed.

Lyons stepped forward until he was nose to nose with the blond astronaut. "I not only have the authority, I've got enough of a free pass to allow you to decide whether you're sitting in the sick bay or on a refrigerated drawer."

Cole bristled. "Was that a threat?"

Lyons maintained eye contact, not blinking. "Just information. If you're too stupid to know what to do with that data, it's your funeral."

Broome rested a hand on Cole's shoulder. "Bi… William, it's cool. We were told by the President himself to keep this as quiet as possible."

Cole glanced to the shuttle commander, then back at Lyons. "I'm not sitting this one out."

"Good. I'd have hated to scrape that pretty-boy face of yours off the concrete," Lyons said.

He dropped his hostility like a curtain and turned, nodding politely to Thet. "When do we begin our preparations for launch, sir?"

"Captain Broome will take you," Thet answered. "You can take that Hummer over there."

"Thank you," Lyons said, and followed Broome.

He paused long enough to look to Cole. "Respect where it's earned, Billy. Remember that."

Cole took a deep breath but held his tongue.

As ABLE TEAM WAS BEING sized up for their space suits, Broome sized up Lyons.

"You and Cole have taken an instant liking to each other," Broome commented sardonically.

Lyons shrugged as he tugged a blue jumpsuit over his powerful frame. A few shrugs, and he was certain that his broad shoulders had enough room for combat maneuvers. "I've been in this business long enough to develop a pretty good nose for bullshit, Captain."

"Call me Jordie," Broome responded.

Lyons nodded. "Right now, I can't really tell if Cole's just a shithead who's gotten under my skin, or something worse."

"I've worked with Cole for years. The man is as red, white and blue as you can get," Broome said.

Lyons zipped up his jumpsuit, then performed his space suit checks, the refresher course on their handling having gone quickly thanks to Able Team's experience. "Patriotism or jingoism?"

Broome ruminated. "It is hard to tell the difference. But if anything, he hasn't shown any racist tendencies."

"Some bigots can bite their tongue enough to achieve any goal," Lyons said. "Just because he's kind to Armin Mustafa doesn't mean he's the prince of peace and tolerance."

"Then why not ground him?" Broome asked.

"There's a reason why 'keep your friends close, keep your enemies closer' is a tired cliché," Lyons explained. "A cliché has a strong core of truth around it. If we go up without Cole... You never know."

Broome frowned. "Someone would try to shoot us down."

"Sounds paranoid, but I've been doing this for a long time," Lyons said. "Not as long as Paul here, but I suspect things were similar before Orville and Wilbur invented flying machines."

Blancanales looked up, then flipped Lyons the bird. "He's just jealous that I ended up with wisdom and good looks."

"I've got my doubts about Cole's culpability," Broome said.

"So do I," Lyons answered. "But if those doubts fade, I wouldn't stand too close to him."

Broome frowned. "And what if I give up the knowledge of your suspicions?"

Lyons looked to Broome, but didn't answer the question. From the scowl on the big man's face, Broome didn't need one.

China

DAVID MCCARTER PULLED OUT a bayonet and rubbed it across the back of Chow Wing's hand.

"That's not sharp," the Chinese turncoat said.

"That's the point," McCarter replied. "Combat blades are supposed to do enormous damage. Their edges are blunt because sharpening them would wear away too much of their structural strength. It's hard, stiff steel, with a chiseled sharp tip."

McCarter ran the point along Wing's fingertip. Blood dripped from the cut digit. The Briton continued his discourse on bayonet design. "See, these are for turning fighting rifles into spears when they're out of ammunition, or are used in close-quarters combat. The weight of a man behind that blunt point produces massive hemorrhaging and tissue destruction, unlike a sharp spear point that glides through human flesh in a streamlined fashion."

"So, it won't cut me up…" Wing began. His eyes widened as he saw McCarter rest the blunted edge against his little finger. "But it'll tear me up."

"I used to be able to take off a finger with an AK bayonet with two blows," McCarter told him, hefting a brick. "Course, they weren't fat asses like you, Wing. This might take four hits to totally crush all the flab wrapping that little sausage."

"You're b-bluffing," Wing stammered.

McCarter looked at him, then shrugged and brought down the brick. Wing howled as he felt his little finger break. Blood poured from ruptured skin as Wing vomited in agony. "Oh look, it might just take only one more shot."

"You didn't even ask me anything!" Wing protested, sputtering chunks of bile through his lips.

McCarter shrugged and lifted the brick again. "If you can't figure out what I want to know, then you're too stupid to have fingers anyway. Can someone get me a mop? I don't want my boots all sticky…"

"Wait! Wait!" Wing protested.

McCarter paused and glared. "I don't hear you saying anything interesting."

Wing spit the acidy taste of bile. "Hard talking after I puked…"

"I want to know something I didn't know before you open your mouth the next time I see your lips move. Otherwise, I'm adding another little piggy to my collection at home," Mc-Carter growled.

Wing's mouth tightened into a thin line and he nodded, weighing his options. "Asmadi wasn't officially sanctioned by Tehran."

McCarter set the brick down gently in Wing's lap. "Go on."

"Like me, he believed more in a good profit than he did in fanatical idealism. And Asmadi worked for General Vali," Wing added.

McCarter reviewed his mental files of the Iranian military's most likely threats to stability for the country. General Raood Vali was one of them, but Vali was not among the opposition party elements who were being wooed by the U.S. government in hopes of introducing a stable regime in the region. Vali was one of an Azeri minority in the predominantly Persian Iranian government. While the Azeris were in a high enough position as the largest minority in Iran, they were still vulnerable to insults such as being ridiculed as cockroaches. Vali was someone who would love for the status quo to change just enough to put him at the top of the Iranian food chain.

"And what about you?" McCarter asked.

Wing nodded. "I'm being paid very well."

"So Vali was offered political power to back this. And how much money are we talking for you to commit suicide like this?"

"Seventy-five million. U.S."

"Whose money?" McCarter asked.

"Technically, it's Chinese money. They did something…"

McCarter snatched up the brick and Wing froze, his eyes wide.

"It was a corporation called DeeDec Enterprises," Wing stated. He spelled the company name.

McCarter frowned.

"That's all I know. Their hackers set up the drain on the Red Chinese treasury, feeding me and my followers," Wing said. "Funneled into Filipino banks."

"Where's DeeDec based?" McCarter asked.

"The United States," Wing answered. "I'm pretty sure it's a cutout."

McCarter took a deep breath and tossed the brick into the corner. "I'm done with you."

"Oh, thank God," Wing whispered.

"Oh, don't thank Him," McCarter replied. He turned and

opened the door to the room. On the other side of the doorway, the grim faces of Ximan, Kinan and several others showed in the gloom of the hall.

Wing knew what they were there for.

Revenge.

McCarter closed the door after the angry former hostages entered, whistling a funeral march to drown out the howls of Wing's tortured screams.

"WE LUCKED OUT," Captain Hau told McCarter after he returned from transmitting Wing's interrogation back to Stony Man Farm. "They didn't have the technicians remove any of the life support from the second rocket."

"Why?" McCarter asked. "I thought these were coming up on autopilot."

"At the last minute, there was a change of plan. A flight crew was going up with the second launch," Hau said. "Pilots for all four orbiters, and the second craft was going to tether the dedicated cargo carrier behind."

"So they weren't quite certain whether their automatic pilot could do the job," Manning surmised. "Just a last-minute, belt-and-suspenders replacement."

"I'm not so certain of that," McCarter countered. "Do we have the pilots in captivity?"

"Yes. Your friends, Farrow and Rey, are looking at them," Hau said. "I had some of my people bolster their numbers for security reasons."

McCarter nodded. "How much longer until you're going to forget we just saved your arses?"

Hau sighed. "More like how long until it looks like I can't avoid my responsibilities to Beijing. I wish I could say long, but once communications come back up, I'm obligated to at least let my supervisors know what's really going on here.

Coming under the threat of execution once in a day is quite enough for me."

McCarter nodded.

"The good news is that with life support on one of the launch craft, and given the nature of your Land Warrior uniforms, we can get you up to the International Space Station long before that uncomfortable duty throws a wrench into your plans to get out of China," Hau added, smiling. "Having those full-face helmets also makes visual and audial identification impossible."

McCarter shook Hau's hand, smiling despite the fact that the Chinese rocket scientist couldn't see through the protective black faceplate. "I'm going to need a patch for my chest."

"A space suit adhesive repair swatch should work as well on your Land Warrior suit as well as an orbital suit," Hau stated. "Roy?"

Manning helped affix the patch to McCarter's knife-slashed battle uniform. "It's not camouflaged, but…"

"Yeah. How many forests are we going to run into in orbit anyhow?" McCarter asked.

Manning grinned under his helmet. "Like the man said, if you're going into combat, you should clash."

That elicited a laugh from Hau. "The repairs on the liquid oxygen lines are almost finished, and the second orbiter is almost in position."

"We'll go up with both?" Manning asked.

"All the better to take the other two craft off guard," McCarter stated. "They'll be expecting two ships."

Manning nodded. "Hopefully, we'll be able to hook up with the others in no time. The course we have plotted for our launch will give us eight hours to reach the International Space Station."

"After liftoff?" McCarter asked.

"No, from the top of the hour," Manning returned. "Which is in two minutes. We'll launch in forty minutes."

"Which will give me enough time to try my hand at the orbiter simulator," McCarter replied. "Captain?"

Hau escorted McCarter. "What aircraft are you checked out on?"

"F-15s and F-16s are in my repertoire," McCarter said, being noncommittal.

"You're in luck. The orbiter has the same responses as those craft," Hau returned. "We copied the schematics for them."

"That's no surprise," McCarter said.

"Which is why I'm not concerned with spilling the beans. Granted, we did adjust the ergonomics for Chinese pilots. You're a good half foot taller than they are, so things will be cramped for most of your team," Hau stated.

"I'm gonna have to have words with my cruise director then," McCarter grumbled. "They promised only the best accommodations."

"I don't suppose you'd give me their business card so I could complain for you?" Hau asked.

"Nice try," McCarter replied.

"Just for the sake of being able to tell Beijing I tried my best to learn about the Americans who rescued us," Hau said.

McCarter paused, looking Hau over. It was obvious that the Briton's accent had marked him as anything but American. The same would go for Encizo's Cuban turn of phrase. Hau smiled. "Come on. I have to check you out on the simulator before we can get you up. We don't have time for you to get all maudlin and thankful for my disinformation."

"You've got that straight," McCarter answered. He followed Hau into the flight simulator room, more than a little grateful for a new ally.

CALVIN JAMES AND RAFAEL Encizo returned from interrogating the pilots, finding Manning and Hawkins testing the adapters that would hook their helmets to oxygen bottles provided by the Chinese.

"What's the word on the captured pilots?" Manning asked.

"A finer group of charm school graduates I've never found," Encizo mentioned.

"It took some effort to deal with them," James said. "They fought the Scopolamine injections, and one of them seized up under the drug."

Manning didn't need to see James's unmasked face to see his grimace. Calvin James was their primary interrogator, utilizing the drug Scopolamine to lower the inhibitions of their prisoners. As a medical man, though, James hated to cause harm, and Scopolamine had the potential to cause cardiac arrest. However, due to time and equipment constraints, the Phoenix Force medic hadn't had the time to run an electrocardiogram on the prisoners. "Did that one survive?"

James shook his head. "The drug loosened up everyone else's tongues though. I found two of them were Russian air force pilots. One's suffering from cancer, so this was his last hurrah. The other wasn't together mentally, but he still wanted to fly. There was also a disgraced French pilot."

"So, three people who had the potential to be suicidal?"

"The only straight one was the one who died under the Scopolamine," Encizo said. "He was going to ferry the crews down in the ISS's own orbiter."

"Space-borne kamikaze." Manning groaned. "But they are four orbiters, and let's not forget the *Arcadia*."

"There was a fifth pilot, but he caught a face full of LOX," James said.

Manning grimaced, remembering the grisly image of a man falling, his head shattering like glass when it struck the railing. Though it was a bloodless demise, the crimson and gray chunks of crystallized brain and skull, tinkling to the catwalk, was a disturbing memory, even for a member of Phoenix Force, who'd encountered stomach-churning atrocities across the breadth of the globe.

"And with the sane pilots on the first two orbiters," Manning said, fighting down the memory of the shattered human, "they'd have three pilots to take two shuttles down."

"Which is cutting the crews thin, but they'll be cramming an assload of people in there," Encizo explained. "Anything that isn't necessary will be stripped out and extra room made for the pirates."

"Pirates?" James asked.

"The best description I can think of for them," Encizo returned. "Except they're going to send their pirate ships down to Earth as kamikaze fighters."

Manning frowned as he performed mental calculations. "The orbiters are each approximately seventy-five tons. They'll be falling through the atmosphere, so we're talking enough power to knock out Manhattan."

"Well, take a look at the Tunguska blast," James mentioned. "The shock waves from that object were heard around the world. Only the fact that it struck in an unpopulated region kept there from being any casualties. I remember watching scientists reconstruct that. It was approximately an eighty-ton object striking the atmosphere at an angle and detonating in the air."

"Air detonation?" Encizo asked.

"It's possible that the object behind Tunguska was composed of rock and frozen gaseous compounds like hydrogen. The heat of reentry could have ignited the hydrogen," Manning explained. "Most of the so-called ice on a comet is composed of solidified elements that are normally gaseous in

Earth's narrow temperature range. Provide enough heat, and those elements go from solid to gaseous or even plasma form in an explosive manner."

Encizo looked toward the Chinese rockets, liquid oxygen fuel being pumped into them. "Hell, just the potential energy released from turning oxygen from liquid to gas form is enough to toss those rockets thousands of miles into space, against the pull of gravity."

One of the technicians who was helping Manning and Hawkins set up the oxygen tanks for the Land Warrior uniforms lifted his head. "That might explain something."

Hawkins regarded the technician. "Explain what?"

"We had to load up extra tanks on the orbiters," Shiong, the tech, said. "Liquid oxygen. Two hundred gallons into specially designed containers."

"Let me guess." Hawkins spoke up. "There were places to load heavy metal rods in the skins?"

Shiong nodded. "The Tunguska blast conversation reminded me of the extra tanks. The people who were loading the tanks were part of Asmadi's international coalition, and they wore radiation suits while handling the metal rods."

"Iridium-192 rods," Manning told them. "We've got two-hundred gallons of liquefied oxygen hitting the atmosphere. The reentry heat would turn that into an air burst bomb. I don't even want to crunch the numbers on the explosive force available from three quarters of a ton of liquefied atmosphere exploding."

"How many tanks were there?" Hawkins asked.

"There were eight of them, loaded into the satellite racks on the orbiters," Shiong told Phoenix Force. "Each was designed to deliver four satellites. We haven't put the other eight on the two ships you're taking up."

"Well, be careful with them," James said. "I-192 puts out

high-energy gamma radiation. You need some serious shielding to protect yourself from that kind of juice."

"When we call the Red Army, we'll tell them to bring in hazmat teams," Shiong answered. "Thanks."

McCarter and Hau burst into the room, Hau looking breathless.

"Time to go," McCarter said. "Are the tanks ready?"

Shiong nodded. "What's—"

"Ximan spotted a Red Army column up the road," Hau said. "We've got ten minutes before they're at the gates."

"Time's up," McCarter told his team. "We either get in the launch vehicle, or we have a very long visit with the SAD."

"And I wouldn't be able to talk you out of the warmest of SAD's accommodations," Hau added.

"Are you checked out on the orbiter?" Manning asked.

McCarter nodded, but the silence was uncomfortable. The Canadian could tell that his friend had familiarized himself with the controls, but it wasn't a comfortable level of acclamation. Though Manning had often complained about McCarter's wild driving and his daring flying abilities, he never truly doubted that the Phoenix Force commander was suicidal. McCarter was as skilled behind a steering wheel and at a joystick as any man alive. The Briton's silence also struck the other three members of Phoenix Force as ominous.

McCarter took a deep breath. "The sky's waiting, lads."

CHAPTER FOURTEEN

Kennedy Space Center

Seven engine funnels, two each on the solid fuel booster rockets and three on the back of the Space shuttle *Arcadia,* which were fed from the massive, missile-shaped bladder tank on the bottom of the spacecraft, yawned and breathed out blazing white cones of light. The sheer tonnage of the combined thrusters lifted the ninety-nine-ton spacecraft off the ground.

Sitting in the acceleration couch, Hermann Schwarz felt as if an elephant suddenly decided to take a seat on his chest. Multiple gravities stacked up on the Able Team electronics genius, the force weighing on his body increasing as the *Arcadia* accelerated to escape velocity, which he knew to be a shade under seven miles in a second. The constant thrust would continue to lean on him until they reached the apex of their orbital path. Though the atmosphere only extended nominally eighty miles from the surface of the Earth, gravity extended much farther. The trip to the top of the troposphere, where there was enough oxygen for a human to breathe was complete in only a moment.

Eleven seconds into the launch, the shuttle began to spin,

but with gravity going in only one direction, in the opposite direction of the acceleration, Schwarz didn't feel as if he were being flipped upside down like a pancake. In fact, without any visual reference through the windshield, the only reason he knew that the *Arcadia* was beginning its roll was when Cole announced the roll maneuver. He knew from the briefing that they were moving at 927 miles per hour, the shuttle sucking oxidation and fuel out of the massive tank greedily.

Looking at the gauges, trying to tear his concentration off gravity, he spotted the compass. They were hurtling from Kennedy Space Center, aiming northeast. At that point, Cole announced the end of the roll maneuver. The six seconds the shuttle had spent spiraling toward its intercept course with the International Space Station felt like six minutes. At this point, the solid rocket boosters had propelled the *Arcadia* to past 1000 miles an hour. When the main engines throttled up six-and-a-half seconds before launch, Schwarz felt as if he were going to shake apart. That was with the *Arcadia* idling, engines revving for the big push. Now, only the construction of his launch suit and the acceleration couch cushioned him against the massive acceleration forces leaning on him.

"You cool, guys?" Broome huffed under the thrust pressure.

"Keep your eyes on the road, Jordie," Lyons grunted. "We'll make it just fine."

Broome managed a chuckle. "Throttling down main engines. Things will go a little more smoothly while we're going through the dense lower atmosphere."

Lyons nodded and looked at Schwarz. "Like going into lower gear on a muddy road."

Schwarz took a deep breath, despite the increased weight of his ribs pressing down on his lungs. "I know you're smart, Carl. Don't have to prove it to me."

"You okay, Pol?" Schwarz asked.

"I'm just enjoying the ride," Blancanales answered. "Relax, Gadgets."

Schwarz grimaced. Up until the rest of Able Team arrived and the scheduled research scrapped for a dedicated rescue mission, he had been warmed up as a flight engineer, one of the crew of the *Arcadia* as it screamed up past thirty miles. He would have held an active role, but that position was being filled by Komalko and Mustafa. Once more, he was just a passenger.

That wasn't a problem when he was riding with pilots like Jack Grimaldi or even David McCarter of Phoenix Force. However, here in the shuttle, surrounded by high-tech systems that he had studied religiously on multiple occasions, it just reminded him of his impotence.

"Throttle to maximum," Cole announced. "Fourteen seconds to Max-Q."

"I'll have a triple thick shake and an order of curly fries," Schwarz muttered too softly to be heard by anyone but himself. It was conditioned reflex to make a quip, but right now, his heart was in his throat. What if he, Manning and the crew at Stony Man Farm were all wrong about the enemy conspiracy's capability of fielding an antispacecraft laser?

Schwarz wasn't afraid of death, but his stomach churned at the thought of hurtling through the sky, as tempting and vulnerable a target as a skeet bird. Only the fact that he knew that their velocity was topping 1500 miles an hour, and at Max-Q they would be protected by atmospheric refraction from any directed energy weapon, calmed him somewhat.

"Thirty seconds to SRB staging," Cole announced.

Something suddenly speared through the sky in the distance, darting across the windshield like a laser bolt effect from a movie. Schwarz tensed, but the angle was all wrong for something coming after the *Arcadia*.

"What the hell?" Cole growled.

"Darkest night…" Broome gasped. "Mission Control, are you tracking that on radar?"

"We're trying. It came within twenty-five miles of your course," Thet said on the other end. "Its trajectory is toward the Caribbean."

"What is it?" Cole asked.

Lyons closed his eyes, jaw set firmly. "It's the opening shot. This war has reached the hot stage."

Gulf of Guancanyabo, Cuba

CAPTAIN ARTURO BONQUILLA steered his boat around the shallow, reef-filled waters of Guancanyabo, wending his way toward Manzanillo. It was a concentration intensive exercise, since his primitive craft didn't have the underwater tracking radar of his American counterparts. One wrong turn and he'd tear open the rusty, barnacle-encrusted belly of his ship, the *Esmerelda*. Here on the back end of Cuba, far from Havana and too close to Guantanamo, he was all too wary.

First, there were still pirates of the Caribbean, and they didn't travel under sail and launch broadsides with ancient cannons. They rode in high-powered speedboats and wielded RPG rockets and machine guns. Also, the coast was of heavy interest to various powers in the region. The U.S. was interested in Cuban activities, and Cuba wanted to know what the U.S. had discovered. The waters were only slightly more dangerous for the intrigue and piracy than it was for the coral reefs, but not by much.

There was a ruckus among his deck hands, and Bonquilla ground the throttle to full stop, grabbing up his AK-47. He rushed out of the pilot house to see Enrique pointing with feverish emphasis toward the sky. *"Mire!"*

Bonquilla turned his head and saw a streak of light extending through the blue-black, star-sprinkled sky. The streak, looking like a knife slash through the night, rocketed downward, having crossed the familiar path of an American space shuttle.

"It's a shooting star," Bonquilla stated. He looked over the railing, wondering if there were any speedboats gliding in like lions in tall grass.

"It's aimed right at Manzanillo!" Enrique said nervously.

It took a moment for Bonquillo to realize that the course of the *Esmerelda* and the strange streak would meet at the apex of the horseshoe-shaped gulf. The coincidence was unnerving to the captain, but he fought to dismiss it. "Shooting stars burn up. It won't hurt the port…"

Enrique's eyes widened as the rocketing streak dropped to the horizon. Suddenly, a bright flare glowed beyond the curve of the distant waters. It didn't light up the sky, but it was noticeable, even twenty miles out. A rumble filled the air, following on the heels of the sudden glow, thunder on a cloudless, stormless night.

Bonquillo felt a chill slice through him, the same eerie tremor that ran up and down his spine when he was a child and the Soviets had parked missiles in the Cuban countryside. His parents had warned him that the Americans would rain nuclear damnation on the defenseless Cuban people to destroy those missiles only ninety miles from U.S. territory.

Now it looked as if that prophecy had come true, if only decades late. He rushed back to the pilot house and turned on the radio. Static and unintelligible, panicked chatter poured out of the speakers. He brought the handset to his lips.

"This is the *Esmerelda*. Repeat, the *Esmerelda*," Bonquillo said. "Is there anyone out there not shitting their pants?"

"Arturo!" came a response after a minute of garbled communication. "Arturo, turn back out of the gulf now!"

"Sammy?"

"Something blew up over the city," Samuel DeSousa explained. "My ship was cracked in half against a pier by the tidal surge."

"Tidal surge?" Bonquillo asked.

"I'm on the shore…I grabbed my CB before my crew pulled me out. A fifteen-foot wall of water rose from the harbor and snapped the boat over the pier. I'm lucky to be alive," DeSousa explained. "Turn your ship around and get to deep water!"

Bonquillo squinted out the windows of the pilot house, but he throttled the *Esmerelda* to full power, steering out toward the opening of the gulf. "The tidal surge caused by the explosion won't have the room to dissipate in the shallow waters of Guancanyabo and the wave could toss us onto the coral, breaking us apart."

"Just move, Arturo," DeSousa said. "Get out of the way of the wave because we need to evacuate. That means every boat we can summon."

"Captain!" Enrique shouted. "There's something on the horizon!"

Bonquillo had the boat turned around and he rode the throttle slowly. By all rights, he'd have at least half an hour to reach deep water. Tidal waves were powerful, but they only had a limited velocity. He looked back and saw the bioluminescent shimmer of the frothing wave top on the horizon behind him. He looked at his watch. The *Esmerelda* was twenty miles from shore, and for the wave to have traveled that distance in the five minutes since Bonquillo had consulted his watch, the crest had to have been moving at blistering speeds. He pushed the throttle to the limit, realizing that if the wave struck his ship, it wouldn't matter if he avoided hull damage against the reefs.

"Brace for impact!" Bonquillo roared to his crew.

MAJOR HONORILLO RUIZ looked out of the cockpit of his MiG as it speared through the night en route to Manzanillo. The *Esmerelda* was only the third of the tidal wave–tossed boats he'd seen wrecked in the Gulf. His wingman, Quesada, called them in as they passed, a grim tally of destruction that was only the preliminaries before they reached the port city.

At only five hundred feet above the waves, moving at a leisurely 400 miles per hour, he could see the flames on the far shore. Whatever had been launched at Manzanillo had produced an air burst. He could tell by the concentric rings of damage. There was a relatively small ground zero where the maximum force of the explosion had touched the ground. A quick swoop, and he could see that flames had spread a mile from the center of the impact.

He checked his gauges and noticed a small sensor light was blinking. It was a radiation meter, built in by the Soviet Union when they'd constructed his plane decades ago.

"Base, be advised, we have radiation signature over ground zero," Ruiz said.

Manza, his ground control, answered quickly. "Havana has been informed of the situation. Someone had launched into orbit, and dropped a form of fuel-air explosive utilizing a radioactive isotope as a shrapnel casing."

"Fuel air explosive from orbit?"

"Liquid oxygen set off by atmospheric friction," Manza said. "What's the damage look like?"

"The docks are a wreck, and like Quesada's been reporting, there are a lot of damaged ships in the harbor due to a tidal wave caused by detonation," Ruiz said.

"I lost count after thirty parked craft," Quesada chimed in.

"The maximum damage caused by the air burst was around the piers. I saw three warehouses flattened, but there is fire and heat damage a mile from the epicenter," Ruiz continued. "You said there was radioactive isotope used as shrapnel?"

"That's what the U.S. Government has informed us. They're very concerned about this attack, since it landed so close to Guantanamo," Manza answered. "We have naval and marine forces in motion to aid in casualty recovery and emergency service, augmenting our own rescue services in the area."

"Glad they're stepping up," Ruiz said. "Things look bad. With a mile radius worth of blast damage, the shrapnel must have affected thousands. I don't know if we'd be able to handle that many casualties."

"You don't think they're covering their asses?" Quesada asked.

"Don't be an idiot," Ruiz growled. "Why would they spike a weapon like this down so close to their own military base? It's not as if Manzanillo has anything truly strategic as an advantage. It's almost pure economic, with a little spy activity on Gitmo."

"Misdirection for something important going down in Guantanamo Bay?" Quesada asked. "They could have had a submarine pop up a SUBROC and it would have come back down. All our eyes are on Manzanillo right now."

Ruiz grimaced. "That's why you're just a wingman. By the time your balls drop and your IQ shoots up a couple points, you'll realize that nuking a nonhostile city isn't the way the Americans work. If they were going to make some real noise, they'd have struck at the northern shore of the island. Not in their backyard."

"I still say a few 20 mm shells across their decks are in order when they pull in," Quesada muttered, dejected.

"You try it, and I'll light you up and piss on the wreckage when you're done roasting," Ruiz snapped. "Behave or go home!"

Quesada snorted angrily but continued his patrol, reporting in on the damage.

Ruiz looked over the shattered port city. Quesada wasn't the only Cuban military man on edge because of the air burst. Ruiz just hoped there were more cool heads like his own to keep them in line, otherwise the burning fires below would only be the first of a conflagration that would engulf the whole of the Caribbean.

Jottunheim Station, the North Sea

DEIDRE TANIT LOOKED AT the news break interruptions flooding into channels around the world about the mysterious explosion over Manzanillo, Cuba. Her smile was sly as nervous newsmen announced what could have been a nuclear attack on the tiny island nation. Of course, the U.S. government had explained to the Cuban government about the presence of Iridium-192 in the fallen liquid oxygen canister, turning it into a deadly, dirty, high-radiation shrapnel grenade capable of flattening everything in a one-mile radius. The metallic rods, propelled by superheated liquid oxygen, had the potential for even further dispersal of death and suffering as even splinters would release gamma rays inducing life-threatening radiation poisoning.

She stepped to the window, looking away from the video monitor wall, and out over the choppy gray waters of the North Atlantic. The starless sky was stretched like a smothering shroud over the world, and she took in a deep breath, controlling the tingling joy running across her skin. "Ah, if you could only see me now, dear brother."

"Deidre?" a deep, sonorous voice called. "Weren't you supposed to make your transmission?"

She looked to her husband, a towering man, close to seven feet tall and topped with a mop of red curly hair that matched his thick beard. Cabled, rippling arms hung from the sleeves of his T-shirt, the cold not even making his forearms dimple with goose bumps despite the fact that she was wrapped in a turtleneck sweater and a warm parka. Tanit smirked, looking over Magni Piarow as he stood like a statue in the center of Jottunheim's command center.

"There isn't quite enough panic," Tanit said.

Piarow nodded. "Should we have the orbiters drop another tank?"

"We want to save them for maximum destruction," Tanit said. "Let's throw Cuba into communications darkness for now. A sky flash, and throw some confusion in on the heels of that…but wait for my command."

Piarow smiled, enjoying his wife's tugging at the puppet strings of fear and media confusion. Tanit walked to one of the monitors, tuned in to the most-watched cable news network in America. The anchorman, a distinguished black man with graying hair, spoke seriously.

"And now we go to Anthony Stephens, our correspondent in Havana," the anchor announced.

"Thanks, Derek," Stephens began. He was on live video feed, speaking into a microphone as he stood on a balcony overlooking Havana. "So far, the only thing we know is that a lance of fiery light sliced down out of the sky, apparently on a course with the opposite end of this island nation…"

"Kill it. Turn the signal into a howl," Tanit ordered.

The live video feed cut out, and even with the volume at the lowest audible setting, she could hear the electronic howl of ravaged technology issue from the monitor's speakers.

The screen snapped back to the anchorman, his normal serious face washed away by a flash of panic that left him looking bug-eyed at the disappearance of his correspondent in Cuba.

"Oops, looks like they're suffering technical problems," Tanit said. She chuckled and walked over to Piarow, running her delicate fingers along his massive, bare arm. "Give it ten minutes for them to really get nervous, and then send the prerecording."

"Don't you want to watch?" Piarow asked, resting one rough hand on her hip.

"I've seen it enough. I'd rather spend some quality time celebrating the upending of the status quo with a little godly thunder," Tanit said.

Piarow chuckled and scooped her up as if she were a child, carrying her out of the communications center and back to their quarters.

Jan Pantopoulos watched the waters of the North Sea slash by in the gloom as he rode the Bell JetRanger from the Scottish coast toward the seemingly dilapidated oil rig. Across from him in the passenger cabin of the helicopter, Gilbert Shane fidgeted, full of nervous energy.

"What are you so worried about?" Pantopoulos asked.

"I looked at my account back at FBI headquarters," Shane said, tapping his laptop. He shook his head. "I went in through a back door and found out that someone in the Justice Department had put a tap on it."

"So they found you out." Pantopoulos sighed, irritated. "And what's so bad about that?"

"They found me out," Shane answered. "They finally figured me out."

"And they found out about that old fuck I used to work for," Pantopoulos mentioned. "One of the boys I'd left behind in Florida told me that someone made a move on him tonight. Guns blazing, and a lot of Russians and local Cuban talent dead."

"You're used to picking up and disappearing. I spent years building a real life, not this gypsy setup you exist in," Shane said.

"So you'd rather be sitting in Washington, D.C., when they drop a satellite or one of their little improvised Daisy Cutters on your ass?" Pantopoulos asked. "You're alive, and you're out of the target zone for a nuclear hand grenade dropped from outer space."

Shane's lips pursed in disgust.

"You're also pretty damned rich," Pantopoulos added.

"My fingerprints are all over this scheme. They might just send a wet works team after me. What am I supposed to be? The richest man in the world living in exile on a rusted-out old hulk in a cold puddle of water?" Shane asked.

Pantopoulos rolled his eyes. "You Americans never just accept all the good that comes your way."

Shane sighed. "Please, give me some credit here. I'm a dead man."

Pantopoulos looked at Shane, then broke into a laugh. "When we're finished, the government will have a lot more on its hands than looking for a crooked Homeland Security agent."

"You really think so?" Shane asked.

"This is the apocalypse, man. The balloon will go up once world capitals are pummeled with satellites and our bombs," Pantopoulos said. "Everyone with a grudge will make their move. Anarchy will rule continents, and even if the current administration in the U.S. survives, they'll be fighting off dozens of factions wanting to set up their own splinter states."

Shane's shoulders untensed. "I hope you're right."

Pantopoulos looked out the window and saw the towering hulk of Jottunheim Station bursting from the choppy waters. "I'm rarely wrong."

The turncoat American agent and the deadly Greek mercenary continued the rest of their trip in uneasy silence.

CHAPTER FIFTEEN

Near Earth Orbit

The *Arcadia* disengaged from her fuel tank, and Broome and Cole steered the ship toward its intercept course with the International Space Station. This allowed the men of Able Team to retire to a communications panel to get their briefing from Stony Man Farm.

"The enemy has blacked out Cuba in the middle of a major news feed," Barbara Price explained.

"That's sure to cause a panic," Lyons said. "What's the situation in Florida?"

"Stores are being hit hard by people looking for survival supplies," Price answered. "Water, canned goods, building supplies and ammunition. We haven't had any fatal shootings yet, but police departments are reporting that their cars are picking up bullet holes from panicked citizens. The situation hasn't deteriorated into looting yet, but I'm only giving it some time."

"What about the rest of the coast?" Blancanales asked.

"New York and Baltimore are reporting riots," Price told

him. "The UN Security Council is in emergency session, and China's complaining about the massive computer crash that hit their country. They're glaring daggers at the U.S., but haven't mentioned incursion into their secret launch facility."

"If they did that, then they'd have to explain why they have a militarized launchpad," Lyons said. "There are treaties against utilizing weapons in space, and we have photographs that show they not only have the capability to engage in clandestine launches, but have a training camp devoted to orbital combat."

"So?" Blancanales asked. "They're not the only people with firepower set up in orbit."

Lyons nodded. "And they know about that. Remember, they made their move to gain control of that platform, too."

"Either way," Schwarz interjected, "we don't have to worry about the UN Security Council just yet. They'll pass a few resolutions, even while the sky is falling on their heads. What we have to worry about are those other orbiters."

"Phoenix is in orbit with you," Price explained. "The Chinese sent them up before the Red Army could arrive at the facility."

"Should we hook up with them?" Lyons asked. "We could plan an intercept course…"

"No," Price cut him off. "All accounts as to the orbiters they went up with are going to be guided in via remote control."

"So we're already too late to the station," Lyons said.

"No activity confirmed on that front," Price stated. "But the enemy seem—"

There was a powerful squelch of static that broke across the signal.

"Barb?" Lyons asked.

"…adjusting for interference." Price's voice was masked by static, but Able Team could understand her.

"What's going on?" Lyons asked.

"Seems to be a multiband broadcast," Price mentioned. "It's showing up on some of our monitors."

There was another squelch, and the monitor was replaced with the image of a woman clad from head to toe in black, her face obscured by a ninja-style mask. Able Team could tell it was a woman because of the curves of her body, long stems of legs crossed as she reclined in a leather-backed office chair. Gloved, delicate fingers were steepled together, and her piercing blue eyes aimed right at the camera.

"Citizens of Earth, the reign of fascism and intolerance is nearly over," she said. "The Celestial Hammer has been loosed from its restraints, and it will smash those who presume to govern over you as if you were sheep."

"Celestial Hammer," Lyons repeated, searching his memory for a similar group. He had nothing, but then, radical groups popped up like weeds across the globe. He was certain, however, that this was just another renamed conglomeration of discordant freaks who had the manpower and money to stage a global crisis. These were the kinds of thugs that Able Team and Phoenix Force had been created to battle, and considering that they had manpower from around the globe, from the Iranian and Chinese governments to expatriated Greek and American mobsters, they weren't going to roll over and die. The combined forces of Stony Man Farm would be pushed to their limits when it came down to stopping this scheme. Something in her message struck a familiar cord in is mind.

"You may wonder what the Celestial Hammer is, but there are those of you out there already familiar with us. We have scourged the world on several occasions, and only by the slimmest chances have we been halted. We will not stop, and this time, we shall turn the very baubles, the expensive playthings of out-of-touch governments, into the rocks with which we shall slay the Goliaths who control humankind. The time of fools who go to war over oil or putrid, failed ideologies is done. Anarchy is our goal, and we will smash the yoke around your necks. Already, those who have been inspired by our message are taking up the reigns of their destiny to do what must be done."

The video image changed to boatloads of gun-toting Cubans at sea. "Those who have been ousted by the still shambling corpse of communism are rising up to purify Cuba."

There was another flashing change, showing Chinese tanks on fire. "In China, justice is being struck for the smothering influence of ancient, corrupt officials."

The scene changed to early morning in Paris. Rioting thugs surged wildly, throwing Molotov cocktails and clashing with the police. "The underclasses around the world have been spurred, taking their battle to the obsolete old men who have strangled the human spirit, while ruling us from silver balconies at the edge of space."

Camera footage of Manzanillo showed up. Wounded civilians cried out in horror as flames smeared the sky a bloody crimson beneath choking black smoke. "There will be some breakage. The world has become too entrenched, and those who insist on being sheep must be reaped along with the slave masters who dared to stand on our necks."

Live footage showed a satellite searing out of the sky, coming down on a city in India. It crashed with a relatively small explosion, not the apocalyptic air blast associated with hundreds of gallons of liquid oxygen detonating. Still, Lyons knew that even a small satellite striking in the middle of an urban area would unleash hellish destruction and sow panic and terror with lethal efficiency. "We are taking away their ability to peer into your lives and steal the freedoms you are entitled to. We are opening the window to give you the sweet air of liberty. All you have to do is reach for it."

The camera turned back to the woman. "We have told many what needs to be done. They are doing it. Follow their lead and break your chains. This is the Celestial Hammer. Over and out."

The signal ended, and Barbara Price was on the monitor, her jaw slack with surprise.

"They took control of another satellite, gave it the command to fire its maneuvering thrusters and dropped it on the subcontinent," Price said.

"It looks like they've set a lot up for this day," Lyons agreed with a grimace. "They somehow have managed to coordinate various anarchist groups around the world to act."

"Anarchist or antiestablishment," Price said. "I'm having the cyberteam look at Coast Guard reports to see if they have a lead on those boats. It seems like the footage was taken earlier today, but they also have access to live feeds. The French riots are going on now."

"What about the situation in China?" Schwarz inquired. "That looked like mass sabotage, rather than any form of real fighting."

"We've already established that Celestial Hammer had some strong influence inside the Communist Chinese government structure," Price said. "I'm so glad we finally have a name for this group."

"Seems like a hand-picked name for this particular plot," Lyons said. "You don't get much more celestial than orbit. And taking a look at the damage in Cuba and India, they've got the hammer part down cold."

Price looked off screen for a moment, then looked to Lyons. "We've got David on hookup with you. He's been briefed on Celestial Hammer."

"How was China?" Lyons asked.

"The usual. Blokes trying to kill us, surrounded by enemies. Made a few temporary friends, though," McCarter answered. "How about you?"

"The usual. Streets filled with body parts, wrecked cars, good times," Lyons said. "What can you tell us about the orbiters?"

"Room for eight passengers," McCarter described. "And according to Captain Hau, there were slots for four of the devices similar to the one that struck Manzanillo."

"And they also seem to have the ability to take over satellites via computer control," Lyons returned. "So we have a double threat."

"Triple threat," Manning interjected. "The station itself is composed of several hundred-ton modules. While we don't have to worry about the ballistic force of the solar panels—they're not dense enough to survive atmospheric reentry—the station's sections have sufficient mass and construction to cause significant damage."

"And all the while, we're factoring the potential radiation hazard caused by isotopes that power satellite batteries," Schwarz added. "Nothing compared to the kind of problems cause by the Iridium, but still significant."

"You think that they might try to crash the station?" Lyons asked.

"Back in '79 there were serious concerns about Skylab coming down in a populated area. Luckily, NASA had steered it into an orbit that had it come apart over the Indian Ocean and unincorporated Australia," Manning explained. "The projections for even one module landing in an urban area called for two thousand casualties."

"How many modules make up the ISS again?" Lyons inquired.

"Enough to take out half the East Coast's major cities," Manning told him. "And from the sound of the Celestial Hammer's rhetoric, Washington, D.C. might receive an extraordinarily focused pounding. There are literally thousands of objects in orbit right now that can be utilized to take out D.C., London, Moscow, Tokyo…all forms of world centers."

"Hang on," McCarter announced. "Control of our craft is being overridden from the ground. Barb…"

"We're triangulating the signals," Price interjected.

"They're not monitoring our communications, are they?" Lyons asked.

"We're working off a focused laser comm beam. Almost impossible to intercept," Price told him.

"Almost impossible," Lyons emphasized.

"If they were listening in, they'd have shot us into a nosedive toward countryside or the Pacific Ocean," McCarter stated. "This is just a controlled roll. They're opening the hatch for one of our tanks."

"Knowing you, they'll only fire blanks," Lyons said.

"Yeah. We emptied the hold," McCarter replied. "If she's expecting a big kaboom, she's going to be disappointed."

Lyons glanced back toward the cockpit, casting a wary eye on William Cole. "Just be ready to override that remote control—"

"Our wing-drone is veering off course," Rafael Encizo's voice cut into the conversation. "It's breaking orbit!"

"Bugger!" McCarter snarled. "They either sensed that the holds were empty, or we've been screwed."

Lyons glanced at Schwarz, not even having to ask his question. The electronics genius had been watching his CPDA and looked up, nodding. "We've got an unaccounted signal heading earthward, from the ship."

Lyons got up. "Hold on, everyone. People to kill."

Cole looked over his shoulder and smirked as Lyons, rising from his seat, floated weightlessly. No longer under constant acceleration, the crew of the *Arcadia* was free to maneuver through the orbiter in a zero gravity environment. Cole touched the throttle and pushed it forward.

Lyons grimaced, reaching for a handhold, but the acceleration of the *Arcadia* returned gravity, momentarily, to the shuttle. Carl Lyons, as well as the rest of Able Team, Broome, Komalko and Mustafa were hurled from their workstations, thrown against bulkheads with stunning force. Lyons fought to remain conscious, fingers clawing to return him to an upright position when Cole speared through the air like a champion swimmer. With two kicks, the astronaut tucked into a somersault and rolled, extending his legs like pistons to catch Lyons in the jaw. As his head struck unyielding metal, Lyons, already hurt by the sudden thrust, was out like a light.

Cole glided to the conference call with Stony Man Farm, pulling a small stun gun "I'm sorry. The party you have been speaking to has been disconnected."

He pulled the trigger on the Taser, taking out the communications board instantly.

The International Space Station

COMMANDER PAVEL ROUSAKIS was aware of the nature of the threat. Stony Man Farm had decided it was in the best interests of the three-man crew manning the orbital habitat that they be informed of the potential of hostile invasion by orbiters packed with zero-gravity trained terrorists. Watching the radar, he saw two craft gliding through space, matching the approach path that the *Arcadia* had been scheduled to take. Dull, stomach-squeezing dread filled Rousakis as the orbiter approached.

"They're not answering hailing signals, Pavel," Emiko Nyoka said. "And that radar profile doesn't match the *Arcadia,* even without its shadow."

"But they still have the proper IFF signal," Rousakis

mused. "NASA was right. Whoever is behind this has put a lot of money and effort into pulling this plan off."

Nyoka wrinkled her nose. "Of all the times to be an unarmed space station."

Rousakis shook his head. "No photon torpedoes or phasers here. We don't even have knives on hand. Signal an all-station alert. We'll try to disengage our orbiter from the station and return to Earth."

"They're approaching quickly, and they'll be in range to ram us before we can disengage," Nyoka answered.

Rousakis looked at the screen for a moment and grimaced as he confirmed that the raiders' ETA was shorter than their emergency disembarkment course. "No way off the station before we can initiate maneuvering jets. They timed it just right. We could detect them, but we couldn't get away from them."

"If I could, I'd suggest that we head to the barracks module and barricade. That's one of the backup systems we have on hand," Dr. Rahir Innuman noted. "They may not have the tools or codes to get through that bulkhead before we engage emergency quarantine protocols."

Rousakis nodded at the Egyptian scientist's evaluation. "All right. Back to the barracks. Emiko, let Earth know that we're shoring up against invaders."

Dr. Innuman's fingers flew across the control board for the life support console. Systems and lights began shutting down through many of the modules. "I'll try to make it as difficult for them to maintain control of the station as possible."

Rousakis joined him in unlatching the control panel. In three hard blows of a wrench, the circuit boards beneath were pounded to useless splinters of plastic and silicate. "Luckily we do have backup controls in the barracks module."

"Not luck. Planning," Innuman stated. "Come on, Pavel. The longer we waste, the more chance we'll be intercepted."

Rousakis paused, looking at the radar screen as the Celestial Hammer's twin raiders closed in on his station. He kicked off, hoping for the safety of a bulkhead, and wishing he had the weapons to fight back.

Launch Vehicle Three

DAVID MCCARTER WATCHED LV Four peel off their combined path. Its hatches were also open, undoubtedly in an effort to launch its payload of nonexistent explosive containers toward hapless targets on the Earth's surface. The Phoenix Force commander glanced back at Manning and Encizo, who were hard at work dismantling the communications system. They'd been able to talk with Stony Man Farm by utilizing McCarter's sat phone hub, rather than airing information over bands monitored by both the Chinese and the Celestial Hammer.

"Give me some good news, lads," McCarter said.

Suddenly LV4 jolted, its thrusters activating.

"When we hit, we absolutely will not have to worry about spending the rest of our days as quadriplegics," Manning said, working hard on the ground control relay. "Any joy on the board, T.J.?"

Hawkins was in McCarter's copilot seat, trying to override the commands beamed up from the Celestial Hammer. "Nothin' yet!"

Manning suddenly hissed as the lights cut out completely on the control panels. "Shock…"

"You okay?" James asked.

"The amperage was too low," Manning rumbled. "It just burned."

"Whatever you did, it was brilliant," McCarter said.

The Phoenix Force orbiter spun, its maneuvering jets spinning it around to intercept the other craft.

"We're in the clear?" Encizo asked.

"Not quite yet. I'd strap in if I were y'all," Hawkins announced. "It looks like we're going after the Celestial Hammer's guided missile."

Manning's eyes widened as he slipped into the seat behind McCarter. "You know this ship doesn't have any guns."

"Well, you can't get a better ramming speed than reentry," McCarter stated.

Encizo made a sign of the cross after clamping into his harness. "Just catch up with that thing, David. It's not like we have many other options."

"We do," McCarter said. "But the distance I'm going to take us to, we might as well be on a collision course."

"That's the man in charge," James said with a bit of hope. "We're not going out like that!"

"Just hold on," McCarter said.

The thrusters roared to full power, maneuvering jets guiding the craft. The responsiveness of the orbiter in a zero-atmosphere environment was a shock to the ace pilot, who was used to having to take into account air resistance. With the Celestial Hammer vehicle, it wasn't as if he could throttle a jet and use the flaps to finesse his movement. He blew the maneuvering jets and had to counter the direction change with a braking thrust, otherwise he'd spiral the orbiter like an out-of-control bottle rocket.

"David, what are you doing?" Barbara Price called over his sat phone.

"My job." McCarter milked more acceleration out of the throttle, spearing the launch vehicle through the ionosphere toward the other craft.

"Aaron says that the launch vehicle is on a course for Washington, D.C.," Price said. "He also says that if you can flip your ship and go maximum burn, you can decelerate enough for the chutes to not be torn off when they deploy."

"Small favors," McCarter said. "What's my distance to the other ship?"

"You're inside 150 kilometers," Price answered.

McCarter could still see the far curves of the Earth in the windshield around him. The Celestial Hammer craft was a distant speck, slowly growing in scope as he hurtled the orbiter after it. Their momentum at this rate had applied several gravities to the members of Phoenix Force inside the craft. He knew that once the acceleration stopped, he wouldn't feel the crushing pressure of artificial gravity weighing on him, but that sudden decrease wouldn't come until he got closer to the enemy craft.

The speck flickered on one side and it rolled, twisting. McCarter realized that the Celestial Hammer had to have known he was hot on their tail and they were adjusting their course. Sooner or later, though, the kamikaze vehicle would have to slide back into the approach angle needed to hit its target. Another jolt to the throttle gave them more speed.

"David, if you use any more fuel and throttle, you'll never be able to decelerate enough," Price said.

"How many citizens are in the D.C. metro area right now?" McCarter asked.

Price remained silent.

"I wish I could have dropped you lads off at the station," McCarter whispered as he gave the main thrusters another jolt.

"And miss your most spectacular landing ever?" Manning asked. "Either way, we'll have a hell of a story when we see Keio and Katz again."

"We're not dead yet," Hawkins said. "Twenty-five klicks to the other ship. Altitude 400 miles and dropping."

McCarter throttled up the maneuvering thrusters. At that speed, any precision movement was an exercise, not only of the Briton's muscle power, but of his experience as a pilot.

He hit the retro rockets, decelerating, but the distance between him and the other plummeting vehicle continued to shrink at lightning speed.

"They've got nothing to maneuver with," Hawkins said. "They fired off the last of their thrusters to settle into the approach toward DC."

"That means we don't have much to maneuver with ourselves," McCarter said, reading the fuel gauges for the retro rockets. "Velocity dropping off, but not much. I'll only have one shot at this."

"Four klicks," Hawkins announced.

McCarter nudged the maneuvering thrusters, a tiny spurt. Kurtzman had sent McCarter a projected image of his path and the other craft's. They'd be parallel inside of fifteen seconds. He went through the countdown, his finger poised over the throttle.

His course was just inside that of the remote drone, and for his plan to work, he had to power up just as he cleared it. The basic principles of rocketry were based on action and reaction. The enemy craft wouldn't change course now unless some outside force were utilized upon it, and short of a broadside collision, there was only one force that could deflect the rocket.

The trio of main boosters on the back of LV3. He'd have to be within yards of the other ship for his plan to work.

LV4 loomed in his vision and his hand was resting on the throttle.

"Guys," he whispered, "let's do it."

He slammed the throttle forward and the orbiter shook violently as it speared past the other vehicle.

"LV4 has been deflected!" Price shouted. "It's going into the Atlan—"

The satellite feed failed, but David McCarter knew he'd stopped one missile from striking Washington, D.C.

Now all he had to do was to change course to keep from doing the Celestial Hammer's job for them.

McCarter hit the retro rockets again. Unfortunately, the controls weren't responding. Maneuvering thrusters were dead, even though the indicator told him they still had a few moments of fuel in their reserve.

"Okay, lads, now we can panic," McCarter said.

Hawkins punched the control panel. "Come on, you piece of shit!"

"This isn't a TV," James admonished.

"It might be an electrical short," Hawkins said. "I might jumble the wires back into place."

McCarter kept trying the controls. The throttle still worked, there was only a short in the maneuvering thrusters. "Gary! See if you can find an override on your panel!"

"I've been looking ever since you first started flipping switches," Manning returned. He grimaced. "Ah hell…"

A loud thump filled the cockpit, and McCarter glanced back to see that the burly Canadian had dropped his fist on the engineering panel like a massive club. He looked back to his console and saw that all the buttons were lit up. All the buttons except the malfunction indicators, which had gone out.

He slammed on the retro rockets to full burn, and LV3 slowed dramatically, turning over as they passed two thousand miles.

"Told ya!" Hawkins said as centrifugal force mashed him into the copilot's seat.

McCarter grinned as he hit the throttle. He had to bleed off their breakneck velocity before they struck the upper atmosphere, otherwise they would be splattered as if they had hit a brick wall. The main boosters burned, the fuel pressure dropping like a rock as the engines converted the remnants of their tanks into energy.

"David, alter your course by thirty degrees. You're com-

ing in too steep. You'll skip across the atmosphere," Kurtzman said as communication was restored.

"What happened to you?" McCarter asked. He worked the
joystick, following the Stony Man cybergenius's instructions.

"The Hammer interrupted our signal. We've found a different frequency," Kurtzman explained. "How's your velocity?"

"Dropping," McCarter answered. Outside the windshield,
he could see the stars hanging above him, a tranquil rhinestone
blanket of placid silence. "What about the other ship?"

"It's in the atmosphere already, but it's on such an oblique
path, reentry friction is tearing it apart," Kurtzman said. "It's
nothing more than a collection of splinters spread over the
mid-Atlantic."

McCarter checked his altitude as he felt a gentle vibration.
The orbiter had hit the outermost atmosphere, 150 miles
above Earth's surface. "Are we going to get a pickup?"

"We've got your course directed," Kurtzman answered. "I
hope you'll get enough time to rest."

The tanks bottomed out. There was nothing left to push
through the engines to slow the craft's drop, except for the
drag chutes, which wouldn't deploy until they were thirty
miles above Earth's surface.

"You're triangulating the lead on the ground control signal to the ships?" McCarter asked.

"Yeah. And since Able Team's busy in orbit, you'll have
to go after the ground element," Kurtzman stated.

McCarter closed his eyes, waiting for the chutes to deploy.
"Just have a cold Coke waiting for me. Saving millions of
Americans is thirsty work."

CHAPTER SIXTEEN

USS Arcadia, Earth Orbit

Carl Lyons's eyes fluttered open and he looked around the flight crew deck, but his peripheral vision had been limited by a flight helmet. His hands were bound tightly behind him, and he cursed himself for letting a little bit of physics pin him down like a sack of useless meat. He tried to make out the manner of the restraints from the feeling in his wrists, but the jumpsuit cuffs made it difficult.

"Gadgets? Pol? You guys awake?" Lyons asked.

"They're still unconscious, Agent Dutse," William Cole said, stepping into view. "I presume you'll want to know where they are, though."

"Probably in a place where you can maintain control of them," Lyons answered. "I'd say an air lock, so you can coerce me into cooperation."

Cole smiled. "You're not as dumb as you look."

"Lot of people have made that mistake, Cole. Most of them are deposited in unmarked graves," Lyons returned.

"Just as well. I already underestimated your physical attributes, and had to kick you in the head with both feet," Cole said. "You stayed conscious through a 2.5 G acceleration hurling you against a bulkhead. Even Komalko, a trained flight engineer, ended up with a broken arm from that."

"You obviously don't want to go into a discussion of weight training minimalizing orthopedic injury potential in athletes," Lyons said. "So make your pitch. What do you need my help with?"

Cole grinned. "Sixteen of my close friends are already on-board the International Space Station, but they're having some trouble convincing the station's crew to let them into the module they've fortified themselves in."

"Sorry. No matter what you threaten Gadgets and Pol with, I'm not going to help you take civilians captive," Lyons said.

"Nothing like that, good man," Cole told him. "In fact, you really don't need to physically do anything."

Cole touched an earphone he wore and nodded. "We're closing in on the ISS. Wait here for a moment, will you?"

Lyons remained silent, trying to twist his forearms and loosen his bonds. Unfortunately, he couldn't get any leverage. The helmet limited his ability to see around, and his legs had been folded beneath him, keeping him from seeing how his ankles were bound. It was a tight spot, but Lyons had been held captive before.

He squinted, looking for a sign of movement around the corner; all the while his powerful arms flexed and pushed, trying to loosen his restraints. He could feel a little give, which immediately retracted when he could no longer apply enough leverage on his arms. That told the Able Team leader that he was held by some form of polymer. It didn't take much imagination to figure that he was held in place by cable ties.

Lyons had broken steel handcuffs on previous occasions, but that was an entirely different form of necessary maneuvering. Those cuffs had a steel joint chain, and Lyons had built up enough pure rage to shatter the links. The slight slack in the chain had helped him build up the force. One explosive surge of muscle power, and his arms were free.

The fibrous nature of the polymer cable ties and the way they cinched tightly around his limbs meant that he wouldn't have the leverage, and even if he did, he couldn't break the semielastic plastic grain. Still, Lyons wasn't a man who utilized a form of restraint without testing escape methods beforehand. As a cop, he used to have a handcuff key that he secreted under a bandage at the small of his back, a habit he'd lapsed in, requiring a display of berserker strength that forged his reputation as Able Team's viking war chief. The steel-hinged handcuffs were impossible for him to snap, reinforced rings and bolts providing too much resistance for any creature short of an elephant to take apart, necessitating a return to a hidden key.

The cable ties required a different strategy, one that took time, patience and endurance. If he could provide an overwhelming amount of force on the polymer strips, he could deform them out of shape.

Lyons dug down and flexed. His wrists felt as if a half dozen piano wires had been yanked tautly across them, and as his forearms and shoulders swelled with the effort, his fingertips grew cold and tingly, the circulation cut off as the multiple cable ties strangled his blood vessels. He flexed for thirty seconds, blood roaring through his ears like a freight train. The rumbling in his skull was almost enough to drown out the dull thud of the *Arcadia* connecting with the umbilical that would allow the crew to board the space station.

Lyons relaxed his arms and the blood rushed back through thirsty vessels, feeding his oxygen starved fingers. Under the helmet, his blond hair was matted to his forehead.

Cole appeared again, this time bracketed by a pair of hard-looking men. Lyons got a good look at one and recognized a set of Slavic features.

"Look at this. I wrap eight cable ties around his wrists and another eight around his ankles, and he thinks he can break them," Cole said with a derisive laugh. "Who do you think you are? The Man of Steel?"

Lyons declined to answer. The burly Russians manhandled him easily in the zero gravity environment.

They were oblivious to the knowledge that they had a trained and ready Ironman in their midst, already one millimeter closer to breaking his bonds.

BLANCANALES LOOKED THROUGH the porthole in the airlock door, watching as Cole's Celestial Hammer compatriots offloaded Broome, Mustafa and Komalko. Lyons had gone first with them, trussed up like a turkey. He glanced to Hermann Schwarz. He'd only woken up a moment before and was rubbing his head where he'd barked it against a bulkhead. Dried blood matted Schwarz's hair to his forehead, and a large goose egg was forming at the hairline.

"Sit still for a moment," Blancanales said. "I'll check to see if you have a concussion."

"What ran over me?" Schwarz asked as Blancanales thumbed his eyelid down, looking for reaction from his partner's irises. Schwarz pulled himself free from his friend's ministerings.

"I'd say the *Arcadia*. How's your mouth?" Blancanales asked.

"A little dry, but I was asleep and drooling," Schwarz said. He brushed his mustache. "Yeah, my flavor saver's full of dried spit."

"Salivating fine?" Blancanales asked.

Schwarz nodded, then winced. "It's just a little blood. No severe loss, no dehydration. I won't be able to tell if my equilibrium's fine because we don't have any gravity—"

"Okay," Blancanales interrupted. "Cole must have emptied our pockets before he tossed us in here."

"Where's Carl?" Schwarz asked, feeling under his jumpsuit.

"I saw them dragging him out another of the airlocks," Blancanales answered. "We must be in the entrance to the cargo hold."

Schwarz unzipped his jumpsuit and reached down into his pant leg

"Tool kit?" Blancanales asked.

"Multitool," Schwarz answered, pulling out a small pair of folding pliers. "Never leave home without one strapped to my calf. I might leave the house without a .45 but—"

"Save the commercial endorsements for later and open up that control panel. Carl might not have a lot of time," Blancanales said.

"You're thinking that he'll be used as the beating horse?" Schwarz asked, extending an Allen wrench. He swiftly set to work unfastening the hex-head screws that held the airlock control panel in place.

"Seems like it. He's the most physically impressive of us. He'll take a far greater amount of torture and pain than Broome, Mustafa or Komalko. Besides which, Komalko was hurt," Blancanales said. "They'll need someone to cow the ISS crew into opening up."

"You've been awake for a while?" Schwarz asked.

"Playing possum and listening at the door. Steel's a good conductor for sound waves," Blancanales said. "Cole said that he had to find some way to get the station crew out of their fortified position. He has Carl cowed into inactivity with the threat of our lives, and he assumed that we were helpless."

Schwarz took the panel down and looked at the circuit boards within. "Shouldn't take too long to get this open. But

I wouldn't count on Cole being stupid enough to leave the air-lock unwatched. He'll think of it sooner or later."

"I'm betting sooner," Blancanales said. "Can you pop the hatch?"

Schwarz moved a few chips around, rerouting the power flow. With the click of a circuit breaker, the door hissed, opening for the Able Team pair. "That answer your question?"

"Goof," Blancanales snapped as he pushed into the flight deck. "Clear."

Schwarz hovered alongside his partner, looking around the crew stations for something. He spotted a pen in a clipboard. He unsnapped the cap, looking at the steel neck before the hard metal nib. The body's construction was also aluminum. Taking the pen's lanyard, he tied the cap across the base of the pen in the shape of an inverted cross, fashioning the writing utensil into a push dagger.

"Hopefully it won't get lodged in bone. That handle won't let you pry it out," Blancanales said.

"It's more to cushion my hand when I ram it into soft viscera," Schwarz replied. He thumbed out the largest blade on his multitool, a three-inch spear point, and closed the legs of the folding pliers to form a pommel for the regular knife. "You have a weapon?"

Blancanales grabbed the back of a chair and kicked at the armrest bases, two steel tubes holding the foam rests to the rest of the chair. With leverage and the strength of both of his legs, the Puerto Rican commando snapped the steel tubes off at the fused joint where they met the seat. Two more kicks knocked the flats of the armrests off the tubes. Though each of them was a mere ten inches long, Blancanales tested their motion in his hands. Though he was an expert in *bo-jutsu,* the Okinawan style of stick-fighting, he was also a student of ku-botan technique. The art of the kubotan was the utilization of a sub-foot long striking implement as a means of effective self-defense.

The mass of the steel pipes would give any blow he struck with them bone-crushing force. In the zero gravity environment, they'd be dangerous weapons, momentum unchecked by their weight. "I'm good to go," Blancanales said.

Schwarz, with his push-dagger and utility knife at the ready, floated to observe the hatch to the umbilical. He frowned. "Clear."

"That won't be for long," Blancanales said. "Who first? There's not going to be any room to leapfrog in that tube."

"I'll go first. If anything happens in the access hatch, it'll be extreme close quarters. I'll have the advantage there," Schwarz replied.

Blancanales gave one of his impact sticks a twirl. "Beauty before age."

Able Team started the stealthy, slow crawl into the International Space Station. If they were detected, they knew that their leader, Carl Lyons, would pay the ultimate price for their failure.

Jottunheim Station, the North Sea

WALTER AND LANCE WOODROW, the hacker twins in the employ of the Piarows, stared at their screens with identical scowls.

"What's wrong, you two?" Deidre Tanit asked, stepping between them, her long delicate fingers touching each on a shoulder.

"We're encountering increased difficulty in hijacking establishment satellites," Lance said. "You told us that the status quo had excellent computer experts in their employ. We were not expecting this level of fluid adaptation on their part. Strategies that we're implementing last only a few minutes before they pick up on them."

Tanit sighed. "Which is why I hired the two of you to be the head of my electronic warfare team. How many satellites have you brought down?"

"On target, or close enough to cause a panic?" Walter asked.

"You're missing?" Tanit asked.

"We dropped two satellites in the outskirts of Canberra, Australia," Lance told her. "A few hundred casualties, nothing like the satellites we dropped in downtown Bangalore or into Le Havre."

"And Des Moines?" Tanit asked.

"Missed completely," Walter explained. "Though the satellite did destroy a small farm three miles outside of the city limits. A family of four was reported—"

"Is that enough to cause chaos and panic?" she asked them.

"There are riots in Iowa and Minnesota, and Chicago and Springfield are under martial law," Lance said.

"Then you're doing a good job," Tanit informed them.

"That was then. Right now, we can't maintain control of a satellite maneuvering system long enough to direct it at an urban population," Walter replied. "They regain control and deflect it off course."

"The International Space Station will be dismantled and dropped in pieces across the globe," she replied. "Have you been able to locate the center of enemy activity?"

"I'm trying," Lance said. "They're elusive, but I'm not giving up. I've got someone working on tracking them down."

"We can hit them with orbital debris, we might be able to distract them long enough to bring the whole sky down," Walter added.

"If not, we have other options," Tanit said. She turned away from the pair, keeping her disappointment under control. It wasn't the Woodrow twins' fault that they were in action against one of the finest cybernetic teams in the world.

Acquaintances of hers had gone up against this particular team and had fallen hard.

She had a tramp freighter positioned off the U.S. Eastern Seaboard equipped with Soviet P-700 Granit guided antiship missiles. The warheads were an impressive 750 kilogram charges. She wished that she had a nuclear warhead or two, but she'd replaced half the warheads with submunition-cluster bombs. As soon as she received the coordinates of her enemy's stronghold, she'd order the tramp to launch its Granit and destroy it. Tanit looked to see that her husband was talking with Jan Pantopoulos. Gilbert Shane was over in the corner, nursing a mug of coffee, his face sallow with fear and doubt.

She walked over to the group.

"Jan," she greeted, opening her slender arms. Pantopoulos turned and embraced her warmly.

"It's good to see you again," the Greek told her. "I was just telling Magni about how I'm certain we attracted the attention of the Death Squad."

"That's what he calls the group of government operators," Magni Piarow said.

"These operatives are in orbit right now," Tanit explained. "William has them as his captives on the *Arcadia.*"

"You're kidding me," Pantopoulos said.

"What about the other group?" Shane spoke up.

Tanit looked to Magni. "They managed to hitch a ride on LV3, and deflected LV4 into the Atlantic."

"Did they die doing it?" Shane asked.

Tanit shook his head. "The U.S. Navy is engaging in search and rescue right now."

"So, we'll still be hunted," Shane muttered. "Just because you took out one of these top secret spook squads doesn't mean the others will be paralyzed with grief."

"Think positive thoughts, Gilbert," Tanit said.

"Oh, I'm positive that we're going to be visited by a squad of commandos who will kill every living creature inside of this oil derrick," Shane snapped.

"Calm down, or I'll calm you down," Piarow said.

Shane looked at the Nordic giant whose deep, calm voice belied the violence in his eyes.

"They're trying to find us, but we will find their masters first," Tanit informed him. "And we have a lot of conventional firepower ready to drop into their laps."

"What?" Shane asked.

"Call it a belt-and-suspenders approach," Tanit stated.

Piarow clapped his massive hand on Shane's shoulder. "One way or another, we're going to throw the world into chaos. A little shopping on the Russian black market has given us what we need to sow terror after terror. No matter what, several world capitals will not survive this day. And Washington, D.C., is going to die in flames."

Shane's face twisted with guilt.

"It's for the best," Tanit told him. "The U.S. government infrastructure has become an inbred forest of rot and decay. We need to excise the tumors that have taken root."

"America, Europe and Asia need this wakeup call. The roots of the tree of liberty have to be fed with the blood of tyrants," Piarow said.

"Thomas Jefferson didn't expect the blood of tyrants to be accompanied by radioactive fallout," Shane muttered.

The nearly seven-foot Norseman laughed. "Don't worry. You seem to forget that D.C. is a city filled with whores, welfare leeches, drug addicts and politicians."

"You mentioned whores twice, Magni," Pantopoulos quipped.

Piarow grinned. "It's not like it's a city full of innocents.

Criminals and thugs dot every street corner. The people in that city can't be bothered to pull themselves up from squalor and corruption. If they disappear in a cloud of submunitions, it's not as if they would be missed."

Shane nodded.

"Besides, you gave Burzyck all that help in eluding police operations," Pantopoulos said.

"For the sake of national security," Shane countered. "You and he were helping us take on the enemies of our nation…"

"And making a handy profit by importing heroin from those same enemies," Pantopoulos admonished. "Where do you think we received most of our contraband from?"

"That was how you kept an eye on them and transmitted their activities to us," Shane said.

Pantopoulos nodded, conceding the point to Shane. "Not that you ever had teams move in and take out these danger-ous terrorists."

"Homeland Security doesn't work that way," Shane said.

Piarow chuckled. "Homeland Security doesn't work. Pe-riod. Full stop. End of statement."

Shane stood, anger crossing his face. "Listen—"

Piarow pushed on Shane's chest, sitting him back down. "I have listened. I've listened to all the incidents of terrorist plots stopped, and you know what? It isn't Homeland Secu-rity's massive, inept bureaucracy that made any difference. If it wasn't the activity of the people fighting us right now, it was lawmen on the street, doing their jobs. You paper-shuffling id-iots claim others' victories as your own. Leeches are more sin-cere than your thieving lot."

Shane's lips quivered as he struggled to maintain his tem-per. He knew that if he had taken a swing at Piarow, the giant would turn him to cream of tomato soup with one punch.

"Lady? Gentlemen?" Walter Woodrow announced. "We

have a video feed from the International Space Station. William is going to provide some entertainment for us."

Tanit grinned. "Now you'll get to see your competition, Gilbert."

Shane shuffled along to the monitor wall.

The International Space Station, Earth Orbit

THEY HADN'T BOTHERED TO do anything more than peel off Carl Lyons's restraining helmet and tear his jumpsuit and T-shirt underneath. His muscular chest rippled freely as he tensed and writhed under the assault of 20,000 volts of extremely low-amperage electricity through prongs jammed through his nipples. Lyons had been subjected to stun guns, as well as to capsicum spray in the course of his many training sessions, so he was familiar with the pain. It wasn't some new shock of lightning dancing across his nervous system, so the agony it cracked open and fried on the blistered surface of his brain was something he could deal with.

It was still agony, and the jolting current tensed his muscles rigidly, paralyzing charges licking at his nerves like the tongues of a thousand pain demons. Cole cut the voltage off and smiled at the captive Able Team commander.

"You see, Commander Rousakis, this man is an elite special operations officer who had been sent to see to the protection of this station," Cole said into the camera. "This is one of the world's greatest combatants, and he's trussed up like a prized goose, and cooking just as well as one."

"Give it up, Billy boy," Lyons sputtered. Tears, sweat and mucus knocked loose by 20,000 volts kicking through his brain and spine flowed from ducts, pores and his nose and mouth. He felt as if he'd been kicked across the circumference of the station's orbit, electricity addled muscles still twitching. "He doesn't know me. And he knows you can't do anything to your copilot or the flight crew, otherwise you'll never get back to Earth. I'm expendable."

Cole sighed deeply, dispelling his rage. He simply pressed the stud on the stun gun, rather than take out his frustration with a backhand across Lyons's jaw. Concentration was impossible with the electricity churning through his body, whipping up his neurons as if they were playing cards in a hurricane. His muscles drew taut, veins and tendons showing in sharp relief under his skin as his whole body convulsed.

The electricity went away, and Lyons's stomach emptied, weightless globules of bile spinning through the air. Cole cursed, slapping at one blob of vomit, then exploded into a whole new level of irate curses as Lyons's stomach contents were smeared across his hand.

"That is sick!" Cole complained. "You did that on purpose!"

Lyons glared at Cole, his fists clenched behind him. He felt the tiniest bit of slack on his wrists, and he hadn't had an opportunity to stress the cable ties to loosen them. He'd only had a millimeter of slack from his first effort, and now he felt much more wiggle room. Lyons looked to the camera with a smile.

"Rousakis, don't pay this little weasel any mind. Keep your crew safe in there," Lyons said.

An Iranian kicked Lyons between his shoulder blades, cursing at him in Farsi.

"Yeah, the Ayatollah got blown by your momma, too," Lyons snapped back.

The Iranian, named Rahim, grabbed the Taser unit from Cole, intending to burn out whatever remained of Lyons's central nervous system with a prolonged blast. Lyons felt his muscles seize, body hard as a rock as the shock slammed into him, forearms swelling and pulling on the cable ties as only the strength provided by electro-convulsive reflex could provide.

"Stop it. If you kill him, we can't get those idiots out of there," Cole said.

"What do you need us for?" Rousakis asked. "It's not like you're going to allow us to live. You could just sever our module and spike it into the center of Europe."

"Please, where's the strategy in that?" Cole asked.

"So what do the brains behind you have in mind?" Lyons asked. "Because sure as shit, you're too simple to even tie your own shoes, Billy."

Cole's boot crashed across Lyons's jaw and he slammed into the floor, bouncing and floating halfway to the ceiling before Rahim caught him.

"If he drifts too far, the Taser barbs will come out of his skin," the Iranian complained.

Lyons tested his wrists again. He had almost a whole centimeter of slack. With a grunt, he dislocated his left thumb, folding it into the palm of his hand as he was dragged back in front of the camera. He didn't know if Blancanales and Schwarz were in position, or if they were still prisoners aboard the *Arcadia*. If he reacted too soon, one of the Celestial Hammer goons could dart across the umbilical and jettison his friends into deep space.

"My name is William Cole, you sack of shit!" Cole snapped. He kicked Lyons in the stomach, but the Able Team commander's abdominal muscles absorbed the impact readily. Meanwhile, Cole had to reach out and grab hold of a strut on the bulkhead to slow his recoil in the low-gravity environment.

"Whatever, Billy," Lyons said. "All I know is, I get to carry out my own imperatives. You just take your orders from a woman in her secret stronghold back on Earth. Really, who's the sack of shit?"

"You're a prisoner, you rotten, thick-browed prick," Cole barked, grabbing Lyons's jaw and pinching his cheeks together.

"I came here willingly. You came under orders," Lyons taunted. He hoped that the Iranian wasn't paying attention to his hands, as his left hand had snaked through four of the cable ties that had been holding his wrists bound together. The dislocated thumb speared agony up his forearm as it ground under the force of the constricting bonds, but he was already hurting so much that he didn't wince as he cleared each tie.

Cole let go. "Commander Rousakis, I need you out of there so I can receive the launch codes for this station's orbiter. If you do not surrender those codes, I'm afraid I'll have no choice but to start killing people, starting with this smart-mouthed establishment ape right here."

Cole pulled out a small box-cutter-style knife, thumbing the blade to full extension. "What do you say?"

"Agent Dutse?" Rousakis asked. "Agent Dutse, what do I do?"

"Personally, I'd tell him to go fuck himself with that pussy-ass little blade, but his asshole's too loose." Lyons grunted.

Rahim's face tightened, trying to fight off a guffaw of laughter. From the crew's fortification, Lyons could hear cheers and chuckles at the astronaut-turncoat's humiliation.

Cole nicked Lyons's cheek, droplets of blood floating into the air between them. "Just for that, I'm going to cut your dick off."

"Come on, Billy. Try for once in your life to be a man and not some pussy ass brown-noser doing what others tell you to."

"Do you realize how insane you are, insulting me when I have a knife to your throat?" Cole asked.

Lyons shrugged. "Saner than you are, chump."

A sudden whip-poor-will chirp filled the air of the station.

"What's that?" Cole asked. He turned back, seeing the smile that had stretched across Carl Lyons's face.

"That's my partners. They're free," Lyons said. "And now, I'm going to kill you."

Cole screamed in fear as Lyons's fingers closed around his throat.

CHAPTER SEVENTEEN

The International Space Station

Schwarz had his improvised pen-dagger ready, and the lock-blade of his multitool rested against his thigh as he reached the end of the umbilical. Rosario Blancanales hovered behind him, a yard back. There was only one advantage up here, Schwarz knew, and that was that firearms would be an exceedingly bad idea for either side. A bullet could pierce the hull of the station or the shuttles, and firearms recoil in zero gravity would throw the shooter off balance. For that matter, thanks to a lack of gravity, the physics of firearms operation and recoil would make accuracy a joke.

Reaching the other end of the umbilical tunnel connecting the *Arcadia* and the space station, he paused, listening to hear if there were enemies waiting in ambush on the other side. He wouldn't put it past the Celestial Hammer's hijackers to give Able Team enough rope to hang themselves, so he held up, waiting.

Schwarz certainly wouldn't hear them walking around the station, so he had to listen for conversation or breathing.

In the distance, he heard the gurgling cries of his partner, Carl Lyons, in pain. The vibrato nature of his grunting informed Schwarz that the enemy was utilizing Tasers. The air-powered darts connected to a high-powered battery were one effective weapon in the zero-gravity environment, since their operation entailed simply Newtonian physics. A pulse of compressed air launched the darts, no need for a rifle barrel or a swinging barrel-link unlocking during firing. The darts would fly true with no difficulty.

He looked back at Blancanales, who'd also heard their leader's suffering. Schwarz nodded to his partner, who tapped his two steel pipes together in a loud clink. If there was anyone on the other side of the hatch, they would have heard that.

Sure enough, a swarthy Iranian face poked around the entrance and Schwarz pistoned his arm straight. The metal point of his pen struck the Celestial Hammer guard in the eye, puncturing the soft orb and plunging through the back of the socket. The brittle bone cradling the Iranian's eye was no impediment to the spearing metal tip as Schwarz's fist stopped against the man's forehead. Three inches of metal were plunged through the orbit, an inch sinking into gray matter.

The Celestial Hammer goon would have let out a cry, but Schwarz brought up his multitool, the three-inch blade spearing through the underside of his jaw. The Iranian's tongue was pinned to the roof of his mouth, jaw clamped shut by the violence of the blow. With two hard twists, he wrenched his weapons loose from the dead man, passing his weightless corpse back through the umbilical. Blancanales pulled the body past him, letting it hang in the middle of the tube as he frisked it for potential weapons.

Schwarz lunged through the hatch, looking around to see if anyone had noticed their sentry had been yanked to his death, but the air-lock chamber was empty. Blancanales popped up behind him, handing a knife, handle-first, to Schwarz.

"Got you a better present than those little stick pins you're packing," Blancanales whispered.

Schwarz took the handle and turned the knife over in his hand. It was a Pakistani knockoff of a Bowie knife, with a seven-and-three-quarter-inch blade. The curved belly of the blade was sharp enough to shave the hairs off his arm, and with enough force, the Bowie would carve through flesh and bone easily. "They sure as hell weren't going to take any chances with the crew."

"More like not take any prisoners," Blancanales answered. "Movement…"

Schwarz kicked off and glided to the corner of the chamber, Blancanales taking the opposite side of the hatch.

"Where the hell did he go?" came a grunt from the other side of the hatch. The voice was thick and heavy with a Russian accent, and a bullet-headed blond figure pushed through the entrance, his forward momentum bringing him right into Blancanales's reach.

Without the ability to put on the brakes in zero gravity, the bulldog-like Celestial Hammer raider flailed wildly as Blancanales snapped one impact weapon across his throat and brought the other down hard on the back of his neck. The two steel pipes struck flesh with incredible force, vertebrae cracking under the neck shot while the Russian's larynx folded under Blancanales's initial swing. Gagging and stunned, the stocky Russian kicked wildly, inadvertently launching his partner, a moon-faced Chinese man, right toward Schwarz.

The Able Team commando lunged with his knife, the point driving into the notch between the Chinese hijacker's throat and collarbone. The powerful blade severed the man's jugular and carotid artery, crimson spilling from the fatal wound before he could recover. Schwarz twisted the blade and slashed the Bowie outward, creating a massive, yawning wound just to make certain his foe was dead.

Blancanales in the meantime had his legs scissored around his opponent's waist, pummeling the Russian in the head with the jagged end of one pipe. The tubular steel tore scalp and broke bone, but the Celestial Hammer bulldog continued to thrash despite violent head trauma. Schwarz was about to come to his partner's aid when a stream of blood and cerebral fluid leaked out of a rift cracked in the raider's skull. Schwarz could tell it was more than just blood because of blobs of diluted fluid mixed in with the thicker blood. The area was filled with floating debris.

Blancanales stuffed his impact weapons down the Russian's collar, drawing an eleven-inch Russian bayonet from the dead man's belt sheath. "At least this crew is keeping in the tradition of the station."

"Iranian, Chinese, Russian," Schwarz said, supplementing his Bowie with a Chinese hatchet that resembled a meat cleaver. "A regular UN of death."

Blancanales nodded. "Time to let Ironman know he doesn't have to worry about our safety."

"All yours," Schwarz said. "You do the bird cries better."

Blancanales cupped his hand over his fist and duplicated the call of a whip-poor-will. The bird cry would carry throughout the station, but would be difficult to target by ear. Blancanales gripped his knife and nodded to Schwarz. "Let's repel boarders."

Schwarz winked. "Aye, aye, me hearty…"

Able Team launched into the next module, blades hungry for flesh.

CARL LYONS, FREED FROM his wrist bindings, lunged with his good hand, protecting his left hand and its dislocated thumb by tucking it against his chest. Iron-strong fingers wrapped around William Cole's throat, but the Iranian Celestial Hammer operative, Rahim, grabbed the Taser and pulled the trigger, spiking 20,000 volts through the barbs inserted in Lyons's chest. The blast of electricity caused Lyons to seize up, his grip increasing exponentially on Cole's throat.

Rahim noticed that Cole's eyes were bulging and he killed the power to the Taser. The end of the voltage broke Lyons's convulsion and he let go of the traitorous astronaut, floating away from him. Rahim yanked hard on the wires connecting the barbs to the Taser's body, raising his foot to hit Lyons in the stomach. The Able Team leader recovered his senses quickly and grabbed the wires, kicking up his feet behind him. Rahim's boot missed his abdomen. Lyons folded, bringing his knees up into Rahim's jaw. The blow snapped the Iranian's head back, jarring the Taser from his grasp.

The blond ex-cop yanked hard, the barbed Taser darts tearing out of the skin on his chest, eliciting a grunt of pain as tines ripped flesh. He threw the wires aside, rotating in the weightless environment. As soon as he was facing the stunned Rahim, he kicked out, feet pushing into the ceiling. To this action, the reaction was iron hard fists crashing into Rahim's chest. The pair dropped to the floor of the station and Lyons grabbed a handful of the Iranian's face, thumb jammed up his nose, ring finger plunged into Rahim's ear hole and fingertips clawing through scalp.

With a snarl, the Able Team leader brought his fist down, sections of scalp ripping loose from Rahim's skull. The Iranian lashed out, trying to rake at Lyons's eyes, but the ex-L.A.P.D. cop blocked the slash with his shoulder, pumping another punch into the gory crater between Rahim's nose and lower lip. Lyons drew back his fist again, cocking it, then speared it down one final time, feeling the crackling of skull bone as he struck Rahim between the eyes. His own knuckles, hardened by countless conflicts and hard-core karate training, were an armored juggernaut that splintered Rahim's maxilofacial structure, plunging those splinters deep into the Iranian's brain.

Lyons looked around, wondering where Cole had gotten to when he spotted Broome struggling to get out of his restraints. Lyons plucked the knife off Rahim's belt and glided across the module.

"You can say I told you so…" Broome began.

"I don't gloat," Lyons said, cutting the pilot free. He turned the knife over to Broome. "Cut the others loose and get back to the *Arcadia*."

Broome nodded and grabbed hold of Lyons. "You'll want those legs free first."

Lyons looked down. "Would be useful."

Broome ran the point across the cable ties wrapped around his shins, and Lyons kicked off, heading toward the next module, giving a sharp whistle as he did so.

SCHWARZ HEARD THE sharp tweet of Carl Lyons, and he knew that his partner was on the loose. He glanced back at Blancanales who had sunk his Russian bayonet deep into the belly of a man who let go of the Bowie knife that he'd tried to use to fillet the Puerto Rican Able veteran. Blancanales twisted the Celestial Hammer mercenary's forearm around violently, dislocating the joint, getting the mercenary's knife pointed away from his own chest.

Schwarz saw a form through the next hatchway and spun to meet it, blades flashing when a stream of pepper spray struck him in the face. The pain was like liquid fire burning across his vulnerable membranes, but he'd been exposed to capsicum-base riot-control sprays before. Though the tissues in his eyes and nose inflamed on contact, he still managed to keep his eyes open enough to see the Celestial Hammer opponent lunge at him.

The marauder with the pepper spray gave a cough as he passed through his own cloud of inflammatory liquid. Even if he hadn't been blasted by his own weapon, he had the misfortune of running into one of the few people ever to go into orbit with not only combat training and experience with tear gas, but the ability to trust senses other than his sight. Schwarz's metaphysical studies had ingrained in him not extra-sensory perception, but the ability to notice things that were on the very periphery of normal perception. While his eyes relayed the image of a blur, lunging with a knife, his adversary's coughing gave a far better "view" of the attacker.

The blinded terrorist's knife whipped through the air, and Schwarz could feel the breeze of its near miss well enough to snap down with the Chinese cleaver hatchet. The sharp blade bit into muscle and bone with savage force, and the pirate screamed as his hand became a useless mass of insensate fingers on the other side of severed nerve endings. Schwarz followed up with his Bowie, spearing the tip down hard. The point glanced off his opponent's skull, splitting the scalp before the point lodged in the attacker's back, stopped by heavy scapula bone.

Schwarz brought his knee up hard, and the Bowie point skittered on the flat plate of bone, carving through connecting muscles that rendered his remaining arm worthless. The tip of the blade glided off the shoulder blade and Schwarz stabbed harder, sinking the fighting knife between ribs close to the spine. He heard a dying wail, and the Able Team warrior let go of the knife, knowing that the steel had become lodged in bone.

"Gadgets!" Lyons grunted from the next module.

"Watch out for the CS, Ironman," Schwarz answered. "I caught a face full of the shit."

"Still managed to take out your dance partner," Lyons noted. Schwarz could feel Lyons take hold of his arm. "Pol! Find some water."

"Got it," Blancanales said. "You need any immediate medical attention, Carl?"

"Flesh wounds only," Lyons replied. "I won't bleed to death from these scratches."

Schwarz rinsed the burning concoction of pepper spray out of his eyes with the damp rag and took a couple of deep breaths. "What were they doing to you?"

"The typical torture shit," Lyons said. "They were trying to get the command codes to the orbiter docked to the station."

"Well, why not just pile everyone on board the *Arcadia?*" Schwarz asked.

"I'll just pretend that the tear gas made you stupid, Gadgets," Lyons answered.

Schwarz grimaced. "Right. They don't have to unbuckle the docked ship. They override the safety measures, hit the thrusters, and they could steer the whole station down."

"One mass breaks up on reentry, and the various modules spin off all along the Eastern Seaboard. If even one strikes a city, the damage would be disastrous," Lyons said.

"I forgot about the lack of maneuvering thrusters on this thing," Schwarz admitted.

"Hey, we just traded places for a second, partner," Lyons told him. "I'll keep your secret if you keep mine."

"When you two love birds are done, there's still a dozen enemies on the loose," Blancanales said. "Where's Cole?"

"He rabbited. You took four?" Lyons asked.

"Five. We're throwing Cole in the final tally," Blancanales stated.

"We've got eleven left. Broome is freeing the rest of the crew. He has a knife with him, but if the Celestial Hammer rushes him…" Lyons began.

"It'll end up bad," Schwarz said. "Lead the way, Ironman."

Lyons whirled and kicked himself back in the direction he came from.

JORDAN BROOME SPOTTED Able Team as they came in and he whipped up his knife, ready to fight. Recognition set in a moment later, and he relaxed.

"These two are my partners," Lyons said to Pavel Rousakis. "Gadgets and Pol."

"No code names?" Broome asked.

"The brain cells storing their cover identities got burned up by Cole's Taser. Commander Rousakis, I think we'd better head to the *Arcadia* before that traitor ends up knocking us out of orbit," Lyons suggested.

Schwarz hovered to a porthole and looked out. "Guys, grab hold of something!"

The ISS crew, the *Arcadia* team and Able Team all seized handholds just a moment before the station jerked violently.

"He's going to use the *Arcadia*'s thrusters to destabilize our orbit," Broome snapped.

"We should have made certain the shuttle was secure before coming here," Lyons grumbled.

Rousakis looked at a workstation monitor and frowned. "Well, the good news is that we've got forty-five minutes before the station is in any position to hit a continent."

The ISS twisted, guided by the maneuvering thrusters on

the *Arcadia*. Lyons dragged himself out of the module, followed by his partners, then Broome and Rousakis.

"Without the emergency shuttle's commands, he's got to aim the station with our ship," Broome mentioned. "But he'll need to save enough fuel to disengage and achieve a controlled glide path."

Lyons grimaced as they entered the airlock. It had been left open, but it would be only a matter of time before the shuttle's twisting broke the interface between it and the station. He glanced at Schwarz. "What are our chances of getting into the *Arcadia* via that airlock?"

"If they'd left me my CPDA, it'd be pretty good. But without it, and with the stresses the engines are putting on the umbilical, we'd be dealing with explosive decompression before I tinkered the panel open," Schwarz said.

"All right," Lyons replied. "Commander, secure this airlock. Gadgets, I don't want Cole getting out of here in one piece."

Schwarz nodded as Rousakis sealed the air lock door. "I've got an idea. When you're done, Commander…"

"Certainly," Rousakis answered.

The electronics genius and the station commander took off through a connecting hatch. Lyons looked to Blancanales. "Pol, go on through and secure the other modules. There's a good chance the Celestial Hammer had sent a suicide squad up here to martyr themselves. I'll check the other…"

The station shook violently, tossing Lyons, Blancanales and Broome around. Lyons dragged himself to a porthole and saw a mechanical arm on the side of the station spearing at the cockpit of the *Arcadia*. Lyons felt a moment of glee as he saw Cole hammering at his windshield, face distorted by angry curses.

"You think Hal's going to take this out of our paychecks?" Blancanales asked.

Lyons watched as the turncoat astronaut and his allies ran off the bridge of the shuttle as Schwarz continued to control the mechanical arm, punching powerful metal claws into the windshield glass. "If he does, it's worth the money."

"I'll wait here," Broome said. "If Cole abandons ship, I want to be here."

Lyons looked at the box-cutter clenched in the astronaut's fist. "Hope you get a crack at him. Pol…"

"I'll stay here and even the odds," Blancanales said.

Lyons leaped through a hatch, beginning his search for members of the Celestial Hammer who'd stayed behind.

WILLIAM COLE HAD BEEN granted reprieve from a very brutal throttling when Rahim jumped "Agent Dutse." He could feel the bruises forming on his ravaged neck and he coughed every other minute to try to dispel the feeling that he had something lodged in his windpipe. He paused at a module and saw several of his Celestial Hammer cohorts preparing high-explosive charges to shear the modules of the International Space Station apart at the seams.

"Cole?" Nang asked, surprised to see him. Nang was the Chinese commander of the Celestial Hammer orbital team. He had been a handpicked member of the conspiracy that Colonel Wing had slipped into the Phoenix Graveyard project.

"Prisoners have escaped," Cole gasped. "Whoever's returning to Earth, we need to get going now!"

Nang sneered. "You should have cut their throats."

"We really don't have time for recriminations," Cole said.

"You're lucky that you're too important for me to just chuck you out into the void," Nang advised. He turned toward six members of his Celestial Hammer team. "Are you ready to be called to free the world?"

The men he addressed clapped their fists against their chests.

Cole violently shook off a chill.

"You've never met someone dedicated to their cause, Cole?" Nang asked.

"There's dedication, and then there's becoming a multiton railroad spike slamming into the heart of a city," Cole returned as he kicked off, heading for the *Arcadia*. Cole spotted the disdain on Nang's face as they headed for the U.S. shuttle. "The prisoners are between us and their shuttle. We'll need to utilize the *Arcadia*'s engines to reposition the station for descent."

"Using up our fuel," Nang complained.

"We'll have enough for a controlled reentry," Cole returned as they entered the air-lock leading to the umbilical. Cole, Nang and the pair of Celestial Hammer operatives who weren't prepared for suicide all paused as they saw two of their compatriots slashed and bludgeoned, hanging lifeless without gravity to deposit them into tidy lumps on the floor. Blood and other fluids hung in the air, indicative of the violence and butchery inflicted upon the pair.

"What about Prahdi?" one of the Celestial Hammer henchmen asked.

Nang floated toward the umbilical and saw Prahdi's corpse suspended in the middle of the interface. He grimaced and reached in, pulling the body out to make room for passage onto the *Arcadia*. He glanced toward his men. "Except for the special team, we're going to have to assume we're the only ones remaining."

The two Celestial Hammer men nodded.

"Cole, get the *Arcadia* going," Nang ordered. "We will be the only survivors of this operation."

Cole floated through, cringing from the globules of blood that had escaped Prahdi's corpse as he was suspended weightless in the station interface tube. He reached the *Arcadia*, wondering if one of the killing machines he'd brought into orbit with him was perched, waiting, like a predator. His luck held out as he cleared his throat, gliding through an empty flight deck toward the cockpit.

Nang buckled into the copilot's seat next to him, and Cole quickly began start-up procedures for the shuttle. The other men took their seats, looking back in the direction of the air lock. Nang had secured both doors, but the umbilical tube was still attached to the shuttle.

"Throttle to fifty percent," Cole announced. The craft shook and even Nang's face tightened with concern as they could hear vibrations of stressed metal through the support struts for the umbilical interface.

"Make sure the station is on target," Nang growled, but any menace that he could summon was diffused by the nervousness in his features.

"I'm working on it. Give me a few minutes here," Cole said.

Nang watched Cole like a hawk, but the astronaut couldn't help thinking of a chimpanzee trying to learn computer code from a top-of-the-line hacker. Cole swallowed, still unable to dispel the feeling of the agent's crushing grasp on his throat as he milked the maneuvering thrusters, swinging the ISS around. He was glad to have the Chinese terrorist quiet for a moment when Nang broke his silence.

"What's that?"

Cole looked up in time to see the manipulator arm dedicated to assisting the *Arcadia*'s positioning air-lock-to-air lock swing toward the shuttle's windshield in a powerful robotic punch. The impact vibrated through the cockpit, and Cole began to scream. He couldn't tell what he was saying, because fear had paralyzed his upper consciousness. All he knew was that his throat had gone sore, and the skin on his cheeks had been drawn as tight as a drum.

Nang unhooked Cole and dragged him out of his seat, growling for him to shut up as he carried Cole like a football tucked under one arm. Finally the Chinese man slapped Cole hard across the face. "Get it together!"

"They were going to break open the cockpit," Cole rasped, his vocal chords destroyed by the panic and rage flooding over them. "They were going to murder us!"

"It's just the same as we were going to do to them," Nang snapped. "Now get your head straight. I don't think they'll be above ruining one ride back to Earth, but they won't be willing to wreck their other ticket home."

Cole nodded, swallowing.

"We're going to clear a path for you," Nang said. "Because if you die, I'm dead. And I'm not as dedicated as the special team."

Cole gulped. "Yes, sir."

Nang drew his knife and opened the air lock, his fellow Celestial Hammer terrorists ready to charge, hot on his heels. "Kill everything in our way."

CHAPTER EIGHTEEN

The Mid-Atlantic

T. J. Hawkins glanced over at David McCarter who fidgeted. The Land Warrior uniforms were great at insulating them from the cool ocean water, which would have thrown them into hypothermia. The life vests they'd removed from the Celestial Hammer launch vehicle kept them afloat and resting, while McCarter's satellite phone sent out a rescue beacon.

"You're more antsy than usual, boss," Hawkins noted.

"Granted, this isn't a Bond movie, otherwise all of you would be beautiful ladies, and we'd have an escape module bobbing, waiting for an aircraft carrier to pick us up," McCarter said.

"I just wish I'd packed some cigarettes away. This waiting is mind-numbing."

Manning reclined on his back placidly in the water. "Patience, David. Didn't you have enough excitement and activity crashing an orbiter into an ocean?"

McCarter grinned. "It was fun, wasn't it?"

"It wasn't," Manning returned. "But I do have to admit that the disembarkment lounge is most comfortable."

"All you need are the umbrella drinks," Encizo quipped. "And yeah, we need more bikini-clad *mamacitas* on hand."

"I heard that, you goofs," Barbara Price's voice cut over their communications net. "We've got a Sea Stallion approaching. You've got about ten minutes before they show up."

"Back to work," James complained. "Back to reality…"

"Such as it is," Manning murmured, drowsily enjoying floating in the calm waters.

"With that tone of voice, it sounds as if you've gotten a lead on the Celestial Hammer's home base?" McCarter asked.

"Not yet," Price returned. "Akira's been repelling attempts to detect us. They've been rolling with our cyberpunches, as if they're drawing us out in a way that they can get the Farm's coordinates."

"A possible attack?" Manning inquired, ending his relaxing float.

"Given the tools that the Celestial Hammer has displayed, it's not impossible that they have something to throw at us," Price said. "They just need a bull's-eye, and we can expect anything from a thermobaric warhead to a low-yield nuke."

"I take it you're already scanning for potential launch platforms on the water," James offered.

"The team's trying," Price informed them. "But with the effort put into stopping satellite orbit adjustments and their interference on our eyes in the sky, Carmen's having to go by radar and communications logs. Dead-reckoning ship positions the old-fashioned way."

"If anyone's smart enough to do that," Manning spoke up, "it's her."

"It's a lot of drudge work, unfortunately," Price stated.

"Any more satellites knocked out of the sky?" McCarter asked.

"Fortunately, we've been able to keep their hackers on the

run, but again, that might just be a feint. They're getting us to overexpose our resources for a cybernetic counterattack," Price explained.

Encizo looked skyward. "I see the helicopter."

"They'll pick you up," Price said. "We've got a quintet of two-seater F-18s on the Stallion's home ship ready to ferry you to your next staging area."

McCarter nodded. "Then you are getting closer."

"We hope," Price said.

"What about Carl and the others?" Manning asked.

"We've lost contact with *Arcadia* and the International Space Station," Price answered after a brief pause. "Although, ground control is reporting that the station has altered its orbit."

McCarter's jaw tightened.

"We're working to reestablish contact," Price said.

"And what about the USAF?" McCarter asked.

"They've scrambled enough to deploy antisatellite missiles on their interceptors," Price replied. "They'll be able to shoot anything heading for a city."

McCarter looked at his teammates, realizing that even if their friends didn't get shot out of the upper atmosphere with antisatellite weaponry, they wouldn't survive a plummet from thousands of miles up. "Just get that helicopter here so we can find the Celestial Hammer's command center."

Price could feel the barely restrained rage in the Briton's voice. "We're on it."

The International Space Station

CARL LYONS SAW THE hulking figure of a man adjusting a shearing charge on the interface between two of the station's modules. The man glared as he noticed Lyons's presence, a heavy beetle brow furrowing at the sight.

"You are the one who keeps our world in shackles," the beast of a man said.

"I didn't come into outer space to debate politics with a nihilist asshole," Lyons returned. "You can just surrender and let me defuse your bomb."

The massive anarchist grinned. "That Taser must have fried your brain. For freedom, I will destroy you!"

The hulking Celestial Hammer warrior lunged toward Lyons, and the Able Team leader didn't flinch, instead launching himself to meet the terrorist head-on. The pair collided and Lyons could feel the breath knocked out of him by the impact, but where his enemy had bulk, Lyons had enough speed and power to counter his mass. The big ex-cop whipped a punch toward the giant thug's kidney, but the blow bounced off powerful oblique muscles. The rabbit punch would have left anyone else folded over and vomiting his guts up, if he didn't go into immediate renal shock from the hit. The Celestial Hammer monster wrapped his hand around Lyons's head and yanked hard. Lyons kept himself from being tossed like a rag doll by snaring his legs around the big man's thigh, his neck muscles screaming in pain as the huge thug tried to twist his head off.

Lyons fired off a flurry of high-speed punches, raining his clubbing knuckles on his larger opponent's ribs and sides, getting off at least three more kidney shots. The effect released a series of grunts from his adversary, who lifted one arm, hand held flat like a hatchet's blade. Before the giant could bring down a chop that would break Lyons's neck, the Able Team leader snapped off a hard blow into his enemy's armpit. With a major juncture of blood vessels, muscles and nerves clumped under the shoulder joint, the punch finally registered more than a wheeze of discomfort. The terrorist let go of Lyons's head and twisted, his arm flopping limply.

Unfortunately for the wounded titan, Lyons was still

wrapped around his thigh, and the big ex-cop formed his hand into a spear, launching his rigid fingers into the hollow of the raider's throat. The giant tried to protect his windpipe by putting his jaw in the way, but he was too slow, and blood vomited from between sputtering lips.

Lyons followed up by untangling his legs from around his adversary's thigh, swinging them up to scissor the choking giant around his neck. Stunned, the big man hammered on Lyons's knees and shins, but the lack of gravity lessened the strength of the blows. Lyons reached up, grabbing two handholds on the side of the module and wrenched his legs hard.

The Celestial Hammer fighter's neck exploded under the horrible power of Lyons's leg muscles, his eyes bulging from their lids, tongue extending like a purple parasite trying to escape dying lips. With another hard twist, he completely destroyed whatever bone structure was in the terrorist's neck, only muscle and sinew keeping the dead man's head on his shoulders. Lyons let go and snaked through the hatch to look over the bomb.

"Heim!" a voice called from the next module. "Heim! Where the hell are you?"

Lyons grabbed the floating body and shoved it in front of him as a shield.

"Oh my God!" the Celestial Hammer martyr gasped, looking at Heim's distorted face and flopping neck.

Lyons shoved the dead man's massive bulk, striking the newcomer and plowing him against the bulkhead. The suicide astronaut snarled angrily, drawing his knife, but with Heim's corpse between them, all he could do was mutilate his lifeless compatriot. Lyons shifted Heim's mass, pinning the knife-man's arm, then he reached around, wrapping his fingers around the space raider's throat.

"Do these bombs have failsafe measures?" Lyons growled,

applying enough force to raise wormlike veins in his captive's forehead.

"No!" the terrorist rasped. "We were going to kill everyone on the station. No one would have been alive to tamper with them. Besides, we were to detonate the charges ourselves."

Lyons squeezed tighter. "If you're lying, I'll take the rest of this station's existence to carve pieces off your body to stuff down your throat."

"You don't…" the Celestial Hammer started, attempting to voice his defiance, but Lyons's fingers had dug into his neck's major blood vessels, and his eyes were blurring. He could barely gasp down a wheeze of breath under the crushing force of the Able Team commander's grip. Suddenly, martyrdom didn't seem so glorious.

"Tamper measures?" Lyons asked.

"None," the terrorist croaked.

Lyons let go of Heim's body, and wrapped his other hand around the martyr's neck. With a surge of his shoulder muscles, he wrenched the terrorist's head 180 degrees, broken vertebral bones slicing though his spinal column. The twist was instantaneous, giving the man a quick, painless death after the uncomfortable interrogation.

Lyons whistled, blaring his tune to sound like a police siren. The whistle would carry through the station, letting his partners know that he had encountered enemy action. He hoped that Schwarz would start looking for him now that he'd shaken up the crew of hijackers who had taken the *Arcadia.*

They needed to fix the orbital path of the space station before it took a crashing nose dive through the atmosphere. And still, there was the menace of the remaining Celestial Hammer martyrs.

SCHWARZ HEARD LYONS'S whistle and wished that he could answer, but he was wrestling with an Iranian for control of his hatchet. The suicide astronaut had come upon him operating the remote manipulator arm, and lunged. Only the growl of anger from the man had given Schwarz enough of a warning to avoid having his back speared by an enemy knife. The pair struggled over the handle of the deadly meat cleaver, knowing that the first one to relent would end up with his head hanging from a thread of skin. The Iranian tried to gouge at Schwarz's eyes, but the electronics genius lowered his head behind his biceps, and brought his knee up with all the force he could muster.

Though his genitals were mashed against his pubic bone, the Iranian's grip on the cleaver didn't relent. In fact, it tightened, his other hand clawing hard into Schwarz's forearm. Nails tore the Stony Man commando's skin, drawing blood. Schwarz grimaced, knowing that his options were running out. He spotted movement in the corner of his eye, and he let go of the cleaver.

Another true believer of the Celestial Hammer speared forward to ambush the Able Team commando, but Schwarz kicked off, putting the newcomer between himself and the Iranian he was battling. The cleaver flicked through the air, its sharp hatchet edge striking the new arrival between his neck and shoulder, snapping the collarbone and several ribs. The Iranian tried to rip the cleaver free, but his blow had been so powerful, the blade was stuck between broken snarls of rib. The mortally wounded raider complicated matters further by grabbing onto the Iranian's wrists, eyes imploring an explanation for the deadly betrayal.

Schwarz didn't waste his opponent's lapse of attention. As if swinging from a trapeze, the Stony Man expert swung on two handholds, his boot heels striking the surprised Iranian in the jaw with enough power to shoot him into the next module.

"I could get used to zero gravity combat," Schwarz muttered as he launched himself after his foe.

The suicide bomber blinked, trying to recover his senses when Schwarz whipped out his multitool, the spear-point blade gleaming from his fist. The Iranian grabbed a clipboard and brought it up just in time to block the spearing knife, two inches of glimmering steel pushing through the lightweight aluminum. The Iranian snarled and twisted the clipboard, popping the multitool free from Schwarz's grasp, only to realize that his opponent hadn't run out of weapons. Schwarz's improvised push dagger, made from the high-tensile-strength metal pen, slashed up and punched into the terrorist's rib cage. The impact and the puncture wound pinned the Iranian to the bulkhead in surprise and pain. Before he could push the Able Team warrior away, Schwarz grabbed a handful of curly black hair and dragged the terrorist's head under his elbow. Forearm closed over the Iranian's throat, Schwarz kicked off from the wall, utilizing his momentum and his foe's bracing to break the man's neck.

The sound of breaking vertebrae was as loud as a gunshot in the space station's module.

Breathless from the effort, Schwarz let his dead foe flop limply in open air.

"Ironman!" he called.

He heard Lyons's curt whistle to his right, and Schwarz looked over to see the Able Team leader floating through a hatch.

"They're setting shearing charges between each of the modules," Lyons said. "But they don't have any tamper-resistant fuses."

"I know. I got a look at three of them before defusing them," Schwarz answered. "Simple, ordinary wads of C-4 with radio detonators."

"Do you think you can do anything with the C-4?" Lyons asked. "I don't know what kind of maneuvering thrusters the space station has, but I doubt that it's not going to be enough to put on the brakes against what Cole did to it."

"The C-4 could be used to generate thrust in order to deflect our course, at least until NASA can launch an emergency operation to stabilize things."

"For every action, there's an equal and opposite reaction," Lyons said. "I figure without much in way of gravity or air resistance…"

"Yeah," Schwarz answered. "I figure the Celestial Hammer brought up about thirty kilos of this stuff. I've recovered two-thirds of it so far."

"And it's likely we've got between two and four of them left behind in the station," Lyons said.

"Wish you'd have thought to recover our communicators," Schwarz muttered. "In case Pol's run into more than he could handle."

"Or we could flip frequencies and talk to Rousakis and his crew," Lyons said.

"They've secured themselves in their reentry vehicle," Schwarz explained. "It's not much, and if we packed in there with the ISS crew, it'd make a sardine can seem spacious."

"I'd been hoping they'd have a shuttle like we had," Lyons admitted.

"No. That doesn't mean that it doesn't have enough thrust to spin the station out of its orbital path like Cole did with the *Arcadia*'s engines," Schwarz said. "Accommodations would just be tight. The station usually only needs to have room for three people. Six would be able to fit, but we've got nine people up here."

"Nine who should go home," Lyons countered. "I've got movement ahead."

Schwarz had recovered the knife that the Iranian had dropped in the manipulator arm control room to replace his lost and used-up weapons. "What's the plan?"

"So far, they haven't gotten it into their heads that they should activate the shearing charges," Lyons said.

"They want to save that for when they hit the atmosphere. The explosions would split the station apart, turning it into multiple projectiles, making it harder for interceptors to blow it out of the sky, and they'll be more likely to strike a population center," Schwarz returned. "Up here, all they would get is us. And while Hal would miss us…"

"Yeah," Lyons said. He looked at the bandages that Blancanales had put on his chest. He tore them off, ripping the scabs off his bleeding pectorals where the Taser darts had ripped his skin. He did the same with the bandage covering his cut and bloody cheek. Schwarz raised an eyebrow, then realized that his partner was caked in blood, and the freshly stripped wounds were bleeding again.

Lyons gave a sickly gurgle, kicking toward the module where the other Celestial Hammer killers were lying in wait. He floated limply, trailing streams of blood.

Schwarz ducked under a console, waiting for his partner's ruse to lure the enemy out.

"It's the blond one," one of the station raiders said, floating through a hatch.

"He doesn't have any weapons, but be careful, Jacques," the other pirate countered.

Jacques reached out to Lyons, prodding him. The Able Team leader remained motionless, doing a perfect imitation of a corpse. "See, Yves? He would have reacted if I'd touched him."

Lyons had been holding his breath, so as not to give away the fact that he was still alive. Yves came into the module, but kept his distance, backing away from the Able Team leader's apparent corpse, retreating down the corridor toward Schwarz.

"Give him another poke, this time with the business end of your knife," Yves said. "He might just be unconscious."

Jacques chuckled. "He's not even breathing."

Jacques's humor disappeared when he spotted Schwarz explode from his hiding space behind Yves. With a swing of an arm around a throat and several deep bites of the combat blade, the terrorist was a bloody mass of twitching flesh in the Stony Man commando's grasp. "Yves!"

Lyons burst into action, throwing a punch that struck Jacques across the jaw, breaking it like a cheap plate. While the Celestial Hammer martyr was stunned, Lyons grabbed a fistful of the man's hair and pushed it against the bulkhead. The Stony Man leader felt bone break on the third crash.

"Gadgets?" Lyons asked.

"I got their radio detonators," Schwarz answered. "Let's whip up an improvised rocket."

"You do that. I have to check to see if we've secured the *Arcadia,*" Lyons returned.

"Good plan. I'll meet you in the manipulator control center," Schwarz said. "There's an intercom that I can talk to Rousakis and his crew."

"Good luck. Keep an eye out in case there are any more of these bastards floating around," Lyons warned.

With that, he headed back to the air lock to reunite with Blancanales and Broome.

CAPTAIN JORDAN BROOME realized he was in trouble when not one but three members of the hijacking squad burst through the umbilical leading from the *Arcadia* into the station's air lock. It was a good thing that he had Rosario Blancanales by his side, however.

The agile veteran of countless wars had a three-foot section of pipe as a weapon, and with his lightning fast *bo-jutsu* strikes, he filled the hatch with stunned terrorists. Utilizing his preferred melee combat tool, Blancanales caught Nang under the chin while staying out of range of the Chinese turncoat's fighting knife. While Nang recoiled off the ceiling of the umbilical, folded in pain, his two allies were snarled behind his stunned form. In slow motion Blancanales lunged like a fencer, spiking the end of his pipe into the forehead of the thug on the left, then looping the length of pipe under Nang's dangling feet to crack the other across the kidney.

The one hit in the kidney winced, but kept coming. Blancanales drew his improvised *bo* back enough to bat the box-cutter out of his hand, the steel proving too much for wrist bone. The terrorist screamed in pain, but kicked off the edge of the hatch, trying to get inside Blancanales's defenses. Instead of getting the jump on the eldest member of Able Team, the hijacker found himself with a broken cheekbone and double vision as Blancanales rapped the pipe across his face.

The other Celestial Hammer minion, his forehead split and bleeding, pushed his boss aside and headed through the air lock, fingers hooked like claws as if he intended to pull Blancanales's entrails out with his bare hands. Blancanales dissuaded that notion with a sharp turn, bringing his foot up to catch the man in the center of his face. The terrorist's nose broke, blood jetting out from the ruptured organ, and he lost his forward momentum, fingers grasping only at empty air.

Blancanales twisted in midair, bringing his feet around to cushion his impact with the far bulkhead.

Broome broke out of his stunned observation of the initial skirmish and lunged into action, grabbing the shuttle thief with the broken cheek and pummeling him in the kidney, utilizing the hilt of his knife as brass knuckles. By the time the astronaut realized that he had a blade with which to cause greater damage to his opponent, the Celestial Hammer fighter brought his elbow down, catching Broome in the temple. The blow stunned him, but only for an instant.

The injured hijacker looked around for his blade, but saw Broome's fist, an emerald ring on his middle finger, flash out of nowhere, catching him on the bridge of the nose. The ring cracked bone, but not enough to be fatal. That didn't matter as Broome pressed his attack, swiping the knife across his opponent's throat. The razor-sharp blade was deflected by the tough, fibrous nature of the human windpipe, the slash only causing ghastly but superficial damage. Blood flew, forming amorphous blobs in the air. Broome turned to go after Nang, but a hand reached out for his collar and pulled hard.

Broome gagged as his collar yanked hard across his larynx, and only the fact that he was weightless kept him from hanging himself on his own jumpsuit. He sailed back against the bulkhead, his shoulders taking most of the impact. It was enough to loosen the knife from his grip, and the Celestial Hammer killer grabbed for it.

Blancanales whirled and cracked his *bo* across the terrorist's arm, hard enough to elicit the crack of breaking forearm bones. The bloodied terrorist curled his arm in, glaring at the Able Team warrior, and when he looked back at Broome, he was surprised to see a pair of boots coming up under his jaw. The Celestial Hammer man was propelled by the powerful muscles in Broome's legs, the top of his skull stopping at the bulkhead. Unfortunately for the bloodied pirate, Broome's boots didn't stop, dislocating the hijacker's jaw with a wet, sickly crunch.

Cole was somewhere on the *Arcadia* and sooner or later he was going to try to go back to the cockpit and disengage the shuttle from the space station. Broome hurtled along, sheer determination taking him to what would be a face-to-face confrontation.

CHAPTER NINETEEN

Fifteen miles off the coast of Virginia

Jack Grimaldi, at the controls of an F/A-18C Hornet, had been in the air for half an hour. Barbara Price knew that the ace Stony Man pilot wouldn't be able to help out Phoenix Force in the mid-Atlantic, and he'd been left behind when Able Team was sent into orbit. Rather than allowing their top wingman to stew, waiting for news about friends far from home, Price had sent him to Naval Station Oceana in Virginia, and got him into the cockpit of the single-seat fighter.

Carmen Delahunt, who was searching for potential hostile craft off the Eastern Seaboard, was directing him toward suspicious freighters that were being tracked by radar. Without satellite observation, denied to them by the Celestial Hammer's team of Walt and Lance Woodrow, Grimaldi was going to have to serve as their eyes in the sky.

Fortunately, in its attack role, the Hornet had excellent eyes and ground-effect radar, enabling the attack fighter to not only be a top dog fighter, but a devastating antiship and antifortification bomber. Grimaldi rode twin 18,000-pound thrust streams blowing out the nacelles of his Hornet's F404 GE engines. He'd hit afterburners after scanning one of Delahunt's suspicious ships, not wanting to waste time getting to the next freighter.

Grimaldi suspected that if the Celestial Hammer had an armed ship out here, the minute they saw him, they'd launch an attack on the coast. Given the number of submarines and missiles that had slipped out of the Russian military's back doors since the collapse of the Soviet Union, Grimaldi was glad for the fact that the F/A-18C had radar good enough to detect submarines. He just knew that if it were a Soviet-era combat sub, they'd be able to dive and fire with relative impunity unless he flashed over them, even with the nacelle sensor pod under his starboard wing, balancing out an AGM-84 Harpoon missile. AIM-120 Slammers were on the outermost pylons, four air-to-air missiles that could hit targets at thirty miles. The inboard wing stations had another four of the Harpoons, perfect if he had to fight off a German wolf pack.

"Are you sure they won't have a sub?" Grimaldi asked.

"I'm not promising you a rose garden, Jack," Delahunt said. "However, enough ships have been engaging in funky activity off the coast. Might just be smuggling, might be something worse. The sensor pod you're packing will let us know if they're packing weaponry."

Grimaldi's lips drew tight. "I'm closing in on your next suspect craft. You picking this up on radar?"

"Men with guns on the rail," Delahunt said. "But nothing on deck that resembles a missile launcher. They're just smugglers. I've got them tagged for the Coast Guard now."

"Why use missile launchers when they're dropping satellites and improvised bombs from orbit?" Grimaldi asked.

"Because dropping things from orbit hasn't been the most successful of ventures," Delahunt replied. "The Celestial

Hammer must have known that it would need backup to make certain that important targets weren't protected by a temperature fluctuation, knocking a reentry path miles off course."

Grimaldi veered away from the ship and darted north, heading for a boat that Delahunt had marked for him on a GPS map. He'd toyed with the idea of cutting loose with the Hornet's 20 mm cannon, giving the armed thugs on the freighter some blind terror in the form of explosive shells. There were important threats out on the sea this morning, though. And there was no guarantee that the armed gunmen weren't just ordinary guards, on alert for pirates or unnerved by the rain of deadly projectiles from orbit.

The suspicious ship was miles behind him, and Grimaldi checked his fuel. He knew that the Hornet could be ferried eighteen hundred nautical miles, but operating in a patrol, his combat radius was less than a quarter of that. Even so, he could engage in combat air patrol for an hour and forty-five minutes on his fuel reserves.

He just wished that Delahunt would steer him toward a target that he could attack. Grimaldi nursed a secret hope that one of her suspect freighters was actually their mobile command center, and that a Harpoon missile would be enough to finish this crisis, bringing his friends back home to recover from their hectic missions.

Grimaldi sighed. He doubted that he would be that lucky. He scanned the horizon, looking for trouble when his threat monitor blazed red.

Someone had locked antiaircraft radar on him.

"Ah, the perfect target for my frustration," Grimaldi said. He was about to hit the chaff, a countermeasure to the radar lock, when he paused.

"Jack, what's wrong?" Delahunt asked.

"Carmen, kill the data link now!" Grimaldi ordered.

"But… Ending link," Delahunt said, sounding a little confused. She'd learned to trust the instincts of the Stony Man field operatives.

Grimaldi saw activity on the deck of the freighter, a 150-footer. Smoke billowed from behind a boxlike object, and he knew that it was already too late.

Jottunheim Station

DEIDRE TANIT RECEIVED THE summons from Walter and Lance Woodrow and rushed to their side, Magni Piarow on her heels.

"What's up?" Tanit asked.

"It seems our opposition has sent up a strike fighter to look for any sign of us along the coast," Walter said.

Lance brought up a radar screen from their tanker, the *Vadim.* "It appears to be a strike fighter. It reached speeds of Mach 2, checking out ships in the area."

Tanit leaned over, peering at the screens. "It could just be a combat air patrol, looking for satellites aimed at the coast or at shipping lanes."

"We've managed to sneak around their push," Walter agreed. "And we've gotten lower priority satellites to adjust out of orbit. Nothing has struck a population greater than 5000 people, but that's because of patrols around the world."

"We mostly plop wreckage into rural communities, or suburban areas when an air-to-air missile deflects the satellite a few degrees," Lance added. "This one, however, was launched from Oceana, but it's not on the Naval communication network."

"Oceana?" Tanit asked.

Piarow nodded. "That's the name for the Naval Air Station in Virginia."

Tanit straightened. "So the enemy managed to snag a strike fighter, and is looking for what?"

"Presumably any backup threats we have on the seaboard, and perhaps, in a fit of egocentricism, thinking that we might have our headquarters close to their shores," Walter said.

"If we could only figure out the fighter's comm frequency, we'd be able to triangulate who it was in communication with," Lance added. "Unfortunately, if we have the *Vadim*'s electronic warfare suite scan it, they'll know who we are and disengage communication before we could acquire a target."

"I've got an idea." Barry LeBlanc spoke up. The Woodrows had called in a friend. "I've been able to narrow down and eliminate comm sources along the Eastern Seaboard. All we have to do is keep their minds off their headquarters, and then we'll have all the targets in the area finalized."

"If we opened fire with our Russian navy surface-to-surface missiles just to take out the covert agency opposing us, the other military bases around Washington, D.C., would track us. We have to hit them all at once, but if we do that without hitting those mystery spooks…" Lance began.

"They'd be able to direct retribution strikes against the *Vadim*," Tanit finished. "I know. They hit that ship, we lose our last ditch against the fascists."

"That's where my idea comes in," LeBlanc said. "Have the *Vadim* light up the enemy fighter with its antiaircraft systems."

Tanit's brow furrowed.

Piarow smiled. "Brilliant. They'll be too interested in analyzing the data from the ship now that it's proved itself hostile, they won't notice you homing in on their data link."

"It's got a sensor suit onboard, and since its data isn't going back to naval command and control, that means it's being piped directly to enemy headquarters," LeBlanc said.

"Do it. Put me through to Manley," Tanit ordered. "That fighter's getting close."

Stony Man Farm, Virginia

CARMEN DELAHUNT GRIMACED as she checked the screen. Someone had managed to locate the data link from the F/A-18C and utilize the signal to home in on the Farm itself. She hit the alarm.

Price and the others whirled as the Klaxons went off.

"The Celestial Hammer has us located," Delahunt said. "The *Vadim* lit up Jack with radar, and that was enough to keep us from noticing that they had dug their claws into the data link."

"What was the last information you got from Grimaldi's plane?" Kurtzman asked, rolling over to her station.

"The *Vadim* had a sixteen-pack missile launcher," Delahunt answered. "From the construction, it's a knockoff of our own Tomahawk systems. The launcher is prepped to fire, and we've got another ten seconds before the Celestial Hammer codes in our coordinates."

Kurtzman grimaced. "The Farm has Phalanx antimissile cannons, but depending on the warheads those things have, it might not be enough."

Price looked at the monitor. "No cybermagic?"

"All we've got is a communications relay from the *Vadim* back to whoever it's talking to," Kurtzman explained. "Akira…"

Tokaido whirled, his fingers flying feverishly across the keyboard. "I'm sending my search results to Strong Base One. If we're torched, Johnny will be able to direct Mack to take out the remnants of the Celestial Hammer."

"I've got Langley Air Field alerted to the threat of the *Vadim*." Hunt Wethers spoke up. "Fighters are launching now, and hopefully they'll be in place to screen the city against the Tomahawk knockoffs."

"How long ago was it that you ended contact with Jack?" Price asked Delahunt.

"We're going on twenty-eight seconds," she told the Stony Man chief officer. "But if he's come under attack from anti-aircraft systems, I don't think that he'll be able to do anything."

Price took a deep breath. "He's one of the best pilots in the world. If anyone can pull our fat out of the fryer, it's him."

"We have radar contact with blips leaving the *Vadim!*" Wethers announced.

"And what about Jack?" Kurtzman asked.

JACK GRIMALDI PULLED THE Hornet up as the first of the *Vadim*'s heat-seeking missiles launched from her deck. Kicking in the afterburner, he stood the strike fighter on its tail, eighteen tons of concentrated thrust throwing the aircraft deep into the sky. With a spin of the stick, he flipped the Hornet upside down and plunged back toward the *Vadim*. The g-forces leaning on Grimaldi's chest were intense, but he reminded himself that it was nothing compared to what his allies in Able Team and Phoenix Force had gone through. Had it not been for the g-suit, utilizing water to cushion his body, he easily could have dislocated limbs or had the breath crushed from his chest.

The high-G turn brought him blasting down the throats of the surface-to-air missiles sent after him, and Grimaldi speared the Hornet between them in a blistering power dive that sent the SAMs spiraling, desperately trying to find the disappearing strike fighter in their forward radar cones. Their processors weren't intelligent enough to imagine that someone had decided to play chicken at over twice the speed of sound.

The brains of the antiaircraft missiles had never been programmed with a flying genius like Jack Grimaldi in mind. The launcher on the deck was hot, according to the infrared scanners on the underwing pod. The Stony Man ace milked the trigger on the Vulcan cannon, spitting a storm of 20 mm rounds down toward the renegade vessel. Though he couldn't see the damage because of the distance, he knew that the explosive rounds were striking the deck with devastating force.

Flames erupted on the *Vadim,* and Grimaldi thought he had done the job in crippling the ship when he saw fiery contrails streaking away from the ship. He recognized them immediately as surface-to-surface missiles. With a twist of the wrist, he yanked out of the power dive, locking his targeting radar on the salvo of SSMs racing toward the coast.

His head's-up display indicated locks on three of the four SSMs and Grimaldi let fly with the Hornet's AIM-120 missiles. The solid-fuel rockets in the Slammers, as the Navy called them, could accelerate the interceptor missiles to Mach 4, matching even the fastest of Tomahawk variants. Leaning into the throttle, he poured on the afterburner power as his Slammers chased down the SSMs. There was one explosion, a brilliant flash filling the air, bright even in broad daylight. A second and a third followed, but he still couldn't get a lock on the fourth SSM as the distance to the coast disappeared.

He clicked on his com link to Stony Man Farm, but found out that he was jammed. Grimaldi idly wondered if that was the work of the Celestial Hammer, or perhaps the Farm had gone on full lockdown. It didn't matter, because the fourth surface-to-surface missile burned a dangerous path toward Washington, D.C. Probably the same interference that kept him from contacting the Farm was protecting the last of the city-smashing warheads in its relentless journey to apocalyptic fulfillment.

"Fuck it," Grimaldi swore, and he triggered the M-61 Vulcan again. The thundering cannon ripped off a twenty-five-round burst, explosive shells slicing through the air in the wake of the Tomahawk knockoff. He adjusted his aim and fired again, 20 mm cannon rounds missing the SSM by a hair. Its own protective radar had picked up the threat of the onslaught of lead from Grimaldi's gun, and it juked to one side to escape destruction.

His cockpit yelled at him, warning of more radar locks on the Hornet, and Grimaldi tripped the chaff launcher, filling the sky behind him with radar-scrambling metal foil. The radar locks disengaged, but at the rate he was eating up sky, he'd be out of the chaff cloud's protective shadow in no time. Grimaldi raked the air again, holding down the trigger for a hundred rounds of explosive damnation, tracer rounds turning the burst into a glowing, curving laser that sliced across the body of the SSM.

Smoke vomited from fatal wounds in the side of the missile, and its kerosene fuel detonated in sympathy with one 20 mm air burst round that had burned its way through its metal hull. A thunderclap split the missile in two, ending its suicide run toward a city of millions. Grimaldi swung the Hornet around, looking for a course back to the *Vadim* when he spotted a squadron of F-15s from Langley Air Force Base lashing through the clouds.

"Jack?" Price's voice cut in. "Jack, can you read us?"

"Loud and clear, where'd you go?" Grimaldi asked.

"Someone was jamming us," Price answered. "We thought we'd have to call in help for you, but it looks like you took out the first wave of enemy missiles."

"One wave down, but according to my sensors, that was a 16-shot launcher," Grimaldi said.

"The F-15s are engaging the subsequent launches. It looks like your strafing run slowed down the firing process enough for the planes out of Langley to intercept them," Price said by way of congratulating him. "I figure you'd want another shot at the *Vadim*."

"Thanks, Barb," Grimaldi answered. He checked his targeting computer. The freighter was a fat, vulnerable target, sitting beyond the horizon, but utilizing the sensors on the Hornet, Grimaldi got a lock. He brought two of his AGM-84 Harpoons on line, then kicked in the afterburners.

He wanted to see the *Vadim* blown to splinters.

The Harpoons took flight to burrow deep into the floating carcass ahead of him, and Grimaldi chased them. The warheads exploded just as the vessel rolled up over the horizon, and Grimaldi could see the impacts of both missiles, twin stars of smoke and debris that looked tiny in the distance. The Stony Man pilot throttled down, swinging closer to the gutted vessel, seeing fat, choking rivers of smoke and fire bleeding out of two massive craters in her side. The Harpoon missiles had a reputation for being ship killers, and even one was enough to break apart a nonmilitary ship. The *Vadim* had been broken into three pieces, only a thin section of railing connecting two segments of the wounded, dying craft.

The gutted sections twisted apart as one piece flopped onto its side, wrenching what was left of its hull and tearing it like a sheet of paper. Grimaldi pulled away from the dying ship, letting out his tension in a single, long breath,

"Celestial Hammer ship scratched. No visible survivors," Grimaldi said.

"Get back to Oceana and refuel," Price ordered.

"Did you find anything useful?" Grimaldi asked.

"We're backtracking their communications," Price replied. "We're working on narrowing things down. You can gas up, and then hop over to Greenland for refueling."

"The North Atlantic?" Grimaldi said, bringing the Hornet around, pointing it toward Oceana.

"It's still a big area, but if we could narrow it down, we'll have the Celestial Hammer in the position of an anvil," Price told him.

"Count me in for that hammer to fall," Grimaldi said, throwing the Hornet into a barrel roll.

He wouldn't miss this kill for the world.

The International Space Station

ROSARIO BLANCANALES HAD launched a wicked strike against the terrorist's throat, his steel pipe crushing the space raider's larynx with brutal force.

Nang recovered from his initial encounter with Blancanales's improvised *bo* and lunged, his blade slashing. Blancanales blocked, steel ringing on steel, the clang echoing through the air lock chamber. The Able Team veteran twisted, barely avoiding having Nang's knife point slice across his ribs. With a hard snap, Blancanales brought up his elbow, crashing it alongside the Celestial Hammer leader's jaw with enough force to make Nang let go of the knife. Clawing fingers wrapped around Blancanales's fighting stick, and the pair was locked in a struggle for control.

Blancanales noticed that Broome had gone through the air lock to get to the *Arcadia*. If any of them were going to get home in one piece, they'd need to secure the space shuttle. He silently wished Broome luck, then let go of the steel pipe. Nang's sudden control of the three-foot weapon came at the expense of his position. The sheer violence with which he tore the pipe away from Blancanales provided him with enough momentum to sail back against the bulkhead.

With the impact against the hull, Nang lost control of yet another weapon in his command. He sneered, blood dribbling in a twisting, weightless thread from his lips.

"Damn you," Nang snarled.

"Just because I was a better study at zero gravity than you are is no reason to get hostile," Blancanales said. He kept his voice light and jaunty, despite the fact that he felt nothing like a swashbuckler. He floated, keeping a smirk on his face, hoping to taunt his opponent into foolish action.

Nang wasn't falling for it, and he held his ground, looking

around. He obviously hoped that one of the weightless weapons floating through the air lock would come into reach. Blancanales kicked and floated to the far side of the chamber, so that he was directly across from the Celestial Hammer leader.

"You won't have me striking out brashly again," Nang said. "I've spent too long in training for this day. I will see this abomination torn from the lap of heaven and smeared in the face of the pathetic little mortals who dare to put the sky and Earth in chains."

"In chains?" Blancanales asked. He snorted in derision. "You really are completely clueless. This station is meant to be a joint effort in exploration. If anything, we're doffing the chains of earthly confinement. Over the next few centuries, humanity will find its freedom in the stars. Provided we get rid of the small-minded scumbags like you and your terrorist kin."

"Sure, wrap your fascism in pretty lies and call it democracy," Nang returned. "Ever find those weapons of mass destruction?"

Blancanales shrugged. "We've found enough. But if you're done with that soapbox, maybe you could grab that knife off to your side and we can get down to serious business."

Nang looked over, noticing the hovering blade. He reached out, scooping it up. A grim smile crossed his Asian features. "You're going to regret letting me arm myself."

"Anything so I don't have to listen to your ignorant nihilism," Blancanales returned.

Nang snarled and lunged, rocketing off the air lock wall. He speared across the space between them, but Blancanales was ready. The Able Team veteran lurched to one side, the knife coming within inches of slicing skin. Blancanales looped his arm around Nang's, then snapped off a short palm-strike that rocked the Chinese terrorist's head on his shoulders.

Nang's eyes unfocused for a moment, and Blancanales

pressed his attack, spearing his knee up into his breastbone. With the air hammered out of his lungs, Nang gagged, trying to pull free from Blancanales's grasp. A knuckle punch stabbed into Nang's temple, rocking him again. With a wild thrash, the Celestial Hammer commander tore his hand loose from his opponent's grasp, but he'd lost his knife.

Frustration filled the Chinese skyjacker, and he swung wildly, trying to connect with Blancanales. The Able Team vet's wiry frame was too flexible and agile for Nang to land a hit, especially since he couldn't find any leverage. Blancanales, however, hooked his leg around the Chinese's, giving himself enough grounding to plant a hard elbow between Nang's shoulder blades. Fetid breath escaped the stunned terrorist, and his arms flailed, looking for a handhold.

Blancanales snaked one arm under Nang's throat, clamping his hand on the back of his head. Nang realized that the headlock was the beginning of the end, and he thrashed his whole body like a wounded shark, trying to buck the Stony Man warrior off his back. However, no force was able to stop Blancanales now.

The Able Team commando stamped his foot against the bulkhead, hooking his toe through a handhold. At the same time, he let Nang anchor himself to a nearby set of handholds. Nang hadn't taken into account the fact that by bracing himself, he left himself vulnerable to a dozen lethal and crippling moves on the wiry Puerto Rican's part. By the time Nang realized his mistake, his head was wrenched to one side at a ninety-degree angle, neck bones popping like overstressed twigs. His snapping spinal cord increased the strength of his grip exponentially, a death grip hooking him to the bulkhead, despite the fact that Nang was dead.

Blancanales let go, breathing hard. He wanted to just float, relaxing his stretched muscles and burning lungs for a moment, but Broome was on the *Arcadia* going up against Cole, and there was the possibility that Schwarz and Lyons were dealing with more threats inside the space station. Torn for a moment, he decided that his partners would be able to fend for themselves, and he dived through the umbilical to aid the space shuttle captain against his turncoat copilot.

CHAPTER TWENTY

William Cole had found a wrench and he gripped it tightly, his heart hammering in his chest so loud, he was certain that whoever was stalking him on the shuttle would hear him. He barely took breaths, his eyes wide in fear.

The sound of death cries from the air lock was an all too clear signal that his bid to foster a new age for the world had come down, not in flames, but via the tried and ancient ways of tooth, nail, club and knife. Here, aboard two exemplars of space-age technology, the *Arcadia* and the International Space Station, the battle for control of Earth's orbit was decided the same way cave men and bronze-aged warriors had fought millennia ago. Blades and brute strength had carried the day, the defenders having proved more ferocious and primitive than the men of the Celestial Hammer.

He spotted Jordan Broome, wielding a knife, floating and searching, moving carefully through the ship. Cole regarded the titanium wrench in his hand. The modern materials of the weapons did nothing to disguise the original natures of their chosen weapons. Cole had a club, no different from an animal bone or a tree branch. Broome had a steel blade, no significant improvement over the chipped edge of obsidian, or a ground-down and fire-hardened stick.

Two astronauts who had traveled 180 miles above where life began, reduced to a sharp stick and a hard club. Cole let out a breath softly, tensing for when Broome would look away from the equipment locker he was hiding in. His legs knotted, muscles starting to cramp, silently wishing for Broome to just expose his back for a few seconds.

Instead, Broome turned and looked right at the equipment lockers, knife wavering in his trembling fist.

"Come on out, William," Broome said.

Cole pushed open the locker door, the wrench locked in his fist.

"Why?" Broome asked.

"An establishment punk like you, kissing up to government stooges like Thet, you'd never understand," Cole answered.

Broome chuckled. "Establishment punk…"

"It's the only reason a screw-job like you could be in command of a better qualified man like myself," Cole continued.

Broome shook his head. "Whatever. Just because you can't make friends…"

"They're our inferiors. Mustafa dislocated his shoulder when I hit the thrusters," Cole said.

"And yet you kept pushing for him to come with us," Broome stated.

Cole smirked. "C'mon. The shuttle is hijacked. And there's a black man with a Muslim name on board. The country would purge itself like lightning. A government on a Saudi leash, and those fat cats in the Middle East keeping them feeding on their oil teat. The bigot backlash would do half the job for us."

"What job?" Broome asked.

"Destroying the fascists controlling the world," Cole said.

Broome frowned. "You really believe that."

"They need guns and tanks to enforce their ever-fraying laws," Cole replied. "A real democracy doesn't have police officers with machine guns and armored vehicles. Only a soul-crush…"

"Shut up," Broome snarled. "The U.S., the world, they're not exactly perfect, but you're grabbing at straws, man."

"Open your eyes," Cole offered. "Together, we can set things right back on track. We have the *Arcadia*. We can drop this ivory tower on the dictators, weakening them enough for the people to rise up."

"My eyes are open. And so's my nose," Broome replied. "And all I smell is bullshit. Twisted, insane bullshit."

Cole's shoulders sagged for a moment. "I should have guessed that you weren't superior enough to want to be a part of our cause."

"I notice you weren't ready to commit suicide. This cause can't mean that much to you," Broome said.

"That's because the inferiors will need an exemplar to show them the true way," Cole answered.

"Meet the new boss, same as the old boss?" Broome asked.

"An exemplar. Not a dictator," Cole countered.

Broome shook his head. "Exemplars don't drop satellites on innocent people. They protect them from that. You're just a fascist trying to justify your garbage."

Cole's face twisted in anger. "Lies."

"Shut up," Broome said. "I'm tired of listening to your crazy talk. Either cave in my skull with that wrench, or give up."

Cole sighed, then lurched out of the locker, kicking off at Broome.

Broome whipped up his knife, the point piercing into Cole's breastbone almost effortlessly. So savage was Cole's launch that the NASA traitor speared his own heart, even through heavy bone. Broome tumbled backward with Cole's suddenly lifeless weight propelling them both up against a hatchway door.

There was movement behind him and Broome turned, realizing that his weapon was lodged in Cole's ribs. Luckily, he didn't need to fight. It was Blancanales and Schwarz.

"Is it over?" Broome asked.

"Not quite," Blancanales said. "We need to stabilize the station."

"We need to check on the fuel status. If not, we'll have to use the C-4," Schwarz added.

Broome looked at the lifeless Cole, hanging in his arms. He pushed the dead man off of him and sighed. "Good. I'm sick of taking lives."

Stony Man Farm, Virginia

BARBARA PRICE TOOK A HIT of Kurtzman's high-test coffee, and grimaced. So far, the Farm's cybercrew had managed to hold off, or at least anticipate satellite orbit readjustments. It was a long, drawn-out battle going on in cyberspace, pushing Kurtzman and his team to their limits. She handed Kurtzman a mug of his own brew, and the big man took a sip and smiled.

"Ah, just what I needed to put some hair back on my chest," Kurtzman said. He blinked and looked at his screen.

"The defenses we laid for this section of satellites is wearing a little thin. I'll have to bolster them with some new layers of black ice."

"We've got a weather satellite coming down around Japan. Its initial trajectory was toward Kyoto, but I've managed to break in and initiate a thruster burn," Tokaido said. "These guys are taking out satellites with as much gusto as those bastards with the hunter-killers."

"Those guys had rail guns on platforms doing the hunting.

No amount of hacking we did could have shielded our satellites from supersonic projectiles," Kurtzman reminded him. "Just keep up the good work."

"Rats, and I was going to punch the clock," Tokaido said.

Kurtzman heaved a small plastic football at Tokaido's head in retaliation for the smart-ass comment. "Hunt, tell me you're narrowing down the location of the Celestial Hammer."

"You want finesse, Aaron," Wethers said. "If I make the wrong move, the enemy will detect my efforts and evacuate to a new location."

"So?" Kurtzman asked. "They evacuate, and they can't continue to knock satellites out of the sky."

"There are twenty air forces around the globe intercepting space debris," Delahunt mentioned. "New riots have broken out in Auckland and Hong Kong."

"It's the Hong Kong riots I'm worried about. The Chinese might not go so lightly on their people, even if they are scared out of their wits," Kurtzman said.

"At least there are elements of the Cuban military who are keeping their more reactionary brethren in check. The Marines and naval personnel engaging in rescue operations at Manzanillo are reporting excellent cooperation," Price noted. "Who knows, this might backfire and strengthen bonds again."

"I've got progress on Jack. He's approaching Scoresby Point Weather station," Delahunt announced. "He must have burned up the sky on that Hornet."

Price looked at her watch. "Phoenix has been on the ground for forty-five minutes. Thank God for supersonic planes."

"Able to Stone House," Herman Schwarz's voice broke over the radio. "Communications have been restored, and station is clear."

"Gadgets!" Price spoke up. "Good to hear you."

"Right now we're crunching the numbers to see what we

need to do to stabilize the station's orbit," Schwarz informed her. "Cole used the *Arcadia*'s engine to alter the course. Innuman's got our path deteriorating, but it'll take four circuits around the Earth to put us in a danger position."

"Whatever you need, you know we've got the best computer setup around," Price stated.

"We've been looking for potential fuel sources, and then we found that there were still three of the liquid oxygen tanks on one of the launch vehicles," Schwarz explained.

"What happened to the other four?" Price asked.

"Near as I can tell from a quick examination with a Geiger counter on a manipulator arm, they didn't put anything onboard," Schwarz explained. "That cargo space was used for C-4, radio detonators and space suits for the first ship's team to board the station."

"The explosives were to separate the modules on reentry?" Price asked.

"Give the lady a cigar," Schwarz answered. "Right now, Nyoka is using the station's manipulator arm to separate the LOX tanks from their radioactive outer shells."

"Safer than doing it in a space suit," Price mentioned.

"Yeah. Even though they do have radiation shielding, gamma rays are powerful stuff. Innuman's sending through some calculations, and we need you to verify them," Schwarz explained.

"You can't double-check?" Price asked.

"Not before we use up the remaining four orbits," Schwarz told her. "This is mathematics on a scale I can only describe in two words. In and tense."

"Shoot 'em down to us, Gadgets," Price said. "With our Crays, we should be able to crunch those numbers. Carmen?"

"I'll observe the calculations on my workstation," Delahunt said. "Whew. Gadgets wasn't kidding. We've got three options. One involves feeding the liquid oxygen into the *Arca-*

dia to make up for the fuel already used. We've got to make certain that the stresses involved won't sheer off the docking structure of the umbilical."

"What about the launch vehicles themselves?" Price asked.

"USAF and the Russians took them out when the Celestial Hammer took remote control of them. One almost hit Los Angeles, while the other was vaporized over St. Petersburg," Tokaido mentioned. "Whoever they sent up there was either going to die for the cause, or they were coming down on the shuttle or the emergency escape vehicle."

Price winced. "Suicide on reentry. Scary shit."

"If they popped the modules apart," Kurtzman reminded her. "Explosive decompression in the upper atmosphere would have spared them a relatively slow death from the heat of reentry. At that speed, even in thin atmosphere, they would have been torn apart on impact with the air."

"So wait…" Price began. "They would come back on the shuttle? Hunt…"

"I'm looking for landing strips that could accommodate a shuttle landing, but there are none of sufficient length," Wethers told her.

"What about a water landing?" Price asked.

"That's a plausible plan. It is in the emergency protocols," Wethers said. "That would require another ship."

"Or a more permanent installation. An island, or maybe an oil derrick," Price offered.

"That doesn't narrow down my search parameters by much," Wethers admitted. "But it's something. I'll keep up the search."

"Don't worry about stealth," Kurtzman ordered. "The moment we get them on the run, the sooner the sky stops falling."

Wethers nodded. "It goes against my grain, but like our

very own Ironman says, sometimes you just have to nut up and do it."

"Less talkie, more scaring the bad guys into retreat," Price told him.

Scoresby Point Weather Station, Iceland

THE F/A-18D FIGHTERS HAD taken Phoenix Force to a supposedly abandoned airfield that had been shut down after the end of the cold war. In reality, the U.S. government kept the station open. Its location a few miles inland from Scoresby Sound in the midst of a barren wasteland provided a position from which to launch covert operations across northern Europe and the former Soviet Union. The facility was far from the closest Inuit settlement, keeping it remote and safe.

"From a tropic paradise to…this," McCarter said, lighting up a Player's cigarette. He took a deep drag and exhaled, letting the smoke hang in the air.

Encizo waved away the fumes with disgust, then went back to reassembling the field-stripped SIG-Sauer 2022 pistol. He racked the slide back, slipped in the 15-round magazine, closed the slide and pressed the decocker to lower the hammer. "I seem to recall you didn't mind polluting the paradise with that cancer stick obsession of yours."

McCarter grinned, thumbing rounds into his M-4 carbine's magazine. The SIG 2022s and the M-4s were on loan from a Special Operations Command armory in the "abandoned" weather station. "I prefer to call it giving the room some atmosphere."

"Whatever, David," Encizo replied. "Why can't you just enjoy brisk air outside like Gary?"

"I've already passed selection, amigo," McCarter replied. "I'm not freezing off my naughty bits unless it's for the chance to put rounds in an enemy. Gary, on the other hand, doesn't mind when it's so cold you can't feel your toes."

McCarter's sat phone warbled and he picked up the handpiece. "Nanook of the North."

"That's right. You just ride the sled pulled by dogs and leave the flying to a real pilot," Grimaldi said over the radio. "I'm just ten minutes out."

"Cripes," McCarter grumbled. "They'll let anyone into a cockpit these days."

"At least I didn't belly flop in the Atlantic," Grimaldi chided.

"Okay…enough grab-assing," McCarter returned. "Glad to have you with us. I take it you're going to be our ticket to the next stage of this mission?"

"Nah. I just thought I'd waste taxpayers' money to visit some godforsaken wastes," Grimaldi replied. "The Farm has narrowed things down to the North Sea, but they're going full court press against the Hammer."

"Get down here," McCarter said. "We've got a C-21A idling to take us to our next staging area. It's sub-mach, so I think you can let me spell you if you get tired."

"Yeah, with your last landing, you've got your crash fix for the next seventy years," Grimaldi answered. "I'll be down in five."

McCarter chuckled and switched the phone over to the Farm. "Barb?"

"David," Price answered. "We heard your chatter with Jack."

"What's the update on the search?" McCarter asked.

"We've got multiple launches emanating from an oil derrick a few hundred miles from Scotland," Price explained. "Seems the Celestial Hammer didn't quite trust the satellites to do the job for them, and they picked up some souvenirs from the Russian navy."

"You don't sound concerned," McCarter stated.

"It's a smoke screen," Price told him. "We pushed the search hard to get them to lay off of the satellite onslaught."

"Russian navy souvenirs. P-700 Granits?" McCarter asked, referring to a ten-meter-long antiship and land-attack capable cruise missile preferred by the Soviet navy since 1980.

"Yeah. How'd you guess?" Price asked.

"Old enough to not raise some panic if they were discovered missing, yet they can carry either 750 kilograms of high explosive or a low-yield nuclear warhead. Either is good enough to raise some mayhem," McCarter said. "They can do about Mach 1.5 if I remember, which means while European Union and Russian fighters will be busy tracking them all down, they won't be unkillable."

"I hope they can be stopped. Three-quarters of a ton of sub munitions or conventional explosives over a city center will cause a lot of death and destruction," Price muttered.

"In the meantime, we still have to nail down the conspirators," McCarter responded.

"While you're in the air, we'll get you on target," Price said. "The Celestial Hammer isn't going to be allowed any respite."

"That's the ticket. What's up with Able?" McCarter inquired.

"Doing some crazy mad science to keep the International Space Station in orbit. Barring that, they're going to try to drop it in the South Pacific," Price returned.

"Oh good. I save Washington, D.C., but the boys get to piss off twenty countries by destroying the biggest joint science project in the world," McCarter grumbled.

"If it means anything, I'm quite certain that the Celestial Hammer would love to pull your nut sack over your head," Price said.

"You're just saying that to make me feel better," McCarter quipped. "Try to keep the station up there. I'd hate to see it all go to waste."

"We will. Carmen's running through the calculations," Price replied. "We've got some good simulations."

McCarter signed off, and went out to the C-21A to wait for Grimaldi's arrival.

Jottunheim Station

PIAROW AND TANIT BOARDED the 152-foot lobster fishing boat that had been moored to the oil derrick. Though technically it was supposed to provide comfortable accommodations for a crew of eighteen and a hold with 220 cubic meters of room, they'd picked the craft, renamed the *Revolution,* because it could easily take all thirty-five of the Jottunheim staff on board with little discomfort. As well, in the cold North Sea waters, the heavy craft would be invisible. With a rusty, barnacle-laden hull, it looked like every other fishing boat operating around the Arctic Circle.

Their captain, Geoffrey McNeal, and his dedicated operations crew scrambled to their positions to get the *Revolution* under way. Tanit knew that the fishing boat wasn't going to be much of a threat if they encountered a naval vessel. The largest weapons on board were assault rifles and grenades, meant for repelling boarders. Their truest defense was the anonymity of the craft, and its 15 knot top speed, taking them as far from Jottunheim Station as possible while the world's attention was directed toward the chaos of cruise missiles and falling satellites.

Walter Woodrow paused, looking to Tanit. "Of course you realize that without the projected damage to the satellite screen, those Granits were wasted."

"Get on the boat. They're buying us time to get to safety," Piarow said. "Right now, we're the most-wanted human beings on the planet. Nothing short of complete extermination will supplicate the operatives on our trail."

Lance Woodrow kept his head low, not daring to incur any more frustration from the giant and his venom-dripping wife. He grabbed at Walter's arm, pulling him onto the motor yacht, feeling fortunate that Magni Piarow's legendary anger hadn't been unleashed on the mousy little hacker.

"And lo, I looked around me, spying my kingdom, composed of only rubble and foam," Piarow said with a sigh.

"Paraphrasing Ozymandias?" Tanit asked.

Piarow chuckled, cupping his wife's cheek. "More or less. Sand just doesn't fit into this scene."

"We've got Jan on our side. If they do come after us, we might be able to fight our way to freedom," Tanit told him. The thrum of massive diesel engines fired up, and the *Revolution* pulled away from the once more abandoned derrick. The place had grown on her, and she knew that she would miss it. However, she had no doubt that the firepower of a dozen navies and air forces wouldn't miss such a target. She'd find a new home base to grow comfortable in.

"Might," Piarow said. "I wonder how many others felt as if they could make a clean getaway. Our opposition was just simply too much, and the lengths they've gone to finish the job are legendary."

Tanit watched as Jottunheim Station receded into the sickly gray distance, feeling a hollowness in her gut as she realized that more years of effort and machination lay ahead. Without the unrelenting waves of apocalypse washing across the planet, fiery thunderbolts from heaven slicing down into the halls of power, the current throes of anarchy convulsing across the globe would wither and die. The uprising she promised had started up with fire and blood, but in the end, all it came down to was a minor skirmish that the world governments would weather. The status quo would come back.

She did smile. Cities had been scarred, and countries had

lost citizens in the brief hours of mayhem that she'd inspired. Without a doubt, the world would remember this day as one when it was proved that no one was safe. Not on the streets of their hometown and not 180 miles into space.

"It's not a defeat, my love," Tanit said to Piarow.

"You're right," the Norse warrior replied. They stood on the stern of the *Revolution,* holding hands until Jottunheim Station disappeared over the horizon.

GILBERT SHANE FLINCHED as he heard the rumble of the fishing boat's engines throb to life. He was expecting his life to end with every breath he took. Panic had seized him and was shaking him like a hound savaging a rabbit until its neck snapped.

He silently wondered if his heart would explode from the stress his fear had put upon him. Tucked into the confines of the prefabricated cabin built into the hold with the Woodrows and Barry LeBlanc, he was surprised that none of them asked what the trip hammer pounding was as it thundered in his rib cage.

"Have a drink," LeBlanc offered. "You look tense."

Shane took the offered tumbler. He didn't know what the brown liquor was, but given their proximity to Scotland, he could hazard a guess that it was some form of whiskey. He took a sip, feeling it burn in his throat. He glanced out the porthole, looking at the receding shape of Jottunheim Station. He wondered if leaving behind a hastily scrawled note was a good idea.

Would the covert operations team that Tanit, Piarow and Pantopoulos feared give him a break for pointing them in the right direction? Shane had left the message to buy himself some forgiveness, but with so many dead and injured across the world, would he be worthy of such consideration?

Perhaps they'd spare a particularly gruesome death for

him simply because he was one of their own, supposedly a defender of the United States of America. As a traitor to his duty, responsible for uncounted numbers of murdered citizens, his only hope was a quick, painless death.

Shane held his tumbler out to LeBlanc. "Fill 'er up. This is going to be one shitty trip."

CHAPTER TWENTY-ONE

Jottunheim Station

David McCarter and Phoenix Force disembarked from the Black Hawk atop the abandoned oil derrick. Their Land Warrior uniforms had been exchanged for dark green flight suits, and the M-4 carbines were familiar tools in their hands as they took down the rig by the numbers. Stony Man Farm had arranged for their strike team to get first crack at the temporary headquarters of the Celestial Hammer. McCarter didn't quite have an exact distance, but from their starting point on Midway Island, and throwing in their flight on the Hammer's launch vehicle, Phoenix Force had traveled far enough in the past couple of days to circle the planet twice.

McCarter had prided himself that his team was low drag and high speed, but with the Mach 2 plus Hornets and their orbital travels, their flight to Scotland on the C-21A had seemed to go at a snail's pace in comparison.

Without any resistance apparent after a thorough search, McCarter gathered his team in a section of the rig that had one wall dominated by video monitors, and a communications and computer setup that looked like an ersatz copy of the Stony Man Farm war room.

"They took off," Hawkins grumbled. "Just when I was hoping to put boot to ass…"

"Things aren't looking too bad," Calvin James said. He held up a folded sheet of paper. "I found this stuffed in the cushions of a chair overlooking the view of the water."

McCarter took the note, unfolding it.

"'To whom it may concern,'" he read, making out the hastily scribbled scrawl. "'My name is Gilbert Shane, and I'm hoping for a token of consideration.'"

"God," Encizo said. "That's the Homeland Security asshole who'd been protecting that smuggler Burzyck."

"And Burzyck's organization has killed a lot of folks," Manning mentioned. "According to Carl, they're responsible for a couple of cops, and dozens of civilians."

"Do you mind?" McCarter asked. "This bloke is pointing us toward where the Hammer is setting up shop."

"Don't keep us in suspense, man," Encizo prompted.

"The Hammer's taking off for a spot twenty miles down the coast from Murmansk," McCarter said. "According to Shane, it's a decommissioned OSNAZ training quarters."

"Russian combat swimmers," James muttered. "Their version of the Navy's SEALs."

"I don't think they'll have any OSNAZ forces on hand," Manning interjected. "But then, you never know what you'll find on the black market in Russia. They managed to get hold of thirty-two Granit missiles."

"It's a bit refreshing that they didn't get the warheads to go with them," Hawkins added. "But then, they spent the money gathering Iridium-192 and mercenaries."

"Even then, many of them were in on this to advance their own agendas," Encizo said. "Colonel Wing was setting up a retirement fund to get himself out of the Red Chinese army. And Vali supplied a load of his followers in an effort to destabilize the Iranian government. Tehran was the other city to be hit by an I-192 charge."

"Not that the mullahs cared. They were safe," James muttered in disgust. "The West didn't even hear about the Tehran explosion until twenty hours had passed. Any rescue assistance was outright refused by their government."

"At least the Farm managed to sneak Tehran information that General Vali wasn't on the up and up," McCarter said. "His planned coup crashed almost immediately."

"He took off," Manning said.

"He'll die another day," McCarter countered. "We've got his scent now. And so do the mullahs and the Mossad. Whoever finds him isn't going to give him any slack."

Manning nodded, checking his watch. "It's been four hours since the Celestial Hammer opened fire with their missile payload. Radar didn't pick up any helicopters, so they must have taken sea craft. Assuming they left immediately afterward, they've got at least a sixty nautical mile head start on us. Too far for Jack to take us in the Black Hawk."

"We pop back to Scotland and arrange transportation to Murmansk," McCarter said. "Let me report in to Barb, so she can get the wheels turning."

The other members of Phoenix Force spread out, double-checking to see if there was any other evidence of their quarry's destination while McCarter raised the Farm on his sat phone.

"David, good news. Able Team's on its way down. They'll be landing at White Sands in half an hour," Price replied. "The station's orbit has been stabilized until the member nations can arrange launches to return it to its original path."

"Great news. We've also got something for you. Could you arrange a ride for us?" McCarter asked.

"No sign of the Celestial Hammer?" Price asked.

"They lit out. We have a destination for them, though," McCarter said. "They're headed for Murmansk."

"Cold, rocky, barren, and on the sea," Price mused. "As if an oil derrick wasn't miserable enough."

"Any idea how we're going to get there?" McCarter asked.

"I'll get the team on it. I should be able to pull enough strings for you to get in with a proper weapon load out," Price replied. "And if we can, we'll see if we can spot them. None of the polar orbit satellites were affected by the Celestial Hammer's rain of satellites."

McCarter took a deep breath, loosening his shoulders. "They weren't knocked out of the sky, but they might be operating with computer-induced blind spots, like the Hammer had done when they were operating on the border."

"We're running checks for tampering on all the satellites we're accessing," Price said. "If there's anything kinky, we'll clean it out and restore it to normal operation."

"And that'll take how long?" McCarter asked.

"Long enough for them to get close enough to the coast and regular shipping lanes to make themselves indistinguishable from normal traffic," Price admitted. "I'm not going to be able to guarantee that you'll intercept them before they reach Murmansk. But we will have eyes on target, free and clear of all interference long before you or they get there."

"Good," McCarter said. "Before we disconnect, get me a bloody Hi-Power. The other blokes might like plastic, but I'm a dyed-in-the-wool steel hand gunner."

"Your wish is my command," Price returned. "Godspeed, Phoenix."

McCarter signed off.

Murmashi, Russia

GENERAL RAOOD VALI GOT off the plane, flanked by his body-guards, eyes scanning for a reception committee. He'd escaped Iran the moment that his friends within VEHAK, the Iranian Ministry of Intelligence and National Security, warned him that they were fully aware of his complicity in the isotope-laden liquid oxygen bombs dropped on Tehran and the port city of Bandar Abbas.

The military units that Vali had maneuvered into position were betrayed by a U.S. government communiqué that had put VEHAK on the alert for his loyal followers. Vali was on the plane at the same time that loyalist Iranian forces and VEHAK counterinsurgency teams gunned down the first motorized infantry companies moving into Tehran and the Naval Command Center at Bandar Abbas. He quickly passed on information to his second- and third-wave units to stand down and his most trusted commanders to flee the country.

His coup had failed, and if it hadn't been for his ability to plan three steps in advance of any situation, he would have been caught flat-footed. Vali had been on the ground in Oslo when the head of VEHAK reached him on his cell phone.

"General, I would advise you to return to Iran immediately and surrender," Director Ali Fahalli told him. "I would hate to have to take action against your family and holdings here."

"There is an old Azeri saying, Ali. It says, 'I was born at night, but not last night,'" Vali answered. "I'd have better luck throwing myself off a cliff into a pack of hungry jackals."

"No harm in asking for a peaceful resolution, Raood," Fahalli said. "But apparently…"

"Apparently nothing," Vali returned. "If you think you can reach anything I truly care about, you're sadly mistaken. Have fun throwing a fit killing people who don't mean goat shit to me."

Vali hung up, then boarded the first flight he could arrange to Murmansk, where Deidre Tanit had told him she'd set up an emergency fall-back point. While on the charter plane, Vali burned up the phone lines, arranging for a meeting with the Russian *mafiya*.

Olef Korolev was an ugly, pinch-faced man with gangly, unseemly limbs that dangled from under the heavy black wool topcoat. When he smiled in greeting to Vali, the effect was a twisted mess of oddly pointing teeth between livid worms of lips. "Welcome, friend."

Vali nodded and extended a hand in greeting, forcing himself not to flinch from the bulbous jointed fingers that reminded him of the pallid legs of a camel spider. "I hope my requests were not too much for you, Olaf."

"Of course not," the Russian mobster said. "I have weapons for your guards, and I myself will lead the extra manpower you have asked for."

"Good. I have a meeting with some people who owe me for failure," Vali told him. Korolev guided Vali toward a BMW. Isham, his bodyguard, elected to ride with Vali in the back seat. Korolev had a stony-faced, grim thug sitting next to him, a suitcase in his lap.

The hardman opened the case and retrieved two pistols, handing them to Vali and Isham.

Korolev sounded like a used-car salesman as he presented the weapons. "I introduce you to the MR-443 Grach. Seventeen-round magazines, double action operation, and ambidextrous safeties. This is the weapon of a real man. No plastic, except for the molded rubber wraparound grips, and exceedingly easy to field strip. To get any simpler, you'd have to sacrifice safety, durability and controllability. The recoil from this is so light my grandmother could use it."

Vali imagined Korolev's grandmother. All he could see

was a scrawny, snaggle-toothed woman resembling the strange creature sitting across from him, except with skin sagging in masses of wrinkles, blue veins and liver spots. Vali tried to kill the image, so he inserted a 17-round magazine, racked the slide and applied the thumb safety. "Do you have long arms for my men?"

The silent bodyguard set the briefcase aside and pulled another display case into his lap. When he pulled the weapon out, Vali thought for a moment that someone had sawn off chunks of an AK-47.

"The Gepard," Korolev introduced. "Nine millimeter, 40-round magazines, and the world renowned and ultimately reliable Kalashnikov action. If you can find a more reliable weapon, I'll buy it for you with my children's own school funds!"

Vali smiled. "Wonderful."

"I have twenty Russian infantrymen with us. They are equipped with the same firearms," Korolev explained. "They're watching the location you mentioned, and so far, no one has shown up."

"Good," Vali said. "It will be fitting to throw them a surprise party."

The BMW and its subsequent convoy rolled on.

Thirty miles off the Kola Peninsula

DEIDRE TANIT STOOD ON the bridge of the fishing-boat-turned-evacuation barge, listening to the radio. The trek through Norwegian coastal waters had been a tense one, but none paid notice to the rusty old ship even as it cut through the sea like an arrow. Tanit was glad they'd replaced the diesel engines with more powerful models, increasing their speed so that the trek from Jottunheim Station wouldn't take long.

Still, her nerves were pulled tight as hair triggers as she stood beside Geoffrey McNeal.

"Deidre?" a voice called to her from behind. She turned to see Barry LeBlanc standing there, his head hunched between tense shoulders, a laptop clenched in his trembling hands. She'd assumed that he was bound up in a ball because of the cold, but even in the warmest cabins of the ship, he was still wound tightly.

"What is it, Barry?" she asked, putting on the charm for the young hacker.

"Our bug-out location has transmitted a security alarm to my laptop," LeBlanc said. "It's a silent alarm, like you wanted."

"I would hope you have surveillance on hand," Tanit told him.

"Absolutely. Security cameras picked this up." LeBlanc set down the notebook computer and opened it up. On the screen was a grainy image of several men in wool coats, carrying assault weapons. He slid his finger over the touch pad, highlighting one of the figures on the screen. With a tap of a control, the image was expanded. It pixelated for a moment, then cleared up. "Image enhancement has it pegged as General Vali, and about thirty of his closest friends."

Tanit took a deep breath, and she vaguely noticed that his attention was suddenly pulled to the swell of her breasts against her tight burgundy turtleneck. Suddenly the mystery of his constant tension faded away. He was restraining his sexual attraction for her.

"It's a shame," Tanit said softly. "Raood would have been welcome in our little compound. He didn't need to bring all those guns."

"Walter is telling Mr. Piarow about them, as well," LeBlanc mentioned, his voice a stuttering stream of uncomfortable syllables trying to push through a tongue-twisted mouth. "Should we change course?"

Tanit looked at the image of the group. "Russian *mafiya*, armed with submachine guns."

"Thirty of them," LeBlanc reminded her.

"It'll be a light workout for Magni and Jan," Tanit said. "And with the rest of the security force, we'll roll right over them all."

LeBlanc nodded. He was about to turn away, when he stopped. "Deidre…I have concerns about Gilbert Shane."

"What's wrong?" Tanit asked.

"He's been drinking constantly," LeBlanc said.

"If he dies of liver failure, he'll save Magni the trouble of listening to his worries," Tanit countered.

LeBlanc shook his head. "I don't think that's the case. He won't talk to anyone, and his paranoia level is off the charts. He nearly shot Lance when he woke Shane up."

"He's worried about our enemies tracking us down," Tanit mused.

LeBlanc pursed his lips. "I don't think that's it. He did something."

"When would he have had a chance to betray us?" Tanit asked.

"I don't believe he did it with electronic communications, but we didn't check every corner of the station. We magnetically erased every bit of data onboard, but something as simple as a piece of paper would point them at us," LeBlanc mentioned.

"That's why we didn't utilize hard copies," Tanit replied. "And we made certain that you and the Woodrows brought your spiral notebooks with."

LeBlanc reached into his pocket and pulled out a small book-style calender, an innocuous little fake leather–bound day planner. He opened it up and Tanit could see one page, brushed with the edge of a pencil tip, the lead smearing across the page, except for where the impressions of an ink pen shone brightly against the cloud of smudge. The frayed edges of a torn sheet showed in the crease.

Tanit read the note and frowned.

"Why didn't you come to me with this sooner?" she asked.

"Because Shane didn't pass out drunk again until just before I got the alarm from the backup location," LeBlanc said. "Walter and Lance have been looking for signs of opposition looking for us, but they're blind to the *Revolution*. Of course, our foes might be operating even more secretly than usual."

Tanit nodded. "Has any action been taken against Vali and his force?"

"None so far," LeBlanc said. "But they might just be waiting for us to arrive."

Tanit frowned. "A three-way dance."

"We could run…" LeBlanc offered.

"And spend more days on a ship already over packed with personnel?" Tanit asked.

LeBlanc chewed on his upper lip and shook his head. The look in his eyes was unmistakable.

Tanit smirked. "Magni will want to meet Vali and the others head-on."

LeBlanc's shoulders sagged, but she ran a long, delicate finger along his jawline. She winked to him and silently mouthed "I'll think about it."

The hacker froze, glancing over at McNeal, who was guiding the *Revolution* to its final port of call. LeBlanc picked up his laptop and returned to his quarters.

Tanit regarded the captain, then went to find Piarow. Let the modern-day Viking rush into the jaws of a trap. Tanit hadn't lived this long by putting her life on the line.

And if she had to rebuild with only one twitchy hacker by her side, then so be it.

Valhalla Gate, Murmansk, Russia

MAGNI PIAROW STOOD ON THE bow of the *Revolution,* looking upon the hard and rocky shore that he would call home. Though his wife had grown tired of Piarow naming their bases based upon Norse mythology, even going so far as to suggest they rename the group from Mjolnir, The Hammer of Thor, Piarow knew that it didn't matter what this stretch of barren, lifeless beach was called. He knew that if they had to fall back to this location, to any location, it would be to set up one glorious, final defense against the forces of law and government.

Piarow had renamed himself for the Polish god of thunder, a personal reinvention that struck him as a more appropriate title evoking power and nobility. He could never understand men who had willingly taken names like the Jackal or the Desert Fox. Born in Zielona Gora, in the southwest region of Poland, his size and strength had obviously been a mix of Nordic genes and the tough Polish peoples. The area had long been contested as owned by Teutonic forces, from the renegade Teutonic Knights to the Third Reich. As a youth, he had accepted his role as a slave of the Soviet Bloc, told that he was just one of millions, nothing special. Only by discovering the history of the Teutonic Knights and their grim, battle-worthy gods, brought down only by the Jagiellon dynasty, Poland's first and greatest kings, did the young man realize the magnificence of the warrior blood running through his veins. Both sides had been influenced by gods of thunder, and the blood of both had run through Magni Gruenfelde's blood.

When he met Deidre Tanit, another rebellious soul who had remade herself in a quest to ascend to godhood by changing the world, he took the title of thunder god.

He didn't mind the group being named the Celestial Ham-

mer. The name sounded Chinese enough to inspire years of
open hostility hotter than the East-West cold war that had gone
on before. He knew though, that his race had been run. He literally had been chased to the end of the Earth, the last open
water port, nestled within the wreckage of the Soviet Union.
To the north, there was only the bitter chill of the Arctic ice
sheet, and all around him was barren, inhospitable soil, the
only life coming from ponding through stone for its precious
metals, or from eking out a harvest from the slender stretch
of unfrozen sea.

Valhalla's Gate was so named because it would be here that
he would pass to the next life.

But like all who were summoned by the Valkyrie, he would
meet his fate with sword in hand, the blood of his enemies
drenching his skin. His roar of defiance would be heard until
the end of time, and they would write songs about how he had
shaken the world.

Ahead of him, General Vali, the Iranian who sought his
own historic change, waited.

McNeal brought the *Revolution* into its berth at the end of
the lonely, decrepit-looking dock. Piarow felt a presence by
his side and turned, knowing it to be Tanit.

"You know about our reception committee?" she asked him.

Piarow rested his hand on the small of her back. "Yes, my
love. But there is hesitation in your voice. Something else has
come up?"

"General Vali may not be alone. Shane left behind a message for those who are hunting us," Tanit told him.

"Then this landing shall be glorious," Piarow said, his tone
wistful. "You wish to make your escape?"

Tanit sighed. "I am not you. I wish to accomplish my goals."

Piarow bent and kissed her cheek. "And you shall, my dar-
ling. And if the gods smile upon me, I may even follow you,

but regardless of the outcome, I shall make certain that none shall detect your departure."

"I love you, my magnificent berserker," Tanit said, embracing him tightly.

"And I you, my weaver of discord," Piarow returned. "The fields of heaven will be dim until we meet again."

Tanit tried to smile, but even she was surprised at the choking emotion catching in her throat, stinging her eyes.

"Say no more and go, little one," Piarow said. "My destiny awaits."

Tanit turned and ran back belowdecks as Pantopoulos came up top. The Greek commando tossed Magni his weapons, twin Steyr TMP machine pistols, weapons large enough for Magni's huge hands, and shaped like hammers.

"Thank you," Piarow said. "Perhaps we shall even have enough ammunition to deal with the death squad."

Pantopoulos smirked. "I've been working with Russians for the past decade. I could mop the floor with them with my eyes closed."

"Then you would miss all the fun," Piarow said.

Pantopoulos tilted his head and grinned. "I would, wouldn't I?"

"Let's go have a chat with General Vali," Piarow suggested.

Pantopoulos, armed with a Heckler and Koch G-36, nodded. "Lead the way."

CHAPTER TWENTY-TWO

Phoenix Force had split into two groups. David McCarter, T. J. Hawkins and Gary Manning had arrived on Suzuki off-road motorcycles, tearing along frost-broken road leading from Murmansk to the Celestial Hammer's backup headquarters, while Calvin James and Rafael Encizo were charging along the coast in a Zodiac boat.

It was traveling along the road that they had spotted General Vali's convoy, and noticed the gunmen that Korolev had assembled for the sake of bringing vengeance down upon the Celestial Hammer. The trio had pulled off the road, hiding themselves behind a boulder to gain more intelligence on the kind of opposition that they would face.

Manning, through his rifle's scope, had counted heads in the bus. "We've got two Russians to every Iranian. It looks like Vali's going to throw a party for the Hammer."

"I knew I should have brought more dip," Hawkins muttered. "The smart thing would be to hang back and let both sides have at each other and then move in to pick up the pieces."

McCarter looked at Hawkins.

"Aw shit, Gary. That crash into the Atlantic must have knocked something loose in his head," Hawkins said. "He looks like he's enjoying himself."

"All we need is an overstuffed Cessna and a crazy-ass distraction, and it'll be just like the good old days," Manning replied.

McCarter ignored the banter between his partners and raised James and Encizo. "New arrivals coming into play. Vali, his bodyguards and about twenty Russian gunmen."

"Woo, we haven't had this kind of mix-up since MERGE and TRIO were going at it tooth and claw," James said.

"Mix-up?" Encizo asked. "It seemed more like a feast to me."

"I take it the plan is still hammer and anvil, right?" James inquired.

"Of course. We can't risk that ship getting out of here," Mc-Carter said. "These bastards have sown too much suffering to reap anything but the best shot we can throw at them."

"Just give the word," Encizo replied. "We're hanging out in a small cove, waiting for the Celestial Hammer's ship to pull past."

McCarter killed the transmission. The plan was simple on Encizo and James's part. The two capable sailors would swing the Zodiac boat up behind the terrorists' ship and attach magnetic charges to the hull. The explosives were overkill, designed for military craft, and would rip open the belly of the old fishing boat. With the *Revolution* going at full power, its diesel engines and the groaning of its superstructure flexing on the choppy waters would drown out the sound of the high-speed raft as it pulled up. Encizo and James were clad in swimsuits the same hue as the turgid, cold waves of the Barents Sea. The synthetic hull of their raft was also camouflaged. The color scheme and pattern stripes would help the craft blend in with the sickly waters they raced upon.

It would be a waiting game, and now, nestled in a vantage point over the old OSNAZ training compound, with the *Revolution* pulling up to the decrepit old pier, McCarter held his breath, feeling the moment coming. With his M-4 rifle off-safe and his scope centered on the spine of an Iranian bodyguard, he waited for the conflict to explode. The antsy edge that always had badgered him in peaceful moments disappeared, his blood humming a song of adrenaline and increased oxygen.

David McCarter was at his calmest just when the world was about to detonate in blood, thunder and fire, and now, serenity filled every fiber of his being.

KOROLEV NEARLY GAGGED WHEN he saw the tall, powerful form of Magni Piarow step off the *Revolution,* walk up the pier. A small man with a knit wool cap pulled over his head ran alongside the giant Piarow, and for a moment, General Vali wondered if the Celestial Hammer leader had brought his young son with him. Only focusing did he realize that the smaller man was fully grown. A dozen others, also heavily armed, swarmed off the boat, following their leader.

"What did you get me into?" Korolev asked.

"Revenge. He's tall, but he's still a man," Vali said. "Wait here."

Vali stepped out into the open and brought a bullhorn to his lips. "Hold it right there, Magni."

"Raood!" Piarow called back, his deep booming voice needing no artificial enhancement to be heard across the distance between the two forces. "I take it you're disappointed in the results in Tehran."

"You people dropped the ball," Vali snarled.

"We utilized no information pertaining to your involvement with our efforts," Piarow said. "Most likely, when the

American team struck in China, they got the information from your own people."

Vali swallowed. "And why would the Americans want to help the Iranian government?"

Piarow threw back his head, red curls spilling off his bare shoulders. "Oh, you're now a friend of the U.S.?"

Vali's face screwed tight with frustration. "Die, you overgrown imbecile!"

One of his bodyguards rose, rifle swinging up to his shoulder to open fire on Piarow and the Celestial Hammer soldiers when a burst of automatic fire ripped up and down his spine. The Iranian bodyguard crashed on the rocks, his weapon silent.

Vali whirled, wondering where the sudden attack had come from.

"Welcome to Valhalla!" Piarow bellowed. "We will dine together in the Great Hall come night!"

Vali dived for cover as a spray of automatic weapons fire raked across the stones he had been standing on only moments ago. He swung up the Gepard, triggering 9 mm rounds wildly, knowing he wouldn't be able to hit a thing, just hoping that he could hit something.

He doubted it.

Bullets flew, spearing through the air, Russians and Iranians crying out as one as Piarow and his followers opened up, moving expertly to and from cover and firing with lethal marksmanship.

When the hull of the *Revolution* ruptured violently in a series of three explosions, he heard the Celestial Hammer commander bellow forlornly.

"Deidre!" Piarow called as the triple thunderclap faded.

Madness had seized General Vali's universe and was tossing it around like a child's plaything.

Jan Pantopoulos hit cover as soon as the first of General
Vali's gunmen was hit, and he fired from his prone position,
stitching a line of 5.56 mm rounds across the chest of a Russian gangster. The burst tore open his target's rib cage, exposing shredded and butchered internal organs and gleaming,
naked bone. Pantopoulos swung his weapon around and
sought another target. The twelve Celestial Hammer fighters
had also dropped deftly behind cover and picked their shots
carefully, not wasting ammunition except to tear apart one of
the Iranian rogue's hired guns.

For a moment Pantopoulos thought that this would only be
a momentary skirmish, a gunfight settled within the space of
a minute.

Then the magnetic mines that had been attached to the
Revolution erupted, high-powered shaped charges shearing
through the hull with rending force. Pantopoulos could feel the
hot rush of superheated air stampede over him and he curled
into a ball, knowing what eventually came on the heels of the
initial flash. Metal pinged and rang out, striking the rocks
around him, shrapnel moving at bulletlike speeds as the old
rusted boat disintegrated under irresistible concussive power.

When the shrapnel wave had finished, he looked up, seeing that two of his Celestial Hammer cohorts were down,
their bodies ravaged by high-velocity shrapnel.

Magni Piarow rose, letting out a long, mournful bellow.
"Deidre!"

Pantopoulos looked back at the *Revolution,* realizing that
anyone on board the ship and belowdecks was either wounded
or dead. He couldn't imagine being trapped inside the ship
when superheated jets of molten metal, propelled at supersonic
speed by high explosives, tore through the bowels of the craft.

"She's dead!" Pantopoulos shouted, and he looked back.

Vali's force was equally as stunned by the explosion on the

ship, and the hired gunmen were torn between firing at the Celestial Hammer strike force, and the mysterious ambushers in the rocks above them.

A sniper rifle cracked, and a Russian stumbled, the top of his head transformed into an empty bowl as hydrostatic shock excavated the brains from his skull. Another rifle stuttered, and a third member of the Hammer's host jerked violently as he was riddled by precision marksmanship.

Pantopoulos cursed and fed a 40 mm shell into his rifle's under-barrel grenade launcher. Sighting on the position he estimated was the source of the sniper shot, he sailed the high-explosive round with a tug of the launcher's trigger. There was a scramble up on the rocks even as Pantopoulos fired his launcher, and scant seconds later the high-explosive round detonated, spitting out a flower of pulverized rock and loose pebbles. The dust rained on Vali's position, but the Greek commando cursed, realizing that he'd just obscured his view of the enemy. One small consolation was that if he couldn't see them, they couldn't see him.

That's when he heard the "bloop" of grenade launchers from behind him. Pantopoulos looked back to see a Zodiac boat floating freely away from the shore. He pushed his feet under him and kicked back toward the water line, running through the countdown in his mind. One grenade landed amid a knot of the Celestial Hammer fighters, and they disappeared in a mangled blossom of shrapnel, shorn limbs and choking dust. Pantopoulos hit the water, diving deep as the second bomb hit where he'd been entrenched only moments before. The shock wave was deflected by the dense water, no crushing compression forces chasing the Greek as he swam submerged to the twisting hulk that used to be the *Revolution*.

Pantopoulos finally broke the surface, gulping down life-giving breath, clutching his rifle to his side. He spotted a figure, half submerged in the icy waters of the Barents, firing an automatic weapon into the Celestial Hammer's exposed flank. The Greek special operations veteran triggered his G-36, a spray of 5.56 mm rounds raking his target's position, but Rafael Encizo had taken his firing roost too well. The Phoenix Force warrior simply ducked down to avoid the splatter of deformed slugs, robbed of their velocity by supersonic impact with the stones he was hiding among.

Encizo popped back up and fired his M-4, ripping off a return burst, but Pantopoulos was also savvy enough to fight from secure cover. The Cuban's salvo pinged off the shattered hull of the ship, ruptured steel still strong enough to protect the wily Greek. Encizo ducked back down only a moment before Pantopoulos's autofire hammered at his position.

"Cal, can you get a line on this guy?" Encizo asked over his LASH communicator.

"I have the wreckage between us, Rafe. He's picked a good spot," James returned. "Let me try something."

Pantopoulos heard a grenade launcher discharge again, and he abandoned his rifle, spearing under the water. The 40 mm shell erupted in the bulkhead just over where he'd been ensconced. With powerful strokes, the Greek drove himself under the waves. If anything, he would have been stuck in a pointless duck and shoot exchange with Encizo, allowing his enemy's four partners to flank him once they finished with Vali's and Piarow's forces.

The only course of action was to take the fight to the enemy up close.

The Barents was cold, but Pantopoulos hadn't been immersed long enough to feel the effects of hypothermia, his muscles flexing and keeping themselves warm as the blood drained from his skin to insulate his internal organs. It would have been bone chilling and crippling for anyone without training, but to Pantopoulos, it was merely a brisk swim.

The real hardship would come when he broke the surface and engaged Rafael Encizo in close combat. He pulled the Glock 19 off of his hip. Like the Greek who carried it, the compact pistol was tough enough to withstand a dip in the frigid Russian waters.

And then, what would happen after he finished that fight?

Pantopoulos only had one answer for that. An old calming phrase he had drilled into himself in response to troubling questions.

What will be, will be.

DAVID MCCARTER SCRAMBLED down the cliff face to avoid the fury of Pantopoulos's grenade. As he skidded down an open stretch of flat rock, he spotted James and Encizo launching their own 40 mm entries into the thunderstorm of conflict raging on this forsaken beach.

An Iranian popped up, swinging his Gepard to hose down the Phoenix Force leader, but McCarter had his M-4 ready. The trigger pulled back, held down for a fraction of a second, long enough to drill a half dozen holes in General Vali's loyal gunman. The lifeless Iranian tumbled backward, sprawling on the hard base of the cliff below. McCarter kicked again, extending his skid on the slippery slope he rode on, looking for more targets as he allowed gravity to pull him closer to General Vali's entrenched position.

Obviously, the general hadn't chosen the right kind of weaponry for this terrain. A Gepard machine pistol was good for a street fight, maybe house-to-house combat, but along this beach and cliff face, you needed a carbine with at least 300 meters of range. McCarter's M-4 was light and handy enough to go quickly through a door, but still hit targets at 400 meters with the right ammunition. Sliding to the edge of his flat, McCarter leaped, landing in a crouch behind a Russian mobster who was bellowing curses and emptying a magazine in panic fire.

The gangster heard McCarter's landing and he whirled, but instead of getting the drop on the Briton, he received a brutal swipe of the rifle's tubular steel stock across his jaw. Mandible shattered and his windpipe collapsed by the violent blow, the Russian flopped into a boneless heap at McCarter's feet.

"David, down!" Hawkins's voice came over his comm. unit.

McCarter ducked, and the Southerner's rifle chattered, high-velocity bullets punching down into another Russian who was rushing to his partner's aid. "Thanks."

There was another explosion on the wreckage of the *Revolution,* drawing McCarter's attention.

Down on the beach, the tall figure of Magni Piarow moved with deceptive quickness, long legs driving the tall warrior along. From the way that Vali and Piarow had traded words, McCarter had no doubt that this man was the highest ranking member of the conspiracy still living. He triggered his M-4, but Piarow's broken-field run was too quick and erratic for the Phoenix Force veteran to get a decent shot.

"Gary! Can you nail that bastard?" McCarter asked.

"It's like trying to hit a rabbit with a fly swatter," Manning complained. "Whoever he is, he's too good."

"You keep missing?" McCarter pressed. He triggered his M-4, ripping a burst through the heart of an Iranian.

"I hit him twice, center of mass, but he's wearing body armor," Manning said. "He's wearing body armor, and he's as tough as Lyons after drinking a pot of Bear's coffee!"

McCarter dived for cover as Piarow straight armed a TMP machine pistol, raking a burst at his spot. The Briton swung his rifle around, emptying his magazine at the flame-haired

Viking, but cursed in disgust as the swift warrior ducked behind cover. A flash of movement drew McCarter's eyes skyward, and he could see the shape of a grenade against the pale, cloudy sky.

"Bugger this!" McCarter snapped, launching himself out of his position and skidding across loose rock and pebbles. Behind him, the grenade landed, detonating in a thunderclap. The Briton knew that if he had been a moment slower, his arms and legs would be occupying separate zip codes.

Unfortunately, his wild dive had torn the rifle from his grasp.

McCarter's hand dropped to the Browning Hi-Power on his hip and he scrambled behind an outcropping before a pair of Celestial Hammer gunmen could nail him. Hawkins's and Manning's rifles barked, peppering the terrorists who tried to murder their friend and leader. Out in the water, McCarter could see Calvin James hard at work harrowing the Celestial Hammer's rear flank, and taking down targets of opportunity among Vali's ever-shrinking revenge squad.

"Cal, where's Rafe?" McCarter asked.

"I lost contact with him," James said. "He's on the other side of the ship."

McCarter looked over his outcropping, seeing a small atoll of rocks where he'd seen Encizo at work. There was no sign of the fiery Cuban, and the Briton's first impulse was to swim out to see what was going on.

That's when seven feet of red-haired Viking came screaming out of the sky, bloody murder churning in his wild eyes.

RAFAEL ENCIZO FIGURED that James's grenade had taken care of Pantopoulos, so he returned to his task of providing the hammer to McCarter's team's anvil. He swiftly stuffed a grenade into the breech of his rifle's M-203, but a sudden erup-

tion of movement in his peripheral vision spurred his reflexes
to hurl him into the chilling Barents Sea.

Pantopoulos's Glock 19 barked, 9 mm rounds screaming
in ricochet off the rocks that Encizo had resided in only moments before, the rapid-fire string of bullets chasing after the
Cuban as he made his dive to escape certain death. The cold
ocean gripped him, even through the insulating layers of his
dry suit, but Encizo didn't slow down, kicking hard.

Pantopoulos rose higher on the rocks, reloading the Glock
with swift, fluid skill. The Greek knew better than to shoot
into the water. Even though his bullets wouldn't detonate on
contact with the waves, like he'd experienced with rifles, the
slow-moving 9 mm rounds would lose velocity after only a
few feet.

Pantopoulos took a deep breath and holstered the Glock.
Drawing his knife as he dived, he plunged into the water after
his quarry.

The Cuban was waiting just below the surface, a Tanto
blade locked in his fist. Pantopoulos smirked and he kicked
after the submerged Phoenix Force diver, fully aware that if
his opponent was willing to have the fight come to him beneath the waves, then this was going to be a tough contest.
Pantopoulos, however, hadn't spent much of his life diving in
the Mediterranean to be concerned with a little underwater
knife-play.

In two kicks of his powerful legs, the Greek was on Encizo. Except for their hair and features, the two men could
have been poured from the same mold, with broad powerful
shoulders and deep, V-shaped chests. The two combatants
had spent much of their lives swimming, in combat and otherwise, and even their breath control would be comparable.
Hands gripped wrists to hold knives at bay, and muscles
surged and swelled with power.

All thought of the biting chill of the Barents Sea had been discarded as the Phoenix Force veteran and the Celestial Hammer hardman struggled beneath the waves.

Rafael Encizo's mind raced as he realized that he and Pantopoulos were too evenly matched, and it would be quite possible that he would run out of air because he'd gone under several moments before the Greek took the dive. Their arms rippled with muscle, each trying to break the other's hold just long enough to spear six inches of razor-sharp steel into vital organs.

Encizo grimaced, feeling his lungs reaching the end of their endurance, when he knew that he had one advantage. Though Encizo was not an official practitioner of any specific martial art, he had learned countless lessons from his friends and partners. He had one trick in his repertoire that came from David McCarter.

With a surge of both his arms, Encizo propelled his forehead like a torpedo into Pantopoulos's face. The impact was lessened by water resistance, but it still shocked the Greek enough to kick away from Encizo. With two powerful kicks, the Cuban broke the surface and gulped down air.

He looked around, trying to see where Pantopoulos had gone, and the Celestial Hammer mercenary broke the surface next to him, shaking off the effects of the head butt. Encizo whirled, swinging his knife at the Greek, but Pantopoulos brought up his foot, catching the Cuban in the chest. Encizo's initial slice only raked at empty air, so he changed his tactics and brought the point spearing down into Pantopoulos's calf. Muscles and skin parted like butter as Encizo's powerful arm propelled the cutting edge. The Greek grunted and twisted below the surface, plunging through the depths.

Encizo had no choice but to follow his opponent into the icy murk, knowing that nothing short of death would bring Pantopoulos to a halt. A few yards below the surface, he caught sight of the Greek, launching himself from the shallow sea floor, knife leading the way. Encizo turned, minimizing the damage, taking the carving point of Pantopoulos's knife across his shoulder rather than his throat. The Greek whirled, trying to follow up on his first blood, but Encizo lashed his legs around his adversary's waist. The Cuban grabbed Pantopoulos's forearm, blocking the follow-up stroke, holding the lethal point at bay.

The Greek grimaced, then expelled a flurry of bubbles as Encizo scissored his legs tightly around the man's abdomen. Suddenly the Celestial Hammer fighter realized that he was in a bad position. With the strength and tactics of an anaconda, the Phoenix Force pro squeezed, forcing his opponent to exhale. With six feet separating him from life-giving air, Pantopoulos kicked violently, giving up his grip on his combat knife.

Rafael Encizo wasn't letting go, crushing the wind from his foe with every ounce of strength he had. Pantopoulos's lungs couldn't help but to vomit more air in a dirge of bubbles, and now they were empty. The Greek glanced down, an angry glare filling his eyes as he fought off the reflex to inhale.

Encizo fired off a punch into Pantopoulos's breastbone, and the Greek's mouth opened, coughing up nothing, and then the water flooded into his lungs. Encizo kept up the hammering with his fist, legs squeezing until Pantopoulos was just another limp corpse, bobbing beneath the waves.

With a kick, the Cuban disengaged and burst to the surface again, seeking the air that his dead enemy so desperately strove for.

From the sounds of gunfire rattling on the beach, the war with the remnants of the Celestial Hammer wasn't over. Encizo pulled his Heckler & Koch USP and swam for the shore.

CHAPTER TWENTY-THREE

General Raood Vali stuffed his last magazine into the well of the Gepard, realizing the futility of this battle. He'd wanted Korolev to give him the firepower he needed to tear into Piarow's crew, and all he'd gotten was outgunned and outflanked. Between the Celestial Hammer and the mystery attackers, his cadre of bodyguards and the Murmansk street thugs were being chopped to ribbons. He knew that if he could get out of the way, neither side would care enough to chase after him.

Vali broke from cover, racing between rocks. Bullets spit after him, but so far, God was watching out for him, his feet moving so fleetly that those who sought his demise wouldn't target him.

"I don't matter!" Vali shouted, finally reaching the OSNAZ compound. He threw himself through a rusted-out hole in the chain-link fence, scrambling wildly on all fours as he crossed half of the ground. Hawkins opened fire, tracking the fleeing Iranian turncoat, but it was useless.

"Vali took off into the barracks," Hawkins said.

"Not like he'll find any weapons in there," Manning returned. "Cal, you reading us?"

"Yeah. Vali's in the barracks?" James asked.

"I don't want to waste ammo shooting blindly through the roof. Light him up," Manning called.

Having scurried through the door, Vali slammed it tightly behind him. The place was clean and livable, and he wondered idly if he could set up shop in the unlit, abandoned barracks. It wouldn't take too much effort to simply fold himself into a corner and sleep until the spring thaw. By that time…

James's first grenade cut through the general's reverie, ripping a gaping hole through the roof. Corrugated aluminum peeled back under the force of six ounces of high-powered RDX. Vali curled into a ball, screaming as a second shell hammered into the back of the building. The thunderbolt blasts rocked Vali's ears, and he could feel blood pouring from ruptured eardrums.

Half mad with fear and pain, Vali stood, pulling out the Grach. He fired a blistering salvo of 9 mm rounds through the gaping holes in the roof, calling upon God to send hordes of sand mites to besiege the conniving bastard who was raining down high-explosive fury on a loyal son of the faith.

Vali realized that he wasn't going to get any results as long as he was inside the grenade-rocked prefab building and he tore open the door, stepping out into the open. Disheveled, ears ruptured, his hair in a flyaway mess, he was the stumbling vision of insanity, stomping with his pistol pointed at the ground.

"Where are you!" Vali bellowed. "Show yourself, you godless infidel!"

The Grach pointed up, burping out rounds, firing at random far and wide.

Korolev had squirmed halfway through the hole that Vali had used to enter the compound. He paused, stunned at the sight of the Iranian caught up in the throes of madness.

"Oh, it's you, you ugly camel spider of a man!" Vali snarled.

Korolev swallowed hard. "General…wait…"

The general brought up his pistol, and Korolev clenched his eyes shut, waiting for the 9 mm bullet that would cut his life short. Instead of the polite bark of the handgun, he was hurled by a concussion wave accompanied by the brutish belch of a high-explosive grenade. The Russian gangster sprawled, looking in shock at the fence, seeing quivering pieces of Vali still twitching in the chain link.

Revulsion ran through the Russian's gut and he vomited.

A 7.62 mm bullet cracked the ground next to Korolev's hand, and the mobster looked up to see Gary Manning, a sniper rifle leveled his head.

"Run for your life," Manning growled in passable Russian.

Korolev didn't even stop, his limbs windmilling in cartoon-ish exaggeration, propelling him up the beach.

Hawkins jogged up beside the burly Canadian. "You're letting him go?"

"He got me on a good day."

Gunfire exploded in the distance, and the Phoenix Force pair whirled at the sound. McCarter was still unaccounted for.

CALVIN JAMES FIRED THE last of his grenades at the barracks building when he saw a disheveled older man slogging out of the water. James recognized him immediately, having reviewed the photographs of the suspected occupants of the *Revolution*. It was Gilbert Shane, and the traitorous Fed had seen better days as he clung to a rock.

James scrambled down the cliff. The bodies of two more men, identical twins by the look of them, bobbed on the waves behind Shane.

"Hold it, Shane!" James shouted.

The Fed looked up, trembling. "The water's too cold. Please…I just want to get out."

"Keep your hands where I can see them," James ordered.

Shane looked down at the ruins that used to be his right arm. Bone showed through peeled back layers of skin and muscle, and he glanced back to the black Phoenix Force medic. "Do I look like I can do anything with this piece of shit? I'm barely holding on to this rock as it is!"

James scanned for remaining enemies, then slung his rifle, advancing through the waves to the wounded turncoat.

"You're not going to execute me?" Shane asked.

"Much as I'd love to, you're no threat to me anymore," James answered. "But try something, and I'll turn you into crab food like the Bobbsey Twins over there."

Shane looked over to the lifeless Woodrows, then began to chuckle. "Bobbsey…they're bobbing in the water."

James could tell that the man had lost it. He was going into shock from exposure and blood loss, and he'd have to drag Shane to shore before even thinking about dealing with the mangled limb. "Just take it easy and give me your hand."

Shane's giggling had taken on a dementia that sent chills of up and down James's spine. "Bob bob bob bob…right?"

"Yeah, now come on," James snapped. "Give me your hand."

Shane's gibbering shook his shoulders, and James could see that his eyes were bloodshot, tears streaming from them. "I'm so fucked."

"You poured the wine. Now it's time to drink it," James told him, grabbing Shane by the wrist. With a hard tug, he pulled the wounded man out of the water.

Shane struggled, trying to pull out of James's grasp. "I want protection. I led you here…"

"Protection from what? If you keep fucking around in this water, your core temperature will drop and you'll die of hypothermia," James said, struggling to bring the madman ashore.

A hard knee snapped up through the water, catching James off guard in the crotch. With a wheezing gasp, the Phoenix Force commando dropped to his knees, planting him waist-deep in the frigid waves. Shane lunged, grabbing at the Colt Python that James had tucked in his shoulder holster.

James cursed himself for being so slow to react, but he'd been distracted, not expecting the wounded man to put up such a fight. Now, Shane's fingers wrapped around the grip of his Magnum revolver, and in a moment, he was going to put a bullet through James's brain. The warrior pro exploded into action, grabbing Shane's wrist again, this time to resist, not to assist.

With a violent twist, James dislocated the traitor's shoulder, shoving Shane face-first into the surf. The Fed still maintained his death grip on the handle of the revolver, trying to pull it out of the holster.

"Blue suicide," James muttered, holding him under. "Getting the cops to kill you because you're too damn stupid to have lived your life right. Well, Shane, I'll oblige you. This one's for the cops in Baltimore that you fucked over."

Shane struggled, but he didn't have any strength left to put up much of a fight. After a few moments, the Python plopped into the water, dragged out by the dead Fed's limp arm.

James took a deep breath, staggering to his feet. He looked around, wondering if there were any more survivors in the wrecked hulk. Just to be sure, he unslung the M-4 and raked it on full-auto. Then he limped up the shore, looking for the rest of his team.

DAVID MCCARTER BARELY GOT out of the way of Magni Pi-arow's flashing fist as the giant came down in full battle lust.

The Briton fired off a quick punch at the towering terrorist leader, knuckles hitting solid abdominal muscles that felt like a brick wall.

"You killed her," Piarow growled. "You killed Deidre."

McCarter assumed that it was the woman who had narrated the worldwide video threat. He brought up his leg, snapping a hard kick into Piarow's side, catching him right over the kidney. The blow staggered Piarow off to one side, and he realized that his Browning Hi-Power had fallen during the attack. McCarter returned his focus to Piarow, who brought around an arm as solid as a tree limb. The Phoenix Force leader turned, catching the impact on his shoulder, but the sheer force of the blow lifted McCarter from the ground and hurled him into the rocky sand four yards away.

Stunned by the sheer power of the Celestial Hammer leader, McCarter struggled to regain his feet. Stovepipe legs took long strides, dragging Piarow to continue the savage conflict, and the Briton kicked out hard, catching the Pole in the ankle. Tripped up, the man flew, landing face-first in the hard, cold beach. McCarter rolled over and got on all fours, then looked Piarow in the face. His beard's red curls had been enhanced by jagged stones that had torn at his cheeks and forehead when he'd fallen.

Piarow lunged, and the Briton lurched to one side, avoiding most of a hammering fist, catching only a graze off massive knuckles. McCarter continued to roll, despite sharp stones jabbing into his back and chest.

"You and I, we will feast in the great hall of Valhalla. The final destination of all great warriors," Piarow explained, out of breath.

"How 'bout a rain check, then? I'll just stop off at Mc-Donald's," McCarter said. Piarow took a long step, and McCarter grabbed a rock and hurled it at the giant's face.

It was no better than spitballs against Godzilla, but it slowed him down enough for the Briton to get back to his feet.

Piarow lashed out with another quick, clublike fist, but this time the Phoenix Force leader ducked it completely, countering with a swift chop across the titan's kidney. Piarow grunted in pain, and crashed his elbow heavily across McCarter's already sore shoulder. The Briton collapsed, his arms wrapped around Piarow's knees, giving the terrorist a moment's pause.

"Begging?" the Celestial Hammer leader asked.

"No. Leverage," McCarter snarled. With a surge of strength, he yanked the man off his feet, dropping him onto his back. Piarow's head bounced off a large rock, his scalp tearing, dying his flame hair a darker, stickier red.

Piarow groaned, stunned, and McCarter saw his Browning lying a few feet away. He went to retrieve it, hoping to end this fight with a bullet to his adversary's head. "This slugging it out is for wankers."

As he stooped and took the Browning, a freight train of human muscle slammed into McCarter, lifting him off his feet. Piarow had charged him, and McCarter was bent over the giant's broad shoulders. The two men crashed into the rocky surf, but McCarter held on to his pistol.

The Stony Man warrior whipped the steel barrel around, opening up a savage gash along Piarow's jawline, blood flying as the front sight snagged skin. The berserker responded with a punch that definitely broke a rib, hurling McCarter backward into the cold water.

"I told you…we're going to Valhalla…" Piarow gasped.

"No. You are," McCarter said. He cut loose with the Browning, burning off a half dozen rounds into the big man's face.

Encizo swam up and dragged himself out of the water, helping McCarter to his feet. Manning, Hawkins and James raced toward the sound of gunfire, and saw their partners leaning against each other in the frigid waves.

"What happened?" James asked.

McCarter pointed to the faceless corpse buffeted by the surf. "Viking funeral."

"Any other survivors?" Encizo asked, panting.

"I ran into Shane," James confessed. "Oh wait. He's not a survivor anymore."

"Carl will be glad for that," Manning grunted. "How about we get back on dry land? There's a nice BMW that'll take us to Murmansk and some warm clothes."

"How fast does it go?" McCarter asked.

Hawkins looked around at the group. "Not that fast. We'd be lucky to get fifty miles an hour."

McCarter nodded. "Just my speed, mates. Let's go home."

Phoenix Force slogged out of the surf, leaving behind the shattered remains of the Celestial Hammer.

ROOM 59

THERE'S A FINE LINE BETWEEN DOING YOUR JOB—AND DOING THE RIGHT THING

After a snatch-and-grab mission on a quiet London street turns sour, new Room 59 operative David Southerland is branded a cowboy. While his quick thinking gained valuable intelligence, breaching procedure is a fatal mistake that can end a career—or a life. With his future on the line, he's tasked with a high-speed chase across London to locate a sexy thief with stolen global-security secrets that have more than one interested—and very dangerous—player in the game....

Look for

THE finish line

by

cliff RYDER

GOLD
EAGLE
®

*Available January
wherever books are sold.*

JAMES AXLER

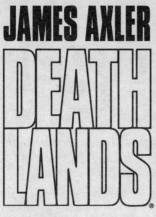

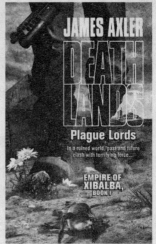

Plague Lords

In a ruined world, past and future clash with terrifying force...

The sulfur-teeming Gulf of Mexico is the poisoned end of earth, but here, Ryan and the others glean rumors of whole cities deep in South America that survived the blast intact. But as the companions contemplate a course of action, a new horror approaches on the horizon. The Lords of Death are Mexican pirates raiding stockpiles with a grim vengeance. When civilization hits rock bottom, a new stone age will emerge, with its own personal day of blood reckoning.

In the Deathlands, the future could always be worse. Now it is...

Available December wherever you buy books.